The Girl and the

Sunbird

Also by Rebecca Stonehill:

The Poet's Wife

The Girl and the

Sunbird

REBECCA STONEHILL

bookouture

Published by Bookouture

An imprint of StoryFire Ltd, 23 Sussex Road, Ickenham, UB10
8PN. United Kingdom

www.bookouture.com

ISBN: 978-1-78681-028-1
eBook ISBN: 978-1-78681-027-4

For Andy, Ya tu sabes

Teach me
how to bare my heart
so that you can touch my vulnerability
with your lips
and I won't cringe under the
spotlight of honesty
and your lips will stay.

Abigail Arunga

PROLOGUE

MAITHO

NAIROBI
1952

It will happen in five days and eight hours.

This man, this man who came last week, he told me, 'I am friend.' I believed him. I wish he would come again. Every day I wait for him. But he is not coming. Strange, I do not know him, who he is. *Why* he is friend. But there is something that connects him to me. To my past, this past of which my questions are not answered.

I keep waiting for this man. If he comes again, I will ask him, 'You know my mother? Real mother? You know my father?'

In five days and eight hours I will die.

PART ONE

CHAPTER ONE

IRIS JOHNSON

CAMBRIDGESHIRE
AUGUST 1903

'I shall never understand you, Iris. Nor why you have made this decision, but there it is.'

Mother stands a shoulder's width apart from me outside The Old Vicarage as we await the landau. I ignore her and stare ahead of me. What kind of a choice is it truly? I fidget with my hat, my eyes drinking in the overgrown brambles, clumps of nettles and winding trellises of bryony that skirt the hedgerows surrounding the house and those wide, endless skies. In what feels like the blink of an eye, I have moved from debutante to would-be wife of a lord to a girl who will be flung unceremoniously across the seas into the waiting arms of a faceless stranger in East Africa.

A chaperone, Miss Logan, has been employed through *The Lady* by Mother to escort me to Mombasa. She arrived yesterday afternoon on the 1.20 from King's Cross and was collected from Cambridge by Papa with her one small valise and chiffon parasol. I want to hate her, this woman who will take me far from all I know and love. But she has small, shrewd eyes and a look of suppressed humour about her that I cannot help being drawn to. Somehow her presence also comforts me, calming the anguish that racks my body in great, nauseous waves at the thought of leaving my beloved papa and brother Arthur with no idea when we may be reunited.

Farewells are brief. Papa looks exhausted, his thick, white dog collar accentuating the pallor of his cheeks. As he grasps both of my hands in his, he parts his lips to say something and then closes them again, simply shaking my hands with emphasis. How curious it should be, I muse, and how gratifying, if we lived in a world in which we were all permitted to say precisely what we were thinking rather than be restrained by convention.

As Miss Logan and I climb into the landau and the horses begin their gentle trot towards the end of the drive, I cast a final look back at The Old Vicarage, large and white and solid. All the staff have come out and I smile sadly as I see Cook waving a white handkerchief at me. How I shall miss her; her smooth, shiny face and the way she would always smuggle me small pieces of Welsh rarebit or lardy cakes when Mother punished me as a child with no luncheon for coming into the house dirty or answering her back. Mother holds her head in that high, imperious way of hers as she watches me leave, relief to see the back of her errant daughter painted in the squint of her eyes and the haughty tilt of her chin. As for Violet, only now that I am on my way do I see that she is crying. It is possible her tears are genuine, but somehow I doubt it. More likely it is for Papa's sake. I feel the slightest pang, wishing, as I have done many times, that my sister and I had shared a closer relationship. Well, it is jolly well too late for all that business now.

Before pulling out of the driveway, I hear the sound of crunching gravel and a shout. Poking my head back out of the carriage, I see Father running after us, spidery black arms waving overhead. I call out to the coachman to stop and Papa approaches, panting.

'Iris, I forgot to give this to you.' He feels around in his pockets before pulling out a small velvet drawstring bag and hands it to me through the window. I stare down at my outstretched palm for a moment before opening the bag. It contains a tidy pile of banknotes, wrapped around something hard. Peeling back the money, I find a small silver medallion, bearing the figure of a saint holding a staff.

'It is St Christopher. The patron saint of travellers. My grandfather gave this to me many, many years ago and it is right that you have it now.'

I close my fingers around the medallion, cool against my skin, and thrust my head further out of the carriage to kiss Papa's familiar cheek and grasp his hand.

'Goodbye, Papa.'

'God bless you, Iris,' he says before nodding to the carriage driver to proceed. 'God speed you…' His voice trails off as I am forced to drop his hand and he is left standing there, forlorn, a figure in black framed against The Old Vicarage. My head out of the window, I tilt it backwards, the cockaded silk hats of the coachmen fluttering in the breeze against the cloudless, blue summer sky.

CHAPTER TWO

PENELOPE LOGAN

Sitting on the train from Cambridge back to London, the air awash with swirls of tobacco and train smoke, I take up my thick, weathered volume of Pearl Rivers and flick through it. I know that my charge is curious about me – I sense her eyes flickering over me and my reading material – but I shall let her talk first, as I always do, in order to find out what kind of a girl she is.

Presently, Miss Johnson clears her throat. 'Miss Logan.'

I look up, removing my spectacles.

'Have you escorted any other young ladies to British East Africa?'

I laugh. 'Heavens, no. Though I have chaperoned girls to other places.'

'Which places?' Miss Johnson asks eagerly, leaning forwards. She is not what one could call classically bonny, with her rather hawkish nose, high forehead and awkward teeth, yet there is certainly an attractiveness about her, soft brown waves of hair pinned up beneath her hat and navy blue eyes, penetrating.

'To Switzerland, Austria. To Denmark.'

'Where is the furthest you have been?'

I raise an eyebrow. 'So many questions, Miss Johnson!'

She blushes and laughs a little, leaning back in her seat. I pause before replacing my spectacles and resuming my reading. Miss Johnson leaves a respectable amount of time before enquiring which book I am engaged in. I peer at my charge before once again removing my spectacles.

'Do you like to read, Miss Johnson?'

'Oh yes! An awful lot.'

'And have you brought suitable reading material for this lengthy journey we are to embark on? Or can I expect you to interrupt me in my own reading at five-minute intervals throughout?'

'No, I did not bring anything to read, apart from *Alice's Adventures in Wonderland*, my favourite childhood book.' She pauses and then adds, rather challengingly, 'My mother does not approve of me using my mind.'

Somehow this surprises me not a bit. The reverend's wife had that sour look of repression about her. I do not say anything, ensuring my face does not betray my thoughts.

'I did try to find a book on East African birdlife but Mother was far more concerned with marching me around the dress shops and milliners' in Cambridge, not the book-shops.' She sighs. 'You know, speaking of Cambridge, I had even made enquiries to study at the university sever-al months ago. In secret of course. But—' Miss Johnson breaks off and her face clouds. 'Girls like me are expected to *marry*, are we not? When Mother found out about it…

well, let us simply say that she was not happy about it.' She bites her bottom lip and turns to stare out of the window.

I study Miss Johnson's face in profile. A frown puckers her forehead. There is a great deal, it is clear, that she holds inside her and I feel an unprecedented stab of sympathy for her. Clearing my throat so that she turns back to me, I present the cover of my book so that she is able to read the name on the front.

'Pearl Rivers! What a beautiful name.'

'It is her *nom de plume*, Miss Johnson. Are you familiar with the writings of Eliza Nicholson?'

She shakes her head.

'She was from the United States of America. A poet and a journalist.'

'*Was?*'

'Indeed. She is no longer alive, more's the pity. Died of influenza some years ago. But this book is a collection of some of her poems and writings from *The Daily Picayune*.'

'What is *The Daily Picayune*?'

'It is quite a forward newspaper in many respects, from New Orleans.'

'Forward. In what way exactly?' Miss Johnson asks, leaning towards me. Her penetrating eyes are glittering and she appears almost breathless with excitement.

'Miss Johnson. This excessive questioning. Has nobody ever intimated that it may be impolite?'

She leans back and smiles in a faux-demure manner that clearly requires some effort.

'I am terribly sorry, Miss Logan. And yes, this has been intimated. *Many* times, I am afraid.' Turning her face towards the window, she gazes out as the fields and pastures roll gently by, a landscape that will soon be a thing of the past for her. I cannot help but admire my charge for her forthrightness. Somehow I suspect she will be rather different from the previous young ladies I have chaperoned.

CHAPTER THREE

IRIS JOHNSON

I feel curiously, deliriously happy, quite belying the reality of my predicament. I am being chaperoned by a woman of learning, not someone stuck in the staidness of Victorian Britain's past. Mother, for example. After the death of Queen Victoria, she made Violet and I wear mourning bracelets for an interminably long time. Such bracelets, woven from locks of their hair, are customarily only worn if a relative dies. I detested the thing with a passion for, as Mother had failed to secure any of the late queen's hair, it was fashioned instead from the mane of a horse and itched dreadfully, causing a rash upon my wrist. As for Mother herself, she wore black gowns well beyond the mourning period and would dissolve into fits of weeping at the slightest reminder of our late queen.

'When I am not engaged with Pearl Rivers,' Miss Logan says quietly, 'perhaps I might permit you to read it. Is that something you might enjoy?'

I feel my corset tightening as my chest heaves out, wondering if I might burst with pleasure. 'Yes,' I whisper. 'Very much.'

Miss Logan has a small frame, a tiny waist and her face is narrow and angular. Her brown hair is pulled back severely and is liberally dusted with grey, but her lips are full and warm and those eyes, I noticed as soon as I met her, are full of a silent intelligence. I have never met a Scottish person before and it is a great pleasure to hear English being spoken in such a lyrical manner with the rolled 'r's and elongated vowels.

The following days pass in a tangle of shades, scents, sounds and birds I have never seen before as we travel through France, Switzerland and Italy. The night before we board the steamer at Naples, we lodge at a small *albergo* close to the harbour, where we dine on seafood fresh from the Tyrrhenian Sea and a glass of Italian wine. It affects my senses almost instantaneously, colour rushing to my cheeks as I fan myself furiously with my table napkin.

'It is terribly hot in Naples, is it not, Miss Logan?'

'Not as hot, Miss Johnson, as I should imagine we shall find it in British East Africa,' she replies in that unruffled tone of hers. I notice that despite the dark, heavy clothes my chaperone wears, she appears quite unaffected by the temperature.

'The heat does not bother you?'

'On the contrary,' she replies with a smile. 'I am from Scotland, land of snow and ice, and to feel a warm wind on my face is rather pleasant.'

I am about to enquire which part of Scotland she is from, and what it is like there, but stop myself in time. It has become quite apparent that my chaperone is congenial only up to the point that I begin asking too many questions. She will then stop talking and purse her small mouth in final, though good-humoured, disapproval. There are so many things I long to ask her, about which other writers she admires or what she thinks about my attempt to study at Cambridge University. Yet I respect Miss Logan so greatly that I take care not to irritate her in any way.

Our berth upon the SS *Juba* is small, sparsely furnished and cramped, but I do not mind. I think, briefly, of my room back at The Old Vicarage, adorned with the most fashionable curtains Mother brought up from London for all our bedrooms, the wardrobe filled with fine dresses and accessories, and my seventeenth-century dressing table, ornate and austere in one corner of the room. I do not miss any of that, though I know I shall miss the garden and Papa and Arthur and the servants. But the truth is, I've scarcely thought of any of them since leaving.

I have never been on a boat before and on the first couple of days of our voyage from Naples to Mombasa, my stomach lurches as I rise in the morning to the rocking sensation. I drink plenty of fresh lime cordial, which is brought to us upon silver trays by white-gloved deckhands, and as I sip from the long, cool glass I lean over the deck with the spume of the ocean blowing up in my face and watch the edge of the wind catch the wings of wheeling seagulls as they chase behind the steamer.

🕊 🕊 🕊

At Port Said, the air redolent with dusty dryness and sweet, fetid smells, the ship docks to refuel. The ship is to remain here overnight and we are to sleep on board. An endless stream of cinnamon-skinned Egyptians come aboard, carrying upon their backs great baskets of coal, which they tip into the bunkers, chanting all the while. Whilst this is happening, a commotion erupts on the other side of the ship. Miss Logan and I hurry over and watch, wide-eyed, as scantily clad men are hoisted on board in large wicker baskets.

'It's the gully-gully men!' I hear a child cry in delight from the deck beside me. The men jump lithely from the baskets, baby chickens clutched under their arms. They hold them out to us, and I see them as clearly as I see Miss Logan beside me, but before I know what is happening, the chickens disappear in a great puff of smoke before my very eyes! Everybody claps and cheers and they bow profusely before the enthusiastic crowd and then hold their hands out towards us. Miss Logan, as unruffled as ever, produces a coin and drops it into the outstretched palm of the nearest conjuror. He rewards her with a wide smile, teeth glinting in the sunlight.

'Come, Miss Johnson. We are permitted to leave the ship.'

Dressed in white deck shoes and clutching my parasol, I feel quite sick with excitement as I feel dry land beneath my feet in a foreign country. I am plunged into sudden shadow as a vast-spanned vulture soars overhead, white against the bleached sky with black-tipped wings. It appears that a number of the passengers have already taken this voyage before, for they instinctively reach into pockets and purses and begin to throw pennies into the sea. At first, I have no idea what they are doing but then small, half-naked boys dive down to reach them, their small bodies gleaming slick as seals.

Miss Logan and I walk along the harbour wall, past numerous men wearing long blue or white gowns that look almost like nightdresses and others who are virtually naked, cloth knotted round their sinewy middles. They have laid out their wares of stuffed camels, fly whisks and scimitars with jewel-encrusted handles that wink at us in the bright sunlight. 'Very cheap! Good price!' they call out to us as we walk past.

We see that several of the passengers are drifting towards a vast, solid building opposite the canal quays with the words 'Simon Artz's Emporium' emblazoned across the top of it. Local men swoop upon us by the entrance, asking if we wish for a quick tour of the Lesseps Statue or 'Native Quarter' in their horse cabs. I glance at the horses, miserable, bedraggled-looking beasts, and shake my head resolutely.

Upon entering the building, we follow the crowd up to the tea terrace where Miss Logan and I sit for some time, enjoying the view of the canal stretching out before us as we sip our refreshing tea. It is served to us in peculiar glasses, but I must say it is the best I have tasted since leaving England. Then we wander from room to room, past hats of all shapes and sizes, shelves of rolled and folded cloth, bottled and pickled eels, lipstick of deep purple hues and dark eyes that stare at us from hidden corners. A young, bare-footed Arab boy dressed in a grubby khaki uniform darts up a ladder at one customer's behest to fetch fabrics from the top of haphazardly layered shelves.

It is terribly hot in here – only a few lethargic fans battling through the air and no windows – but I am so fascinated by all this that I do not mind. I try to picture Mother in this strange place, then swiftly push it from my mind. She would be horrified, yet this voyage is of her making and I care not a jot anyway. As I walk through the glittering hall, I glance at Miss Logan, who is peering with great interest at a cluster of peacock feathers in a narrow porcelain jar. I feel a great wave of affection for her. She is such a small, delicate-looking woman, with her tiny waist and pointed features, yet despite this she inhabits her space fully, so that the air around her almost moulds to her formidable presence. It is unlikely Miss Logan is even aware of it, yet I feel its potency even from the other side of the Emporium.

What a far cry this all is from my months of frivolity and parading as a debutante. How entirely unsuited I was for all that and how ill our family could afford it. Mother had to pull a great many strings in order to see me part of the great debutante debacle, or the Marriage Mart, as Lord Byron so aptly called it. Why could she not have just waited and seen her wish fulfilled with Violet – pretty, fussy Violet – who longed for the debutante season with the same fervour that I eschewed it? But no, Mother was determined to see me married off into a wealthy home. Of course she was simply living out her own frustrations that she herself was never granted the opportunity to come out in society, having to settle instead for being the wife of a provincial vicar rather than that of a naval captain or city lawyer.

🕊 🕊 🕊

Five days into our three-week voyage, I awake with a heaviness upon my chest. I have done so well during my passage, scarcely thinking of Mr Lawrence at all. But this morning, he slips into my mind like a dark shadow. I sit upright in my narrow berth as both he and my previous would-be suitor jostle for space in my mind. I shudder, sending a silent prayer out that Mr Lawrence is nothing like Lord Sidcup.

I am still bewildered by how it could have happened. But after one of those dreadful white-lace-and-taffeta society balls, following an exhausting week of teas and charity bazaars, I awoke in the bedroom of my aunt and uncle's house in Mayfair to Mother bustling in with the news that a lord from the ball wished to call upon me.

'I don't know who Lord Sidcup is, Mother,' I replied, leaning back into the pillow and closing my eyes. 'He must be mistaken. Or *you* must be mistaken.'

'*No*, darling.'

I had scarcely looked at anybody the previous day, let alone spoken to them. I stared straight ahead of me, summer light slanting through the window and landing on the dressing table, with all the paraphernalia from the previous day: hairpins, fresh flowers, gloves, rouge and lipstick, all tidied up and the surface left gleaming and bare. What did I think of that? I thought it was a terrible, terrible mistake.

'Well?' Mother pressed. 'Is that not marvellous news?'

I stared up at her. She was, of course, in her element in London, wearing a matching blush-pink Eton jacket and full-flare skirt, with her fair hair pinned up in a peculiar sweeping style that was no doubt all the rage of the season. At that moment, she seemed more of a stranger than ever before.

That very evening, I was dressed up for dinner with the abominable Lord Sidcup. Mother pulled my corset strings until I was forced to turn round and cry that I might very well faint if she persevered. If he had kept his mouth firmly closed, perhaps all should have been well. But his discourse was bombastic, ill-informed and, frankly, unintelligent. He was concerned only with frivolous society gossip and chattered gaily and inconsequentially beside me throughout the entire meal whilst I remained silent.

By the time our dessert of ladyfingers with strawberries had arrived, I was exhausted. I could not have been more relieved when the gentlemen retreated to the smoking room for brandy and cigars, even when I had to listen to Mother scolding me for behaving like a petulant child.

Perhaps I was, for he encouraged such behaviour in me. And yet, despite all that, I was horrified to discover a few days later that he wished to call upon me back at home in Bourn.

> > >

It was a bright spring morning, one that in other circumstances should have made my heart sing. But the only thing that was singing was a sparrow perched upon a branch of

an apple tree as I walked through the orchard with Lord
Sidcup; or rather, I walked several paces ahead of him. But
the moment I had been dreading came. He did not ask me
outright, but told me he had a question he wished to ask
me. I skirted around the subject, pointing out that I was not
a young lady who enjoyed the gaiety of London society: tea
parties and grand dinners and the like; and that surely he
would feel more comfortable with a girl of this kind instead.
But he seemed not to hear me, telling me about Dervish
Hall where he resided, and how he would try to be a good
husband to me.

I decided I had no other choice but to inform him, without further delay, that even should I accept his offer, I had
every intention of going to university. Never could I have
predicted his reaction, even from a man like him. For he
stated, categorically, that such a notion was quite impossible and – I remember his exact words – that 'young ladies
do not go to university'.

I did not want to spend a single moment more in his
company, and pushed past him, striding back towards The
Old Vicarage. He hurried after me and caught the crook
of my arm, swinging me round and pulling me close. I
could smell his skin, cologne and garlic, and noticed the
thick black eyelashes that fanned out across his cheek as
he breathed down his nose at me. I was about to wrench
my way free when he moved one hand up to my shoulder,
grasped it roughly and pressed his lips hard upon mine. The
feel of his moist tongue flickering around in my mouth was
unbearable but when I tried to wrench free from him, he

tightened his grip. I placed my hands against his chest and, with all my might, pushed against him. Lord Sidcup staggered backwards, tumbling with a great thump onto the lawn.

He stood up, brushing the grass from his trousers, and fixed his eyes upon me. To my great horror, he was laughing. 'You see, Miss Johnson, that is what I like about you. You have spirit. Not one of those yes-Sir, no-Sir girls that can be found at every society event the length and breadth of this country. *This* is why we shall make such a formidable match.'

I had heard quite enough. I walked up to the house, went directly to my bedroom and locked the door.

❧ ❧ ❧

I refused to leave the room for three days in a row. I would not come out for dinner or, indeed, any food at all; I would not come out to see my brother Arthur, who had been called back from Cambridge to talk sense into me, and I would not even come out for some fresh air. The offer of marriage to Lord Sidcup arrived nevertheless. And with it, an ultimatum.

On the fourth day of my self-imposed confinement, the waves of hunger overwhelmed me and I allowed Papa to come in with bread and soup. I gobbled it down and he called the maid to bring more. He stood by the window, staring morosely out at the front lawns and fields beyond them, before turning and telling me that if I did not agree to marry Lord Sidcup – a future that would ensure me a title and land and inheritance for my children – the fate that awaited me would be far less desirable.

'What do you mean, Papa?' I asked, bread lodging in my throat.

Without quite meeting my eye, he began to quietly speak. 'Mother has found an advertisement in *The Lady*.'

'An advertisement?'

'Yes… for a gentleman who requires a wife.'

'I see.' I clasped my hands in my lap. 'Where?' I envisaged a far-flung corner of rural Wales or Cornwall, many miles from the nearest university where women were permitted.

Papa sighed and turned away from me, furrows interweaving across his brow. 'British East Africa.'

I let out a shrill, high laugh. He was joking, of course. But he did not smile. He simply stared at his feet, grimacing.

'Papa!' I cried. 'Tell me you cannot be serious. Please!'

'I have never been more serious, Iris.'

I began to laugh again, bitterly. 'To be fed to the lions or fed to the lord! How *lucky* I am, to be given such a choice.'

Papa's face turned red and his eyes, the exact same shade as mine, narrowed. 'You are behaving like a child, Iris. You are eighteen years of age now. You *must* face up to this.' His words were quiet but I could see him quivering with rage in a way I had never before witnessed in my quiet, gentle father. For a single moment, I felt guilty that I had angered him, my beloved papa, who had always been my ally, for as long as I could remember. But then I felt myself responding with my own fury. I *wasn't* going to accept it just like that, I simply was *not!* Of all people, from him I expected far, far more.

I jumped up from my bed. 'I see that I am quite alone in the world!' I cried. '*You* studied at Christ's College in Cambridge, Papa! How can it possibly be just that you are afforded such an opportunity in life and I am not? Tell me!'

At that, Papa took a sharp intake of breath, clenched his fists and marched to the door. After pulling it open, he spun upon his heels and stared at me long and hard. 'There has been quite enough melodrama, Iris. You need to make a decision, and make one quickly. Lord Sidcup or the East Africa Protectorate.'

And with that he was gone, pulling the door firmly shut behind him.

The following days were endless as I agonised over the choice I was required to make. Perhaps, just perhaps, in Lord Sidcup's vast country manor we should not see too much of one another. But then, I remembered with what scorn and derision he had treated me that day he came to dine; how he had forced his large, wet mouth upon mine. I found myself physically shuddering, closing my eyes to steady myself. *No*, I thought, if he could treat me in such a way before we were even married, how much more of a bully would he be were I his wife?

And yet... East Africa. A vast, unknown territory, flooded with sunlight and... what else? I did not know. I could scarcely begin to imagine it. Papa had kept fantail pigeons for as long as I could remember and I spent far longer than normal in the pigeon house during those days, safe in the warm, musty gloom. There, I let my tears flow freely and one pigeon, as though sensing my distress,

flew to my shoulder, where it perched, making soft coo-
ing noises.

❧ ❧ ❧

An entire week passed before we had that terrible conversation, the one that will remain forever seared on my memory.
Mother sat primly at the head of the dinner table, informing me that I must give her and Father my decision.

'You say, Mother,' I began to say slowly, 'that I have a
choice; that I am lucky to be afforded this. Yet what you
fail to see is that it is not *really* a choice.' Mother opened
her mouth, about to protest in horror, but I pressed on,
determined to speak. 'Am I to be married to an unrefined
man whom I abhor, who I have no doubt should mistreat
me, or am I to be married to a man I know nothing of – you
have not, incidentally, even thought to tell me his name – in
a place I know nothing of; a man who, potentially, could
conduct himself even more deplorably than Lord Sidcup?
This is what you call a choice?'

Mother's face turned quite crimson at my speech and
she opened and closed her mouth as though gasping for air.
Clearly finding no words, she turned to Papa and dug him
sharply in the ribs.

'What is your decision, Iris? To marry Lord Sidcup or
Mr Lawrence?' Papa asked wearily, staring down at his half-
eaten meal.

'Mr Lawrence. So that is his name. My decision, *not* my
choice, is that I go to the East Africa Protectorate. I have no
knowledge of what to expect there. But at least it is a new

life and I can hope that this man is kind and learned and possesses dignity, unlike Lord Sidcup.' I pushed my chair back abruptly. 'My decision gives me no pleasure, but the matter is now decided.' I glanced at Papa, who appeared stunned, a genuine expression of horror framing his features. Mother, on the other hand? Her entire bearing softened and what I read on her face was unmistakable: relief.

❧ ❧ ❧

I remember little of my last few weeks at The Old Vicarage. Cases and clothes and accessories were ordered for me, in which I took no interest, more arriving each day. I started spending longer and longer in the pigeon house and furiously knocking croquet balls across the lawn and, for once, Mother neither commented upon this nor called me in. My brother Arthur came from Cambridge to spend the day with me shortly before I departed. How I adored that brother of mine! We shared a different relationship to how it was between Violet and myself: a yawning chasm of indifferent misunderstanding.

His arm was linked through mine as we trod over the crisp grass. 'I should imagine it will be thrilling being in Africa. In a way I envy you. *Not –*' he added hurriedly – 'the marriage business. I mean simply being there. It must be terribly beautiful.'

'Do you think so?'

'Of course. It's the wild, untamed continent. Miles upon miles of wilderness and animals: elephant, lion, leopard. How ripping to see all that.'

I bit my bottom lip. 'Perhaps you can come and visit me,' I said, with little conviction.

'Perhaps I can,' he replied cheerfully. 'The East African railway that has been built from Mombasa into the interior sounds like the greatest of its kind anywhere in the world.'

'Arthur,' I said as I stopped walking, taking my arm from his to look at him properly. 'Is there anything about Mr Lawrence you know that I do not?'

He paused, brushing a leaf from his trousers. 'The mater really hasn't told you anything?'

'Not a thing.'

'Well…' He frowned. 'I don't know much, but here's what I do know. His name is Jeremy Lawrence. He's British…' he paused, 'obviously. But he's lived out there for five years or so. I'm not sure what he does now the railway is finished; he was stationed in Mombasa for some time but is now in Nairobi, where you will be going.'

'Nairobi?'

'Yes. It's the new administrative headquarters of the region. I don't know anything about it, I'm afraid. But after his first wife died—'

My fingers involuntarily fluttered. 'His first wife died?'

Arthur stared at his hands. 'Yes.'

'What did she die of?'

He paused. 'I don't know, old girl—'

'Tell me, Arthur.'

He was silent for a few moments as I listened to the distant call of a thrush and the breeze murmuring in the leaves.

'She died of malaria, Iris…'

'Which is why he wants another wife, to replace the wife who died.'

'I suppose so. But look upon it as an adventure.' Arthur was attempting a strained smile.

'An adventure in which I may come back in a coffin like my predecessor.'

He sighed. 'Don't think like that, old girl. You must think the best. See it as something…' He floundered, 'something *new*, something different. Iris…' He reached out and took one of my hands in his. 'Frankly speaking, you don't fit into this life here. You know what I am speaking of.' Tears sprang to my eyes. 'Perhaps… I do hate to say this, Iris, because I shall hate losing you, but perhaps this is for the best. To have a break from Mother – you do rankle one another terribly. If anybody can do this, you can. You're intelligent and strong – far stronger than Violet or I.'

I hung my head. 'Strong?' I sobbed. 'Look at me! Just look at me!'

'You *are* strong, Iris. You are the strongest person I know,' he said firmly. 'Make a success of it. Don't be beaten. Show Mother that you can take a situation like this and rise above it.'

I shook my head. 'No,' I replied sadly, 'I do not wish to prove anything to Mother—' I broke off and looked upwards to a small bird that circled overhead. 'Arthur, look – a swallow!' I pointed towards the bird that wheeled gracefully in the sky.

He shielded his eyes against the brightness of the sky. 'Yes. This is your bird, Iris. He shall migrate to Africa once the summer is over here, so you can follow him.' We both stared upwards at the glossy blue-black of the swallow's back and its streaming, forked tail.

'Yes, little swallow,' I say, 'I shall go before you and welcome you when you arrive in Africa. Arthur…' I pull my eyes away from the bird, 'if you ever find a book of African birds in Cambridge, could you buy it and send it to me?'

'Of *course*, Iris. I shall make a point of looking in all the shops I can think of.'

'Thank you, Arthur,' I whisper. I look back up for the swallow, but it is already long gone.

CHAPTER FOUR

PENELOPE LOGAN

We have reached the long red furrow of the Suez Canal and Miss Johnson and I stand up on deck as the ship's bow pushes her way through the baked sands and stony banks. Once this is behind us, we move slowly past the hazy, sun-smitten mountains of the Sinai. It is beautiful, but my charge is looking weary.

'Miss Johnson,' I say, 'let us go below deck to take some tea and a rest, perhaps.'

She turns her head towards me, her eyes unnaturally bright. 'Oh, thank you, Miss Logan. But I should far rather stay up here. I would hate to miss anything.'

I frown. 'Come, Miss Johnson. The heat is terribly damp and oppressive here, and it is not sensible to remain so long beneath the sun.'

Still, she does not move. I find myself becoming impatient but, at the same time, cannot help but admire her stubborn spirit. I only hope that her husband-to-be is tolerant of it.

'*Please*, Miss Logan.' She narrows her attractive eyes. 'My hat is quite broad enough to protect me from the sun. I...'

she hesitates. 'I do so thrive upon fresh air, you see, and this is the first ship I have ever sailed on.'

I sigh, and nod my head briefly. Let me leave the girl where she is. Neither of us can know the kind of man I am to deliver her to in Mombasa and these are her last days of being quite alone.

I myself retire to the cabin for a rest. Upon awaking, I hurry back up on deck, where I find my charge in the exact same spot where I left her. The crystal waters of the Red Sea glimmer and lap against the shore as we steam into the port, which is dotted with wooden fishing boats and, in the distance, towers and humble homes.

Miss Johnson turns to me, her eyes gleaming with excitement. 'We are in Port Sudan!' she cries. 'I overheard somebody saying so. And look, Miss Logan, look!' I follow her outstretched finger and see, on land, the most curious humped creatures with long-lashed eyes. 'What *are* they?'

I peer at them. 'Camels, I should say.'

'How terribly exciting! Have you seen them before?'

'I have not,' I admit. 'But I have seen them depicted in paintings and so forth. Are they not peculiar to look at?'

Miss Johnson throws her head back and laughs as gleefully as a child. 'I should say they are rather beautiful. Exotic!' she replies.

She leans precariously far over the railing. I am about to reach out to restrain her, but bring my hand back. I *must* allow Miss Johnson these small pleasures.

As we reach the harbour, once I have stopped gazing at the camels, I notice the people who are leading them. I am

acutely aware that this is the first time in my life I have seen
men with ink-black skin, not the lighter colour of earth we
have seen up until this point. Yet they mingle with Arabs,
who wear fringed headdresses, dark scarves wrapped round
their hair and mouths, leaving only the tops of their honey-
coloured noses and eyes uncovered, giving them a furtive
appearance. They are awaiting smaller boats at the harbour,
heaving in chests and packages from the water's edge and
staring at the likes of us, who gaze down from the wooden
barriers of the steamer.

⟩ ⟩ ⟩

The wind becomes warmer the further south we travel,
yet the nights are chill and clear. Once Miss Johnson has
watched the sun vanish into the horizon, she agrees to come
down below deck and play a hand of cards with me before dinnertime. The food is terrible, almost inedible, but
thankfully, due to the heat, neither of us has much of an
appetite in any case.

The next port town the steamer pulls into is Aden.
We stop so infrequently that all the passengers are eager
to disembark and I am pushed aside by a group of excit-
able young children, their nannies blustering after them. As
soon as we are on land, Miss Johnson and I are met by the
peculiar sight of a stuffed mermaid in a glass case; she looks
almost lifelike, with her waxen skin and forlorn, glassy gaze.
I frown, shaking my head, and turn to look at my charge,
her nose quite wrinkled up.

'What *is* that smell?' Miss Johnson asks.

'*Smells*, I should say,' I reply as I thrust my nose upwards and breathe in the air, pungent with spices and the dung of animals, seaweed and fish. Miss Johnson places a handkerchief beneath her nose as she walks alongside me. 'Would you like a camel ride?'

She bursts out laughing, shaking her head. 'I should think not.'

I give a small, curt nod. 'Very well,' I say and hand a boy a coin. Within moments, I am being hoisted by two men on to the dip between the two humps of a tethered camel. Miss Johnson, below me, claps a hand to her mouth in an attempt to stifle a laugh. The truth is, it is not terribly comfortable up here – the creature's back is hard and bony and I do not feel very dignified sitting with my legs astride so. As it begins to move, I clutch the leather strap round its neck, yanking hard at it. The camel stops, turns its face back and blinks at me, eyes perturbed beneath its long eyelashes. After some moments, however, I begin to relax and from high up here I realise I can see hills folding gently in on themselves, washed golden in the sunlight and dotted with dwellings and towering minarets. It is really a tremendous view and I am, despite the discomfort, rather disappointed when I am brought down from the camel and Miss Johnson and I walk back to the ship.

I have been employed by the reverend and his wife to chaperone Miss Johnson to Mombasa, remain with her there for the wedding and then travel back by steamer. I am to stay in East Africa for no longer, yet as I stand on deck now and watch this young girl, with her face turned towards the sun bleeding into the horizon, dark strands of hair coming loose and blowing about her, I experience a strange, unexpected sensation: something maternal, protective. The Lord knows I have acted as chaperone enough times in the course of my life. I have chaperoned silly girls, spiteful girls, unintelligent and unfeeling girls. And there have, of course, been sweet girls as well. Yet Iris Johnson is none of these. She reminds me of a caged bird that beats its wings in a passionate fury to leave its prison, yet remains shackled. There is something about Miss Johnson that worries me – I cannot quite say what – and though it is quite impossible, I should like to stay longer with her and travel onwards to Nairobi where she is to make her new life.

These weeks we have spent at sea together have been rather pleasant. Miss Johnson has enjoyed reading Pearl Rivers, which I am delighted to see, and we have played numerous entertaining games of whist and gin rummy. She is rather clever with a hand of cards. She is, in fact, rather clever at everything. She is quick to speak and thus does not possess a measured intellect, but beneath her passionate discourse runs a vein of warmth, depth and wisdom I have never before experienced in an eighteen-year-old girl. I only hope that Mr Lawrence can match her intelligence, for never have I seen a happy match when a wife's intellect exceeds her husband's.

At Cape Guardafui, the sea grows restless from the southwest monsoon and the rocky Somalian coast spreads out along our starboard side as we draw ever nearer to Mombasa. Miss Johnson begins to look quite green about the gills. If only I could put this down to seasickness, but of course we both know it is nothing of the sort. It would be frivolous and of scant help to offer any words of comfort to her at this stage. I had a sweetheart once. He grew up, like me, in Inverness and though marriage was never mentioned between us, it did not need to be. I could read it in his eyes. Yet he died of influenza that bitter winter of 1870 that had us snowed in for weeks, unable to leave our homes for food or medicine. I decided after that that I should never marry and I never regretted my decision. As I look now at Miss Johnson, I feel a flash of anger twist within me that women must be subjected to this. Where are the liberals, the progressives? Why must women be prevented from being involved in such decisions?

CHAPTER FIVE

IRIS JOHNSON

Mombasa Island. My heart sinks as we approach.

As SS *Juba* steams into port, the anchor is lowered a stone's throw from the shore. Everyone is flung into a frenzy of excited activity: porters carry trunks from the berths; a young child, her noisy sobs rending the air, is reprimanded sternly by her nanny; a fashionable lady treads purposefully along the deck, with a wide-brimmed parasol and high-necked dress with leg-of-mutton sleeves, looking far better suited to the streets of Mayfair; a gaggle of young men in khaki uniform, with strange, bell-like helmets upon their heads, nod at me as they walk past. Who are all these people, I think, and what is their business here?

'Miss Johnson, are you quite well?' Miss Logan says. I am gripping the railing and leaning far over, staring into the clear azure waters of the ocean. I feel a firm arm round my waist and a hand grasping my elbow as I am steered back from the railing. For such a small woman, Miss Logan's strength is astonishing.

'I am not sure…' I falter, craning my neck round to stare into the small, bright eyes of my chaperone as people jostle past us on all sides, 'I am not sure I can do this. Be here. Marry this man.'

To her credit, Miss Logan is silent for several moments before replying, blinking her bird-like eyes at me. 'Miss Johnson,' she says eventually in a small but firm voice. 'Have you looked around you? Have you seen how very beautiful this place is? I myself have never seen a land of such splendour. Look!'

I cast my eyes around desperately, following her wiry, outstretched finger, and take a sharp intake of breath. I cannot deny it: it is an astonishing sight. The red-roofed houses of Mombasa Island drip with flowering shrubs of colours so bright and so brilliant I could never have imagined they truly existed.

'Do you see those?' Miss Logan points to a cluster of smaller trees beside the palms, the branches weighed down with large, orange fruits. 'Mango trees, I am fairly certain.'

I nod my head mutely. I have no idea what mango is. No doubt I shall find out soon enough though. The harbour is crowded with white-sailed wooden boats as well as smaller rowing boats and tall, elegant buildings with shutters glowing the colour of beeswax in the late afternoon sun. Thatched bungalows made from wood are flanked by graceful, bending palm trees and dark-skinned men weave through the groves with bright turbans wound about their heads.

I hear what I am sure is a distant woodpecker – a persistent knocking against wood – and I scan around for it. But my attention is pulled back to the boat as I become aware of a great number of men surrounding us, pushing, jostling and gesticulating this way and that as they cry in broken English through blackened teeth, 'Madams! We row you ashore!' before pointing to the line of wooden boats steadily making their way to the mainland. I take a deep breath, feeling overwhelmed and as wobbly as those simple little vessels that are travelling across the harbour.

Miss Logan squeezes my arm. 'Come,' she says decisively. 'Let us go and meet Mr Lawrence.'

We row ashore in the small boat and I clutch Miss Logan's arm as though my life depends on it. Terrified as I feel, my curiosity overcomes me and I slowly lift my head and scan the nearing shoreline for signs of Mr Lawrence. Immediately, I spy a tall, solitary figure standing upon the harbour wall, stiff and ramrod straight, hands clasped behind his back and pipe in his mouth.

Despite the heat's intensity, he is dressed in thick, white linens, replete with waistcoat, jacket and cummerbund. The relentless sun is beating down upon his peculiar helmet, of the kind that all the gentlemen on the ship wore whilst on deck. I am close enough now to see that one of his eyes is glinting: he is wearing a glass monocle. He looks terribly old.

I am trapped in some kind of dreadful dream, the tropical heat extracting small rivers of sweat from places I never imagined possible. We approach the shore and the gentleman on the wall takes one step forwards, removing the pipe from his mouth. So, it *is* him. He grasps my hand and helps Miss Logan and me unsteadily out of the boat before taking my hand once more and shaking it firmly. It is cool, despite the heat. I look from his lined hand up into his face and, up close, he looks even older. Older than Papa, even. His monocle glints fiercely in the sun and a wisp of fair but greying hair has escaped from beneath his sturdy helmet. He looks as though he is about to go into battle.

'Miss Johnson,' he says. 'I am Jeremy Lawrence. And Mrs…' He shoots her a cursory glance.

'Miss Logan,' she says, nodding briskly at him.

He turns away from her, enquiring after the luggage. He has brought two men with him and directs them towards the cases. They are being heaved up from the rowing boat onto the quayside.

'This way, Miss Johnson. Miss Logan. Follow me please, ladies.'

We walk away from the wharf behind Mr Lawrence and the luggage-bearers towards a narrow street. The sailors in their turbans fan out at either side and craftsmen ply their trades from open-fronted dwellings along the harbour. I feel sick with the heat and the strangeness of it all.

Before long, we arrive at what looks like an open trolley car. As the men load the trunks into one of these, Mr Lawrence calls back over his shoulder. 'These carts are known as garries here. They travel upon old, abandoned railway lines.'

'Indeed!' Miss Logan replies, but I notice that Mr Lawrence ignores her, only helping me and not my chaperone to climb into one of the two garries beneath its canvas awning.

As soon as we are seated, we are propelled forwards by native boys who push us from behind and begin to travel through a warren of narrow streets, past what look like

government offices and grand residences with arched doorways. It is quite unlike anything I have seen before. Scarlet
blazes of red-petalled flowers and rich sprays of white and
purple bougainvillea fan out against wood-and-corrugated-
iron buildings on either side. The town is built in shades of
rose, chestnut and lemon, its hues enhanced by the light of
late afternoon. Clearly Miss Logan is marvelling at the very
same thing, for at that moment she turns from her garry in
front and calls to Mr Lawrence, sitting beside me, to ask
what the building material is.

'Coral-rock,' he replies shortly.

There is also a rather fine view of a fort en route, glowing
a majestic deep apricot colour. Mr Lawrence sees me staring
at it.

'Fort Jesus,' he tells me. 'Interesting history actually. Built
around five hundred years ago by the Portuguese to guard
the harbour. Over the years, it's been changed by both the
Omani Arabs and the British. In fact, up until…'

The gentle rocking of the trolley car lulls me into a deep
weariness and I hear none of his subsequent words. As my
eyelids begin to droop, I suddenly feel a dreadful jolt. I clasp
on to the side of the trolley, eyes wide open now, and see
a white-robed Arab sitting astride a donkey moving in the
opposite direction from us along the narrow lane. The poor
beast is also laden down with baskets, its owner kicking its
flanks to make it carry on whilst Mr Lawrence stiffens beside me.

'*Quite* unacceptable,' he mutters irritably, 'that natives,
particularly with animals, should be permitted down these

same streets demarcated for garries.' I have no idea how to respond to this so I remain silent. Whilst we are delayed, a young beggar approaches the tramcar and thrusts a bowl, encrusted with grime, beneath my nose. He is quite the filthiest and poorest-looking child I have ever seen. I am about to look for a coin of some sort when Mr Lawrence clutches the sides of the garry, stands up and shouts at him. '*Kwenda uno! Kwenda, kwenda!*' He then calls something with equal ferocity to the garry boys and we jolt back into motion.

I take in less and less of our surroundings and once again am overcome with fatigue and the heat. Much as I enjoyed the sea passage, I didn't sleep terribly well and now that we are here in Mombasa, my future husband sitting beside me in this cramped tramcar with the heat and smells of sweat and spice more powerful than anything I have previously experienced, I feel quite overwhelmed by it all.

Jeremy Lawrence looks just like the frog footman in livery from *Alice's Adventures in Wonderland*. He has a vast Adam's apple and protruding eyes, watery blue and unblinking and one made even larger as a result of that thick monocle he removes at intervals to clean with a handkerchief. His moustache, which I can see he has spent considerable time grooming, is thick and yellow-grey.

We arrive at an attractive, tumbledown building named Africa Hotel with thatched roofs, latticed balconies and a grand, carved door studded with brass and surrounded by coconut palms. I accept Mr Lawrence's proffered hand to help me clamber out of the garry, but again he makes no move to assist my chaperone. Miss Logan and I are ushered inside to a dim room of dark wood panelling. Several Arab servants with skin the colour of rich honey stand around in long white gowns and caps. They give us something to drink; I have no idea what it is and though the coolness revives me, all I can think of is lying down. Once I have tipped the contents of the glass down my throat, I look about until I see Mr Lawrence, who is issuing orders for our cases to be taken to our rooms. We are shown the way by one of the servants, tall and slender, the hem of his gown brushing the floor. The dark wooden staircase, curiously, is external to the building and, like the balcony, intricately carved and latticed. Miss Logan is exclaiming and marvelling and tutting, more to herself than anyone else, and I envy her more at that moment than I have ever envied another soul. She is here as a casual observer, a traveller to this distant land, and she is free to turn her back on it all.

What a relief it is when I am shown to my bedroom and realise that Mr Lawrence and I are not yet expected to share! Now that he is here, in the flesh, however, I realise with startling clarity that the time for this will surely be soon upon me and I must submit to whatever it is that is expected of me. It makes me feel ill to the core as I look at him in his linen trousers and waistcoat, not wishing to know what lies beneath in the curves and folds of his body. He takes off his pith helmet and tucks it beneath his arm, revealing that his fair hair is thinning at the temples. He has large lips that look out of place on his narrow face and his eyes are pale blue – not, I think, unlike the shade of my mother's. He is smiling at me and yet his face is distant. The door to my room is opened, revealing a grand, mosquito-netted four-poster bed, and I stand on the threshold for an awkward moment, longing to go in and lie down but unable to do so quite yet whilst he is still standing there.

Mr Lawrence clears his thoat. 'Ladies, I am going to the club now. But please make yourselves comfortable. If you would like tea, cold drinks, something to eat, just ring the bell in your room and anything can be brought up to you. We shall dine at seven downstairs, so…' he hesitates, running a hand through his thin hair, 'until then.'

He nods curtly and then vanishes, his shoes clattering down the wooden staircase. I stare at Miss Logan rather helplessly and she raises both her thin eyebrows at me.

'Miss Johnson, you look exhausted. Get some rest.'

CHAPTER SIX

PENELOPE LOGAN

Expect nothing and you're bound to be pleasantly surprised,' that's what my mother always said. But I expected nothing of Mr Lawrence and have received rather less, I'm afraid. The man is prejudiced, that much is clear. Prejudiced against the natives around him, prejudiced against the Scottish and prejudiced against women.

My heart truly aches for Miss Johnson; I know a bad egg when I see one. Of all the girls I have chaperoned in my time, Miss Johnson is the very least suited to Mr Lawrence. I have a good mind to take her back with me in two days' time and thwart this marriage. But of course I cannot and shall not. Miss Johnson is an adult, eighteen years of age, and I only hope and pray that her spirit is not broken by him.

I glance up at the ineffective wooden ceiling fan, then walk to the windows. I throw back the shutters, smelling the salt from the ocean and feeling the wind on my face. My *History of Trade in Mombasa* volume tells me that this wind is the *kusi*, blowing in a southerly direction to take the

traders away from Mombasa and north up the coast. As I
close my eyes, it certainly feels like a southerly wind against
my face: warm and welcoming.

It begins on the bare toes of my left foot and steals up to
my ankle. At first, it is merely a slight irritation, like a fly.
But then I feel the sharp pain in my toes, my ankle, my heel
and further up towards the shin. It is as though a thousand
tiny little needles are being pushed in simultaneously and
I look down and see dozens upon dozens of small, black
creatures. They look like ants but never have I known them
to bite so viciously, or to bite at all for that matter. I grimace
and stoop down to brush them from me and succeed in dis-
lodging one or two, yet the majority remain entrenched and
the pain, to be sure, is quite unlike anything I have experienced. Try as I might to prevent myself from crying out, I
shriek. I clamp one hand over my mouth and with the other
I swipe frenziedly to expel these devilish African ants from
my toes and ankle. But there are too many of them and the
pain escalates and I scream with all my might – long and
hard and clear.

Miss Johnson appears in the doorframe, her eyes huge
and concerned and her thick brown hair loose about her
shoulders. And then, I am sorry to say, Mr Lawrence is behind her, his tall, gaunt figure looming with all its foreboding menace. He pushes past Miss Lawrence, dashes across
the room to the window and grasps my ankle roughly between his large, weather-worn hands before plucking each
small beast individually from my bare skin and hurling
them through the window. Had the pain not been so in-

tense, I should be mortified that Mr Lawrence is witnessing the sight of my naked skin. Once the operation is finished, he brushes his hand, not gently, one final time over my ankle and foot and stands up, pulling the window shut behind me. I lean back against the wooden shutters, panting from the exertion.

'*Siafu*. They are biting ants, common in these parts,' Mr Lawrence says. His words are kind, but his tone and expression are not and he looks at me with unveiled distaste. I catch my breath and compose myself. I am about to say something to him when he presses on. 'There is a reason why the windows remain closed, Miss Logan, and why there are fans in the rooms. You would do well to keep them shut from now on.'

I open my mouth and close it again. He takes his leave, whilst Miss Johnson and I remain in the room, our eyes locked. She looks desperate, her eyes searching mine as she no doubt considers the man she is to marry just two days henceforth. And then the look of tension in her face melts, her lips part and she begins to laugh. A laugh so open and so unrestrained that despite the aching, lingering pain of the ants, I cannot help but join her. What a sight we must look, me with my un-stockinged legs and she with her hair loose and wild!

CHAPTER SEVEN

IRIS JOHNSON

Approaching Emmanuel Church, I feel nauseous. I try to focus on concrete things; the church itself, for example, blindingly white beneath the glare of the sunshine, fiercer than ever though it is now four in the afternoon. The church crumbles into the sea on one side and, on the other, is partly shaded by a huge, ancient-looking tree, several black crows staring down at me from the bare branches.

Miss Logan is at my side and, were it not for her presence, I truly do not know how I should even be able to place one foot in front of the other to reach the pulpit and await Mr Lawrence.

'That is a baobab tree, Miss Johnson,' she murmurs into my ear, pointing at the curious old tree that looks as though its roots are sticking into the bright blue sky. 'If I am not mistaken, they are amongst the oldest trees on this planet.'

'Oh!' I exclaim, and can think of nothing else to say beyond that. I am shaking slightly, and Miss Logan grasps my arm in that firm way of hers. I am certain that she is actually holding me up.

I feel the wind upon my face and the discomfort and itch of my corset beneath my clothes, and little else. Miss Logan told me, on the long sea voyage, that slavery is common in these parts, particularly Mombasa. Slaves are bargained for and sold as readily as spices, sugar and tea. As I stand there, on the threshold of the church, in my starched white cotton dress with a lace frill round my neckline, white embroidered slippers and a corsage of fresh lilies pinned to my chest, I feel, unequivocally, like a slave. My family has sold me to a man in a far-off land and how shall I ever bring myself to forgive them?

Last night, I fell asleep clutching the St Christopher pendant in my hands. I cried as I thought of my dear papa in Bourn and how he must suffer the wrath of Mother now without me to come to his defence. Today, however, I feel none of this empathy, only the dull thud of betrayal.

Miss Logan walks me to the front of the church, close to the pulpit and the short, bulbous-nosed vicar, with his bright, cheerful eyes the same colour as the Mombasa sea and a thick thatch of peppery white hair, then she squeezes my arm once more and removes herself to sit on a pew. Without her arm on mine, I feel as though I might dissolve into a watery puddle on the church floor. I turn to look at her.

Miss Logan gives me a kind, firm smile, narrowing her shrewd eyes and inclining her head at me. I try to smile back but my mouth is frozen; in fact, my entire body is frozen, despite the heat. But then I hear the sharp clip of footsteps along the aisle behind me. I stare fixedly at the vicar's nose, the odd purplish shade and roundness of it, and even when I feel that Mr Lawrence is standing directly next to me, I cannot bring myself to turn my head and look at him.

The vicar presides over us and I mumble in the pauses, as expected. I hear the sudden flurry of wings and I look round to the church entrance. A black crow caws and beats against the faded interior of the church. My mind is taken immediately to the fantail pigeons back home and I feel a pang of remorse that I shall not see them again for a long time. Father, I know, goes in there to tend to them, but does he ever speak to them like I did?

I pull my attention back to Mr Lawrence and the vicar and suddenly the ring is being placed upon my finger and my veil is being lifted and I feel Mr Lawrence's face close to mine. His proximity takes me by surprise and I feel a sudden roughness in my throat that I try to remove by coughing. I bring my hand to my mouth whilst Mr Lawrence, narrowing his eyes, draws away. 'Sorry,' I whisper.

I glance at the vicar, whose bushy white eyebrows are raised in surprise. The moment for the kiss, it appears, has passed and instead Mr Lawrence brushes his lips awkwardly against my cheek as I attempt to smile at him, though I am unsure if this bid is translated to my lips for it feels more like a grimace.

Man and wife, man and wife. Those words echo as hollow as the empty church and before I know it, I am signing my name upon a piece of paper. We stand now before the vicar as he gives us one final blessing, before turning and walking down the aisle, my arm through my husband's. There is no music, no fanfare, not that I ever desired any of that.

🕊 🕊 🕊

Mr Lawrence and I – of course I am to call him Jeremy now, though I do not know when I shall be able – dine alone that evening at the Africa Hotel in the dining room beside the wide verandah that overlooks the open sea. We are the only people eating here, the sound of our cutlery scraping against fine china echoing around the cavernous room. Every time I move my fork, the flash of silver upon my left ring finger startles me and that curious sensation of a dry, irritated throat starts up again.

'Do you have a cold, Iris?' Mr Lawrence asks me and, again, the sound of my Christian name emanating from his lips startles me. I lay down my cutlery and cough behind my linen napkin.

'A cold? No, I think not. Perhaps I am not accustomed to Mombasa's dust.'

He nods and smiles briefly before placing a forkful of chicken in his mouth. The meat within the strange, spiced sauce is tough and the vegetables bland.

'This food is… what exactly?'

'Curry,' Mr Lawrence replies, dabbing the corner of his mouth with a napkin. 'It's what the Asians eat. A chap called de Souza opened this hotel. Runs a general store next door and he hasn't quite… well, managed to employ a European cook yet.'

I nod mutely. How I long for Cook's steak and kidney pie or cream of asparagus soup.

What is one to say to a man one does not know, yet has just married? Does a manual exist, I wonder, in which topics of conversation are put forth to advise a young, newly married woman? Or should I simply remain silent and allow my husband to talk? My mother was always terribly fond of manuals and, alongside Papa's encyclopedias and volumes of Tennyson and Milton, our library at home was filled with *The Scholar's Handbook of Household Management and Cookery* and *The New and Revised Edition of Cassell's Household Guide*. I remember on more than one occasion Mother leaving a book open in the drawing room so that I might be inclined to read it. Of course I never did, instead always banging it shut and replacing it on the shelf. Yet as I sit here now opposite my new husband, I wonder if within those heavy, bound pages of *Cassell's* or the *Scholar's Handbook* there was advice for a new wife. Not that there is anything scholarly about my predicament. If only there were.

I am not sure if Mr Lawrence is nervous or simply not inclined to talk, for most of the rest of the meal passes in pained silence, alleviated only by the hushed murmurs of the hovering servants, dressed in their long, white robes, offering more wine or water. By dessert, a sweet melon cut up in its skin, I can bear the silence no longer.

'Tell me about your work, Mr Lawrence.'

He finishes his mouthful, leans back and eyes me rather strangely. 'I know it will take a little while to get used to, but you are to call me Jeremy now.'

I take a sip of wine and then dab at the corner of my mouth with my napkin. 'I know,' I reply quietly, 'I am sure it will come eventually.'

He is silent for a while longer and I am just thinking that he is going to ignore my question when he clears his throat.

'I'm not sure how much you already know about what I do?'

Nothing. I know nothing at all about this man, about what he does. But I do not want to seem too ignorant. 'Not a great deal.'

'I am a member of the administration of the British colonial authority, based up in Nairobi. As I'm sure you're aware, I was previously stationed here in Mombasa, overseeing the coolie labour on the construction of the railway. But a new district commissioner post came up in Nairobi to work for the Farmers and Planters Association and it was thought I was just the chap for it. So I have been in Nairobi the past few months, setting up a home...' he hesitates, 'for us.'

I nod, in recognition of his last words, and eat a small slice of melon. It is the best melon I have ever tasted. As I allow its sweetness to dissolve in my mouth, I consider Mr Lawrence's words, realising I am none the wiser.

'Forgive me,' I say, laying down my spoon, 'but I am still not clear what it is you actually do.'

Mr Lawrence looks at me in surprise, his pale blue eyes widening and a small muscle in the corner of his mouth twitching. 'What I *do,*' he says, 'is to help our government encourage settlers to come out from Britain to start farms, opening the land up to economic use. Of course there is also the business of pushing the frontiers of respectability into the wilderness; to assist in civilising the Africans.'

'Civilising the Africans?'

'Indeed.'

I become aware of the man who has just poured water for me, standing in one corner of the room in his long white gown, with his tall and proud bearing, the very picture of civilisation and no doubt listening to our every word. As though reading my thoughts, Mr Lawrence continues.

'You have just disembarked from the ship, Miss... *Iris*, and Mombasa, you must know, has been established for many hundreds of years already. Nairobi is...' His words break off.

'Yes?'

'Nairobi...' he repeats, and then stops again, avoiding eye contact. 'Well, you will see presently how different it is to Mombasa. The good thing is,' he continues in a more cheerful voice, 'that it is not nearly as infernally hot as Mombasa, due to its altitude. It is almost six thousand feet above sea level, you know. And it is,' he adds, 'non-malarial.'

'I... I am sorry about what happened to your first wife,' I blurt out.

Again, the muscle in the corner of his mouth twitches and he stares at me, stricken, and I wish desperately that I could take my words back.

He looks down and begins to attack the remaining melon on his plate with great fervour. I feel guilt sear through me, yet also something else: frustration that I cannot express sympathy without it being taken as a slight.

I sigh, rather louder than I had intended, and then determine to encourage Mr Lawrence to talk again. How I wish Miss Logan were with us. She would know what to say.

'Please do tell me about the house in Nairobi, Mr Lawrence,' I say. 'Jeremy,' I add hastily. But no, it sounds strange and insincere. I am quite certain I shall never be able to comfortably call him Jeremy.

He finishes his melon and pushes his chair back slightly, both hands resting on the table.

'It is not so much a house as a kind of…' he hesitates and I see that he is itching to take his leave, for this meal to be over. 'It is… a kind of *boma*.'

I raise an eyebrow at him. He must know, surely, I have no idea what he means by that. 'A *boma*,' he continues in a voice so quiet I can barely hear him, 'is a homestead, a smallholding of sorts. And now, Iris, I shall let you settle into the new room while I go to my club, and I shall be back a little later. I bid you a good evening.' He lights his pipe, then nods at me, and I stare miserably back at the lank, fair hair that covers his scalp and frames his thin face.

When he has taken his leave, I sit turning the tumbler of water round on the table with my thumb and forefinger. Here I am, on the evening of my wedding, newly married to a man intent on civilising the Africans, a man whom I am expected to call Jeremy and whose will I am expected to submit to in the bedroom. I have, of course, no idea what to expect. Whether it is painful, whether I must be fully or partially undressed. Whether I am expected to undress myself or leave that matter to my husband. I catch the eye of the hovering servant and find myself blushing furiously, a hot pink creeping up my neck.

'Can I get you anything else, Madam?' he asks quietly and smiles at me demurely.

'No.' I shake my head. 'No, thank you. I think I shall just… go to my room now.'

He nods and bows slightly, starting to clear away the dishes. Is this, I think, what is meant by civilising the Africans? To teach them to speak like us? I force myself to smile back at him and push my chair back to make the journey upstairs, which I should like to last for ever.

I don't know for how many hours Mr Lawrence has been out at his club, but what I do know is that by the time he returns he has had more than a little to drink. As he leans over me in the darkness, I can smell the thick stench of whisky upon his breath and am determined to feign sleep. I feel both disgusted and terrified in equal measure as he lies down beside me and runs his fingers up and down my arm. I lie stiff as a board, relieved by how dark it is so that he is unable to see my eyelids fluttering. He grunts, kissing my shoulder a few times before hooking one thin leg over mine, and I think for one dreadful moment he is going to force himself upon me. But he evidently thinks better of it before unhooking himself and lying back on the bed in a stupor. I lie on the bed, but unlike that sensation of frozenness in the church earlier, my body is burning and sweating. It does so for hours after Mr Lawrence has fallen asleep.

How shall I possibly perform what is expected of me? I shall have to keep my eyes closed, but I only hope I am able to also close my ears, and everything else for that matter. I shudder at the thought of it, turning away from the loud snorts emanating from Mr Lawrence – my husband – and listen to the whine of mosquitoes from the other side of the net, high-pitched and accusing, and the thick whir of the wooden ceiling fan as it battles through the cloying air, hoping it will eventually lull me into some kind of sleep.

In the morning, when Mr Lawrence has already gone downstairs, I realise that this is it. I am married, I am leaving Miss Logan today and there is nothing at all that can prevent me from travelling to Nairobi. Sitting at the dressing table, the heat thick despite the early hour, I feel too weak to even attend to my hair.

There is a light knock on the door and my heart lifts; I know it must be Miss Logan. For Mr Lawrence would not, of course, knock on his own door.

'Yes?' I call.

'It's me, Miss Johnson. May I come in?'

I notice instantly that she has not called me Mrs Lawrence, and feel nothing but gratitude. I stand and hurry to the door, opening it. Never have I been so relieved to see anyone. Miss Logan peers down the corridor before quietly closing the door behind her. 'Mr Lawrence is reading his newspaper downstairs,' she says. 'I just wanted to come and see… how you were.'

I smile weakly at her. Grasping both my hands, she smiles at me warmly. 'Let me arrange your hair, my dear.'

She leads me, much like a child, over to the dressing table and I sit obediently still as she takes out my brush and pulls it through the tangles. The humidity has played havoc with my hair. A halo of frizz has formed over the top of my head and it looks quite unruly. I have dark circles beneath my eyes as well, for I scarcely slept last night.

My eyes fill with tears. I close them tightly to stem them and feel Miss Logan's hands, large and firm and warm, upon both of my shoulders.

'Iris,' she says, in her lovely, lilting voice. It is the first time she has called me Iris.

I look at her in the mirror behind me, her slight yet imposing figure. I blink back the tears.

'Iris,' she says again. 'Do not be afraid. You are stronger than you think.'

A sob escapes my lips as I drop my head and a hand comes up to press deeply into my eyelids.

'I think not,' I whisper.

'Yes,' she says firmly, 'yes, my dear, you are.'

I stare through my tears at her as she continues with my hair. Suddenly she lays the brush down with a loud clunk and produces a small piece of paper from a fold in her skirt. 'I wanted to give this to you now, in case there is no opportunity later on.'

'What is it?'

'My address in England, in Durham. If there is ever anything I can do for you. Anything you need…' She trails off.

'But I shall be here, in East Africa.'

'Yes. But perhaps you should like to write me a letter. To tell me how you are. It will take a good many weeks to arrive. But nevertheless, I should like to receive news from you.'

I close my fingers around the paper and smile at her. It is remarkable, the effect that this woman has on me, for beside her I feel as though anything is possible. I am to lose her very soon, and yet, perhaps she will be not quite so lost if we are able to keep communicating.

>> >> >>

Mombasa railway station takes my breath away with its throng of humanity carrying mangoes and chickens and crates filled with eggs. Women bear babies on their backs and I hear talking, shouting, laughing in foreign tongues everywhere. The air smells pungent, thick with sweetness and spiciness of unknown origins. One terrified young girl is crying, whilst her parents clutch her from both sides, laughing and pointing at the trains.

'What is the matter with that girl?' I ask Mr Lawrence.

'Oh,' he laughs, 'she is just scared. This is still a relatively new sight for people here. Remember the line only reached Nairobi in 1899 and its final destination of Port Florence in 1901. Personally, I am rather gratified that such a fuss is made over the great Uganda Railway, for great it is and shall, I have no doubt, always remain.'

I stare at him, my mouth falling slightly ajar at his pompous little speech. But I have no time to think of it any longer, for as we continue walking we are confronted by a crowd on the platform so immense that I cannot help wondering with a surge of panic if all these people are to board the train with us, to sit beside us in our compartment. As though reading my thoughts, Miss Logan points towards the far end of the platform and says, 'Presumably your first-class carriage is down there.'

At this, Mr Lawrence spins round on his heels to face her and replies, 'Yes, Miss Logan. Third class is for the natives, second class for the Asians and first class, naturally, is reserved for Europeans and a handful of wealthy Asians.' He is talking down his nose at her and I should like very much to push him. 'A tremendous amount of soot billows out from the coal train towards the second- and third-class carriages,' he continues, 'and in first class we are, naturally, spared such an aversion. I thank you, Miss Logan, for bringing Iris thus far. But we have no further need of your services. I wish you a pleasant journey back home.'

She is being dismissed. Mr Lawrence had not even wanted her to come with us to the railway station. 'I'm not at all sure about these needlessly sentimental, drawn-out farewells, Iris,' he had said at the Africa Hotel, drawing me aside.

'Oh *please*, Mr Lawrence, she has been so terribly good to me these past weeks.'

He had tutted and shaken his head. 'Very well, then. But you *must* call me Jeremy.'

We knew, of course, that this moment would come and Miss Logan grasps my hands as Mr Lawrence continues walking. I see that she has brought Pearl Rivers with her, and now she is pressing the book into my hands. 'This is for you.'

'But Miss Logan—'

'No buts. This is for you to keep, my dear. God bless you.'

I clasp the book to my chest and perhaps it is a trick of the light streaming onto the platform, but I am certain I see a stout tear form in the corner of Miss Logan's eye.

'Iris!' Mr Lawrence says sharply and I gaze at Miss Logan one final time. She is standing on the platform, her small, formidable figure filling the space around her. She raises a hand to me and I stare at her until I am forced to turn back.

I cannot help but stare at the third-class carriages, in which vast numbers of locals are sitting on wooden benches, large, handwoven baskets on the floor beside them. Just before I board the train, I turn and Miss Logan is still standing there, in the exact same spot. She lifts one hand above her head, holds it there and smiles at me.

❧ ❧ ❧

As we pull out of the station, I look out of the window and see the track winding away amongst luxuriant hills and foliage, the bright sky dotted with cawing, wheeling birds. As we pull away from Mombasa Island and Miss Logan, Mr Lawrence's spirits appear to improve considerably. He chatters incessantly about how marvellous the Uganda Railway is; that the sheer cunning of this engineering accomplishment can be likened to nothing else in this world.

'I feel damned proud to be British at times like this,' he is saying. 'What other nation could have built the most magnificent railway on this planet, securing British predominance upon the Upper Nile and gaining access to the fertile richness of Uganda?'

I nod mutely, hardly in the mood for a lesson on the history of East African colonialism. But my silence does not deter him. He keeps up a steady patter of facts but I only catch fragments: 'Kilindini... grand bridge... Mombasa Island... elephant grass.' Had I been taking this journey with Miss Logan, I should indeed have been terribly interested, particularly if we had been gleaning this information from a book, or even a native. But the ostentatious manner in which the words leave Mr Lawrence's mouth, almost as though he is custodian of everything that surrounds us, greatly lessens its appeal.

Gazing through the window, I see glades of palms and creeper-covered trees. After a mere fifteen minutes, the country begins to open up and become wilder, great tracts of red earth and thorny trees. I imagine all those people crammed into third class and then look around our own spacious carriage, the mahogany panelling and padded, green leather seats the height of class and comfort.

Every few miles we stop at trim little stations in order, Mr Lawrence tells me, for the boilers to be refilled with water. I notice numbered telegraph poles dug into the ground and the stations are replete with signals, water tanks, ticket offices and flower beds, not unlike a village station in England. Mr Lawrence drones on, and I do so wish he would be quiet so I could at least close my eyes. I even try opening Pearl Rivers at one stage but he glares at it as though I am holding something devilish between my hands. I wonder what he will think of *Alice's Adventures in Wonderland*!

❧ ❧ ❧

As the sun dies across the great expanse of land, the jungle slowly blending into forest, Mr Lawrence witters on still about the building of this great railway across the heart of Africa. Can he not see that I need a little peace, to be alone with my thoughts? But then I think to myself, I am not being terribly fair. At least I am witnessing Mr Lawrence in a state of enthusiasm about something. I will myself to concentrate on his words.

'Communications, you see, were terrible at that time as giraffes were constantly making their way over the line and removing parts of the telegraph wire.'

'Giraffes?'

'Yes, indeed. Do you know what a giraffe is?'

I inwardly grimace. I may well have been raised in rural England, but I have not led such a sheltered life as to not be aware of a number of African animals.

'Of course,' I say evenly. 'I have visited the Natural History Museum in London on two or three occasions with Papa. There are all kinds of drawings and lifesize models that—'

'There were also the dreadful Nandi and such other tribes who would brazenly steal the telegraph wire, not to mention attack railway escorts, burning telegraph offices and killing soldiers. And the lions that would make off with the coolies and railway workers! Gracious, it's a wonder this line was ever completed.' He sits back against the upholstered seat, crosses his arms and looks tremendously pleased with himself for this assertion. I force myself not to frown at him by looking out of the window once more and staring at the undeniably beautiful golden-green landscape rolling past. I cannot help but close my eyes – I am so terribly exhausted – and before I know it I have fallen into a deep, dreamless sleep.

I do not know how long I have slept for, but the train is shuddering to a halt.

'Come, Iris. We are at Voi.'

'What happens here?' I say, stretching luxuriantly, feeling a great deal better.

'There is a small settlement here. First town since Mombasa. We are to dine in the dak bungalow.'

Mr Lawrence, I have noticed, often speaks to me as though I should know what certain things are, as though I have not stepped off the steamer mere days ago. Yet this is combined with a certain condescending tone. He does not even wait to hear my response. I find myself shaking my head in frustration, but I must confess I am in far better spirits than when we boarded the train and I am also terribly hungry.

Servants have already bustled into our carriage and are busy with rolls of bedding, which they are beginning to spread out over the seats for us to sleep on after dinner. I follow Mr Lawrence out of the compartment and along the narrow corridor until we arrive at the ladder that has been lowered to the ground. With the other first-class passengers, we make our way along a narrow path hewn into the long grass across to the bungalows, guided by the light of paraffin lamps. A painted sign above the bungalows reads 'Nazareth Brothers' and I ask Mr Lawrence who they are.

'Goan chaps that run the station restaurant,' he replies.

The lamps are placed on tables inside the bungalows and we're served with brown Windsor soup, followed by cutlets that Mr Lawrence, always keen to inform, tells me come from gazelle, and a hash of some sort. The cutlets are terribly tough and gristly, and despite my hunger, I find myself losing my appetite as I attempt desperately to knife my way through them.

'Why aren't you eating, Iris?' Mr Lawrence turns to me, the lines on his gaunt face accentuated by the flicker of the paraffin lamp.

'I *am*…' I hesitate, 'but I am not finding the cutlets that palatable.' I know I sound very fussy. The truth is I am not a fussy eater at all and I feel another pang of longing for Cook's pies and succulent roasts and tender vegetables back at The Old Vicarage.

Mr Lawrence grunts. 'Nora had a tremendous appetite. Never let the slightest morsel go to waste.'

A tiny piece of gristle lodges in my throat. Nora. So that was his first wife's name. Although I was curious about her, hearing her being spoken of now in this manner makes me feel distinctly uncomfortable. I gulp down some water and stare straight ahead whilst Mr Lawrence clears his throat awkwardly beside me. It seems he had not meant to speak quite so frankly.

I focus on the muted conversations around me, certain that from the far end of the table I can hear German being spoken. I peer down to locate the owners of the voices and see a couple of older gentlemen. Mr Lawrence, possibly keen to dispel the feeling left over from the mention of Nora, murmurs in lowered tones that there are a number of Germans in Voi due to the proximity to German East Africa.

'Oh! Does East Africa belong to the Germans as well then?' I ask.

'*No*, Iris,' Mr Lawrence chides, immediately making me feel foolish. 'East Africa belongs to Great Britain and Tanganyika to the Germans.'

I am grateful that dessert promptly follows, tinned pears in syrup. I eat every last mouthful of this, despite its curious metallic taste. Once dinner is over, Mr Lawrence turns to me and, not quite looking me in the eye, says, 'I am going for a quick brandy and cigar. Can you find your way back to the compartment?'

'Of course.' I am relieved to have a little time alone, to collect my thoughts. *Nora had a tremendous appetite.* Nora. What was she like, this ghost from the past? I walk back to the train, its iron hulk gleaming in the moonlight. The guards and drivers are changing over and I hear the rustles and squeaks of the wild closing in around me from all sides. I am not scared though; in fact, I take some kind of comfort from these small sounds of nature unfolding around me. There are also a number of passengers surrounding me, many of them Asians. When Mr Lawrence returns, I question him about our fellow passengers.

'Ah yes, the Asians,' he replies, taking out his pipe and filling it with tobacco. 'This new breed of East African. Many of them came over to help build the railway and have done rather well since.'

I nod my head. 'What have they—'

'Thieving and wily, of course, to have this kind of money. Don't trust them, but they're an enterprising sort, can't deny them that. In fact, I've employed one as my tailor in Nairobi, a Mohammedan chap by the name of Ahmed. Must say I'm not displeased with the clothes the fellow's made. Perhaps—' he breaks off and surveys my skirt and blouse, 'you'd appreciate some new attire from him when we arrive?'

'Oh, that is very kind, but I have bought a great deal of clothes with me—'

'I somehow think, my dear, that the climate you will find in Nairobi is not the same as that of Cambridgeshire. Frankly, some of the clothes I have seen you dressed in thus far have been... well, a little *inappropriate*, shall we say.'

I frown at him and glance down at my trumpet-skirt and shirtwaist. Why does whatever comes from his mouth sound so critical?

'You weren't to know.'

I am reluctant to bring my mother up, but I do not wish him to have the last word on the subject. 'My mother went to great lengths to procure suitable attire for me for East Africa.'

'I am sure she did, Iris. But that does not mean she got it quite right.'

Detestable man! I take a deep intake of breath and try to steady myself against the irritation I feel building up inside me. 'Well,' I say decisively, 'as long as I myself am comfortable.' Mr Lawrence opens his mouth to respond to this, but I cut him off. 'Are we to get changed for bed now?'

He looks at me, mouth agape and cheeks reddening. One would think I had just asked him to jump from the carriage window.

'There is a separate room with basin and lavatory. Otherwise, I shall move outside whilst you… arrange yourself.' I nod and he pulls the compartment door across, vanishing. My nightclothes have been laid out upon my pillow and I remove my clothes, hastily folding them and placing them in the valise under the bed. I pull on my nightgown before jumping into bed and tugging the linen sheet up beneath my chin. Please, *please* let him not come to me tonight. I squeeze my eyes tightly shut again as, after some time, Mr Lawrence re-enters. I know he is looking at me, but all I hear is a loud sigh and then the clink of a glass as the unmistakable smell of whisky infuses the carriage.

Once the paraffin lamp has finally been extinguished, my eyes flicker open and I see dim grey shapes moving about in the darkness whilst the carriage sighs, clatters and squeaks. The sounds and the motion are not unpleasant and after some time they lull me into sleep.

When I awake, I have no idea what time it is. It is still dark outside, yet with the faintest hint of pale amber light gleaming through the curtained window to signal the approach of dawn. I can hear Mr Lawrence snoring in the bed above me and I push the sheets back with my toes and wriggle forwards to press my nose against the glass. It is blackened by soot and I am unable to see much. I glance backwards; Mr Lawrence does not appear to have moved and I decide to chance it. I first peel back some hastily applied wire netting from the window, then push it down. It is stiff and at first will not yield, but I try with all my might and eventually I am able to thrust it down with my elbows and put my face against the whistling wind and dust swept up from beneath us.

What I see, early that morning, I know I shall never see again. At least, not with such intensity. The wakening dawn is splashed with gold, painting everything it touches in gentle, glowing hues. Across the wild scrub, thorny, hostile trees are dotted, their shadows defined against the rolling plains. Three giraffes are silhouetted against the hills, startled, staring at the train whistling past, gangly yet graceful as their necks stretch heavenwards. Nearby, a number of antelope scamper around, scared by the rumbling of this iron hulk, their sinewy bodies gleaming in the sunlight. I smile, wishing that Papa, Arthur and Miss Logan could see this. And just as I am thinking that, a vast flock of birds soars overhead, the tips of their wings edged with burning gold.

Above the noise of the steam train, I hear a high-pitched whistle, rising and falling upon the wind. I stare down the length of the carriages and then up to the top, attempting to find the noise's source, but it stops and starts and I cannot identify it. The air is warm and as I turn my face into the buffeted breeze, I close my eyes and let my hair flicker about my face. Beneath my closed lids, I feel the tears escaping and, for the first time since leaving England, my tears are not shed due to unhappiness. I feel alive, I feel fortunate, something within me opening up and turning outwards like a flower craning towards the light. As the tears spill down my cheeks, salt mingling with soot and the breath of the warm African wind, I resolve to try. I am here, in East Africa, and whilst Mr Lawrence does not seem by any stretch of the imagination a warm, nurturing man, I have not truly given him a chance. I open my eyes to see the sun burst above the horizon in all its burnished glory and I think I fall a little in love with Africa right at that moment.

When I hear Mr Lawrence stirring and awakening in the compartment behind me, I pull my head back in through the window and turn round to face him, smiling broadly.

'Good heavens!' he says, sitting upright and rubbing at his eyes.

'Is something wrong?' I ask cheerfully.

'Iris, what have you been doing? You *cannot* put your head out of the window. The soot has dirtied your face. Do you realise you have black lines streaking your nose and forehead? We shall be breakfasting soon and you need to get yourself cleaned up.'

'Cleaned up?' I ask, still grinning at him.

'Yes, Iris. Have you a looking glass?'

'Well…' Now I draw myself completely back into the carriage and pull the window shut. 'Somewhere I do, in all my belongings. It's simply splendid out there at this time of morning, isn't it?'

Mr Lawrence's face softens a little.

'Yes, isn't it? A little later, after breakfast, I shall go on the cowcatcher if you should care to join me.'

'What is that?'

'You've not heard of it? It's a wooden bench attached to the front of the train. Marvellous platform for viewing game.'

At that, I cannot help but clap my hands together, my smile widening. 'Oh, I should *love* to!'

He looks, frankly, shocked by my enthusiasm and clears his throat, telling me he will wait outside the compartment whilst I dress. When I enter the small washroom, I almost burst out laughing when I see my wavy hair untended and coal smudged across my face. I begin to scrub my skin with a flannel.

After Mr Lawrence and I have had our fill of scrambled eggs and steaming tea, he leads me up to the cowcatcher as the sun continues its strengthening ascent to the east. He hands me a pair of goggles to protect my eyes against the red dust.

'Do you not wear them?' I ask, shouting above the noise of the engine.

'Oh no. A servant is bringing me up my .303 rifle and goggles only inhibit my ability to spot game. This early hour tends to be a favourable time when the heat of the day has not begun in earnest and many of the animals are moving about. We shall soon stop at Mtito Andei, though.'

'Mtito Andei?'

'Yes, it's a station coming up. Means "Place of the Vultures". It's the major hunting post on this route. But until then, I should like to sit on the right of you, please,' he says standing up and moving to the other side of me. I raise an eyebrow.

'On the right side of the train, over here,' he says, pointing to the vast expanse of land beside me, 'one can shoot game.'

I turn to him in shock. 'Whatever do you mean?'

'I *mean*,' his voice is impatient, 'that the land on the left, this is protected. But everything on the right side is considered unprotected, and therefore game.'

'But what if there is an animal right in the middle, not on the left side *or* the right?' I ask emphatically.

He stares at me, aghast. Perhaps he thinks I am trying to rile him, yet I ask in earnest.

'If it is on the *track*, my dear, it will be mown down and dead in an instant.'

I frown, fold my hands in my lap and bite my bottom lip. The servant arrives with Mr Lawrence's huge gun, which my husband handles as though it is pure gold, his eyes gleaming with fervour. Moments later, he points over to his right-hand side, shouting 'Ostrich!' I look out and see the huge, ungainly bird running alongside the train, not ten metres away, its vast wings flapping frantically at its sides.

'What an easy target!' he cries, and I think that this is the most animated I have seen him so far. 'It would be senseless, cruel even, as a sportsman, not to take a shot.' I watch as he lifts his rifle, follows the bird for a little while and then shoots. To my relief, he is way off the mark. He curses.

'Why must you shoot the poor creature? We are on its territory after all, not the other way round.'

'Not from a hunting family?' he asks, frowning. I ignore his comment and he raises the barrel to take another shot. This time he hits the ostrich, but only one of its legs, and it stumbles and sinks to the ground, flapping its great, useless wings. I gasp as he turns into the wind, shooting again and putting the creature out of its misery. Satisfied, he turns back round, readjusting his pith helmet, which has been sitting awry on his head.

Eventually, Mr Lawrence turns to face me. I have one hand pressed firmly down on the top of my hat and the other hand covers my mouth. My eyes, I know – I cannot help it – are narrowed and accusing.

'What is the sense in that?' I know he will not appreciate my tone but I do not care.

'In what?'

'That. Killing that defenceless beast.'

'Iris!' He looks intensely irritated. 'This is Africa. This is what people *do* here. They hunt. Even the natives, the local tribespeople, *especially* these local tribespeople, they hunt from the land. The Maasai have an initiation ceremony, that when a boy turns into a man he must slay a lion. That is certainly not in order to eat the flesh of the animal. It is a ritual.'

'A ritual?' I ask. 'So killing the ostrich was a ritual for you?'

He pauses. 'Yes, in a way. Iris, if you are to live in East Africa, you will have to put aside your prejudices. People hunt here. *Everybody* hunts here.'

I open my mouth to say something but promptly close it again and we continue the journey in preferable silence. We pass through Mtito Andei and onwards, and I keep to myself the many questions swarming around in my head. As the train pulls into the station, I see all kinds of animal tusks, hides, horns and skins lined up on the platform.

Some of them are being packed up and others are being sold to the Europeans who step down from the train to admire them. Mr Lawrence, to my surprise, does not join them on the platform, but I suppose if he is so fond of hunting, he probably has enough such items of his own. People around the Cambridgeshire villages do, of course, hunt for foxes but I've never been terribly fond of that either. I simply cannot understand why some feel compelled to kill animals for sport. On that subject, I doubt Mr Lawrence and I shall ever see eye to eye.

☙ ☙ ☙

When the train finally pulls into Nairobi railway station, I feel great relief as I step on to the wooden platform. I am eager to stretch my limbs and see my new home. As the servants are unloading our cases from the locomotive, I hear a great squawking and a thunderous flapping of wings from above and I look up to see a number of large birds with long necks and curved beaks flying up towards the corrugated-iron roofing, making an awful lot of noise, almost like a braying sound, their wings catching the light with a shiny iridescence.

'Mr Lawrence!' I exclaim. 'What is the name of those birds?'

He looks up, shielding his eyes against the sun. 'Which birds?'

'Those huge ones.' I point into the distance. 'They have just flown over us.'

'Not the slightest idea,' he replies, before he busies himself with organising the servants and our cases. Not a bird man, clearly. No doubt he would have much the same opinion of Papa's pigeons as Mother does.

The railway station, just like Mombasa's, is chaotic. There are people everywhere I look, climbing down from the train, carrying cardboard suitcases tied up with string, selling bananas and sucking from curious, long, woody sticks. Crowds are flooding onto the single platform from outside, staring and pointing at the train, which has pulled to a decisive halt and now stands shuddering beside the platform. A huge kitchen clock hangs above the main door and I notice that it has taken us more than a full day to arrive at our destination.

The level of noise is astonishing and I experience an unexpected flip of excitement in my stomach, for it will be fascinating to see Nairobi, this vibrant new township. A few porters appear and begin loading our cases onto a wheeled contraption. Mr Lawrence bustles me along the platform towards the exit. I notice immediately that the heat is not nearly as cloying as it was in Mombasa; it is, in fact, rather cool here and I draw my shawl tighter around me.

We stand beside the porters in front of the railway station with a sweep of curving road before us, flanked by a few makeshift shops constructed with planks of wood and palm fronds, one-storeyed tin houses scattered here and there. I stand on tiptoe to ascertain what is beyond this road, but it is difficult to see much else.

'Mr Lawrence.' I turn to face my husband and he grimaces at me. How can I possibly call him Jeremy? I blush and look down, kicking my foot at a large stone lying on the ground. 'Sorry,' I mumble, before looking back up at him and smiling brightly. 'Where is the town?'

'The town?' he asks in surprise. 'Why, this *is* the town.'

'Oh,' I reply. 'I… I thought…' I know I am stammering, but I find it hard to extract my words.

'You thought…?' He peers as me glassily through his monocle.

'Oh, it is nothing. I merely thought Nairobi may have been a little… larger.'

'I don't know what gave you *that* impression. You are aware, Iris, are you not, that this town was established a mere few years ago?'

'Well, yes but—'

'Mile Number 327 of the Uganda Railway. Frankly, you should have seen it back then. There was *nothing* here, save bleak plains, antagonistic natives and even more hostile animals.'

'Yes,' I say, wishing I had never voiced my thoughts. I realise I shall have to keep a great deal more to myself in the future if I am not to be ridiculed.

'Do you know what one engineer said to me, whom I met a few years ago? "Who will ever want to live on this swampy stretch of godforsaken land? Nobody, that's for sure." Well!' he smirks, 'there are plenty of people that should like to live here now, I can tell you that much. The truth is, however –' he stands straight and grasps his hands behind his back, sweeping his eyes over the bleak stretch of land ahead of us – 'that Nairobi was never intended as a permanent base. Yet now with each new settlement establishing and business opening, it will be more and more difficult for the government to relocate.'

'Relocate?'

'Yes. Now and again, the colonial government still talks about abandoning Nairobi for Kikuyu, a higher tract of land. It is less inhospitable up there. So we may be lucky.'

The words 'inhospitable' and 'lucky' jar, spoken in the same sentence, and I frown at him, but he ploughs on. 'You see, this place used to be the last open space along the plains before the railway began its steep climb up the Kikuyu escarpment, providing space for the locomotives to shunt. Not a terribly auspicious beginning for a township.'

He is talking to himself more than to me; he is not even looking in my direction. I squint at him beneath the wide brow of my hat. If he is trying to put me at my ease, to tell me how Nairobi has grown and bettered itself, he is failing. Yet I am determined not to let Mr Lawrence spoil my optimistic mood of earlier and I flash a brief, bright smile at him before he turns and calls out to a man seated on a mule trap. I think of the journey to my debutante ball in a horse-drawn landau mere months before and cannot help but laugh at the prospect of now being pulled by a mule. If only Mother could see this! Mr Lawrence eyes me strangely at my outburst, but remains silent, helping the native driver to pile our luggage into a trap. Once loaded, the driver tinkles a bell to clear our path, and before I know it Mr Lawrence is off again, reeling off one fact after another.

He informs me – and I must confess I *am* interested in this – that only last year the entire township had to begin all over again on account of being burnt to the ground. Everything went up in the flames: military lines, bazaar, railway workshops, native villages – all of it. His words are defensive as he explains the diminutive size of Nairobi, almost as though his very manhood is under assault.

I swallow. 'An accident?'

'No. Bubonic plague. Couldn't take risks in those sorts of conditions. It was decided that the whole place should be razed to the ground.'

'Gracious.' I suddenly find myself wondering again about Nora Lawrence, his previous wife, considering how she may have reacted to her first time on East African soil. I suspect I am nothing like Nora.

I can scarcely see a tree anywhere. A few scrubby bushes dot the terrain and small black-and-white birds, their tails wagging up and down, flit around, but that is about it. We rattle past corrugated-iron sheds and a few tracks running off the road from the station that seem to be inhabited in some way, yet become fewer in number the further we travel until I can see almost nothing around me. Simply miles and miles of – what? Of rain and sun-cracked earth, of sky and of silver-tinged, scudding clouds.

Yet as the trap driver draws to a steady halt, I notice a sudden change in the topography of the land. For we are at the foot of a gently inclining hill and I am being told we must continue on foot. Relieved to stretch my legs, I climb out and see a muddy brown river ahead of us with large stones sliced neatly across it.

'Government buildings, hospitals and barracks up here, as well as the Europeans' houses,' Mr Lawrence announces. 'And this,' he points ahead to a muddy little stream, 'is the Nairobi River.' I am about to say that it appears to be more of a stream than a river, not dissimilar to the ford in Bourn, before I think better of it and close my mouth.

How on earth will the driver be able to carry all our luggage single-handedly across the river and up the hill? Without a moment's further thought, I turn to him and ask if I can assist. But no sooner have I done so than Mr Lawrence grasps me firmly in the crook of my elbow and steers me away from the small, wiry driver.

'Iris,' he mutters sharply. 'I am sure you were not required to help with luggage at home. It is *no* different here.' He purses his thin lips at me.

'But that is not the same. It is impossible that the driver will manage all our belongings up the—'

'Ah, but that is where you are quite wrong. He will make as many journeys back and forth as necessary. Now. You are a country girl, I'm sure you will have no difficulty crossing the river.'

He is absolutely right, of course. Jumping from one stepping stone to the next will give me nothing but pleasure; yet his voice is filled with disdain, as though I should be ashamed of my country origins. Raising my head an inch, I stride ahead of him to the bank, hitch my skirt up a little on either side and move forwards. I am glad that Mr Lawrence is behind me, for the smile that stretches across my face is as wide as Nairobi's plains.

At the top of the hill, there exist a few newly cut roads, official-looking residences and bungalows on stilts, quite unlike what I saw on the lower ground near to the railway.

'This way, Iris. Not far now,' Mr Lawrence says as he veers off the path and we walk for another five minutes or so until we reach a bungalow, all on its own with nothing close to it, a thorny bush encircling it.

'For what reason is the bush here?' I ask Mr Lawrence, and he eyes me strangely, turning his head away slightly as he mumbles some reply about every house here being built in such a style to keep the natives' goats and oxen out.

I look at him with impatience. 'The truth please?' I raise my eyebrows at him and he is, I can see, shocked by my forthrightness. But if I am to live here, I shall not be deceived.

He clears his throat and tugs his waistcoat down. 'On occasion, rhino and leopards and suchlike are known to wander around, hence the need for the thorn fence. It is for our own safety.'

I nod my head, satisfied. That is more like it.

Mr Lawrence points the way through a metal gate separating the fence and stands in front of the small homestead, his eyes slightly cast down. He looks cowed, in a way, to be introducing this place to me. Perhaps it is not what he was accustomed to in Mombasa when he lived there with Nora. But I truly do not mind; in fact, the bungalow looks rather charming to me, especially the tins lining the verandah, painted blue and serving as ornamental flowerpots. I cannot imagine Mr Lawrence being involved himself in such an aesthetic touch and wonder whose work this is. I feel ever so slightly sorry for him at that moment and am determined to appear enthusiastic about our home.

Ducking my head, I walk inside. Mr Lawrence, I notice, does not take his pith helmet off inside the bungalow. When I myself remove my osprey-trimmed felt hat that is slowly roasting my head, he turns to me rather sharply and says 'I advise you not to do that.'

'Why ever not? We are no longer beneath the sun's rays.'

'I wouldn't be so sure about that,' he replies, pointing up to the slanted metal sheets that constitute the bungalow's roof. 'You see, this corrugated iron can only offer so much protection from the equatorial sun. It is even thought that the rays can damage one's brain. Yet until we can find a more substantial material for the roof, the hat,' he pauses and taps his own helmet, 'stays on.'

Before I am able to stop myself, a nervous laugh escapes from my lips and I immediately clamp a hand over my mouth to prevent more from coming. The absurdity and nonsense of it! As if sunlight could pass through such metal sheets! Mr Lawrence looks at me and frowns deeply, lines carving across his face that make him look older than ever. How terribly *difficult* it is to retain sympathy for this man for any length of time!

'Is there something you find amusing?'

'No!' I say, shaking my head resolutely as I try desperately to think of something morose to push down the rising peals of laughter.

He pauses, peering at me strangely, and then nods his head, turning away and striding across the room as I take a deep, calming breath and keep my hat on, knowing full well that I shall not be doing so when Mr Lawrence is not in the house.

I notice that all the legs of the table and chairs – curiously, fashioned from empty packing cases – are placed inside kerosene tins just like those being used as flowerpots on the verandah. When Mr Lawrence sees me staring at them, he offers an explanation. 'They are to keep the rats and *siafu* away.'

The floor is hard, packed earth covered here and there with animal skins and there is a rather shabby-looking horsehair sofa in one corner.

The bedroom is a room off the main living area, simple and sparse, containing only a small, wooden bed (will that really be big enough for the two of us?) with a mosquito net shrouding it, a plain wardrobe and a tiny dressing table with a wooden stool.

'A mosquito net?' I turn to Mr Lawrence. 'I thought that—'

'Non-malarial,' he responds, 'so nothing to fear on that front. But even if they are non-malarial, they can still be irritating and one gets bitten. Particularly at night.'

He exits the bedroom and I am about to follow him when I notice a photograph in a frame sitting upon the dressing table. Ensuring that he has quite left the room, I walk to it and lift the frame up, studying it. A woman, in her late twenties I should say, stares out at me from beneath an ornate feathered hat, eyes dark, cheekbones high and nose pointed. Nora. I feel that same nervous cough build-ing up from my chest, a momentary chill passing through me. Is she to watch me in my bedroom as well?

Frowning, I replace the frame quickly when I hear Mr Lawrence calling my name. I leave the bedroom and walk out to the side of the house, where there is a small attached hut with a simple curtain cloth pulled over as a door. I peer in and see nothing save another kerosene tin, suspended from a string, high in the air.

'Water can be boiled once a day in order for you to bathe in. I fear...' he hesitates, '...it is not quite what you are ac-customed to. But I daresay you will get used to it. Also,' Mr Lawrence is striding back through the yard already, 'I do plan to have a proper bathroom built within the house at some stage, but it is damned difficult to get one's hands on a tin bathtub and sink in this town.' He shrugs and there it is, that cowed look again, and I try to offer him a bright smile. I look back at the kerosene tin hanging from the top of the bathing hut, wondering how on earth it possibly works and if anyone will give me instruction. But no doubt it will all come clear in time.

The kitchen is separate, in a corrugated-iron lean-to with yet another kerosene tin rather ingeniously used as an oven and one tacked to the wall that looks as though it may serve as a boiler. After I am shown the 'long-drop' (simply a pit with a wooden box hanging over a hole in the ground), I am about to follow Mr Lawrence back into the house when I see a native woman unlatching the gate and walking in. She is young, not much older than myself. Her hair is cropped short and springy and she has a shy, yet warm smile that at once puts me at my ease.

'Ah!' exclaims Mr Lawrence. 'There you are. Muthoni, this is the memsaab, Mrs Lawrence.'

She approaches and bows her head, saying in a deep, rich voice, enunciating each syllable, 'Memsaab Lawrence. Wel-come.'

'Thank you,' I say and I smile back at her.

'Muthoni does the cooking and cleaning and laundry and so forth,' Mr Lawrence says. 'She barely speaks a word of English. Her native tongue is Kikuyu. That being said, compared to most of the natives, she has quite a few words. At any rate, I'm sure you will understand one another somehow.'

I glance at Muthoni, who is being spoken about as though she were not standing right before us, but her face gives nothing away.

'Anything you need,' Mr Lawrence continues as he ducks his head and walks into the house, 'Muthoni can arrange for you, though you may have to use sign language of some sort. Oh, you might like to teach her to cook some dishes from back home, because at the moment I've been eating an awful lot of African food and it hasn't been wonderful for my digestion.'

Me, cook? Mr Lawrence must know, surely, that I grew up with a cook and have not the foggiest. I clear my throat. 'I am surprised you can get hold of English ingredients here.'

Mr Lawrence turns to me, his thin face twisted into a question mark. 'Such as?'

'Such as…' I search my memory for all those stolen moments spent in the kitchen with Cook whilst growing up. 'Suet?'

'Suet?' He wrinkles his nose up. 'Well. Suet, granted, that might not be the easiest thing to acquire. But there are always substitutes. Anyway...' he flounders, clearly unhappy to be discussing these matters of the female domain, 'you'd be surprised what you *can* get here. There are a number of Indian *dukas* cropping up and of course the goods that come in by train from Mombasa.'

Mr Lawrence clicks his heels together impatiently and strides purposefully back to the kitchen, where he points to a well. It makes me think, with a small pang of longing, of the well in the kitchen of The Old Vicarage. 'You can pump ground water up from this or, if you find it too difficult, ask Muthoni. The water's perfectly safe to drink and of course, it's also used for bathing in and cooking and everything else.'

I am about to ask him a question about this, but before I have a chance he is striding off once more, this time back into the house. I cast a look at Muthoni and she smiles at me, a little more openly, before we both enter the bungalow. Mr Lawrence is talking again, from the bedroom, and I go and stand near the door so I can hear what he is saying. His voice is starting to irritate me – loud and self-important.

'I shall make room for your dresses in the wardrobe,' he is saying, 'though I shall take the liberty of arranging for the tailor to come round first thing tomorrow morning. As I mentioned on the train, I predicted in advance that you would not have the appropriate attire for living in such a climate. Most of these Asians are a public health hazard, riddled with the plague and such like. But Ahmed's a pleasant enough chap. Better than most of them. You shan't find him lacking, I'm sure.'

'Perhaps I can go to him, to take a walk through Nairobi?'

'Walk to Bazaar Street?' he scoffs. 'I think not. Dreadful, fetid place. Filled with rats. Vertibable breeding ground for typhus. No, he will come here. I shall be gone all day, at work. I leave first thing in the morning and return for dinner around seven, later if I go to the club.'

Club. Of course. Another one of those. It amazes me, given the size of Nairobi, that there could be an established one here. I watch Mr Lawrence as he makes the slightest space in the wardrobe, sighing impatiently as his clothes bounce back again on their wooden hangers. Does he really expect all my dresses, as well as the new ones that are to be made, to fit in? 'Remember that we are near the equator so dusk falls the same time every night year round, around 6.30 p.m. Ensure you are safely inside the house, as animals will be hunting by then.'

'Besides rhino and leopards, which animals?'

He frowns and waves a derisive hand through the air. 'Oh, *animals*. The kind we saw from the train. This is not the village of Bourn,' he adds, 'so we are not talking about cows and sheep here.' As I remember Mr Lawrence and his rifle on the train's cowcatcher, a vision comes to me of him doing the same from the verandah.

I lean on the doorframe. 'And when you are at work,' I say, my optimism rapidly diminishing 'what am I to do all day?'

He actually begins to laugh then, and it must be something to do with the evening light streaming in through the window behind him, but I notice for the very first time that his teeth are stained yellow.

'Good Lord, Iris! What kind of a question is that?'

I stand my ground and stare at him, waiting for him to say something else. Given my circumstances – I have been plucked from everything I know and am familiar with – it is a very reasonable question. In England, I filled my days with lessons and then, when Mother would let me avoid it not a moment longer, pianoforte, needlework and flower arranging. And for my own pleasure, I would take walks through the garden or surrounding fields, play croquet and visit Papa's pigeons at least once a day. Of course there were also so many of Papa's books I could read. Yet here? I cast my eyes around the small bungalow, which Muthoni is now illuminating with small paraffin lamps. There appears to be not a single book, save for the Bible (which Papa would be relieved to see), unless perhaps they are hidden away somewhere. And I am at the mercy of the wild animals if I should like to take a walk. That is, if Mr Lawrence does not shoot all the animals within a twenty-mile radius of Nairobi.

'I am simply wondering –' I clear my throat – 'what is expected of me? How do you foresee me filling my time?' I trust that my voice sounds sufficiently calm, but the truth is I feel angry with this man.

Mr Lawrence smooths back strands of his thinning hair that have dislodged themselves and hang down over his craggy face. He looks directly at me. 'You seem like a re-

sourceful young woman, I'm sure you will find plenty to
do.'

'I suppose I can take walks during the day?'

He clears his throat. 'I should certainly not advise that.
Walk a little if you must. Or go and take tea at Wood's. But
you would be far wiser to stay close to the house. This is
hostile land, make no mistake. But frankly, how you choose
to spend your time during the day, Iris, is your concern.'

I stare back at him and find that a small knot of dread
has formed in the pit of my stomach. *During the day...* Is
he referring to the wifely duties that are expected of me at
night? I am aware that my time is running out; I have been
spared the past few nights, but it is unlikely I shall be spared
again. Stretching both hands out to plant them against the
doorframe, I squeeze my eyes shut for it is, I realise, terror
that clutches at me.

'Is there something the matter?' I hear him asking.

My eyes spring open again. 'No.'

'Jolly good.' He is brushing past me into the main living
area. 'I am going to the club for an hour or two, let you get
settled. Then I shall see you back here later.'

I am silent for a moment and when my stomach rumbles in
protest at the lack of a proper meal in some time, I say, 'Supper.'

He picks up one of the paraffin lamps. He is about to
duck out of the front door.

'Supper,' I say again, in a firmer voice. 'I am hungry. Are
you not?'

'Of course. I shall have a quick bite at the club and Muthoni will prepare something for you now. Food, Muthoni!'

He turns, almost shouting at her. 'Food!' As though saying it louder, she may understand better.

'Yes, bwana.' She nods meekly, averting her gaze.

'Oh! One more thing. Should you need to visit the lavatory after dark, you must take a gun with you. This one here.' He taps the nose of a rifle propped up behind the door. 'And the lamp, of course. You need to check for snakes curled up on or near the seat before you sit on it.'

My breath catches. 'Are they poisonous?'

He smiles at me in that tight-lipped, lofty way of his and says, 'This is not the Cambridgeshire countryside, my dear.'

I continue to stand there, held by the doorframe as my new husband, rifle in one hand, paraffin lamp in the other, vanishes into the night.

My stomach growls again and I wonder if I am expected to help Muthoni prepare food. I imagine not. Yet I do not know what else to do with myself, so I approach her.

'Muthoni…' She turns round and smiles at me. Without the presence of Mr Lawrence, her smile is more open and natural. She is the first native woman I have spoken to and I suddenly feel tongue-tied. 'I… I help you?'

She raises both eyebrows quizzically.

'Help. With the dinner?'

Muthoni laughs lightly and shakes her head. How am I to make myself understood?

I pick up a paraffin lamp and beckon her outside to the makeshift kitchen. In a box there are a few vegetables: some potatoes and tomatoes and another swarthy, brown-skinned one I do not recognise. I take one potato and mime cutting into it, then turn to her.

'Ah!' Recognition glows in her eyes. She says something I do not understand, shaking her head, but I merely nod. Muthoni raises her eyebrows again, but then shrugs and hands me a knife and slab of wood. She peels the potatoes whilst I chop them and we stand there side by side in the flickering darkness as I listen to the unfamiliar whistling, hissing and calling from the Nairobi plains.

Mr Lawrence comes back a few hours later and as he enters the bedroom, placing his rifle on the bedside table, I keep my eyes shut. He bunches the mosquito net up a little so that he is sitting on the side of the bed and although my eyes are closed, I sense he is watching me. His hand lightly touches my shoulder, but forgetting the mosquito net is in the way, he curses beneath his breath as his hand snags in it. I hear his breathing grow louder and more ragged as he roughly hauls up the net and clambers upon the bed, so close to me I can feel his breath upon my skin. My eyes flicker open with terror and I cannot quite look at him, so I look beyond him.

'Iris, my dear,' he breathes and runs a finger down my arm. I flinch, continuing to lie ramrod straight upon the narrow bed. My arms are thrust out to either side, still as a corpse. I am covered with a blanket and a sheet that travels to just above my breasts and tucks into either side of the bed. Hands trembling, Mr Lawrence hooks both thumbs into the sheet and draws them down to my waist. I know that he can see my breasts rising beneath my cotton night-dress and I sense his excitement building and feel sick to the core. He scoops his hands beneath the small of my back and draws me up towards him, groaning as he buries his head in my hair that falls in thick waves down my back.

I feel violated, though nothing has happened yet. What next? What now?

'Iris,' he breathes, his eyes travelling down my body. 'How lovely you are.'

I cannot move. I can scarcely even blink, so overcome am I with terror. Now he is removing his own clothes, quickly, urgently, and I cannot watch him. I can only hear the shedding of shirt and trousers, the rasping breaths.

'Iris, will you not yield to me?' he says. But I do not know what he can mean by that. What does he want me to do? Yet I have no doubt that whatever it is, I will not do it. I simply cannot.

'*Iris*,' he says again, and this time his voice has a hard edge to it. I stare at him, wide-eyed. 'I have been patient these past days. *More* than patient. And the time has come. Do you understand?'

I realise this must happen, but I cannot be part of it. I am frozen with fear and disgust and a wordless horror and I will myself away from my body so that it feels as though I am watching this from afar, or observing it happening to another.

Mr Lawrence presses his lips upon mine and moves them, waiting for some kind of response. But when this does not come, he stands up and impatiently pulls down his underpants. The mosquito net is hindering him once again. He curses beneath his breath as he pushes it aside and dives back on to the bed.

His lips are against my ear. 'You are so beautiful. So desirable.' I know he is making an effort of some kind, possibly to make me feel less horrified and more at ease. Does he think these are the kinds of things a woman likes to hear? His irritation with me is obviously building, but I am powerless to do anything to resolve that. And clearly my attitude does not serve to dispel his desire in any way. With both hands, he pushes my nightdress up to my waist. The thought that he is staring at my thighs, at parts of me that are dark and secret, causes me to close my eyes again. I feel my face screwing up; scrunching, folding in upon itself like a sheet of paper. *No… please… no…*

He climbs on top of me, plunging deep down into me, a painful parting and ripping. I gasp; but no, it is more than a gasp. It is almost a scream, like that of a startled animal, short but loud, and Mr Lawrence instantly clamps his hand down over my mouth. Why he is doing this I have no idea; it is not as though there are neighbours to hear me and the nearest house to ours is a few hundred metres away. But with my eyes closed, we remain like that for some time, his hand over my mouth, as he rocks back and forth on the narrow, creaking bed. I force myself to concentrate upon the sounds from beyond our bedroom; the distant night creatures, a curious high-pitched whistling sound and the wind that howls across the empty plains of this lonely British outpost.

The morning after that first night, after Mr Lawrence has left, I walk out of the gate in front of the bungalow and trudge along the track that leads further up the hill. I want to be anywhere but at home; the memory of the previous night is pressing on my shoulders, pushing against my chest, an angry, throbbing soreness between my legs. It is a clear morning and I pass a smattering of other small houses and strange, thorny shrubs skirting the path. I pant with the exertion – the air feels so thin – and once I have walked as far as I feel like going, I clear the ground beneath a large bush and sit in the shade. The tears flow silently and I wipe them away and take in large, deep gulps of cool morning air.

Gazing upwards, I see clouds dotted across the sky, casting a patchwork of moving shadows across the plains. My eyes scan the horizon and that is when I see it, far in the distance: the snow-clad peak of a mountain. I had no idea there were mountains in this region, but it calms me, the sight of this one, and I stretch out my fingertips so they look as though they are resting on top of the peak until my breathing returns to normal. In this strange land there is snow, just like the snow around Bourn in winter.

I pick at a tuft of scrubby, yellow grass beside me. A curious little bird with a yellow neck, a generous body and short, waddling legs moves past me, oblivious to my presence. It is followed by a number of young, tiny cheeping things. I smile, wiping the last tear from my cheek.

Further up the hill, I hear the bark of instructions issuing from the long, squat army barracks. The voices are so very English and I close my eyes, imagining I am back in my homeland. But it brings me little solace and my eyes flicker open as I push out my bottom lip and blow upwards so that my escaping strands of hair flutter. I scratch at my cheek absently and that is when I spy it – a long, sturdy piece of wood lying not a few metres away. An idea comes to me right away. All sadness dispelled, I jump up, stride over to the stick and pick it up, surveying it. It is perfect.

Back at the bungalow, Muthoni is cleaning the bedroom, down on her hands and knees as she scrubs at the wooden floorboards with soapy water from a zinc bucket.

'Muthoni!' She stops work and spins her head round to face me. Her sleeves are rolled up to her elbows and her dark arms are thin but muscular. 'Can you help me?' I say slowly. She raises an eyebrow.

'I need…' How to explain it in simple language? 'Ah!' I have an idea. I fetch *Alice's Adventures in Wonderland* from the bedside table, the weight and feel of the book in my hands as comforting as any soothing words. I flick through its pages and then turn it round to show Muthoni the illustration of Alice playing croquet with a mallet.

'I want to make this,' I say, pointing at the mallet in the picture, 'with this stick.' I hold it up to her and she cocks her head on one side. 'Now,' I continue, 'I only need *this*.' I point to the mallet head in the illustration, look back at Muthoni and smile hopefully.

She narrows her eyes in deep concentration, frowning. But, miraculously, she must understand me for she beckons me to follow her. We walk out of the back door. From beneath a long table Muthoni pulls out a box that is filled with all kinds of odds and ends. She rifles around in it, then pulls out a tin can filled with rusty old nails. Upending the can so that the nails clink out into the palm of her hand, she shrugs and hands me the can. Her eyes ask me, *Is this alright?* and I nod and smile. This will be my mallet head.

'Thank you in Kikuyu?' I say.

'*Nĩ ngatho.*'

'*Nĩ ngatho,*' I attempt and she laughs gently at my pronunciation. '*Nĩ ngatho,*' I try again.

Muthoni places her hands on her hips, nods her head and smiles warmly at me.

CHAPTER EIGHT

FAZAL AHMED

Mr Lawrence is an honest man but he is not a kind man. He has paid me for all my work on time. I cannot complain. But does that mean I must like him? I do not think so. There is a hard steeliness in his eyes and one thing I am certain of: I should never cross this man. I have seen his type before; he and men like him demand complete authority, and those who fall short of his exacting standards are at the mercy of his wrath. He does not suffer fools. In fact, he does not suffer very many people: natives, Indians, insubordinates of any kind. I once heard him remark that the Africans are idle and incapable of working, lolling about whilst their three or four wives earn a living for them. Yet, for some reason, he has accepted me. This, I am sure, is because of the reference I arrived in Nairobi with.

It was signed by the captain of the ship that brought me to Mombasa in 1896 and read as follows:

Mr Fazal J. Ahmed is a fine, upstanding gentleman with superior character attributes and a strong command of the English language. I would heartily recommend him for a favourable posting upon embarkation in Mombasa. Captain Timothy Rodgerson.

What happened, you see, on that journey over is that we all came as equals. Hundreds upon hundreds of us men and boys crammed into every space on that ship. Brought over by the English government to East Africa to work as coolies. To build their railway into the heart of Africa. To beat the Germans in the imperial race for African domination. To bring civilisation to the uncivilised world; farm tea and coffee at the beginning of the line and mine for copper at the end of it.

Almost every man on that boat was educated; amongst my fellow passengers I met lawyers and craftsmen, doctors and painters. We all knew that we were pawns in this imperial game. Yet we were not wealthy men and when we were told that this new, fertile land could make us rich, we were blinded by greed. If we had known the cost of laying those tracks, would we have gone? No, I say emphatically. No. For the cost was too high.

I left my young bride in Karachi. I told her I would wait until I was established in Africa and then I would send for her. This was six years ago. I send money to her every few months but I know I am too proud; I wish for everything to be perfect before she comes, for a tailor's business and a shop in Nairobi's Bazaar Street with my name hanging proudly outside. It is still far from that.

Yet that reference changed everything. There was a terrible storm during the crossing. The monsoon deluge raged and lashed and there was nothing to protect us up on deck from the vagaries of the wind and rain as we begged Allah's clemency on our soaked and battered prayer rugs. I remember it then, that feeling of injustice. It bubbled up in my gut, as though I had eaten too many chapatis with raw mango chutney, but with a hard shell of anger. How, I thought to myself, *how* does this British government expect us to build a railway for them if a great number of the men arrive half-dead? We needed proper sustenance and shelter on the crossing. Instead, men were dying.

Thus I made a decision. Late one night, as I watched a man shivering wretchedly, his poorly clothed body dripping from the monsoon rains, I crept from the deck and demanded an audience with Captain Timothy Rodgerson. I did not know his name until that evening but as I shook his hand, taking in his surprised expression, I told him that I was Mr Fazal J. Ahmed and he was...

'Captain Timothy Rodgerson.'

'Captain Rodgerson. It is a great pleasure, Sir, to meet you.'

'Mr Ahmed, is there something I can assist you with?'

'As a matter of fact, Sir, yes. There is.'

And I led him, without protest, along the decks as the ship swayed and sighed up to where the men lay unprotected from the elements – groaning, shivering, their insides spilled out of them, gleaming silver in the rain.

'This, Captain Rodgerson,' I said, pointing, 'with all due respect, is not acceptable. If we are to work upon arrival, we must be in a condition to work. Do you see why I am telling you this?'

Captain Rodgerson stared at the men, taking in the misery, the squalor, the poor health of many of them, and he ran a hand roughly over his face, blinking several times. I thought he was about to move away from them, but then he pressed his face into the wind and rain, clenched his jaw, and he said 'Mr Ahmed, we must get the sickest of these men downstairs into a cabin immediately and I shall ensure that the ship doctor attends to them at once. And for those who remain up here, a tarpaulin must be constructed to protect everyone.' Then he looked at me with his light brown eyes, nodded and asked me to assist him.

That was all it took, an act of human kindness, and when we were leaving the ship days later he drew me aside and wrote my reference for me. So this, you see, was what ensured my position as supervisor amongst a large group of men on the railway; my command of English and my reference, which I only needed to hand over a single time, without saying a single word. That was enough.

Thus I supervised on the railway and I was spared from the gruelling work myself. Yet I loathed it in a way I had never thought possible. I loathed it because it mattered not what I did or how fairly I treated my men; people were being lost each and every day, thirty-eight men per month, to be precise: to dysentery, to malaria, to conflict, even to the jaws of wild beasts. That first year a mere six kilometres were constructed – six! – from Mombasa, so great were the obstacles. And all the while I longed for my wife and my small workshop and my quiet life, and questioned every waking hour of every day why I had decided to leave everything I knew and understood for this life. But I know, of course, the answer to this question. The lure of adventure to a young man and the promise of wealth. I was just twenty-two years of age. I was foolish, my head firmly in the stars, for as a boy I had stood on the shore on Manora Beach in Karachi and stared at the dancing waves and wondered, again and again, what was beyond those seas.

Yet do I regret my decision? I cannot say that I do. I regret that I lack the courage to bring my wife here, though it will come. But I am building a name for myself. From those early days as part-time supervisor and part-time tailor whilst the Uganda Railway was laid deep into the African earth, word spread of my ability. By the time Mile 327 was reached, turning into Nairobi, I decided to go no further. Nobody objected. I was supervisor, after all, and a supervisor with a clear trade behind me. And though my heart and soul still ached for the waves and the wind of Karachi; for camaraderie and for family; for buying a sweet, spiced chai and crunchy, freshly fried pakora, piping hot and wrapped in old newspaper, I wanted to make a success of it here. For people back home to say, 'Fazal went to Africa, see what he has become? See how he has built himself up?'

The shop with the letters of my name hanging outside is still a dream in the making, for I have not the capital to achieve this at present. Yet I have a very small workshop, I pay a reasonable number of rupees a month for it and it holds all my working materials and the single photograph I own of my wife. It holds all my dreams. And it was to this workshop, you see, that a young girl came one morning. She simply pushed aside the curtain, looked at me with solemn black eyes and handed me a note that read, 'I am in need of a good tailor. Please contact me at the above address. Yours, Jeremy Lawrence, Esq.' I had not yet done any jobs for the *wazungu*, the white folk. But somehow I sensed that this was my opportunity and I must say yes right away, before the girl vanished and tried the next tailor along.

I returned with the girl there and then, stepping across the filth of Bazaar Street, over the stepping stones of the Nairobi River and up the hill to the bwana's house. From the very first time he looked at me, I knew that he would have liked a tailor with skin the shade of curdled milk, just like him. But he knew, and I knew, no such tailor existed in Nairobi at that time. So he would have to just make do with me. He told me that he was making a home here and waiting for his new bride to arrive and I thought wistfully of my own bride in Karachi, her misty eyes and radiant smile. What he wanted was new trousers and shirts, not just one pair but several, and I determined to do a fine job for him.

Yesterday they arrived by railway from Mombasa and I have been called to come to their house to measure the new mistress for dresses, 'appropriate,' Mr Lawrence stressed, 'for Nairobi's climate'. So I stand on the threshold of their home, a few plants scattered in haphazard *debbes* across the small verandah. The housegirl answers the door, that very same girl who found me in Bazaar Street those months before. She smiles at me, that shy smile I remember, with the corners of her lips raised, but her eyes dark and serious. I enter the house and the memsaab is sitting at the kitchen

table, her pale hands clasped around a teacup, though more
for strength than warmth, I'm sure, as it is surprisingly mild
– the mornings here in Nairobi can be bitterly cold.

I take my hat off and clasp it in front of me with both
hands, bowing my head to her. 'Mrs Lawrence. It is a great
pleasure to meet you.'

Incredible, those few words, *it is a great pleasure…* how far
they can carry a person when they are needed. I don't know
why it was that I had a gift for English as a child in the schoolroom; that while the other boys were throwing balls of paper
above our heads, I diligently sat there and drank in the ca-
dence and rhythm of this strange-sounding language. When I
asked *Amma* if I could have English lessons at home, she swat-
ted me over the head and laughed fondly. She thought I was
joking, you see, for I was a joker by heart and always playing
the fool when I had the opportunity. But I persisted, asking
again and again until, one day, she swung on her heels, her
hands flying to her hips as she looked down at me, wide-eyed,
realising finally that I was serious. So the teacher came to my
house, every Saturday morning for two hours whilst the other
boys played cricket and pelted stones through the window at
me – 'English boy! English boy!' they screeched. And it was
this teacher, who had once spent two years in England, who
told me what the other boys did not want to hear; that if you
said to a person, 'It is a great pleasure to meet you', they would
pay attention and listen to you, for only a person of refined
manners and background would say such a thing.

And as I say it this morning to Mrs Lawrence and introduce myself, I understand once again how this simple

expression has the power to open doors. For she looks up from her tea and she smiles at me. It is, however, a strained smile. Of course I know about arranged marriages. My own marriage was arranged by my parents and many times it can work and write its own story of happiness as the years go by. I have yet to know with certainty if this will be the situation with my own wife, for we have spent a mere six months in one another's company.

She gets up from behind the table and comes round to stand in front of me.

'Mr Ahmed. It is a pleasure to meet you too.' She has a pleasant voice, low and melodic. 'And you are from…?'

'India. I am from India, Memsaab.'

'India,' she replies and nods her head understandingly. 'So we are both foreigners here, Mr Ahmed.'

I incline my head and she smiles at me again and her smile is open and warm. I laugh and place my bag on the kitchen table, rummaging in it for my tape measure.

'Mr Lawrence is here, Madam?'

'No. He left early for work.'

'Not a problem,' I assure her. 'Let us get started straight away, shall we? Mr Lawrence told me you would be in need of some new dresses, is that correct?'

She doesn't say anything as I pull out the tape and begin the measurements.

'I have just the calico material you need, but any preference for colour, Mrs Lawrence?'

She blinks once, twice, her lips set into a determined line. 'I should like you to choose, Mr Ahmed.'

I straighten up and indicate for her to hold her arms straight out to either side of her whilst I measure them. She has long, graceful arms. I chuckle softly. 'Come now, Mrs Lawrence, you must surely have a preference.'

'I do,' she says firmly. 'But I should like you to choose.'

I scribble a measurement on a piece of paper and continue. 'Why is that, Mrs Lawrence?'

Her shoulders rise in a hint of a shrug and she looks at me, her gaze steady. Her eyes are the colour of the skies above Karachi, just before the rains. 'Because I trust you, Mr Ahmed.'

It is strange. I do not know why she trusts me, but I do believe it to be so. 'Very well, Mrs Lawrence. I am happy to choose your colours. I think I know which may be suiting you.'

I fold up the tape measure and the paper and place them back in my bag. 'I shall make three to begin with and if they are to your satisfaction, we can see about making more. Mrs Lawrence –' I smile at her – 'it has been a great pleasure to—'

'Oh!' she exclaims, her eyes widening as she takes a step towards me. 'You are not leaving already, are you?'

I don't say anything.

'But you must stay for some tea. Please do, Mr Ahmed. Muthoni!' She spins round on her heels and mimes drinking to the servant girl. 'Tea for Mr Ahmed and myself, please?'

'Chai?' Muthoni asks and Mrs Lawrence nods.

I see that I have not been left with a great deal of choice. I cannot say that I mind, for I am in no particular rush to get back to Bazaar Street. She motions for us to go outside on to the verandah, which I have always thought has a tremendous view down the hill and into the valley. This town might be small now, but it will not always be so and before much more time goes by, the valley will fill with houses and streets and commerce. Even now, it seems that every day there is a new business going up. Yet it is still on a small scale and, in the meantime, we must enjoy the view and peace of the township.

Mrs Lawrence dusts off two iron chairs and looks at them apologetically. 'I am terribly sorry there is nothing more comfortable to sit on.'

I wave my hand dismissively. 'Please. I do not mind.'

We sit in silence for several minutes, during which Muthoni brings us the tea and places it on a small wooden table between us. Drinking tea in East Africa always makes me long for home quite unlike anything else. For it is insipid, bland, lacking the sweet, smoky spiciness of the chai I grew up with. Yet it is warm and quite pleasant to sit here with Mrs Lawrence on this bright morning, cool and clear. A light mist clings to the valley and we sit and drink, listening to the echoing chimes of chisel and hammer against metal and the interlinking melodies of birdsong from the thorny acacia tree in front of us. I prefer these hostile trees in the wet season, when they are draped with a mass of convolvulus creepers, transforming their gaunt, spiny appearance to something gentler and more graceful. But now, in the dry season, these trees look like bony old men.

Mrs Lawrence does not talk, but simply sits with her hands round the teacup, staring out towards the horizon. There is a particular quality of sadness that exists in this

young woman; a sadness that does not seem right or fair
for someone of her age. For whilst I cannot be sure of how
old she is, I suspect she is a good five years younger than me
and not yet out of her teens. I never met Mr Lawrence's first
wife but he speaks fondly of her, his hard-edged face almost
softening. Of course I don't yet know the current Mrs Lawrence, but somehow I cannot picture his face softening in
the same way when he talks about her. Though I could, I
realise, be wrong and should not jump to such conclusions.
It is merely my intuition – which, over the years, has rarely
failed me.

'What is that sound, Mr Ahmed?' she asks.

'Sound?' I listen, but can hear nothing save the customary noises of buildings going up and call of birds.

'That – listen.'

I cock my head on one side and, indeed, hear a high,
whistling noise. I strain to establish its origins but the
truth is, I do not know the answer and tell Mrs Lawrence
as much. 'This African savannah is often still a mystery to
me,' I tell her, disappointed at my ignorance, but she smiles
warmly at me.

We continue to sit there, sipping at our tea, until Mrs
Lawrence lets out a startling and sudden cry, hastily jumping to her feet and, as she does so, upsetting her teacup
so that a brown stain of liquid fans out around her feet. I
jump up to assist her with the fallen cup, but she is paying
not the least attention to that. She stands in rapt attention,
both hands clasped to her chest. I look in the direction she
is gazing and see that in front of the verandah gate, where a

potted plant sits, is a small, colourful bird, partially hidden amongst its leaves.

'What is it?' Mrs Lawrence asks, in barely more than a whisper. As attractive as the birds are here, I have never taken the trouble to find out their names, and tell her as much.

'Oh,' she replies, her face a little crestfallen as she keeps her eyes on the small bird. 'It is so beautiful,' she murmurs, barely moving her lips, as though the slightest movement might scare it away. I take a good look at it and have to agree with Mrs Lawrence: it has a red breast with a tuft of yellow on each side and its plumage is green and shiny. With its sharp, curved little beak and beady black eyes, it truly provides a welcome burst of colour against the arid yellows and browns of the *nyika*.

And then the small bird darts off across the plains, a rainbow burst of colour bolting through the air. Mrs Lawrence hurries towards the gate, pushes it open and stands staring after it, both hands shielding her eyes against the strengthening sunlight. When she eventually turns round, she drops her hands and smiles at me, her face lighting up with warmth. She walks back through the gate, closes it and then sits back down with a sigh.

'My father keeps pigeons in England. I was always rather fond of them. In fact, I am rather fond of all birds.'

'You have come to the right place, Mrs Lawrence. The birds here are spectacular. I only wish I knew the names for them, but it is not my strong point.'

'I am sure you are a first-rate tailor, though.'

A laugh escapes my mouth. 'Well,' I say. The warmth of the day spreads across the dusty little verandah and we sit in companionable silence, watching rays of strengthening light slant across our knees. 'Well,' I say again.

CHAPTER NINE

IRIS LAWRENCE

The first time was far worse than I ever feared it could be and thus I deduced that it could subsequently only get better. But no. He hurts me, perhaps not deliberately, but in a way that shows that he holds me in no regard and truly I could be anyone beneath him. He talks incessantly throughout and I can never make head nor tail of what he is saying. Nor do I want to. It sounds to me like a stream of nonsense words that remind me very much of the March Hare in *Alice's Adventures in Wonderland*. And when he eventually reaches the point to which he wishes to get, the cry he lets out is one of both great anguish and satisfaction, and it is at this stage that I too feel the crashing waves of relief flood through me for I know that it is over, at least for one night.

There is one simple word that I make out occasionally during the times Mr Lawrence climbs on top of me. A name: Nora. I think he is unaware that he even utters it, for it comes at the very point when he reaches the pinnacle of his gratification and has entered another realm entirely. He says her name only once, a guttural cry that at first horrifies me, leaving me weeping and sore in the outside bathroom as I empty *debbe* after *debbe* of cold water over my head to banish the presence of both my husband and the woman I share him with. Yet now, when he plunges deeply inside me and I hear those two short syllables, I tell this ghost in my head that she is welcome to him.

Mr Lawrence is predictable in his habits. Each and every day he returns from work, pours himself a whisky and water, and sits on the verandah and drinks it whilst smoking his pipe. We then eat dinner together, a quiet and subdued affair during which I am asked no questions. I am learning to not bother offering any information either. I always place myself at the table with my back to the heads and horns of his trophies that line the wall, as they quite put me off my food.

'What is the mountain visible from the top of the hill?' I ask him one evening.

'I advised you not to walk around, did I not?' He surveys me coolly, his thin moustache twitching.

'Yes. But advice must be taken in the same spirit with which it is meted out, as something that *is*, quite simply, a suggestion.'

Mr Lawrence's pale eyes narrow and I place a forkful of sautéed potato in my mouth, chewing it slowly and deliberately. He clears his throat and takes a long sip of his whisky and water. 'Well, Iris. You are not a child.'

Stop treating me as one, then.

'Are you referring to the series of smoothly rounded hills? They are the Ngong Hills.'

I finish chewing and shake my head. 'No. It is a single, serrated summit.'

'Ah. That is Mount Kirinyaga. More often than not the air is too hazy to see that from Nairobi, for it is more than one hundred miles away. You were lucky to see it.'

I nod, satisfied. Mount Kirinyaga. I would like to visit this place. I shall have to ask Mr Ahmed more about it next time I see him. I think of his kind, chestnut eyes and how much I would like to take tea with him again.

If the mood so takes me, I enquire after my husband's day but he tells me little or, if he does talk, seems to do so only in heavily veiled colonial-speak or briefly laments the caprices of the most recent settlers. Once the evening meal is over, he drinks more whisky, this time with less water, smokes more of his pipe and more often than not polishes his already immaculate rifles with a care and tenderness I have never seen him extend to humans. As he strokes the smooth handles of the guns, perhaps he likes to imagine they are Nora's body. On occasion, he also wanders round to the back of the house where he remains for some time, engaged in I am not sure what.

I then go to the bedroom and read a little Pearl Rivers or *Alice's Adventures in Wonderland* whilst I await my husband. Sometimes I fall asleep before he comes but this makes no difference; he always wakes me, each and every night. There have been occasions on which I have awoken to find my nightdress already hitched up to the waist, him roughly straddling me, the heft and weight and click of his hips as he rolls on top of me and pins my arms down above my head. It is all I can do to prevent myself from screaming out in pure terror. He makes a great deal of noise, yet if I ever cry out in pain when he handles me like a piece of meat on a butcher's slab, he always reacts the same way: by clamping his large, dry hand over my mouth.

I have been tempted to bite this hand of his on many occasions, so that when he rides me, thrusting deeper and deeper, he too should experience pain. But I have always restrained myself, for I do not know how he should react. And though I have never been afraid of anyone my entire life, the truth is that I am a little afraid of Mr Lawrence. Muthoni, also, is fearful of him; one can see it in the way she is unable to look at him when he addresses her, her black eyes darting around nervously. I wonder if he has ever beaten her? Yet we can never talk about Mr Lawrence; our mutual dislike simply hangs, heavy and wordless, in the air between us.

⚐ ⚐ ⚐

A few weeks after my arrival in Nairobi, I wake to the sound of hammering. It takes me some time to realise that the noise is coming from the drumming of rain on our corrugated-iron roof. Groggy from sleep, I push myself up to my elbows and tilt my chin up to the roof. I smile. It is the first time I have heard rain since I have been on African soil. I see in the half-light of the bedroom that Mr Lawrence is dressing to leave for work, so it must still be early.

'Good morning,' I murmur.

He is fastening his breeches and glances at me over his shoulder. 'Morning. I'm just leaving.'

'It's… it's raining.'

'Yes. Short rains have come early. I won't be back till late tonight. There's a function at the club.'

I sit upright and push my hair out of my eyes, watching as he quickly combs his thin hair in front of the mirror, glances briefly at Nora and then strides towards the door. 'Oh!' he exclaims, turning back to me. 'It slipped my mind to tell you last night. Word came to me at work yesterday from Ahmed to let me know that he has finished your dresses and will be here this morning at eleven to deliver them.' And with that, he is gone.

Once I hear the front door firmly close behind him, I tilt my face upwards again to welcome the sound of the rain, close my eyes and smile.

There have been so many opportunities presented to me when I might take a walk further away than my mountain viewpoint; when Mr Lawrence has been at work and I have had nothing to occupy myself with. Long days of cool, misty mornings before the sun burns through into hazy afternoons, the kind of days that would be perfect for walking to better acquaint myself with my surroundings. Curious then, I think as I stand at the front door of the bungalow, the rain teeming down in vertical sheets, that I should chose a day such as this to take my first walk.

Muthoni has brought me my raincoat and galoshes and I push my hair up beneath the wide-brimmed, waterproof hat. Muthoni's black eyes are filled with concern. 'Rain. Too much.'

I smile at her and shake my head. 'Muthoni,' I say impulsively. 'I wish I could talk to you.'

'Hmm?' Her arched eyebrows incline.

'I *know*,' I press on. 'I know you cannot understand me. And that I cannot understand you. Yet—' I break off as she gazes at me, an expression of bemused incomprehension upon her face. 'Yet I believe you are my friend. Thank you, Muthoni.'

'Thank you!' She opens her mouth and smiles widely, her teeth glinting. Evidently she knows these words, for she is nodding her head and repeating them, again and again. 'Thank you, thank you!'

We both laugh, and I am about to turn and walk away when she clasps me in the crook of my arm with an unexpected strength.

'*Nĩndakena nĩ gũkũmenya.*'

We look at one another for a moment longer. And though I have no idea what she said, somehow it does not matter.

'Thank you, Muthoni,' I whisper. 'Thank you.'

❦ ❦ ❦

I have never been bothered or put off by the weather in the way people often seem to be. My mother, for instance, the moment the sky threatens a drop of rain, throws her hands in the air, wringing them as though somebody has died and announcing that her plans have been *spoiled, all spoiled.* I don't think Mother has ever quite made the connection that water is life and this means rain too.

Then again, I think as I step off the verandah, I have never experienced the African rains before, only British rain, which feels far more genteel. Although I have not yet walked to Bazaar Street, I remember the correct direction from the first time I came here from the railway station. It is not difficult and should only take fifteen or twenty minutes. Before long, I am enjoying the rhythmic splash of my footsteps through the mud as I wind down the narrow track on the hill. After mere moments, I feel my shoulders pushing themselves back as I breathe in the scent of the red earth drinking in the rain.

In Bourn, I used to love making my way from The Old Vicarage, fording the brook and walking through meadows, more often than not alone, but sometimes with Arthur and Papa. For me, Bourn was not only The Old Vicarage but also the hills and meadows, small streams and wide skies. If it were not surrounded by this natural environment, The Old Vicarage would have lost its soul.

I walk through clumps of papyrus strewn haphazardly about and back over the stepping stones of the Nairobi River, now running freer. As I near Victoria Street, I breathe in sharply, for it looks as though the heavy rains have rendered it almost impassable; only a few people are picking their way gingerly through the deep swamp that the street has become. I bite my bottom lip and brush raindrops from my face, considering for a moment turning round and returning to the bungalow. But *no*. I have come this far, and got this wet. It would make no sense whatsoever to return now. And besides, I think brightly, it oughtn't be far from here.

The mud is deeper than I had imagined possible and I find myself sinking down as soon as I step from the verge on to Victoria Street, almost to the tops of my galoshes. I no-

tice an abandoned ox-wagon at the side of the road and try
to pay no heed to the unpleasant smell rising from the bog
beneath me and the row of raggle-taggle shops that flank
me. Presently, I pass a post office, which is where, I realise,
Muthoni must be sending and receiving my letters from. I
also pass some kind of soda water factory and a rickety tim-
ber structure with the name 'Wood's Hotel' on the façade.
I stop for a while to look at it, wondering who might be
staying in Nairobi's only hotel and see that it also appears
to double as a general store. I wish I had a little money with
me, for I should like to go and buy something just for the
sake of it, but of course I have carried not a single rupee on
me since I arrived here.

I make slow progress through the mud. An old settler
passes me in a brown flannel shirt cut off at the elbows, khaki knickerbockers, boots and a pair of putties. His face and
arms are burnt dark brown by the sun and he nods at me in
a friendly manner as we walk past one another. The settler
aside, there is barely a soul around; everyone, no doubt, with
the exception of myself, is doing the sensible thing and shel-
tering from the rain. Yet suddenly I am startled, having been
fixed upon my feet and not the road ahead of me, to look up
and see a woman passing in the other direction. She is dressed
in scarcely more than rags, with nothing to protect her from
the rain, and is weighed down by a leather strap that passes
across her forehead like a headband and reaches behind to
an enormous bundle of dried maize stalks. I cannot imagine
how heavy it must be. I look back into the face of the woman.
I am unable to age her, even approximately; she has young

eyes and her face is unlined, with beautiful, high cheekbones and full lips – yet she has the body of an old woman. Her hands are like the gnarled trunk of an ancient oak and her arms look thin and frail, though clearly they cannot be to carry such a load. Rain gathers in a pond at the hollow of her neck and pours down her face and she blinks her thick lashes often to keep it out of her eyes.

We stand, the two of us, ankle-deep in mud, and simply stare at one another. I notice the large, multiple-looped earrings that pass through every discernible part of her ear, from the lobe all the way to the top. How foreign we are to one another. What is she seeing as she looks at me? And then, something I do not expect: she parts her full, rounded lips and smiles at me. Her smile is so open and spontaneous that my heart soars at the sight of it. There is nothing in the woman's mouth save for a few broken, cracked teeth. I smile back at her.

'Hello,' I say and feel immediately foolish for not speaking in her language. Yet I do not know what her language is.

She inclines her head towards me and makes a noise of greeting; a noise that sounds like a door creaking open. 'Eeeee!'

I cannot help but laugh, it is such a curious sound. 'Eeeee!' I respond and she smiles her cracked-tooth grin at me, readjusts the leather strap across her forehead with her gnarled hands and then continues on her journey. I stand and look back, watching her placing one bare foot carefully in front of the other. It was such a small exchange, and yet it has somehow made me feel that my life here in Nairobi is only just beginning.

CHAPTER TEN

FAZAL AHMED

When Mrs Lawrence arrives at the workshop, she is thoroughly soaked through and her teeth are chattering from the cold. She is wearing a raincoat but it is not, I'm afraid, designed with the monsoon rains in mind. Despite this, Mrs Lawrence is in immeasurably good spirits, laughing and chattering jovially as though we were old friends. My heart aches unexpectedly for Maliha for I know somehow that, should they meet, a friendship would arise between them. I find myself thinking, more in earnest than I have done since arriving on African soil, that I should wait no longer; that Maliha of all people would not mind that my workshop is small and that my living quarters are not as grand as I should like.

I am snapped out of these daydreams by the bright face of Mrs Lawrence in front of me and I suddenly wonder what it is she is doing here. I, of course, had planned to come to her bungalow with the dresses. I tell her as much but she smiles openly.

'No, no Mr Ahmed, I assure you,' she says, in such a joyful tone that I wonder if indeed this is the same downhearted young woman whom I came to measure, 'I wanted to walk. I *longed* to walk. I have not walked, you see, since arriving here and I think my muscles had stiffened into rods of iron!' Mrs Lawrence opens her mouth wider and emits a hearty laugh, full-throated and charming, and I cannot help but chuckle along with her. Despite her favourable mood, though, it is clear she is terribly cold and I guide her towards the small hearth I have in the corner of my workshop and pull a chair up for her, then bend down to light the fire.

'How kind, Mr Ahmed. But you needn't light it on my account.'

'Of course I should, Mrs Lawrence. You will catch a nasty cold otherwise and we cannot have that.'

She smiles at me gratefully as she removes her soaked outer layer raincoat and mud-caked galoshes and receives the blanket I hand her, placing it around her narrow shoulders. As I light the fire, I glance back at her huddled inside the blanket and marvel, once again, at how young she looks. Before I can stop myself, I say 'I think you are very brave, Mrs Lawrence.'

She laughs again, but this time her laugh is more uncertain. 'Brave?' she asks in a voice that sounds like a child's.

'Yes,' I say as I turn away from her and blow into the fire. She pauses. 'Why?'

I hesitate. It is not my place to speak to Mrs Lawrence in such a familiar manner. I am her tailor, and tailor to her husband, that is all. However, I cannot say such a thing and not explain myself in some way.

'You are brave for coming here, Mrs Lawrence. To this inhospitable land. And you are brave for walking here today alone.'

She pulls the blanket tighter round her shoulders and stretches her stockinged feet out towards the fire, inclining her head on one side and narrowing her eyes as though she is considering my words. Eventually, she speaks.

'That is very kind of you, Mr Ahmed. But you see, it really has nothing to do with bravery – coming out here to East Africa, I mean. I did not have a choice.'

I nod my head. 'I understand.'

Her head moves back up so that it is straight and she looks directly at me, all trace of earlier humour vanished.

'You do?'

I stand and pull up a chair beside her. I cannot, of course, truly understand her predicament. What it means for a young girl of her age to come here to Nairobi to marry a man she has never met, most probably against her will. I myself came to Africa of my own volition. I do not, and cannot, know what it is like to make such a journey. And yet, there are some things that I do understand: I understand what it is to be alone, and to be lonely, even in the midst of people. I understand how it feels to be an outsider; to have the wrong colour skin, the wrong look, the wrong language. Yet we are all misfits in this barren land, all of us, with the exception of the people who have inhabited these plains for centuries. I shall never fit in for I am not from here nor from there – that place thousands of miles away called Great Britain, whose people are now claiming this land as their own. But now, the Britishers are pushing the native people out, further and further, and this young woman who sits in front of me, her husband is one of them. But this has nothing to do with her. So yes, in a way, I understand.

I smile at her and nod briefly and she smiles back at me. For several minutes we sit in silence as the warmth from the fire permeates the room.

'Oh! Mr Ahmed! Before I forget... do you like to read?'

'To read?'

'Yes. Literature. Poetry. Anything, really. You see, I only had space to bring one book with me and another was a gift from my chaperone but – I have read them rather a lot. Mr Lawrence is not much of a reader and, well... I am very fond of reading. I don't suppose you could lend my anything?'

'I could indeed.' I lean forwards in my chair and stroke my chin. 'I have a number of books. I am not certain however if they would be to your liking—'

'Oh, but anything at all you feel able to part with for a short while.'

'Let me see. I have a couple of works of William Morris, Dickens of course, Conrad. I'm sure I must have others – but female authors,' I cough, 'I'm afraid are conspicuous by their absence. Are any of those male authors though of interest to you?'

She claps her hands together. 'Oh, yes! *More* than of interest.'

Her enthusiasm really is quite touching.

I smile and nod. 'Very well, Mrs Lawrence. I shall see that I get some of my novels to you. As soon as possible.'

We sit in silence for a few moments and then I rise from my chair and move towards the small stove I keep in one corner of the workshop for the purpose of making tea. 'May I make you some chai? It will help warm you.' It's not quite the same as English tea. Or Kenyan tea, for that matter. It is Indian tea made with spices.'

'I would love to try it.'

I light the stove with a match and stir the still-warm liquid from earlier, dropping in a few extra cardamom pods and black peppercorns. Whilst it is heating, I walk to the back of the workshop where I have Mrs Lawrence's dresses in a box, ready to deliver to her.

'Would you like to see what I have made you, Mrs Lawrence?'

'Very much so. Oh, but Mr Ahmed, I must tell you. I keep seeing that bird, you remember the one I am referring to? That colourful little creature with the curved beak. She pauses and laughs. 'I have learnt to be stealthy and managed to draw fairly close to it on one or two occasions for a proper look.' She sighs and smiles. 'How I should like to know what it is.'

I unwrap the paper from around the dress box and take the lid off. 'I remember the bird well, Mrs Lawrence. You are right, it was very beautiful indeed.'

At the very moment that I draw the first dress from its box, swathes of Indian cotton billowing to the ground, a thought comes to me and I laugh out loud for not having thought of it before. Mrs Lawrence's eyes widen in surprise at my small outburst.

'Forgive me,' I chuckle, 'but I have thought of something – or someone, I should say, who may be of interest to you. Oh, the chai!'

I have put it on too high and it is boiling over on the stove. I lay down the bottle-green dress on the table and rush to it, extinguishing the fire. 'I am terribly sorry. But perhaps there is still enough here for one cup.'

'Mr Ahmed, please do not trouble yourself. I am perfectly warm here by the fire.'

I turn and find that she has a smile to match her cheerful voice. I reach for a cup and the pot of sugar on the small wooden shelf I constructed above the stove and carefully strain the remaining chai. 'How much sugar would you like?'

'Oh…' She hesitates. 'I don't know. I think I have never drunk tea with sugar before.'

'You have not?' I say in surprise. 'That is probably because you have never drunk Indian chai before.'

'Is it so very different?'

I smile and hand Mrs Lawrence the cup. She works her hands free from the folds of the blanket and lowers her face to the rising steam. She closes her eyes and smiles. 'I can certainly smell how different it is from English tea.' Opening her eyes, she takes a sip and then her eyes flicker to mine, wide with surprise, before drinking again. 'Mr Ahmed,' she says in a very serious tone. I freeze for a moment. She does not like it. Perhaps I should not have put in the extra peppercorns. 'Mr Ahmed,' she says again, bringing the cup up to warm her cheek, 'this is the best thing I have tasted in a very, very long time.'

I feel my heart lift and cannot help but beam at her.

'I must take your recipe and ask Muthoni to make it at home. What were you going to tell me earlier, Mr Ahmed?' She looks up over her cup at me expectantly.

'There is a man I know here in Nairobi, a local Kikuyu man. His name is Benedict Kamau. He can help you with your interest in birds, I am certain of it.'

She leans forward in the chair and looks at me intently. Her eyes are such an unusual shade of blue that I find myself blinking under their gaze.

'I met him several months ago. He turned up here one day, asking if I knew of anyone who could make shoes for him, so I pointed him in the right direction. He is a cultured man, educated by the missionaries, I believe, and with a better grasp of the English language than I.' I break off, chuckling. 'Anyway, a month or two later he returned to my workshop to tell me that the fellow I told him about who made him shoes had done a marvellous job. He said he would also like a shirt for his teaching.'

'He is a teacher?'

'Yes. As I understand it, there is a school at the western end of the Nairobi River where he teaches young Kikuyu children. When I had made his shirt, I went to deliver it to the school for I was not sure where he lived and did not know how to reach him. I sat outside his classroom and waited for the lesson to be over, then when he came out, he shook my hand and suddenly whispered, 'Wait!' I did not know what it was that I was to wait for, but I realised quickly that he was looking over my head. When I turned round, I saw that he was staring at a bird hopping along the ground. He told me that he had not seen such a bird in more than a few years.'

'What bird was it?' Mrs Lawrence asks, her violet eyes shining.

I shake my head apologetically. 'I am sorry. As you know, I have no head or memory for the names of birds. He did tell me, I am sure. I had quite forgotten about him until now, for apart from waving at him across Victoria Street on a couple of occasions, I have not seen him since. But if you would like me to contact him, Mrs Lawrence, I am sure he can identify your bird with the curved beak. Or any bird, for that matter. I do not know him well, but he is a good man. Of this, one has a sense, would you not agree?'

Mrs Lawrence does not say anything, but leans back in the chair, both of her hands still clasping her cup. She looks reflective and stares for several moments at some point beyond before turning to me and inclining her head. 'Yes, I should say so.'

CHAPTER ELEVEN

IRIS LAWRENCE

A few weeks pass before I next see Mr Ahmed. During this time, I have so little else to occupy myself with that I decide to begin writing down descriptions of the birds I see, hoping very much that over time I shall be able to identify them. My new notes begin with a bird I see up at my lookout spot. Truly, it gave me a tremendous scare. It was vast, not far off the size of an ostrich, and it looked so *odd*, almost like an accident of nature.

'Huge wingspan,' I scribble, 'spindly legs, enormous beak and curious tufty, white hair. Very solemn-looking, as though he were on his way to a funeral.'

Just as I am giving up hope that Mr Ahmed might visit me or deliver any novels and I think I may walk once more to Bazaar Street, he comes. I am sitting out on the verandah when I see a figure making its way towards the bungalow. I stand and walk towards the gate as a sudden gust of wind almost blows my hat off. When the figure nears and I see that it is Mr Ahmed, several books tucked beneath his arm, my heart contracts with an absurd joy and it is all I can do to prevent myself from flinging my arms over my head and jumping up and down on the spot with joy. He approaches, puffed out from the climb up the hill but still with his customary mirthful expression.

'Mrs Lawrence, it is a great pleasure to see you again. And look what I have finally brought you!'

'Mr Ahmed,' I say, grinning like the Cheshire Cat, a wide smile that is stupid, desperate, sincere, 'the pleasure is all mine.'

CHAPTER TWELVE

FAZAL AHMED

Mrs Lawrence chatters all the way down the hill and has not paused for breath even by the time we begin to walk along the banks of the Nairobi River. This river was, when I first arrived here, clear and free-flowing, yet now it looks turgid, carrying all of the township's effluence downriver with it. Mrs Lawrence is certainly not perturbed by this and is in high spirits. I do hope she will not be too shocked by what she is to encounter here. Though looking at her determined, steadfast step ahead of me, I think not.

We reach a bend in the river and I tell her that it is not far from here, pointing out a swampy clump of papyrus, beyond which sits the schoolhouse. We can already hear the shrill cries and chatter of the children being dismissed for the day and my heart contracts a little at the sound of it as I wonder how far in the future it will be until I hear these same sounds in my own home. I notice that Mrs Lawrence's fashionable boots with buttons up the side are caked in mud, but she does not seem to mind or be aware of this and she stands back to let me pass her on the narrow path in order for me to lead the way.

Young children are now pouring out of the schoolhouse door, dressed in the traditional Kikuyu manner in simple drapes, adorned with varying amounts of jewellery. All of them go barefoot and a memory of my own schooldays rises, how we would be beaten mercilessly if we were not dressed impeccably with neatly combed hair. But as I watch these skinny youngsters stream out of the door, I marvel that they are being given an education at all as I cannot imagine there are many native schools in Nairobi.

All at once, it seems, they notice the two of us approaching them and a wave of awed excitement and even fear ripples through them.

'*Mundu mweru! Mundu mweru!*' one boy at the front screeches and, before long, they are all calling out, pointing and staring and murmuring. A small child starts to wail and they all push one another forward, thrilled and horrified and excited.

Kamau soon emerges from the schoolhouse and first of all looks at the sobbing child before he looks at Mrs Lawrence and me. He begins to laugh and scoops the child up in his arms before pacing towards us. The child writhes and screams and Kamau rubs his back in circular motions, murmuring reassurances. As he stands in front of us, the young boy squirms in his arms and turns to bury his face in Kamau's chest.

He first shakes my hand, smiling warmly at me, and then turns to greet Mrs Lawrence, manoeuvring the child in his arms to make this possible.

'Mr Ahmed. Mrs…'

'Lawrence,' she says in a low, firm voice.

'Mrs Lawrence,' he repeats. 'It is wonderful to see you both.'

'I am afraid I have scared your pupils,' Mrs Lawrence remarks.

Kamau laughs generously and replies, 'It is true that they are not accustomed to seeing white people such as yourself. But do not worry, they are excited, not scared.'

Mrs Lawrence laughs too. We all know, of course, that this is not quite true as we look at the face of the small child in Kamau's arms, who stares at her, wide-eyed and petrified. Kamau continues to murmur to the child in his own tongue and slowly, the corner of the little boy's mouth starts to twitch in a smile. I see that Mrs Lawrence is beaming at him, her hands clasped in front of her.

'Please,' Kamau says as he slowly lowers the child to the ground so he can scamper off. 'Will you not come this way?' He motions to the schoolhouse behind him and Mrs Lawrence and I make our way through the throng of children.

CHAPTER THIRTEEN

IRIS LAWRENCE

I know I should not be here. I half expect Mr Lawrence to come in at any moment and march me home. But then the voice of reason tells me this could not happen, that he is at work and is as predictable in his habits as day turning to night and, besides, I shan't be here for long.

I try to relax and focus upon what Kamau is saying. The first thing I notice about him is his command of the English language. His voice is accented, yet he speaks with ease and fluidity, and I remember Mr Ahmed telling me he was educated by missionaries. Kamau offers us both a seat on a small wooden bench inside the schoolhouse and makes a gesture around the cramped room.

'I have to teach forty-three children in here. Not much room, is there?'

Mr Ahmed emits a sympathetic low chuckle and I carefully look around me. A ray of afternoon light is streaming through the single high window. It is no more than a wooden hut really and though there are a number of benches, there are no desks.

'The children keep their books on their…?' I ask.

'Their laps,' Kamau replies. 'Yes. I am thinking about having another room built and dividing the class into two so that it is more age-appropriate. But,' he shrugs, 'their parents are paying one rupee each month per child and with this kind of money it will be a while before I can employ another teacher or pay for building materials.'

Mr Ahmed stands up and walks towards the blackboard, studying the day's lessons. 'It is honourable work you are doing here, Kamau.'

He doesn't say anything, but sits in the single ray of light pouring through the window, dust motes dancing, the tips of his fingers lightly touching and his head down as though in contemplation. We are a mere forty-five-minute walk from the bungalow and yet I feel, for the first time since setting foot on this land, that I am really in Africa. As though reading my thoughts, Kamau raises his head, looks directly at me and smiles.

'And so, Mrs Lawrence,' he says. 'Our friend Mr Ahmed here says you have an interest in African birdlife.'

It is curious; there is no real reason for this, but I suddenly feel eight years old as both men look at me expectantly, as though what I say next will define me for evermore in both their eyes. I am silent for a few moments, aware of the few children lingering by the door and the dark eyes that peer in through the gaps in the wooden planks of the schoolhouse. I also think again of Mr Lawrence, knowing too well the horror he would feel seeing me here.

Pushing such thoughts aside, I reply. 'That is correct. The truth is I know very little about them. And... well... I have a fondness for them.'

I fear that my words sound foolish and childish but neither Kamau nor Mr Ahmed react as though they think so. On the contrary, Kamau only smiles widely, displaying white, even teeth. 'I also have a fondness for birds, Mrs Lawrence.'

Round his neck he has a piece of string, to which is attached a pouch that hangs in front of his chest. A small button holds the pouch together and I watch as he unclasps this and then draws out a notebook and pencil before handing me the book. He nods at me, encouraging me to open it, and I carefully do so, taking in the detailed sketches of birds with both their common and Latin names written beneath them. I find a smile creeping to my lips as I turn from one page to the next, moving my fingers over the lovingly rendered drawings.

'These are wonderful,' I say, raising my head to meet his eyes before looking down again.

Kamau is silent; it is clear he is not fond of being complimented. After a while, Mr Ahmed agrees with me, commenting that he has also seen the small book on one occasion. Kamau shifts on the hard wooden bench, planting his broad hands squarely on his knees. 'It is a hobby of mine. It started when I was a child with the missionaries. There was one man, a Reverend Dutton, who passed on his interest in birds to me. He was never without his identification book wherever we went.'

'Was that here, in Nairobi?' I ask.

Kamau laughs slightly. 'No,' he replies. 'Nairobi did not exist when I was growing up.'

I blush, feeling very young again. I know, of course, that this township has been in existence for scant years but it had momentarily slipped my mind.

'This was in Kikuyuland, where I grew up. I only arrived in Nairobi one year ago, to see what this new place was like that everybody talked of.'

I have a number of questions and open my mouth to start asking them, but am nervous about sounding gushing and close it again. Looking back at his small sketchbook, I reluctantly hand it back to Kamau. He places a hand out to stop me. 'No. Don't give it back just yet. Why don't you look through it again? See if the bird you wish to identify is there?'

I smile and nod my head and Mr Ahmed comes to stand behind me. After all, he was there the first time I saw it and I am certain he also would recognise it. We spend some time there in the schoolhouse as the ray of light fades and vanishes, the eyes behind the wooden slats tire of waiting and move away and Kamau treads noiselessly around the room tidying up. Our task of identification is harder than I might imagine, for, detailed as Kamau's drawings are, they are without colour. I do not wish to say as much, however, for fear that my words should sound critical. But, again as though he is reading my mind, he speaks from the far end of the room.

'Perhaps it is hard without the colour in the pictures?'

'Oh no,' I say, a little too quickly.

'The other thing,' he continues, 'is that within a species there are a number of sub-varieties.'

I continue to look through the book, marvelling at the detail whilst Mr Ahmed stands at my shoulder, making small murmurs of appreciation. I turn a page and pause, my fingers suspended as it rests above the book. 'This… this one, perhaps?'

Mr Ahmed peers down and reads, 'Little Bee-eater, *Merops pusillus*.'

'Little Bee-eater?' Kamau comments from the other side of the room. 'This may well be what you are looking for. There are at least fifteen varieties of bee-eater here, very attractive plumage, so I'm not surprised it caught your eye.'

'But…' I say, biting my bottom lip.

'Yes?'

'The beak. I am not sure. I think the beak of the bird I saw is more curved. Mr Ahmed, what do you think?'

He shakes his head and chuckles and I cannot help smiling, for it is such a mirthful laugh. 'Mrs Lawrence,' he says, 'as you know I do not have a memory for birds, neither for their names nor their forms. The Indian koel from my native land, now that is a bird I remember.'

'What is a koel?' asks Kamau with great interest, and they embark on an animated discussion of this Indian bird. My attention drifts in and out of their conversation and I continue to turn the pages of the book. I am unconvinced by this bee-eater, attractive though it is; it is the beak I keep thinking of. I pass through rollers and hornbills, barbets and greenbuls.

'This must be quite a work in progress,' I comment, once Mr Ahmed and Kamau have stopped talking.

'Indeed it is,' Kamau agrees, smiling broadly. 'I have to keep attaching more pages to the back. Soon –' he taps on the pouch hanging against his chest – 'the book will not even be able to fit in here.'

'Would you mind very much providing me with a piece of paper and pencil? You see, I am making notes of the birds I am seeing at home and can identify several now from your marvellous book.'

He looks pleased, nodding at me. Kamau rises and fetches what I ask for and I flick back through the book, writing down 'Hadada ibis, pied wagtail, maribou stork, mousebird'.

I want to ask him more; I want to keep looking at these pictures, yet I am aware that the schoolroom is growing dim and that the walk home will take a while. I must arrive back at the bungalow before Mr Lawrence, because I am no good at lying and know that my visit here to the schoolhouse today with Mr Ahmed is not something I can share with him.

I sigh, far louder than I intended to, and both Kamau and Mr Ahmed look at me in surprise. I blush. 'Do either of you know what the time is?'

Mr Ahmed glances at his wristwatch. 'Just gone four o'clock.'

I spring to my feet. What if I am unlucky this one day and Mr Lawrence comes home early? 'I really ought to be getting back.'

Kamau stands up and spreads his hands wide. 'I am afraid I have not helped you in your search, Mrs Lawrence. If we had more time—'

'Oh no!' I cry. 'Quite the contrary. You have been marvellously helpful. Both of you – Mr Ahmed for bringing me here and you, Kamau, for showing me your wonderful book. How I wish I had your skill to draw like that. I do not doubt for an instant that the bird I am looking for is in here somewhere, but I am afraid I *must* go.'

He nods his head, grasps his hands in front of him and stands for a few moments in silent contemplation, his face serious all of a sudden as Mr Ahmed prepares himself to leave.

I go to shake his hand and he accepts warmly. 'Perhaps we can do this again sometime, Mrs Lawrence.' It is more of a statement than a question. I should like this terribly but I cannot say that in so many words, so I nod and stammer some insubstantial reply to the affirmative whilst making no firm commitment.

We all bid our farewells and Mr Ahmed and I begin to make our way back along the twist of Nairobi River that gleams and gurgles beneath the fading day.

CHAPTER FOURTEEN

BENEDICT KAMAU

Her teeth are crooked, only slightly. The front ones. So that when she smiles it gives her the appearance of… what? Of a young woman whose mouth is still growing into itself? When she takes her hat off inside the schoolhouse, her hair is dark but at the same time there is a lightness to it, a soft sheen. And though I have seen plenty of *mundu mweru* by now, these white folk who are colonising our lands and calling them their own, I have never seen skin the colour of this woman's. For I cannot call it white, though neither is it brown like our friend Mr Ahmed's. To call it pink would do it no justice, but cream would make it sound like porcelain; breakable, fragile. And there is nothing fragile about her, not at all.

When they leave, I sit for some time on the bench in the schoolhouse. I try to think about my lessons for the following day, but my mind keeps returning to her; to the curve of her bottom lip, which is slightly fuller than the top one; to her narrow wrists and the gleam of the wedding band that sits on a finger of her left hand, winking scornfully at me.

At one stage I pinch myself, physically, to dispel these ridiculous thoughts that crowd my head. I have lessons to prepare. Places to go. People to see. Things I must do. And yet, as I finally lock up the schoolhouse to return home, how can I possibly deny to myself that I know – of course I know – the name of the bird to which she referred? The truth is there, yet I do not wish to face it. I did not tell her the name, for I wish her to keep searching. Yes, I wish to see her again.

CHAPTER FIFTEEN

IRIS LAWRENCE

I have found thin, bendy twigs from all around my Mount Kirinyaga viewpoint. These serve as croquet hoops and I have succeeded in attaching them to the only level patch of shrubby grass above the bungalow by winding string around the bottom of the hoops to the longer blades. The mallet that Muthoni helped me to make is perfect, though I used to hit the ball very hard when playing back at The Old Vicarage with Arthur and suspect I shall have to replace the tin can now and again. But then again, the ball we used in England was so hard and firm; here, I have had to satisfy myself with old bits of cloth from my sewing basket sewn together into a globe shape.

After a few mornings of knocking my makeshift ball around, one Monday morning I beckon Muthoni to follow me after Mr Lawrence has left for work. She walks beside me through the front gate and follows me up to the level patch where I lift up the mallet and show her how to hit the ball through the hoops. She stands, hands resting on her slim hips and eyebrows raised as she watches me, then smiles openly, nodding her head. I hold the mallet out to her, but a hand flies to her mouth and she laughs self-consciously, shaking her head.

'Yes!' I cry. 'Muthoni, please try. It is fun.' I walk to her, gently lift up one of her hands and place the mallet in it. She laughs again and shakes her head. 'Please.'

She raises an eyebrow. '*Daakuhoya.*'

'That means "please" in Kikuyu?'

She nods.

'*Daakuhoya.*'

Muthoni accepts the mallet and hits at the ball, completely missing. She stamps her foot playfully and cries out in Kikuyu, then tries again. But then I see her looking over the top of my head and her face clouds. I turn. Mr Lawrence is standing there, forehead puckered into a deep, black frown. Muthoni drops the mallet as though is it a burning coal, buries her chin to her chest and hurries back towards the bungalow.

For heaven's sake, what is he doing back here? Besides, all we were doing was playing croquet. Or is that not permitted, as Muthoni is a native? Something wells up inside me, hot little sparks of fury. I stride up to him. 'Why are you back?'

'I left something behind. But I see it is just as well I did. Iris, what are you *thinking*?'

I smile tightly at him. 'About what?'

'You jolly well know about what,' he snaps. 'Playing croquet is one thing, but doing so with a *servant*. I'm sure you would not have behaved that way back in your village in England with the servants.'

Perhaps, but I had other things to do, other people to talk to back there. I glare at him. 'I was simply showing her how to use a croquet mallet. I see no harm in that.'

'*Iris,*' he barks, grasping my arm hard, in exactly the same way Lord Sidcup did that time in The Old Vicarage garden. I shudder, shaking myself free. But he looks angry in a way I have not seen before, pale eyes twitching, shoulders hunched and quivering. 'You will *not* play games with a servant. And you will not play games with me; make a fool of me. Do I make myself clear?'

But who is there to make a fool in front of! I want to scream at him. *We are always alone, quite alone, here.* But I do not say anything; I just continue to glare at him before I nod my head curtly and walk past him to the bungalow.

❧ ❧ ❧

On Saturday and Sunday afternoons, Mr Lawrence often goes hunting. After such an escapade one Saturday, he returns late, a dead, bloodied zebra laid out on an ox-cart pulled by two natives behind him. I immediately enter the bungalow, for I have no wish to see what will be done with the beast. What I do know is that somehow its head will be separated from its body and its glassy eyes will someday soon be staring at the back of my head as I sit at the dinner table. Up to now, I have not had the slightest curiosity as to the workings of this process. Yet on this night – I am unsure why – I stand silently in the shadow of the doorway, unnoticed.

Along with the two native men, whom I have never seen before but who no doubt have assisted him in his hunting, he has hauled the dead beast up so that it is hanging by its head, a coarse rope looped round the neck and its mouth stretched open, huge teeth protruding as though it were slaughtered mid-cry. With a large knife, Mr Lawrence is cutting into the greying flesh of its neck. I do not wish to watch and tell myself to turn back into the bungalow, yet my revulsion has frozen me and not only do I find myself unable to move, but I can scarcely blink.

Once he has finished with the neck, he starts on the zebra's front legs, cutting in precise lines into the beautiful striped fur so that it falls away from the bone with great ease, like a camisole falling from a body. I never imagined the skin of an animal could separate with such ease from the flesh of its owner, the flesh that had lived and breathed and moved over sinewy limbs. If Mr Lawrence were to skin me, I find myself wondering, would my skin separate so readily from my flesh?

He is now starting on the hind legs, the flesh beneath the skin a mottled tapestry of reds and creamy whites. It all happens so quickly – so surprisingly, effortlessly quickly. After he has skinned his trophy, his assistants help him to move it to a long wooden plank and Mr Lawrence gently rubs wood ash into the hide and then stretches it out, long and lean, onto a portable frame. Only the heads and the skins of the animals ever remain; the rest is discarded into a tin bucket, destined for I do not know where. Then they move the wooden plank to a spot where the bungalow's roof does not shade it so, I suppose, the skins may dry in the sun.

It is not so much the actions he is performing that I am so disturbed by; it is more his manner. For as he attacks the back legs, I can see his face clearly as the dying light falls upon it. In his frenzy to carry out the task, I recognise the very same expression as the one he wears when he looms over me in the semi-darkness and cries out the name of his dead wife. It is fervour, it is single-minded determination and it is lust – the lust of the kill. Is it that each time he violently takes me, he is killing me? A small part of me? My stomach suddenly contracts in outrage at this thought and I clutch my arms firmly round myself and turn away from Mr Lawrence and his half-skinned zebra, hurrying back into the bungalow. But it is too late; I have not given myself enough time to reach the lavatory outside. As I fling open the front door, I heave as everything I have eaten that day spills out of me across the wooden panelling. Doubled over, I heave until there is nothing left save the bitter taste of bile and disgust in my mouth. I stare at it, spattered across the verandah, as it gleams in the vanishing dusk and flies congregate at once to feast.

The following morning, Mr Lawrence and I walk to church together. I do not wish to think of the previous evening and what I witnessed and yet, like a moth to the light, I cannot help myself.

'Once the heads and skins of your animals are dried, what happens to them? I mean… before they are hung upon our wall?'

He must mistake my question for interest or enthusiasm in his activities, for he turns to me immediately in surprise. 'Well,' he says, his voice threaded with delight, 'I pack them into tin-lined cases, accompanied by plenty of moth killer. Then I spend some time labelling them for train and shipment back to England.'

He waits for me to say something, but when I do not, he continues, his voice puffed up with pride. 'They are delivered to Rowland Ward of Piccadilly. You must have heard of them.'

Of course I have not and I open my mouth to tell him as much before thinking better of it and closing it again and simply nodding. Did Nora, I wonder, take an interest in Mr Lawrence's hunting? Somehow I suspect she must have done. How I should like to magic her back to life for a single afternoon so that I might know what kind of a person she was and how she endured our husband. I do not mind any longer that I am to share him. In fact, I often feel I would willingly give him over entirely to the spirit of the deceased and that we should both be happier this way.

I continue thinking of Nora in church as Reverend Ellis stands at the makeshift pulpit and preaches of redemption and spreading the Good Word across these heathen lands. I also think of Papa – I do miss him dreadfully and should like more than anything for him to be giving the sermon today. I want to write to him, to Arthur also. But I can only bring myself to write to Miss Logan for the time being.

Nairobi
18 September, 1903

Dear Miss Logan,

I am settling into life in Nairobi. The climate is temperate, thus I am not unduly bothered by the heat. We are now awaiting what is known as the short rains, the settler farmers more than any.

From our bungalow, we can sometimes see elephant or giraffe loping across the plains and vast herds of zebra and all kinds of antelope too. I have not seen a lion but have heard one at night. I am not scared, for the bungalow is surrounded by a thorny bush that a wild animal should not be able to pass through, as indeed are all the homes of the settlers. More than the animals, however, I am fascinated by the birdlife here. It is truly spectacular, a riot of colour, shape, size and plumage. I should so enjoy being able to identify them but Mr Lawrence is not in the least interested in birds and cannot enlighten me in this department. He is extremely busy with his hunting at the weekends and work during the week. He has not told me too much about it, but I do know that the settlers he deals with are experiencing manifest challenges, ranging from rain failure to stock theft by African tribes, livestock succumbing to unfamiliar diseases and locust swarms that are able to wipe out an entire coffee plantation in a single morning.

Life for myself is rather quiet. Mr Lawrence often goes in the evenings to the Nairobi Club, which I believe is a social club for settlers. Perhaps on one occasion I shall accompany him and meet some of the settlers' wives, for at present I have only seen them on Nairobi's principle thoroughfare, Government Road.

Do write to me, won't you?

Yours,

Iris Lawrence

Do I ever wish I had accepted Lord Sidcup's hand? No, I cannot say that I do. For whilst I know that Mr Lawrence will never be a gentle husband, sometimes I feel that his neglect of me has also, in some strange way, been my saving grace. Lord Sidcup's disdain of women was all too apparent and whilst Mr Lawrence's opinion of the fairer sex is none too high, he does at least leave me to my own devices, save for at night. It is peculiar though; when we walk to church, he expects that I should take his arm. It is, of course, all for the sake of appearances as no intimacy occurs between us otherwise and it always comes as a surprise to see the crook of his arm so proffered once a week. I take it, for what else am I to do?

I wait in great anticipation for the trains to arrive from Mombasa, as they bring with them news from home and replies to my own letters. It should come as no surprise and yet, somehow, it still does, that the very first letter I receive from England comes from Miss Logan and not from any of my family members. I stand with it in my hands, staring down at the sloped writing, and it feels like the greatest treasure I shall ever receive. I almost do not wish to open it, for fear that it might disintegrate, a figment of my longing imagination.

45 Hawthorne Terrace
Durham

November 13, 1903

Dear Iris,

I hope that this finds you well. Thank you so much for your letter, I was extremely happy to hear from you and learn more about the house you are living in and, to a certain extent, the daily rhythm of your life in Nairobi.

As for myself, I have decided to take an intermission from my chaperoning work. I do not yet know for how long, but I am not as young as I once was and these long journeys are beginning to tire me somewhat. Perhaps I shall only accept the shorter-distance posts for the time being. Besides, I keep myself very busy here in Durham with various activities, most notably the Fabian Society. No doubt you are familiar with them? The society advocates liberal reform and social justice and is tremendously progressive. Are you aware that the Labour Party formation in 1900 was in large part thanks to the participation of the Fabians? I am immensely proud to be part of such a group, despite the fact that the Durham branch is only in its infancy. I have no doubt, however, that it will grow. The greater momentum we gain, the more likely we are to see the back of our ineffective prime minister. Balfour, in my opinion, is a disaster in every respect. Who ever heard of a prime minister who was a Right Honourable Earl, for a start? I fear that it is his social standing in society as opposed to any sensible or intelligent political opinion that has ensured his continued position in government.

There is something else I feel rather excited by and wish to share with you. Last month, a Women's Social and Political Union (WSPU) was founded in Manchester by six women, two of whom are a mother and daughter partnership, Emmeline and Sylvia Pankhurst. They are to campaign for women's suffrage and social reform and since its inception, there have been mur-

murings of a branch opening in Durham. If this happens, I shall certainly be amongst the first of its members. I feel absolutely certain that one day us women shall enjoy equal rights to our male counterparts. I have always felt a deep injustice that I work, pay my taxes and own property and yet, have no political leverage. How can this be right?

Forgive me, my dear. I do get rather carried away on this subject. Do you think that such a movement might exist amongst the women settlers of Nairobi? Even if it is in its early stages, I have no doubt you should enjoy debating the issues surrounding women's suffrage. I enclose a copy of the St Pancras Gazette *that I am sure you will find interesting.*

Please do keep me informed, of how you are. I look forward to hearing from you and do hope that you are happy – or, at least, that you are not unhappy.

Yours,

Penelope Logan

CHAPTER SIXTEEN

BENEDICT KAMAU

Mrs Lawrence occupies my thoughts. I tell myself that the desire I feel to see her again is purely transactional, for I wish to expand her knowledge of East African birdlife. Yet the more I tell myself this story, the more it rings hollow.

I know nothing of her husband, whether he is a good man or not. But I visit Fazal Ahmed one afternoon to have two pairs of trousers and a shirt repaired and, after I have been at his workshop for some time and he has served me tea and really it is time for me to be on my way, I scan the room and ask him a question in as casual a manner as I can.

'Mrs Lawrence. Has she been here for a long time?'

'Mrs Lawrence?' Fazal looks at me with his steady gaze. 'No, not very long.'

'Do you make clothes for her husband?'

'I have done, though he has not needed anything recently. Mrs Lawrence, too. I have made a few dresses for her.'

I nod, standing up and striding to the window so that he cannot see my face. 'What is Mr Lawrence like?'

Fazal doesn't say anything and I am eventually forced to turn round to face him. 'Why do you ask?' he says after some time.

'Simple curiosity,' I reply with a shrug. 'I don't know many of the *mundu mweru* here.'

'No,' Fazal agrees and he doesn't reply for a while and I think that perhaps he will not answer me, but then he sighs and shakes his head.

'Well,' he says. I wait. 'Actually it is difficult to say. I do not know him really. And he has been perfectly civil to me, but I do not find him an easy man to like.'

I feel the warm breeze from the open door and the screech of a whydah calling from the distance. 'In what way?'

He shakes his head again. 'Difficult to say. He is…' Fazal scratches his cheek. 'Cold. Distant. I see a hint of cruelty in him.'

I feel my pulse quickening and the question slips out before I can stop myself. 'Do you think he mistreats her?'

Fazal clears his throat and frowns, looking away. 'I certainly hope not.'

I remain with my back to the door, the breeze tingling the backs of my legs through my thin cotton trousers.

Fazal begins to murmur about having a great deal to get on with and I know I must finally go. I shake his hand and bid him farewell. Leaving his workshop, I make my way past the dusty warren of *dukas* and over the pockmarked terrain of Bazaar Street.

CHAPTER SEVENTEEN

IRIS LAWRENCE

The days turn on their axis beneath the wide Nairobi skies. I take short walks in the vicinity of the bungalow, watch the birds intently, finish reading the works of Pearl Rivers and go straight back to the beginning to start again. I sit on the verandah and drink tea and stare across the plains as papyrus is slashed down, Maasai kraals shifted, the soil tilled whilst tents, buildings and shanties rise like grey phantoms out of the newly drained swamps.

Muthoni and I converse a little and I teach her some English – she is coming along with it tremendously well. She is keen and quick, a good listener, and I suspect if I begin to teach her in earnest she will be a fast learner. Muthoni's native tongue is Kikuyu and I have been muddling my way through a few words and phrases that she has taught me – *Ndeithia, metha, thani, tigwo na wega*. I do so with grave incompetence, but each time I make an effort, she claps her hands together and laughs with such wild pleasure and abandon that I feel a deep well of joy stir within me, a desire to keep trying.

I know Muthoni is a good person; goodness can so often be read in someone's eyes and in hers I see only decency and warmth. Yet I know so little about her: where she lives, what age she is, with whom she lives, what brought her to this township.

I enjoy watching her at her work, using old tea leaves for polishing glass and wood and endlessly sweeping small piles of red dust from corners of the bungalow with a brush fashioned from twigs and leaves. There is a grace and fluidity to her easy movements that I admire and she never appears to grumble. One evening after dinner, I help her carry the dishes to the outside kitchen as I always do. But this time, rather than leaving her to wash up alone, I remain there as she fills the sink with water from a zinc bucket below and lathers a little soap on to a brush. I move beside her and reach my hands into the sink.

'I do it, Muthoni.'

She looks at me uncomprehendingly, her sleeves already rolled up and her hands wet.

'*Me.*' I do the same as her, rolling the sleeves of my blouse up, taking a plate and dunking it into the sink, the water flickering in the light of the paraffin lamp.

'No, Memsaab!' she cries. 'No, *no*!'

'Yes!' I laugh. '*Please.*'

I feel so idle most of the time. I long to be of use – somehow, *anyhow.*

She shrugs, standing aside, her long, graceful arms out and hands planted on her hips. And after some time, I feel myself relaxing into the rhythmic splashing of the dishes against the soapsuds. Muthoni picks up a rag cloth beside me and begins to dry. She catches my eye and smiles at me and I begin to hum to the tune of 'My Bonnie Lies Over the Ocean'. This is the first time in my eighteen years that I have washed dishes.

The Old Vicarage
Bourn
Cambridgeshire
November 5, 1903

My dearest Iris,

Thank you for your letters. Judging by the dates of them, it takes around seven weeks for mail to reach Bourn from Nairobi. I am rather impressed by this; I should have thought it would take a good deal longer.

We are all fine, but missing you. The Old Vicarage is not quite the same without you here, and the pigeons, I have no doubt, have noted your absence as seem quite unsettled. I am busy with my normal round of morning services, vespers, births, deaths and marriages. We have a new organist at St Helena and St Mary by the name of Christine Thompson – yes, a woman, you'll be pleased to hear! She is a jolly soul and has been doing a marvellous job.

Mother, Violet and Arthur are all well. Mother is busy with her At Homes which she seems to have a growing number of women from the village attend. I make myself scarce on these days, as you can imagine! Actually, Mother and her group have a new cause. I'm not sure if you remember the Matlock family who live up at the top end of Gills Hill? If so, you'll recall that their son Lawrence was wounded terribly in the Boer War – lost his sight and one of his legs. He had been convalescing in a home somewhere but has now returned to Bourn with his family. Mother and her friends are determined to get him together with wounded men from surrounding villages, to help organise a social life with concerts and games of cards and so forth.

Violet is starting to be primed for the upcoming debutante season which, I am sure this will come as no surprise, she is approaching with rather more enthusiasm than you. As for Arthur, I shan't tell you too much as I know he wants to write himself, but he is preparing for his final-year exams. He is working very hard, but also playing rather hard as far as I can gather. We don't see much of him at The Old Vicarage and, when we do, it is normally when he is longing for one of Cook's steak and kidney pies or lardy cakes!

It has been terribly cold this winter and we are all eagerly waiting for the first snowdrops. It is hard to imagine you out there in East Africa beneath the blazing sunshine. I am sorry this is not a long letter but I am eager to catch the afternoon post. I do miss you dreadfully, Iris. I should like more than anything to visit you, but I am not sure I could convince Mother to come to Africa. That aside, I am fairly certain that my salary will not cover the passage to Mombasa. I am sorry, dearest.

Take heart that you are in my thoughts constantly.

Ah, I must not forget. A message from Arthur: He says he has searched high and low for your East African birdlife book in all the best Cambridge bookshops, to no avail. He did say, however, that there is an international journal of avian science called Ibis. *I know it was not quite what you were looking for, but could it be of interest? Failing that, I am sure you can find an amateur ornithologist type of sorts in Nairobi, can you not?*

Take heart that you are in my thoughts constantly.

God Bless you,

Papa

I smile at his final paragraph. Little does Papa know that I have found this 'ornathologist type', except... it is a few weeks now since I met him and I cannot very well return to the schoolhouse and say to him, 'Are you *sure* you do not know which bird I am looking for?'

I read Papa's letter again and then place it back in its envelope and watch Muthoni as she works. Most of the time she winds a length of colourful material round her head, to keep her hair from dirtying, I suppose, whilst she is cleaning. But there are occasions, like today, when she does not do this and leaves her hair free, and it is then that I cannot help but stare, transfixed. For crowning her head is a dense thatch of what looks to me like black moss, beautifully soft and deep and springy. How I long to sink my hand into that hair, to know how it feels against the palm of my hand.

Muthoni sweeps around the ochre-coloured dust that somehow settles in small piles beneath the windows, even when they are closed. She has pulled back the animal skins from the ground and is sprinkling the hard-packed earth floor with Jeyes fluid to keep away white ants and jiggers, which, so Mr Lawrence tells me, can burrow beneath one's toenails and cause considerable discomfort. Finally, my curiosity overwhelms me. I place my pencil on the table and stand. 'Muthoni,' I say.

She turns to me, her dark, liquid eyes like black ink and her lips slightly parted, revealing the whiteness of her teeth.

I laugh, even before my request to her has been imparted, for I know how foolish it will sound. But suddenly I do not care at all. 'Muthoni,' I say again, making gestures. 'I should like to touch your hair, please.'

Her eyes narrow in confusion and I repeat my words more slowly, pointing from my hand to her hair. Now she understands and she begins to giggle in embarrassment. I laugh along with her.

'I…' she falters, 'no understand. No understand.'

'Yes,' I reply. 'Yes, you *do* understand. I am sorry. I know it is strange.' I move towards her. 'May I touch your hair?'

'Hair?' She lifts one graceful hand up to her head and pulls at a black coil.

'Yes,' I say. 'Hair.'

Muthoni laughs again and I realise this is the closest I have ever stood to her and now, looking at her so near to me, I suspect that she is younger than I had previously thought. Possibly the same age as myself. She has a luminous beauty and softness of skin, which I marvel at, but it is still the hair I am most fascinated by.

'*Nguri*,' she says as she continues to tug at it.

'*Nguri*,' I repeat and she nods her head, satisfied.

She motions to my own hair and I can only assume she would also like to touch mine. This feels like a fair exchange and I nod. She is laughing again, but this time her face shows less restraint and first of all I lift up my hand and place it gently against the top of her head. Muthoni's hair feels like all that it should; everything and more. Up and down I gently press my hand through her tight coils of black moss and it is warm and wonderful and comforting. She has stopped laughing and is only smiling at me, a smile that is open and sincere. And before I know it, she has raised her own hand. I realise immediately how difficult it will be for her to properly feel my hair, as I have arranged it as I do every morning, haphazardly pinning it up.

'Wait,' I tell her, and I reach both hands back to pull out a few pins so that it falls down on one side. Now she can draw her fingers through my long strands, which are not as well brushed as when I lived in England and had somebody to do it for me. With her fingertips in my hair, she gasps in surprise, her smile widening and her eyes narrowing. Muthoni continues to do that for some time and then a curious thing happens: I feel a dampness against my cheek and I instinctively look up to see if there is a small leak in the bungalow roof but then I realise that there is, of course, no leak and that the wetness is my own tears. And I think to myself as Muthoni continues to draw her long fingers through my hair, I have been lonely, so lonely. And this sudden human contact takes my breath away.

I keep seeing the bird, resting on the flower of a potted plant, from the bedroom window. I hold very still so as not to frighten it. I scarcely want to breathe for fear of losing sight of this enchanting creature but, of course, it is always only a matter of moments before it darts off again, leaving me transfixed in its shining wake.

At our evening meal, I ask Mr Lawrence if he might know what the bird is, going to great lengths to describe its appearance. I know he is not really listening and that I might have known better than to entrust him with such a question. For he merely chews upon his tough beef, his thin mouth working up and down with great deliberation, and then when he finishes, clears his throat and says, 'Beasts of the land are more my thing, not beasts of the air. Haven't the faintest, Iris.'

Yes, beasts of the land certainly are his sort of thing, but not for marvelling at their beauty, strength and agility. Only for bagging them, as he calls it, so he can brag about it at the club. He must see the revulsion in my eyes when he brings home dead ostriches, zebra and gazelles at the weekends, for he likes to remind me at every opportunity that this is Africa, not England, and people have been hunting here since time immemorial. That may be so, but must I be required to like it?

I should so like to see Mr Ahmed again, or Kamau. I consider telling Mr Lawrence I need new clothes to be made up, just for the sake of some decent conversation, but on the afternoon of New Year's Eve, he takes me to the Nairobi Club, an unattractive building of corrugated iron and wood panels. *Perhaps, just perhaps*, I think, *I shall meet some interesting ladies here.* One day a week for two hours, wives are permitted into the reading room, but it takes very little time for me to decide that I shall never step foot in the club again. For it is filled with the worst kind of people; those who bring back the memory of Lord Sidcup and all his prejudices. I cannot help but laugh to myself when I think of Miss Logan's letter, encouraging me to find ladies with whom to discuss women's suffrage. For these are the very *last* people I should imagine concerning themselves with such a topic. There are a few other British wives there, whom I sit with, drinking tea from cracked porcelain cups, whilst the gentlemen next door smoke cigars and drink brandy beneath the hanging, mounted trophies of elephant tusk, rhino horn and antlers of various kinds.

The women complain bitterly about the climate, food, natives of Nairobi and their husbands, all in equal measure. It is curious, because perhaps I am not so different from them as I like to think. Together, we are locked into marriages that we must endure; we are all foreigners here and it might help me to talk about the difficulties I encounter. And yet, I find I am unable to contribute to their conversation that chases endless threads of disdain and contempt and unhappiness. How, I wonder, am I to find equilibrium with myself if I keep the company of such women?

'And you, Mrs Lawrence?' One woman with tight, pursed lips and a purple vein that throbs in one cheek turns her attention to me and I wish to shrink like Alice. 'How does life in Nairobi suit you?' I feel all eyes upon me and I know I could confide in them. But I will not and cannot. Instead, I mumble something about quite enjoying the experience, to which the woman who addressed me remarks that I am young and of course it is easier for the young. So when, after inviting me on two more occasions to accompany him to the club only for me to decline both times, Mr Lawrence does not ask again, this comes only as a relief.

Nairobi
8 January, 1904

Dear Miss Logan,

What a joy it has been to receive your letters. Do please continue sending them to me. You are quite right – the WSPU sounds fascinating and I am very happy that a branch has been formed in Durham that you can involve yourself in. There is nothing like that here. I am sorry to say that we are light years away in Nairobi from such progressive thinking.

It is a rather tense time here at the moment as it is terribly hot and dry with cattle and crops dying. This has made Mr Lawrence more bad-tempered than usual. I do not wish to lie to you, for I feel increasingly distant from him. I know there is nothing you can say in response to this; the situation is as it is and is unlikely to change. All I can do is remain optimistic and focus on the areas of my life that bring me happiness; the glorious landscape, for example, which I shall never tire of.

I am not as lonely as I once was, for despite scarcely being able to converse with Muthoni, our housegirl, I feel a friendship growing between us. She is a lovely girl, very natural and good-natured. I know she is scared of Mr Lawrence, for whenever he appears her entire countenance and body language change.

I pause as I write, staring up from my writing desk and out across the plains, dotted with distant, roaming animals. There is a great deal more I should like to confide in Miss Logan about my husband but cannot. For example, I should like to tell her that he continues to come to me at night, these couplings stretching across a vast chasm of grey emptiness.

I know that Mr Lawrence wishes for a child. He hopes that I should fall pregnant quickly. But each and every month, I find myself folding my cloth in three and fastening it to my belt. At the end of the day, I leave the cloths in the chamber-pot beneath the bed, filled with salted water, for Muthoni to wash. I push it as far beneath the bed as I can, for otherwise it stares at me accusingly, a combination of relief – for a large part of me does not want to bear Mr Lawrence a child – and regret. For if I should fall pregnant he would, for several months at least, not continue to violate me.

I force my thoughts away from Mr Lawrence and back to the letter in hand, but I find my appetite for writing about anything of significance has diminished.

Do you remember those dreadful siafu, *the biting ants you had the misfortune of encountering in Mombasa? They are rife in Nairobi as well, but the curious thing is they enjoy biting not* only human flesh but also wood, in the form of the dining room table legs. The table legs stand in tins of kerosene to keep the ants away, and the rats too apparently. We do the same with the meat which is kept in a wire safe raised above kerosene tins. Speaking of meat, I have eaten enough gazelle chops to last me a lifetime since I have been here. Either that or mutton (which is actually goat) which Muthoni buys from a local Somali butcher. The meat is cooked in our primitive clay oven and served on Spode china plates to make it look more fancy, but all the meat is terribly tough and chewy, no matter how it is prepared.

I look forward to meeting with you again, Miss Logan. I have lost count of the number of times I have read Pearl Rivers:

'With windows low and narrow too, Where birds came peeping in To wake me up at early morn And oft I used to win.'

Thankfully, Mr Ahmed, my tailor, has provided me with reading material. Have you ever read any of William Morris? I am quite taken by him, particularly The Wood Beyond the World. Also, my brother Arthur managed to track down an ornithology journal by the name of Ibis. He bought it, but ended not sending it to me as most of the reports from that edition were focused on South American and Persian birdlife – a pity. But never mind, for Mr Ahmed has introduced me to a local fellow who is very knowledgeable about the birds here so I am hoping very much to learn more through him.

Yours, with great affection

Iris Lawrence

On a fresh sheet of writing paper, I begin to sketch for the umpteenth time the small bird that I am so curious about. I stare down at it critically and am about to alter the beak when I hear a knock at the door. Muthoni answers it and then calls to me. It is Kamau, the very last person I was expecting to see. He is wearing a hat, not one of those helmets that Mr Lawrence favours but something of less substantial material and rather floppy, but offering protection from the sun nonetheless. Upon seeing me approach, he pulls the hat from his head and clasps it in front of him.

Away from his own surroundings, Kamau looks altogether different: less at ease. Endearingly nervous, in fact, as he grasps the hat as though his life depends on it. He raises his eyebrows, almost apologetically, and smiles at me. I notice at once how white his teeth are, whiter than any I have seen before. I stare at them for a few moments before pulling my attention back up to his dark eyes, burning coals, flecked with warmer, honey tones.

I know I must put him at his ease and I ask Muthoni to make some tea for us. I am about to invite him into the bungalow and then hesitate; scornful though I am of the mores and expectations of a single man not being in a married woman's house without her husband present, I also see no reason why I should make life more difficult for myself. I do not think it is time for Mr Lawrence to return home yet but nevertheless, it is not wise for Kamau to be here any longer than necessary. It is quite possible somebody might walk past and see him. And how would I explain this to my husband?

Thus, I propose we sit on the verandah beneath the over-hanging roof, which still offers sufficient shade and, I hope, makes it difficult for anybody walking past to see us. I do not know whether his nerves have an effect on me, but as I move the chairs into the shade, I find that I too feel at a slight loss for words. I do not, after all, know the purpose of his visit yet. Though perhaps he was passing and this is simply a social call. No sooner have I had this thought, however, than I dismiss it. Kamau, like Mr Ahmed, is a busy man and not in the habit, I am certain, of making social calls.

Muthoni brings our tea and serves it to us on the small wooden table that I absently think would benefit from some kind of attractive cloth placed over it. She has never met Kamau before, but must know that Kikuyu is his native tongue, for she asks him something I do not understand before spooning two teaspoons of sugar into his cup, smiling at me and vanishing back into the darkness of the bungalow.

I turn my head to look out over the parched plains and detect movement in the distance. Focusing on it, I see that it is a Masaai man herding cattle, most probably searching the arid plateau for a water source. I look back at Kamau, clear my throat and then open my mouth to comment on the weather, but he begins speaking at the exact same moment. We both stop, embarrassed, and laugh.

'Sorry, what were you going to say?' he asks.

'Oh,' I reply, pressing my little finger into a tiny crystal of sugar that has escaped from the spoon and placing it in my mouth. A memory rises, unbidden, of my mother, who always said that taking sugar with one's tea was a vulgar habit. To dispel this thought, I quickly heap a second spoonful into my teacup and stir it vigorously. 'Nothing. I was only going to comment that it is rather hot today.'

'Yes,' he agrees, lapsing back into silence. I feel rather frustrated. Why has he become so tongue-tied? Where is that self-assured man I met not long ago? I note with delight that his pouch is still tied round his neck and that if conversation should become terribly stilted, at least this will be a subject to fall back on.

'Are you not teaching today?' I ask him.

'Oh yes,' he replies, looking more like the man I remember from our first meeting. 'But I only teach half-days on Fridays.'

Kamau takes a long sip of tea. I am not sure of the time, but know that it will not be that long before Mr Lawrence returns and I know with great certainty that I do not want the two of them to meet. There is no doubt at all in my mind that Mr Lawrence would be horrified to discover I am entertaining a native, even one educated by missionaries. I am all too aware that Mr Lawrence regards natives as inferior to Europeans – mentally, physiologically and in any other way he can think of.

I take a deep breath. 'I have made a few sketches of the bird, you remember, the one whose identity I am seeking?'

I never previously imagined it could be possible to smile with one's entire face, but now Kamau does, from the mouth to the eyes and even to more unexpected parts such as the forehead and cheekbones, every part of his face lifting and shining.

'Ah!' he replies. 'May I see?'

'They are terrible little drawings, truly. Nothing at all like yours.' I feel myself blushing and intertwine my fingers in my lap.

'It does not matter,' Kamau replies in an encouraging voice. 'May I see them?'

I give a little laugh and shrug my shoulders. 'Very well.'

I stand up and walk into the bungalow, briefly plunged into pitch blackness after the strength of the light outside, but it does not take long for my eyes to adjust. In the bedroom, I walk to the bureau and pull out the few thin sheets of drawings. I frown again, shaking my head. I am about to show these paltry efforts to an artist. Yet at the same time, I chide myself for this vanity of sorts, for the entire purpose of doing so is that he might help me with its identification.

I walk back outside, clutching my drawings, and hand them over to him. He doesn't say anything for some time, simply moves from one sheet to the next, nodding as he does so. I hover beside him feeling, as I inexplicably do in Kamau's presence, rather foolish and young.

'Yes,' he says eventually, turning to me and smiling.

'Yes?'

'I know what your bird is.'

I cannot help myself – I clap my hands together gleefully. His smile grows but he says not a word.

'Well?' I cry. 'What is it?'

Still, he does not say anything.

CHAPTER EIGHTEEN

BENEDICT KAMAU

Ludicrous, that I do not want to tell her. Such a simple thing, two such modest little syllables. Yet I nonetheless have an irrational fear that if I tell her, she may evaporate before my very eyes. Instead, I find myself laughing whilst she stands beside me, staring wide-eyed with those eyes, one shade darker than a jacaranda blossom, and her lips parted expectantly.

I look back at Mrs Lawrence's drawings and turn them over once more. The sketches are firm and impressively to scale, if rather childlike. I know I could continue to profess ignorance, but somehow I feel sure she will not believe me. She knows that my knowledge of East African birds is extensive and, simple though her drawings are, it is clear what I am looking at.

I take a sharp intake of breath, place the papers on the table beneath a teacup and stand up.

'Mrs Lawrence,' I say. 'This is a sunbird.'

'A sunbird?' she breathes, and her face is suddenly serious and her eyes narrowed.

I nod my head. 'Yes. Without doubt. It is a sunbird. Mrs Lawrence, do you have any flowering plants around the house?'

'Why, yes,' she says and points to the tubs of adenium a few metres along one side of the bungalow.

'Good.'

'Good?'

I walk up to one of the pots. She follows me and watches as I take one vase-like flower between thumb and forefinger and turn it up to her so that she can look down into the gentle pink glow of its mouth.

'You see how narrow this is?' I ask. Mrs Lawrence nods her head. 'That is why the sunbird has a small, curved beak. So that it can reach the nectar right inside flowers of this type. Pollen sticks to their beaks and even feathers so that when they visit the next flower, it rubs off, helping to fertilise it. You are lucky that you have flowers like this so close to your house. No doubt this is why you keep seeing the sunbirds. I—'

Right at that moment, I realise I have lost her attention – I see her eyes dart to one side of me and then an expression flitter across them – fear? surprise? – before she turns to look at me again and says urgently, 'You must go.'

I raise my eyebrows and she tilts her chin in the direction of the hill behind me. 'My husband is on his way home.'

I turn my head and sure enough, I can see a small figure making its way along the jagged path. I don't say another word, just nod my head. She stretches her hand out towards me and I grasp it as she smiles at me. I would like to remain in her smile, its warmth and vitality, for a great deal longer. But I know I must leave.

I hurry down the hill, overwhelmingly happy to have seen Mrs Lawrence again. I decide to run some errands in town. There are Asian *dukas* emitting strange and wonderful scents, the grand and towering constructions of stone that play host to the official duties of the Europeans and carefully paved roads stretching the township out in all directions. I walk through the landies, squat wooden shacks built hastily, that lean into one another so tightly that all natural light is shut out. My own home is humble, but it is not like these tightly clustered dwellings, which seem almost uninhabitable for the piles of rotting garbage that lie around them in stinking, steaming heaps. And yet, this is where most of Nairobi's inhabitants live.

The *mundu mweru* reside comfortably up on the hill, not only so they command the finest views but also so that all their effluence can drain down here to this warren of shacks, out of sight. And yet, I think, as my breath is caught short, they are not all bad people, these *mundu mweru*. I think first of a woman who has very much been occupying my thoughts these past weeks and then I turn my mind further back, to the man who raised me.

I am proud to hail from Kikuyuland. Around the same time my family died, the British missionaries came and I was taken into the orphanage. I remember little of my first year there, though strange visions of nameless faces as pale as goat's milk still come to me now and again. I remember very little at all until I was taught to read and write by a pastor. His name was Reverend Jonas Dutton and I shall never forget him. He never wore a hat, even beneath the glare of the midday sun, and he had eyes that drooped down at the corners when he smiled, deep lines entrenched like gulleys down both his cheeks and wispy white hair combed untidily into a side parting. But he was my hero when I was a young boy. He realised I wanted to learn to read and write, to understand numbers. And he had a great passion for ornithology, which he shared with me. Once he confessed that his love of birdlife was greater than his desire to save souls, but that he was lucky because he had managed to make both work alongside one another. I was confused.

'Do I need saving?' I asked him once.

And he laughed, his kind blue eyes turning downwards, and patted my shoulder. 'Benedict,' he replied. 'We're all lost. All of us.' For that is the name I was christened with and it was only when I left the orphanage that I reverted to Kamau.

I did not understand his words, but it didn't matter. I trusted him with every bone in my body. You could say he found in me a protégé and, whilst I never witnessed him being unkind to anybody, I always felt that he looked out for me particularly. Perhaps this is only what I wanted to believe, but this is how it seemed to me and this is how I remember it. As well as calling me Benedict, he named me Quiet Warrior, for I did not speak much. As for warrior? Perhaps he saw a strength in me that even I myself did not recognise.

Jonas Dutton died when I was twelve years old and was buried behind the orphanage. I stood at his graveside beneath the scant shade of a euphorbia tree and I wept bitterly. I could not imagine my life without him and, judging by the tears of the other children around me, neither could anybody else. The orphanage struggled on after his death, yet without his vision and passion, it came to represent a place of sadness and stagnation. And hunger. I remember several nights when, the roaring of my belly preventing me from sleeping, I and a few other boys crept from the dormitories and threw stones at the unsuspecting rock hyraxes that lived in the stony terrain around the building and then pushed sticks through their bodies before roasting them on an open fire. Never had food tasted so good. But there were, of course, also many nights that we returned empty-handed, with the growls in our bellies even worse.

By the time I reached the age of thirteen, I knew there was no future for me at the orphanage, but neither did I know where to go. The people half-heartedly running it were not sorry to see me leave; I was one less mouth to feed. But I could not persuade the other Kikuyu boys to come with me. They said that at least they knew where their next meal was coming from. 'But you,' they told me, 'you are a quiet warrior. You will survive.' I pleaded against their logic but not one would join me.

And so, wearing my short trousers, I packed one small cotton bag with the rest of my belongings: two pairs of underwear, one woollen jumper, a pair of long trousers and two torn shirts. The orphanage gave me a bunch of small, sweet bananas and a block of arrowroot and told me to go well. And the boys who had been my friends stood at the door and waved frantically. Every ten steps or so, I would turn and look back at them as their moving hands and smiling faces receded further and further into the distance. Several times, my courage almost failed me and I thought of turning back. But then I said out loud to myself, 'No. I am Kamau. I am the Quiet Warrior.'

Jonas Dutton had given me a great deal more than kindness and a love of birdlife. He had given me the gift of literacy and the ability to speak a foreign tongue as easily as my own. I could not let this gift be wasted and stay in this orphanage, languishing in Kikuyuland, when I had this gift at my fingertips. As I walked away from it that day, I had not the slightest idea of where I was going or how I would survive. But far more important than the clothes and food I carried in my bag, I held within me this weightless, priceless gift that I treasured above all else: I was literate. I knew, somehow, that this would guide my way.

CHAPTER NINETEEN

IRIS LAWRENCE

It is not until several hours later, whilst Mr Lawrence gasps and thrusts above me in the pitch black, that I think of Kamau, his dusky eyes that gleamed in the light of the lowering sun and the strength of his handshake. I did not want to take my hand from his.

Mr Lawrence grunts and rolls off me and within seconds I hear his heavy, guttural breathing in the narrow bed beside me. I feel a sticky patch on my stomach and mechanically reach for the rag beneath my bed and wipe it away before pulling down my cotton nightgown. I close my eyes, but sleep does not come. Mr Lawrence shifts beside me and groans in his sleep and I push myself over so that I am lying on my side, facing away from him. I stare at the dim, dusky outline of my dressing table on the other side of the mosquito net and listen to the croaks of the night frogs and the distant whistle, long and shrill, of a reedbuck. And I find that I have a ludicrous, senseless smile on my face that I am unable to rub away.

❧ ❧ ❧

I spend more and more time sitting on the verandah, very still, close to the potted adenium, in the hope that the sunbirds may appear. I want to learn *everything* there is to know about these exquisite creatures. And then, one does. It flits close to the tiny bulb of the flower and hovers, its wings quivering in the slanted afternoon light. I stare at it, not blinking, scarcely breathing. I think of Kamau and the day he visited me. I recall the contours of his collarbone. The precise shade of his skin, ink black with burnished, lighter undertones. The liquid warmth of his eyes.

I shake my head, trying to dispel these thoughts from my mind. But the sudden movement scares away the sunbird and it skims away over the wooden verandah railing, making a whirring noise like the wheel of a cog as it goes. I stand and lean out over the fence, watching until it becomes smaller than a full stop and vanishes.

I want to see it again. See *him* again. I stand there beneath the high heat of the afternoon, experiencing the unfamiliar sensation of the sun beating down upon my hatless head. It does not feel unpleasant and I close my eyes to experience the moment more fully. As I do so, the image of the sunbird flies instantly into my mind, beating its gossamer wings against my eyelids. But no sooner do I think of the sunbird than the features of Kamau arise, unbidden, his dark eyes and the beating wings merging into one.

᙮ ᙮ ᙮

'Iris, I shall go hunting in two weekends' time and be away on the Saturday night.' It is one of the rare evenings that

Mr Lawrence is not taking dinner at the club, but dining at home with me instead. I confess I had wondered what the occasion was, and now I know; he needed to impart this news to me. And instantly, just like that, my mood lifts. I can think of no greater gift.

I look up from my mutton stew and smile at him, a smile that – I am surprised to discover – is almost natural. 'What is it you are aiming to hunt?'

I know that by asking him such a question, I can guarantee an enthusiastic response. He will no longer be speaking to me, though, but rather just speaking. I do not mind at all on this occasion.

'Iris.' He pushes away his bowl of stew and leans back in the chair, his thin features animated. 'Do you know what I am now able to count amongst my trophies?'

I do not, but he will, of course, tell me. 'Several ostrich, two rhino, four zebra, the head and splendid horns of several varieties of antelope; even the glossy skin of a leopard. I am not terribly interested in bagging an elephant. Oh, I know, I know,' he laughs to himself, 'but no matter that it is the largest beast of the plains. The tusks, I cannot deny it, are attractive. A great number of people I know here think of nothing but the elephant when they hunt. But no, it is not for me. For I have my sights set on something far greater; far harder to hunt, the king of all beasts.'

He pauses, possibly for dramatic effect, and looks at me, raising one bushy eyebrow.

'Lion,' he breathes, and there is a quiver in his voice. 'How I should like to rub wood ash into the skin of this elusive animal. It is so beautiful. I sometimes envy those chaps who worked on the railway down near Tsavo. Of course it cannot be a pleasant end to be taken by a lion. But for Whitehouse and the other engineers working on the line, what a thrill to be confronted nightly by this magnificent creature stalking around their tents! The fellows who are organising the trip for me, they know the right places to go. And the headman, an experienced chap by the name of Mwangi, tells me that several lions have been sighted in the area in which we shall be walking. It was all I could do to stop myself from hugging this ugly little man! We shall leave at the crack of dawn on Saturday morning and come back on Sunday night. I have never before dedicated two entire days to the single-minded pursuit of hunting a lion, and a lion only.'

His eyes are gleaming and he pauses for a moment to look, not through me but rather directly *at* me. 'I don't suppose… would you like to come too, Iris?'

I stare at him in horror. Surely he must know by now I have no interest in his trophy bagging?

'Oh – well, I…' I do not know how to say the words, but I do not need to. The gleam in his eye vanishes and he pushes his chair back. He looks crestfallen and for one peculiar moment I feel guilty that I am not the kind of wife he would like me to be.

'No,' he says brusquely, standing up from the table. 'Of course not. What was I thinking?'

'It's just that—'

'No. I quite understand,' he interrupts. A small window existed, perhaps, in which I could have connected with him in some way, or at least made an attempt to connect with him, but I have lost him again. He begins to mumble beneath his breath so I can barely hear him. I know he is simply filling an empty space and is talking more to himself than to me. 'I must send Muthoni down to Ahmed's tomorrow. I need new wash-leather gloves; my current pair are quite worn through.' As he walks off towards the bedroom, he continues muttering to himself. I remain seated at the table, staring into my half-eaten bowl of stew, feeling both a stab of guilt and a profound sense of relief.

I see very little of Mr Lawrence over the next couple of weeks. I know he is earnestly preparing for his trip, for I see lists lying around the house of items he must remember to take on his hunting trip, with ticks beside them. One such list reads thus:

Light mackintosh (wet weather), pipe, tobacco, warm overcoat (cool evenings), hunting & skinning knife, field glass, collapsible bath (dusty evenings), Monocle x 2, Jaeger blankets x 2, Rifles x 3 (.303, .477 & 12 bore shotgun) Kodak camera (ensure Mr Young can develop once back.)

I am very much left to my own devices, even at night. I think of Mr Ahmed and even more of Kamau, and how I should like to see him, to see *both* of them. Ever since Kamau abruptly left the bungalow that day, he has been in my thoughts a great deal. I am curious about him. More than curious, if I am being honest with myself.

And therefore, one day, emboldened by the long stretches of time Mr Lawrence is now spending at work, I decide to go to the schoolhouse. I justify it by telling myself that I cannot simply sit at home day in, day out, pushing aside the knowledge that Mr Lawrence would be incandescent with rage if he found out. I also tell myself that the purpose of my visit is simply to let Kamau know that I have been watching and waiting near the potted flowering plants in front of the bungalow and have been rewarded a number of times by the appearance of one species of sunbird or another, a small flash of iridescent light by the plant before it bolts away. I have noticed how they are almost constantly on the move but can hover for brief spaces of time. One of them was entirely black from the back, but when it turned I was presented with the most glorious shiny scarlet chest. I have also heard them sing – the melody is extremely fast and sounds a little like *si-sit-swit-chichichichi*. Some of them have a bright, iridescent plumage whilst others are paler; presumably these are the males and females, though I cannot know for certain. I am hoping Kamau can confirm this.

When Muthoni arrives at the bungalow, I point to myself and then open my left hand out. With two fingers, I make stepping motions over my palm to signal that I am going out.

'Walk?' she asks shyly.

'Yes,' I smile. 'Walk.'

As we go outside to the verandah, Muthoni points in concern to the strengthening sun and the bright band of unbroken, shimmering blue sky.

'It is fine,' I say, pointing to the wide brim of my hat.

'Fine?' she repeats.

'Yes.' I nod. I am about to leave when Muthoni holds up a hand and dashes inside. She returns with a teacup of water and puts it in my hands.

'Hot.' She points again to the sun. 'Hot.'

I grin at her and drink. The water, the morning's dappled sunlight, the kindness of Muthoni, the absence of Mr Lawrence and the anticipation of seeing Kamau… I feel intensely alive.

Before long, I find myself at the bottom of the hill, winding my way alongside the thorny, gorse-like shrubs that skirt the twists and turns of the Nairobi River. Dust swirls in ascending spirals up from the parched earth from all directions, concealing the herd of bell-ringing goats that are walking towards me from downriver. When the dust clears, I see the owner of the animals, a tall, lean Maasai with no teeth and his elongated earlobes carrying numerous adornments, pushing his goats along with a stick. I smile as I walk past him but he only stares back at me in bewilderment.

When I arrive at the schoolhouse, the door is open to allow a breeze to reach the children inside. I stand at some distance, being able to see not Kamau but only the heads of several children bent over their laps, diligently working on something. I have no idea of the timetable and I am not happy to interrupt the class whilst in progress, so I sit a little way off in the shade and listen to the murmur of the river and the occasional low word from Kamau. I feel a nervous awkwardness and I chide myself for feeling this way as I twist my hands in my lap.

Presently, I hear the sound of scuffling and the children pour through the small door, pushing one another aside in their eagerness to get out. Most of them do not see me sitting, as I am, some way off, but a few of them stand stock-still and point to me, their shrill voices screeching over and over again those words that I am becoming quite accustomed to: '*Mundu mweru!*' I stand up and smile at them, sincerely hoping I shall not reduce another child to tears like last time. Their cries bring Kamau to the door and he looks at me for a moment with an expression of surprise on his face before a smile spreads across his features, so warm and open and sincere that I cannot help but smile back at him, realising I feel quite giddy with happiness and the heat.

As I come towards him, I stretch out my hand and he takes it in his own. 'Mrs Lawrence…' he says before trailing off. I realise that I need to think quickly of an explanation for why I should have suddenly appeared without warning in the middle of his teaching day. I feel myself blushing furiously and am only grateful for the heat that is no doubt reddening my cheeks.

'I am sorry to interrupt you like this whilst you are teaching.'

'It is no interruption. The children are now on break time.'

I nod and glance at the children, most of whom are now ignoring me and proceeding with their play, standing in a circle and throwing small stones to try to hit a bigger one in the centre. But others are pushing one another towards me or staring up at me with huge, dark eyes. I am about to open my mouth to tell him why, ostensibly, I am here but he quickly asks me if I would like some water. I tell him I would as my own flask is empty and, as he guides me to the schoolhouse, he remarks on the heat of the day.

It is a curious thing, but after only a few minutes I realise that I need not offer any explanation as to why I have come. The simple fact is that I am here. He pours water into a small tumbler from an earthenware jug and I tip it down my throat. He pours me another, watching me as I drink. Once I have finished, he takes the tumbler from me and places it decisively on his desk. Then he says something to me that I am not expecting at all. Smiling brightly, he spreads his hands out before him and says, 'Would you like to teach?'

CHAPTER TWENTY

BENEDICT KAMAU

The very minute I ask her that question, her face lights up; I can see that one tooth slightly crossing over the other at the front as her shiny lips part.

'Me, teach? I have never taught anything in my life!'

'I do not think that matters. The children… they would love it.'

She closes her mouth and looks at me, suddenly a little shy, and lowers her voice.

'But what should I teach them?'

'English, of course. A few words. That is all.'

Mrs Lawrence is silent, yet it is as though I can see the thoughts passing through her, swarming around her head like bees. I wait and watch her face, deep in thought as she considers my question. She is biting her bottom lip – and then she looks up at me brightly with those dark blue eyes and smiles.

'Very well,' she says. 'I cannot see that teaching them a few words can be so difficult.'

'Good,' I say. I feel absurdly happy. I smile back at her and cannot help but notice the colour rising up from her neck to her cheeks, one of the same colours painted by a Kikuyuland sunset. She looks away and fiddles with a thin silver bracelet on her wrist.

I ring the bell and the children come pouring in through the door and take their seats. Mrs Lawrence looks at me uncertainly and I nod. She clears her throat, frowns momentarily and then walks to the front of the classroom. Every single pair of eyes turns towards her and their chattering ceases in an instant, as rapidly as arrowroot dropping into boiling water.

'Good morning,' she calls out. Nobody says a word; the children only stare at her solemnly. The silence in the schoolroom is profound. The only thing I can hear is the gentle clink of glass beads on wrists, necks and ankles as the children turn to one another questioningly. I desperately do not wish this to be a painful experience for her and am about to step in to translate when Mrs Lawrence moves forwards and repeats the two words, her strong voice filling the room. 'Good morning!'

'*Gud ma-neeng*,' chirrups one little voice from the front like a shrike and the entire class erupts into laughter, the silence broken.

'Yes, yes!' Mrs Lawrence claps her hands together, her eyes burning. 'That is right!' She moves closer to the child, a young girl named Wangari.

'*Gud ma-neeng…?*' Wangari hesitates.

Mrs Lawrence nods at her enthusiastically and motions for her to come out to the front of the room. More laughter and Wangari shakes her head, pushing her skinny shoulders back into the seat.

'Yes!' Mrs Lawrence is smiling at her, her face radiating goodwill as she holds her hand out. Wangari hesitates a moment longer, looking from one child to another, before she pushes herself upwards. She takes her new teacher's hand and is led to the front, where Mrs Lawrence gently but firmly clasps the child's shoulders and turns her to face her classmates before motioning with her hand that she should repeat the words.

Wangari looks proud but terrified. She takes a big gulp of air before saying 'Good morning' once more, in her heavily accented voice, to the room full of expectant faces. Mrs Lawrence now gestures to the class that they should all repeat the phrase. Emboldened by not being singled out as their classmate has been, they begin, haltingly at first, until the room is filled with the sound of dozens of confident 'Good mornings', of all sounds and volumes.

Mrs Lawrence now takes Wangari back to her seat before striding towards the entrance and pointing at it. 'Door!' she says. She is slim-waisted, with long, lithe arms and graceful hands. But despite her slimness, there is a strength and sturdiness about her. Her steps are confident and she moves freely in her body with not the slightest hint of self-consiousness.

'Door!' echoes back the class. 'Door!'

She walks to the window and does the same. 'Window!' they call out.

Mrs Lawrence turns to me, her blue eyes gleaming. It would not be difficult to lose oneself in those eyes. 'May I have some water please?' she asks in a low voice. I look at her for a moment longer before jumping up from my seat; I almost forgot that I am not also a pupil, so enraptured are we all by her teaching.

'Of course.' I pour her some from the earthenware jug into a tumbler and hand it to her, watching her white throat as she tips her head backwards and drinks. She makes a noise of satisfaction once her thirst is quenched and then points to the tumbler. 'Water!' she says to the class.

'*Watter!*'

'*Wooor*-ter.' She emphasises the first syllable and, between muted giggling, they all attempt the word again.

She is a natural, I know even though I have not seen many other teachers in my life. Of course, part of her appeal is the colour of her skin: moon reflected on water, the still paleness of a Nairobi dawn. There is also the fact that the children are out of their routine and this can only be exciting for them. But it is more than that. There is an invisible line that travels between Mrs Lawrence and these children and as she moves freely and animatedly around the schoolroom, I know that she feels it too and is emboldened by this knowledge.

I have never met her husband, this Mr Lawrence; I have only seen him from a distance. But suddenly my thoughts turn to him and I feel three things, almost simultaneously: I feel envy that he is married to this enchanting woman; I feel anger, for I instinctively know he is undeserving of her, and I feel a flicker of fear, for as much as I want her to be here, I know that she should not be.

I wonder what Mrs Lawrence's Christian name is as I watch her tread across the floor and listen to her low, musical voice. But no names come to me, for the truth is that, with the exception of a few European women who passed through the orphanage, I do not know any ladies from her country. The girls at my orphanage were given good, Christian names such as Hope and Charity and Innocence. Yet somehow Mrs Lawrence does not look like a Hope or Charity or Innocence.

The children are laughing now and Mrs Lawrence turns to me, raises her eyebrows and shrugs. When she turns back to the class, they all burst into spontaneous applause and she smiles at them, throws her head back and laughs.

CHAPTER TWENTY-ONE

IRIS LAWRENCE

I was going to finish there, but then I am struck with an-other idea. I walk to Kamau and extend my hand to his. He looks a little surprised but then takes it with his warm and firm hand and we shake and I say loudly 'Hello, how are you?' I nod at him to reply.

After a little hesitation, he replies 'Very well, thank you.'

'Good,' I say softly to him and he smiles deeply at me, every part of his face lifting. I look away for a moment be-fore turning back to him. 'Hello, how are you?' I repeat.

'Very well, thank you.' He says the words slowly and clearly so that the class can hear him. After one more round of this, I walk to the children and shake the hand of the same small girl at the front of the class, sending the whole room into peals of laughter.

Embarrassed, a small hand flies to her mouth but I smile at her encouragingly and, in a faltering voice, she says '*Ver-tee* well, *tank* you.'

I nod my head and then say 'Ve-*ry*.'

'*Ver-tee*.'

'Ve-*ry*.'

The class are laughing again and I turn to them, fixing them all with what I hope is my most admonishing stare. I cannot quite believe it, but just like that they fall silent again. Encouraged, the little girl makes another attempt.

'*Ve-ree* well, *tank* you.'

'Yes!' I cry. 'Well done, that is it!' I clap my hands together and gesture that she should extend the greeting to the boy sitting beside her, before walking to the back of the classroom and starting it off there. It is like magic, for before I know it and with very little effort from myself, the greeting and reply gather momentum and move like flowing water from one child to the next. I stand transfixed for several moments before turning my head to Kamau. There is a hint of a smile tugging his lips upwards but his dark eyes are solemn. He has his hands clasped behind his back and is standing tall and strong and I think what an impressive figure he cuts in his well-tailored clothes made by Mr Ahmed. I blink a couple of times and I do not know why I do it, what I am thinking, but I hold his gaze for a few further moments before I turn away.

I am coming alive, settling into my skin, every nerve ending tingling with the sheer exuberance of this experience. For a child to suddenly understand something I teach; to witness their eyes light up with comprehension and with joy – this sensation is quite unparalleled. Knowing this is something I am good at fills me with gratitude and the first real optimism I have experienced since arriving in Nairobi. And then: Kamau. He is not looking at the class. He is looking at me. I can feel his eyes upon me, warmth permeating through my entire body beneath his gaze. It scares me. Yet at the same time it fills me with something majestic, something beautiful. His eyes on me make me acutely aware of being a woman.

When I walk home at the end of that day, I am almost flying over the churned dust track. I feel connected to everything around me: to the slanting shadows that filter through the branches of the thorny acacia trees on to the gurgling river; to the papyrus fronds that sway and bend towards me; to the bright flash of a yellow weaver bird as it darts directly over my head, tiny twigs drooping from its beak.

The minute I am home, I greet Muthoni, fetch some paper and my fountain pen and go straight to the verandah. Pulling the pen's lid off, I write at the top of the page in big, bold letters, 'TEACHING NOTES'. Then I write down everything I taught today, all the words, all the little tricks and techniques that came to me. I chew the end of my pen and consider what I can teach next and how I can do it, then continue making notes. And then at the bottom, I take great pleasure in writing 'Assistant Teacher: Kamau'. I lean back in the chair, close my eyes and smile.

¥ ¥ ¥

Two days later, I return. I know it is foolhardy. It is a great, great risk. But it is, I realise, one that I am prepared to take; to teach, that is, and come alive through this. As for the pleasure of Kamau's attention and the way it makes me feel, these emotions are far less defined and I wish not to dwell on them for any length of time. I wanted to return to the schoolhouse the following day but talked myself out of it. What would he think if I came back so quickly? What would he read from this? Even two days later… as I walk beneath my parasol, I shake my head to dispel these thoughts. Does it matter what he reads from my presence, when I think I already know? At one stage, I stop beside the river and peer down, looking at the fluid silhouette of my murky reflection staring up at me. Whilst the river is far too muddy to really see what I look like, for the first time *ever* I truly care about my appearance. I raise a hand to my hair and smooth over it. How does he see me? Does he simply see me as a white woman or as something else?

Kamau is greeting the children at the door of the schoolhouse. It is the small girl who helped me out two days ago who first notices my presence. She jumps up and down, her tiny feet pounding dust, and then a cascade of falling dominoes as one by one they turn and see me and cheer. Kamau looks up and gives me that smile I am beginning to wait for; the one where the sides of his mouth tug upwards only slightly, for the real smile emanates from his eyes.

He holds a finger up towards me. 'One moment please, Mrs Lawrence.'

I stand and watch as he continues to greet the children, who all cast furtive backwards glances at me. One by one, they vanish into the schoolroom until Kamau stands, alone, by the front door. I walk to him and he holds out his hand.

'Here I am again,' I say.

'Yes.' He shakes my hand, keeping it in his a moment longer than necessary. 'Here you are again. You are very welcome.'

Yes, I am welcome here. Is this the first place I have felt truly welcome in all my life? I never imagined it would be in an environment such as this. As we move inside the dim room, he places his palm against the small of my back and I jump, startled both by this unexpected contact and by the pleasurable sensation that fizzes at my nerve endings. He removes his hand and now I am more aware of its absence than of anything else.

Once we are standing at the front of the classroom, Kamau says something in Kikuyu to the children, gesturing to me, and they all break out into applause again.

'They are very happy you are here,' he tells me.

'I am very happy to *be* here.' I scan their expectant faces, a number of them now familiar.

'Today you will learn some nature words in English,' I tell them. I walk to the blackboard and look around for the chalk, but before I know it, Kamau is beside me, holding out a stick.

'Thank you.' I take it from him, my fingertips fusing with his for an instant, and then look away. I feel colour rising into my face and am relieved that my back is now turned to everyone. I draw a rainbow and a flower, a tree and a bird and write the names beneath them. One by one, we go through the pronunciation.

'*Bud, bud!*' they call.

These children are bright and quick to learn and I have nothing but admiration for their eagerness. They draw pictures on their slates of the items from the board and copy the English words down. I then add to the pictures with a river, sun and moon. I feel Kamau's presence not far behind me. My neck feels hot, as though a warm wind is blowing against it, and I draw my hand up and rub the clammy spot beneath my hairline.

'How can I explain to them,' I say to Kamau, turning to him, 'that I would like them to go into pairs, draw a single image on their slates and then show it to their partners in order for them to say the word in English?'

Kamau's hands are clasped behind his back. He always looks so imposing, like a sentry standing to attention, though rather less stiff.

He takes a step closer towards me. 'Would you like me to stand in? To be frank, I do not think you need me to. I think you are doing a very good job on your own.'

I smile at him gratefully. Perhaps I ought to continue alone. Instinctively, asking Kamau to always translate to the children does not feel like the right thing to do. I need to demonstrate what I want, somehow, by example.

'Do you have a spare slate?' I ask Kamau. He nods and walks to a cupboard, opening it and producing one, which he hands to me. I clap my hands together to get the attention of the children and then draw a large sun on the slate. I show it to all the children and then to Kamau, motioning that he should say the word.

'Sun,' he says.

I smile. 'Yes! Your turn.' I hand him the slate – again, our fingers brush against one another. What is this? Is he intentionally making contact with me? Am I inadvertently making physical contact with him? Suddenly, this feels not enough.

I want him to hug me; I want to feel his warm, strong arms around me and to rest in this space for a long time. Yet in reality, this is a space that could not be more dangerous.

Kamau has rubbed out my picture and is drawing with great concentration. When he has finished, he turns the slate round to the class so they can all see his picture and then shows me.

'Rainbow?' I ask.

He shakes his head. 'No.'

'River?'

'No.'

I smile and scratch my head. 'Hmmm…'

Kamau looks at his picture, at the beautifully rendered bird. In mock horror, he raises both eyebrows. 'You cannot tell from my drawing?'

'*Bud! Bud!*' shout one or two children and Kamau looks at them and bows slightly. I feel like we are acting in front of them, performing our own elaborate theatre between the two of us, the children both our audience and our safety net. It can be no other way.

Together, we divide the entire class into pairs and they immediately begin their exercise. I am amazed – it worked. They know exactly what it is they are required to do, and without a word of Kikuyu from myself or any intervention from Kamau!

He comes and stands beside me as we watch the children drawing and correct a few pronunciations. Without looking at him, I lean slightly towards Kamau and said 'I knew it was a bird really.'

'I know you did.' He pauses. 'And I knew it was a sun-bird really.'

I frown. What does he mean? I do not have long to dwell on it, for a small commotion erupts at the back of the classroom and Kamau is swallowed into a sea of faces.

But later, walking home, his words return to me and I understand. The jolt of recognition, the significance of his words, make me stop in my tracks and begin to fiddle with a tassel from my parasol. What are we doing?

🐦 🐦 🐦

This time I leave longer between visits to the schoolhouse. I want to go more than anything; I am bursting with ideas and have written upon countless sheets of paper both a log of English taught and ideas for the future. I am a teacher. *I am a teacher!* And somebody notices me. For who I am – not for who he thinks I should be or could be, simply for myself. I know, however, that it is more than this. That something has grown very rapidly between us that should not have done.

Greeting Kamau at the door to the schoolhouse, on this third occasion, I feel tongue-tied. Something has shifted between us and we both feel it immediately.

'I hope…'

'Yes?'

'I hope that I am not disturbing you by coming here. Interrupting your teaching plans, I mean.'

'Quite the contrary,' he replies. His voice is soft and serious. 'It is always such a pleasure for us all when you turn up.'

I flush with gladness and look away.

'You are, you know…' he glances at the sun, 'a little early, though. The children will not be here for another quarter of an hour or so.'

I bite my bottom lip and look away. 'I can wait out here if it—'

'No! No. I didn't mean that. Come in, please. Wait with me inside. I simply need to prepare a few things before they arrive.'

I smile and nod, and we walk together the last few paces to the schoolhouse. I watch Kamau's long, slender fingers as they unbolt the lock and push the wooden door open into the comparative gloom inside.

'Please.' He pulls a chair out from beneath his desk for me.

'So,' he says, perching on the end of the desk a mere metre from me, 'how is life progressing for you in our little township?'

I look at him in surprise. I thought he was going to prepare for his class.

'Oh! It is… not what I am accustomed to, of course. But I think I am growing used to it, little by little.'

He nods his head, looking at me intently.

'And this…' I continue.

'Yes?'

I take a sharp intake of breath. 'Well, this helps me.'

'What, exactly?'

I pause, listening to the shout of an approaching child.

'Teaching. Being here.' I shift a little on my seat.

'I am very glad, Mrs Lawrence.'

'You are?'

'Of course. It helps me also, your presence here.'

I almost feel as though I cannot breathe; that everything else has gone out of focus save for the contours of his face. I try not to look at him but I cannot look anywhere else. The moments drag but at the same time stand still. I am aware of his scent, the curve of his lips, the unusual shape of his eyes and slant of his cheekbones.

Two boys poke their heads round the door, their tanned leather garments rustling like leaves, and I twitch with surprise.

'*Tee-cha!*' they cry. Kamau says something to them in Kikuyu and they move back outside reluctantly.

'They are early,' Kamau says apologetically, his face solemn. I would like to lay my hand against his cheek, to see if it is as smooth as I imagine it to be.

'Like me.' I shrug.

'Yes,' Kamau says, not taking his eyes from me. 'Like you.' He is tapping the end of his pencil on the desk. 'Mrs Lawrence…'

'Yes?'

His dark eyes dart around. He takes a deep breath and then laughs nervously. 'Nothing. It is nothing.'

'No, *please* tell me what you were going to say.'

We both become aware at the same moment of the room suddenly darkening. Looking across, we see several faces in the open windows, blocking out the light.

Kamau looks back at me, leans his head on one side and says, 'Another time.'

The children file in and wave at me excitedly. I wave back, happiness washing through me.

I am distracted today, nervous. And despite all the ideas I wrote down at home, now that I am here they have all fled from my mind. As though reading my mind, Kamau is beside me.

'What will you teach today?'

'I… I don't know.'

He looks thoughtful. 'Perhaps we can teach some English together.'

My stomach contracts. 'Yes.'

'For example,' he takes half a step closer to me, 'we can pose some questions together, and put them into pairs again to practise the questions and answers.'

I nod.

I am aware of every pair of eyes on the benches staring at us, waiting for the lesson to start. I am aware of the light falling into the room, casting one half of Kamau's face in shadow. I am aware of the distance that exists between us, both physically and by the conventions we must adhere to. And yet… the very fact that I am here. A line has already been crossed and we both know it.

He is opposite me, a head's distance away. He is looking directly at me.

'What is your name?' he says slowly and loudly.

'My name is Mrs Lawrence.'

He shakes his head. 'No,' he whispers, '*Christian* name. Let us begin again.' He clears his throat. 'What is your name?'

'My name…' I hesitate. Yet another boundary being crossed. 'My name is Iris.'

'Iris,' he repeats. He does not take his eyes from me. 'Iris.'

He nods, gesturing that I now ask him. 'What is your name?'

'My name is Kamau.'

Kamau. I would like to know what it means, this two-syllabled, lyrical name. I like the way it sounds in his mouth, different from how I say it or how Mr Ahmed says it; there is a rich undertone in his accent, redolent of the African earth from which he hails.

He nods in the direction of one end of the classroom, meaning for me to walk over there, and he walks to the other and I start to hear it again, spreading like water over the classroom. 'What is your name? My name is…'

We stand at our opposite ends, correcting pronunciation and providing encouragement, but my mind is not on what I am doing. My voice is with the children but my mind is on him, and him alone. I glance in his direction but he is already looking at me. I hold his gaze for an instant and then look away, back at the children, my cheeks burning. *Stop!* I scream to myself. *Stop this foolishness! It cannot be, not now and not ever. It is impossible!*

Yet despite the impossibility of it, when we bid each other farewell at the end of the morning, my hand stays in his for far longer than I should let it, something vital fusing. And all I can think when I look at his strong, handsome face is, *When can I see you again?*

🕊 🕊 🕊

I stand at the door of the bungalow early on Saturday morning and bid Mr Lawrence farewell. It is barely half past four and I can scarcely open my eyes, they feel so filled with sleep. He nods at me curtly, almost as though I was not there, and once he has left I grope my way back through the darkness to the bedroom, where I fall once again into a deep, dreamless sleep.

When I wake up some time later, I turn on to my side and look at the clock hanging on the wall. I can scarcely believe it, but it is already past half past eight. I do not think I have ever slept in so late since being here. I continue to lie in bed, feeling the absence of Mr Lawrence keenly, in such a manner that I am unable to prevent the smile from creeping up my face. An entire two days free from his ghastly monocle that makes one oily blue eye appear larger than the other, and free from his constant air of disapproval and free from *him*, simply him.

Pushing the mosquito net up, I place the clock back on the dresser, then open the curtains an inch or so and stretch out like a cat as I feel the warmth of the day trickle through the window on to my pillow. Although I am filled with a wonderful contentment, I do not quite feel like beginning my day yet. Revelling in this luxury, I pull *Alice's Adventures in Wonderland* into bed with me, thinking, as I so often do when I read it, of my father. Opening it at random, I fall upon a passage from the Mad Hatter's tea party and read out loud.

The March Hare took the watch and looked at it gloomily: then he dipped it into his cup of tea and looked at it again: but he could think of nothing better to say than his first remark, 'It was the best butter, you know.'

I laugh out loud; truly it is the most wonderful, peculiar, curious book that I know. I continue to read to myself until I hear the pull of the door and the gentle tinkering of Muthoni from outside the bedroom and the brightness of the day can keep me in bed no longer. Opening the door of my wardrobe, I select one of Mr Ahmed's dresses. Wearing something that my friend has made for me – for yes, I do regard him as my friend – cannot fail to give me a favourable start to the day.

Muthoni looks surprised to see me appear from the bedroom at such a late hour, but she smiles warmly at me and – do I truly see this or am I just imagining it? – a look of complicity passes between us; a look that reads: he is not here. And perhaps we are both able to breathe a little easier for that knowledge.

She has already prepared breakfast for me outside: a pot of English breakfast tea, half a mango – its rich flesh scooped into a bowl – and a poached egg dusted with salt and pepper. If all those years at The Old Vicarage spent in the kitchen with Cook taught me anything, it was how to make a poached egg. I am ashamed to confess I am able to cook little else, but there was something about watching Cook drop that soft gelatinous form into the bubbling water, that gentle hardening and moulding into its perfect little oval shape, that fascinated me. So not long after I arrived in Nairobi, I taught Muthoni how to make a poached egg. She can cook them now quite to perfection and I eat them most mornings, crowned with the smallest pinch of salt and pepper.

Thoughts of Kamau involuntarily spring to mind and I try to dismiss them as quickly as can. But he intrigues me, the sincerity and openness of his gaze as well as the fact that I do surprisingly, yet undeniably, find him attractive in a way I wish I did not. Alongside this wish, however, is an edge of something else: the slightest frisson of excitement and warmth that travels along my nerve endings in a manner I am quite unfamiliar with.

Decisively, I get to my feet, more than anything else in a feeble attempt to dispel such nonsensical thoughts. I shall take a walk; that is what I shall do on this morning, rich with colour and light and warmth. I shall not follow the river that snakes westwards towards Kamau's schoolhouse, though that is where my feet should like to take me.

No, I shall walk towards Nairobi.

Except that my feet do not take me there. As I begin walking, my intention is to go to the General Merchants on Victoria Street, where we have credit to buy a few supplies and perhaps take a cup of tea. Instead, I find I am walking in the direction of the Nairobi River. 'What are you *doing*, Iris?' I ask myself out loud. 'It is Saturday, and even if it were not Saturday, well, what are you *doing*?'

As so often happens, Mother unwittingly edges her way into my mind. I write to her occasionally out of some sense of duty, yet these letters to her are hastily assembled. As the months have passed, I have become increasingly aware of the tightening knot of resentment that has formed deep within me and the belief – it matters not how accurate it is – that Mother sold me to Africa.

Yet despite that betrayal that smarts like an open wound, Africa, I realise, is slowly becoming part of me: who I am, who I will be, what I am becoming. The birdsong that filters through to my consciousness each morning before I am really awake; the hawking cry of the hadada ibis that fly over the bungalow roof each day; the distant death calls from the wilds as animals hunt one another, caught up in nature's endless spiral; the distinct redness of the earth, this rich soil that can support growth no matter the month; even the people stopping and staring, slack-jawed at the sight of a white woman walking alone, or the terrified screech from a native child at seeing me – this scarcely registers now. And whilst I do not understand this land in many ways and no doubt shall never succeed in doing so, my admiration for it grows a little deeper each day.

Upon reaching the schoolhouse, just as I imagined should be the case, it is closed and locked up and Kamau is nowhere to be seen. I chide myself for the undeniable disappointment I feel and walk out a little further beyond the schoolhouse, which I have not yet done. My parasol keeps slipping out of my hands, so I close it and lay it beneath a tree as I continue to enjoy the walk along the papyrus-fringed river. There is a rattling sound echoing from beyond. I pick my way over the track, which becomes less of a path and more like shrubby grassland with clods of uneven earth that snag at my boots as I walk. A mere 200 metres or so beyond the schoolhouse I stop abruptly.

Before me is a patch of dry grassland and upon this are several tower-like structures that appear to be moulded from the earth. A large number of young boys surround the chimney-like towers, sitting in circles around them, and as I watch, I see that the boys are holding various items: some are clasping broad, green leaves, others pitchers of water and more still have their hands dirtied by thick, muddy clay that they are passing from one hand to the other before shaping it into long tubes.

I stand at a distance, for I wish to watch whatever is happening unobserved so that I do not divert their attention. The mud is a curious colour, very nearly blue in fact, and once the boys have shaped it, they place it against the tower so that the tubes stand out at an angle. For the first time, I see that there are a number of holes all over the towers and it is against these holes that the boys are placing their tubes.

I am mesmerised. These children have clearly been through the same process a great number of times before; the self-assuredness and fluidity of their movements attests to this. None of them speak a word to one another. In fact, their faces are rather solemn but purposeful and I feel as though I am witnessing the unfolding of some great secret, for I have not the slightest idea of what they are doing or what they might achieve. It appears that all the groups are engaged in the same activity, so I fix my eyes upon the small party that is the closest to me. Now that all the tubes are attached to the sides of the towers, the boys with the leaves roll them up and insert them into the ducts before water is trickled down and a small cap rolled from the clay is placed on the tube opening.

The boys go diligently about all the shafts around the towers. I am still uncertain whether they have made these themselves or if it is some natural phenomenon. Once all these cap-like discs have been placed upon the openings, a sudden and almost eerie calm falls upon the group and I find myself holding my breath a little, concerned that I shall be seen at any moment and the spontaneity of this ceremony be lost. But I needn't have worried. They are paying me no attention.

And then it begins – that same noise which drew me here in the first place, a beating sound that starts off low and dim, but increases slowly in energy and volume. Each of the boys has taken up two short sticks and they are hitting them rhythmically upon a third, longer one. This continues for what feels like a very long time, to the point that I wonder if this is it and the ceremony will go no further. They are deep in concentration as the pounding goes on and on. How I should like to know what they are doing. And why.

'You know,' says a low voice behind me, 'this is what I did as a child.'

I gasp in surprise and spin round, my hand to my chest.

Kamau puts his hand out apologetically. 'I am sorry, Mrs Lawrence. I did not mean to frighten you. I came to the schoolhouse to collect a few things and saw your parasol by the door. I thought I should come and find you.'

'Thank you,' I reply. 'That was kind.'

I am still holding my hand against my heart, which beats furiously, both because of the shock he gave me and something else I do not wish to identify. He looks genuinely alarmed and remains at some distance from me. 'I thought perhaps you heard my footsteps approaching.'

I shake my head and laugh. 'No. I am fine. Truly.' I turn my head and glance at the boys again, wondering if they were disturbed, but they have not even noticed and are still intent on their pounding. Curiosity overcomes the panic I felt and I look back at Kamau. 'What are they *doing?*'

He pauses, smiles thoughtfully for a moment and then comes to stand beside me.

'You know that these are termite mounds.'

'Oh!' I exclaim. 'No, I did not realise.'

'When the water is poured into the holes, one termite says to another "Look! It is raining! Can you see?" And this message is passed from one creature to the other until they all know and they are all talking about it.'

He pauses again, his hands behind him, back straight. I watch his face in profile, a small smile creeping his lips upwards.

'Then what happens?' I ask.

He doesn't look at me. 'Watch,' he replies quietly.

And so I watch as the beating continues; I see the look of stern concentration on the faces of these small boys with their lithe bodies and powerful arms and the determination etched into every fibre of their beings. Presently, a few boys begin to peel back the moulded lids and peer inside before placing them back and continuing with their rhythmic beating. And whilst this goes on for what feels like an age, the patience of these boys far outweighing my own, I become keenly aware of Kamau's presence beside me. There are possibly a few inches separating his left shoulder and my right, yet those few inches feel heavy with distance.

After a few minutes, the boys look again beneath the lids. I begin to wish that I had not acted so impulsively in leaving my parasol at the schoolhouse, for the heat of the day is increasing and, this being the dry season, it is likely to become a great deal hotter. I think how horrified Mr Lawrence should be to see me walking without my parasol, he who wears his pith helmet even inside the bungalow. But I push any thoughts of Mr Lawrence aside, for I know very well that my lack of parasol would be the least of his horrors should he see me here.

Finally it happens and, quite extraordinarily, this appears to come about almost simultaneously for several of the boys, upon lifting the caps, are now shrieking with excitement, dropping their sticks and scooping their small hands into the shafts. I turn to look at Kamau. He has his arms folded in front of him and begins to laugh, his dark eyes shining. Looking back, I see what look like white ants flying above the openings and the boys grabbing them by the handfuls and cramming the insects into their mouths, munching and muttering and chattering away as more and more come, a never-ending supply of these small white delicacies. Fists continue to fly in all directions as the termites are caught and eaten, whilst other boys enfold them into the blankets that they have brought along.

I start to laugh as well, for it is one of the strangest sights I have ever seen, a sight more suited to the pages of *Alice's Adventures in Wonderland*. After several more minutes of watchful silence I take a deep breath and turn to Kamau.

'Well,' I say emphatically. 'I certainly was not expecting that.'

'Really?'

I shake my head.

'What were you expecting?'

'I… I walked past the schoolhouse and I heard this beating noise and I thought I might come and investigate. But I had no idea the towers would have all these termites inside them.'

Silence catches between us and he smiles at me, a glint of humour in his eyes. 'Come,' he says and he motions towards the group of boys, still wildly thrashing about and grabbing great fistfuls of the ill-fated creatures. Rather gingerly, I follow him and he says something in Kikuyu so that they turn to me, wide-eyed. But unlike Kamau's own pupils, who were initially terrified of me, these boys appear shocked at the sight of me but not scared. Their excited clamour falls silent, a hush descending upon the small group as I feel dozens of eyes upon me.

Sensing my discomfort, Kamau says something else to one boy and immediately he produces a few termites for him from within the folds of his blanket, hurriedly closing it up again lest more escape. Kamau puts them straight into his mouth before they can fly away and I find myself wincing slightly as he chews at the same time as grinning, which I should not have thought possible, before removing what look like the wings and dropping them on to the floor.

'Do they taste good?' I ask uncertainly.

'Not especially,' Kamau admits. 'I liked them very much as a boy. Catching them is part of the fun, as you have seen.'

I smile and nod, aware of the sun that is climbing higher in the sky with each passing minute.

'Would you like to try one?' he continues.

'Ah. No, thank you.'

'Are you sure? An African speciality? I am sure you do not eat these at home.'

I laugh. 'That much is certain.'

What possesses me to perform my next action I am not entirely certain. Perhaps it is the intensity of the sun that is making me feel light-headed. Or perhaps it is the desire to show this man I am not like all the other *mundu mweru* who come here to their land with their customs and their clothes and their strange foods and think that all of this is superior to what they encounter. But I find myself saying to him, 'Fine. I shall try one.'

'Are you sure?'

'Yes,' I say quickly, before I can change my mind.

He says something to a boy and a termite is offered to me, the child's face solemn as he clasps the writhing creature by its wings. What I am doing? I have nothing to prove; nobody here truly expects me to do this ridiculous thing – yet strangely, I want to feel the crunch of this creature's tiny frame inside my mouth. I do not think more on the matter, instead taking the insect the child is proffering and putting it straight into my mouth, closing my lips around it. The creature is still alive and I feel it flitting about, in a desperate search for an opening. I attempt to manoeuvre it between my teeth to bite down, but it is intent on moving away and I can feel the horrid sensation of it crashing against the roof of my mouth in its bid for freedom.

I spend some time attempting to trap it, doubtless making peculiar contortions with my mouth, but to no avail. I am quite the spectacle now. I long to open my mouth, and in one great gush of frustration and desperation to breathe more freely, I part my lips a fraction. The termite immediately shoots out of them and flies away in a confused line.

The boys erupt into peals of excited laughter, clapping one another on the back and swinging on each other's arms. Kamau too is laughing, not with the wild abandon of the boys but slowly, carefully, kindly. I feel rather idiotic, but of course I can see the humour in the situation and, despite myself, I begin to laugh along with them. What a curious sight we all must be, I think. A white-skinned woman without parasol near the banks of the curving Nairobi River with a termite fleeing from her mouth, alongside a group of skinny boys wearing almost nothing and a tall, simply but elegantly dressed schoolteacher.

Presently, the boys lose interest and disperse whilst I, almost recovered from the incident, consider again the rising temperature and my need for water.

'I must get into the shade,' I tell Kamau.

We turn and begin to make our way back in the direction of the schoolhouse.

'How are you?' he asks.

I keep my eyes fixed on the uneven path ahead of me. 'I am well, thank you. A little hot, though,' I say with a small laugh. 'It was foolish to have left my parasol at the schoolhouse. I thought I would not need it, but it has suddenly got terribly hot.'

'Yes,' Kamau replies. 'The heat here is deceptive.'

We continue to walk in silence until we reach the school-house. Kamau reaches the door first, picks up my parasol and holds it between his hands for a moment before smiling and handing it to me.

CHAPTER TWENTY-TWO

BENEDICT KAMAU

Mrs Lawrence puts up her parasol and exhales a small sigh of relief. She looks like she is going to leave and I ask her which direction she is walking, not that there are many ways she possibly could go.

'Well,' she says, inclining her head in the direction of the town, 'I am going to my house.'

'Can I accompany you? I need to go that way to visit Fazal about some orders I placed.'

This is not entirely true, as he told me he would send word once finished.

'Fazal?' she asks, her dark blue eyes widening.

'Mr Ahmed.'

She laughs, a gloved hand flying to her mouth. How she can bear to wear gloves in this heat, even those light ones, I do not know. 'Mr Ahmed,' she replies. 'Of course.'

As we walk, I ask her if she has seen any more sunbirds.

'Yes,' she replies, smiling. 'They like our verandah a great deal. I often see them there near the potted plants, particularly when I am having breakfast.'

'Their nests are fascinating. If I see one, I shall let you know. They use a lot of spiderwebs to build them—'

'*Spiderwebs?*' Mrs Lawrence stops walking and turns to me in surprise.

'Yes. The females build the nests, which hang from a tree like a little bag. They are incredibly intricate. It is astonishing how they construct them. The females also incubate the eggs, but the males are known to assist in rearing the chicks. There are a number of species around the world, over one hundred I believe. But in East Africa there are around thirty species.'

'So many?'

I nod.

'I wonder which one it is that visits my verandah so regularly.'

'It is most probably a collared sunbird. Look.' I stop walking and pick up a stick, then begin drawing in the dusty ground. 'This is what the sunbird's tongue looks like, a long tube that is good for sucking up tiny little invertebrates like spiders and termites.'

'So it's not only small boys who are fond of this delicacy.'

'Exactly.' I lean on my stick and turn to her. 'Larger insects they catch with their beaks, often even catching them in flight and feeding them to their young.'

She looks at me, her eyes wide with amazement. 'How do you know all of these things, Kamau?'

'Father Dutton – do you remember me mentioning him? I learnt all I know of birds from him.'

'Yes. Of course. But your degree of knowledge… well, to me it is extraordinary.' She smiles widely and then turns and continues to walk along the rugged track, looking around her with great interest as she goes, pausing to inspect a frond of papyrus.

'What about you?' I ask her. 'I have told you where my interest in birds derives from. But what is it all about for you?'

'I suppose it all started with my father's pigeons. I used to adore them as a child and right up until I left, actually. They were so gentle. So responsive, somehow. But I think there is another reason I love birds so much…'

'Yes?'

She is walking ahead of me and she stops, looking back over one shoulder. 'I think it is because they are free. And I am not.'

I catch up with her and reach a hand out, touching her lightly on the elbow. She stops walking. 'You feel like a prisoner, Mrs Lawrence?'

'I *am* a prisoner. I have been all my life.' She frowns deeply, her forehead puckering, and continues walking so that my hand drops from her elbow. I have opened up something deeply painful to her and I long to take her in my arms and tell her that everything will be fine. Yet how can I possibly know this? I have no idea at all what it is like to be a woman in her situation.

After a few more minutes of silent walking, Mrs Lawrence's shoulders relax once again and she begins to take in everything around her, pausing every few moments to study a leaf or brush her fingers against something. This is not how other white women are, the ones I have seen picking their way down Victoria Street and Government Road with that look of distaste brandished like an indelible mark across their features: eyes squinted and nose upturned. Mrs Lawrence looks around her. She sees things in a way that other people do not – honestly, openly.

'You must miss him,' she says, 'Father Dutton.'

'Every day,' I admit. 'But I have the children to think of now, just as Reverend Dutton once thought of me, of all of us in the orphanage.'

'If they weren't going to school, what would they be doing?'

'These children I teach?'

'Yes.'

'Before they even arrive at school, they help in the house, or on the *shamba*, the family plot of land. And that is exactly what they will continue to do when they get home. Many of the families were highly sceptical about their children attending school. They could not see the point of it. I had to go round each family personally and talk to them, to explain the benefits of an education, particularly now that Nairobi is a rapidly growing town. When these children reach our age, there will be so many more opportunities for them.'

Mrs Lawrence nods thoughtfully and I steal a glance at her face in profile, the determined brow and smooth skin.

'Did you help in the same way when you were a child, Kamau?'

'Of course. Did you not?'

She laughs and reaches a hand out to absently pluck at a leaf hanging from a bush. 'Not really. At least, I did a little in the kitchen, much to the horror of my mother. You see, I wasn't allowed in the kitchen.'

Mrs Lawrence's forehead creases and I leave a respectable pause. 'You're not close to your mother?'

'No,' she answers quickly. 'I never have been. My father and I were always on better terms. And my brother, Arthur. But…' She turns enthusiastically to me, her eyes gleaming like a young girl's. 'But let us not talk about me. Your story is so much more interesting!'

'My story?'

'Yes, to me it is. I know that whatever you grow up with, well, it is just normal, is it not? But I cannot quite imagine you growing up here, particularly when there was no Nairobi. What is it like, this place you are from?'

'Kikuyuland… I haven't been there for a few years.'

'Not even to visit family?'

'No,' I reply simply.

'You do not miss it?'

I'm not sure if she sees my face or if she stops of her own accord, but she pauses again and shakes her head. 'Forgive me,' she says, 'I am asking too many questions. You don't have to answer any of them.'

I laugh lightly as I stop and face her. Long strands of her dark hair have escaped from beneath her hat and a few of them are sticking against her forehead. I suppress an urge to reach out and smooth them away. 'It's fine.' And it really is, given what a private person I am. 'Kikuyuland. It has been a few years, but it is not the kind of place you can forget in a hurry. It is not like Nairobi. Kikuyuland is dominated by Mount Kirinyaga—'

'...which I can sometimes see from Nairobi!'

'Yes. On very clear days. There is always snow on the highest peaks and this leads down to a network of rivers that water the land and make it some of the most fertile and abundant earth for miles around. It is dotted with traditional homesteads, thatched huts and there are goats everywhere and small *shambas* and what I remember above all else is how green it always was. Not a normal kind of green, but a colour so dazzlingly bright, perhaps because we were so high. There was one time though the colour faded—' I break off and clear my throat and she turns expectantly towards me.

'What happened?'

'Drought,' I say quietly, and I know there is also drought in my throat, for no more words will come.

Mrs Lawrence seems more interested in my roots even than myself. I am proud of where and what I have come from, but in many ways I have renounced this part of myself. For Kikuyu men do not stand at the front of schoolrooms teaching mathematics and geography and science. Kikuyu men do not wear these linen trousers and tailored shirts. Yet I am flattered by her attention and her genuine interest that seems so genuine and I find that we are talking so intently, for the whole walk back, that by the time I reach the turning that will take me to Bazaar Street, it feels like only a few minutes have passed and not over half an hour.

We pause on the outcrop. 'Bazaar Street is this way,' I say, gesturing down the track that leads to the cluster of workshops. I shall have to think of some excuse for dropping in on Fazal.

'Yes, well, I am going this way,' she says and then adds quickly, her face shining, 'Oh! Something I meant to ask you. That sound, the high-pitched whistling – what is it? I have asked Mr Lawrence and Mr Ahmed and neither of them know the answer. I cannot hear it all the time, it comes and goes. But I can hear it now. Listen!'

I fall silent, knowing exactly what she is referring to. I smile and walk towards a bush, plucking from it a circular, black bulb with two sharp, protruding thorns. 'It is this, Mrs Lawrence, known as whistling thorn.'

Her face breaks out into a beautiful smile and I want to re-member that smile for ever. 'But why does it make that noise?'

'There is a simple answer to that. Look here.' I pull one from the bush and dig my fingernail into the hard flesh of the bulb. 'The swollen thorns are hollow, see? Now, look inside it – no, don't hold it, you'll see why in a minute.'

She squints, drawing her face close and then, with a sud-den gasp, pulling it away. 'Ants!'

'Yes. Vicious little biting ants live inside the bulbs, often huge numbers inside a single bulb. If elephants or giraffes try to eat the bulbs, the ants swarm out and give the ani-mals a nasty shock. But as for the noise – after the ants have moved on and when the wind blows over the bulbs, which it often does on these plains, it gusts through the tiny little entry and exit holes that the ants have made and makes that low, whistling sound we hear.'

She raises her eyebrows. 'Astonishing. I certainly am learning a great deal today.' She goes on, 'I remember something else I wanted to ask you. Your name, Kamau. What does it mean?'

I laugh, wondering suddenly how old Mrs Lawrence is. Because there are times when I feel as though I am talking to a woman far wiser than her years. Yet at other times, like now, when her features are illuminated with such childlike eagerness, I wonder if she is younger than I believe her to be.

'My name?'

'Yes,' she enthuses. 'It must mean something. In the Kikuyu tradition, I mean.'

'Well, you are right. It does.'

She nods her head, eagerly waiting.

'Kamau means quiet warrior.' I know that when I say those words, my voice drops to the calm stillness of its meaning.

'Oh!' she gasps, 'But that is wonderful! I mean, how marvellous to be called something with a meaning like that.'

I laugh. I cannot help it. 'And you? What does Iris mean?'

'Well, it is nothing as spectacular as *yours,* I'm afraid. It has two meanings. First of all, an iris is a flower. Do you know what an iris looks like?'

I turn my palms upwards and shrug. 'I am afraid I do not. I do not think we have such flowers here.'

'They are tall plants and the flowers are quite often blue or purple in colour. They are quite pretty.' She turns to look at me directly and beams that smile of hers that opens her entire face up.

I clasp my hands behind my back and I feel them shaking a little. 'I am sure they are.'

She nods and blows upwards, so that the escaped strands of hair around her ears and forehead flutter and settle.

'And the second meaning?' I ask.

'It is the coloured part of your eye that circles the pupil.'

'Really? I never learnt that word with Father Dutton. Perhaps because we all had the same colour irises.'

'Oh no,' she enthuses, 'not at all. I have seen many different shades of brown and black since I have been here. More than I imagined possible.'

She looks away, as though suddenly feeling embarrassed. I press on. 'And yours are?'

Turning her face back, she looks puzzled. 'I'm sorry?'

'Your irises. What colour are they?'

I know the exact shade of them, but I want to hear how she describes them herself. 'Oh. The same shade as my father's, *precisely* the same. They are… well, just blue.'

'Not just blue.' The words slip out before I have a chance to stop them. 'What I mean,' I continue hurriedly, 'is that they are a very unusual shade. I have never seen eyes that colour before. Or *irises* that colour, I should say.'

Mrs Lawrence looks at me intently for a moment. Then she clears her throat. 'I oughtn't stay out much longer, I'm afraid. I never remember sensible things like bringing water with me.'

'Yes, of course. Well… it was good to see you.'

She smiles and we shake hands. 'Yes, it was. I hope to see you…' She trails off and this final sentence is left hanging in the air between us, as thick and warm as the high heat of the midday sun. She hesitates, then nods and turns, beginning to move away from me. On an impulse, I call after her.

'Mrs Lawrence!'

She spins round, both eyebrows raised.

'Would you – when might the children next have the pleasure of being taught by you?'

She pauses, her hands resting on her hips. 'Next week, perhaps?'

I grin at her stupidly. 'Very well,' I say, in as solemn a tone as I can gather.

'Very well,' she repeats, and then her slim frame turns, and she is gone.

CHAPTER TWENTY-THREE

AHMED FAZAL

I make chai for us both but I can tell he is agitated. I do not know Kamau so very well, yet I have spent enough time with this man to know when he is feeling not quite comfortable. It is very clear, because he moves around a great deal, picking things up and then putting them down again.

'Your shirt will be ready, I would say, in about four more days.'

'That is perfect, thank you.'

I hand Kamau the cup of steaming tea. At least that will give him something to do with his hands.

'Delicious,' he murmurs. 'You people make good tea.'

I raise an eyebrow. 'You people?'

'Yes. You – you Indian people. I intend no disrespect by that. The orphanage where I grew up, Father Dutton. He was a man of letters, a wise man.' He pauses and takes another sip, curling both of his large hands round the cup. 'But the tea he made, it tasted like the dirty water thrown out after washing clothes.'

He bursts out laughing and I cannot help but join in; there is an infectious humour and lightness about this man it is impossible not to admire.

'I have been busy these past couple of weeks,' I tell him. 'I have a couple of new clients.' I am eager to keep the pride from my voice but uncertain I am able to achieve it. 'I think Mr Lawrence might have given my name to one or two of his associates. And then I also finished some trousers appropriate for a hunting trip for Mr Lawrence himself. He has an expedition this weekend.'

'Does Mrs Lawrence,' he asks, a little too quickly, 'also enjoy the hunting expeditions?'

I raise an eyebrow. 'Somehow, I cannot imagine so.'

Kamau mumbles something. Yet he is not with me; I still feel it and wonder if it is something he will choose to share with me, or whether I ought to ask him outright what is bothering him. At the same time, I am not entirely sure I *want* to know.

So I let him sit there, leaning forwards on the chair as he drinks the chai, and I chatter to him about this and that, waiting for him to open up to me. I tell him about my work and some of my clients and how I dream of a larger workshop and the words 'Ahmed and Sons' on a board outside… 'when, of course,' I chuckle, 'I am blessed with any sons.'

'But Fazal,' Kamau says suddenly and rather loudly, his dark eyes looking up and staring right at me, 'when will you bring— forgive me, I have forgotten your wife's name.'

'Maliha.'

'Maliha. That is it. Why will you not send for her? She must be eagerly awaiting your word.'

I sigh. I do not enjoy conversations such as these. I know he is right; I have thought it a great many times myself and of course, Ahmed and Sons will continue to remain a dream whilst Maliha is still far away in India.

'It is pride,' I reply, 'I know that. But I always wished to be more established before she comes. To have...' I pause, frowning, 'a little more capital to my name.'

Kamau leans back in the chair and looks around the workshop. 'I am not sure I can agree with you, my friend. All I can see is that you have a great deal to be proud of, and the wife you have chosen is sure to see your achievements.'

I smile at him gratefully and clasp my hands together. 'You are right. I know you are right.'

'Well then,' he laughs. 'No more excuses. Maliha – what is she like?'

'In what way?'

'Well.' Kamau stands up and strides to the doorway. He is listening, but he is edgy, a moth flitting around a kerosene lamp. 'How did you meet, for example?'

'Ah. We had an arranged marriage. She came from a village not far from mine and she was from a good family and... well, that is how it works in my place. And here? You will also have an arranged marriage?'

Kamau looks thoughtful for a moment, leaning into the doorframe and staring out at Bazaar Street. 'This is the Kikuyu custom, yes. But my parents are not alive and I do not have other family members.' He shrugs. 'So this takes off the pressure, I suppose.'

'Do you not want to get married?'

Kamau does not look comfortable talking about this, I do not know why. He mumbles something about marrying one day, perhaps. When he looks back at me I smile at him and raise an eyebrow. 'You are still young. You have plenty of time.'

He snorts. 'Not so young, Fazal. How old are you?'

'I am twenty-four.'

'In that case I am only two years younger than you. Anyway...' He glances at his watch. 'I should go, and let you continue with your work. Do you have a lot on at the moment?'

'Well, my largest order so far was Mr Lawrence's hunting clothes. I have a small break now, but I do need to begin making a few shirts for another client soon.'

Kamau stands in the doorway, his face deep in concentration as he absently drums his fingers against the doorframe.

'Is there...' I hesitate, 'is there something bothering you, Kamau?'

He looks at me sharply. 'Why do you ask that?'

I pause for a moment. 'You seem distracted. Not quite yourself. If something is troubling you, I hope you feel you could tell me about it.'

He smiles, looks down and then turns decisively for the door, dismissing what I have said with a laugh. 'Thank you, Fazal,' he replies over his shoulder. 'I appreciate that. But I have no troubles.'

Why is it I do not believe him? Just as he is about to leave the workshop I say his name firmly. He turns to look at me. His eyes are shaped like almonds, the dusky colour of roasted ural dal. 'Yes?' He looks at me in surprise.

'Be careful, Kamau.'

'Of what?'

I stand before him in the doorway, wishing more than anything he would confide in me, but knowing that he will not.

'Just…' I falter, 'be careful.'

But he just smiles, his almond eyes creasing, paper-white teeth flashing, nods briefly and then vanishes into the clamour of Bazaar Street.

CHAPTER TWENTY-FOUR

IRIS LAWRENCE

The Nairobi sky is beginning to darken, a deep blue fringe around a pale, cloudy white, and the croaking frogs strike up their cacophony as they do each and every evening. I sit on the verandah with a blanket wrapped around my shoulders, taking in the subtle shifts in shade and temperature.

I have been so happy today. The walk I took this morning, watching the boys beating for locusts, meeting Kamau and then coming back to the bungalow, knowing that I have the entire long afternoon and evening to myself. I have just finished writing a letter to Miss Logan and really ought to write now to Mother to respond to her recent letter filled with nothing of any import or interest, but find I have not the inclination. Instead, I sit on the chair with the corners of my two-page letter fluttering beneath the heavy stone I have placed on top of it, hugging the blanket around my shoulders as the sound of night birds and croaking frogs settles on to the cool, Nairobi evening. I could, I think to myself, live here alone quite happily.

CHAPTER TWENTY-FIVE

BENEDICT KAMAU

Night falls quickly here, a heavy black shadow devouring everything in its path. Night can hide anything and everything: the wild animals in their stealthy tread as they nudge their way beneath the netting of the homesteads, carrying away goats and sheep and cows after one fatal, silent bite. It can hide the winged creatures of the night: the owls and the bats; slim flicks of dark wing flapping against the edge of blackness. And it can hide our faces, because we are as dark as the night. We can move around beneath a moonless sky, tracking our movements from the constellations. A compass runs through my veins, for it is does not matter what fancy clothes I wear, nor what fancy figures of speech I adopt, my Kikuyu blood flows as freely as the rivers that stream from Mount Kirinyaga's summit.

I know I must heed Fazal's warning, but I cannot. He is a wise man, for I have told him nothing, but he knows. I make myself a simple dinner of *irio* over the fire outside my hut, carefully folding in the pumpkin leaves and watching as they curl and wilt. As the flames flicker upwards, I see the brightness of her face in them. She is smiling. She is *always* smiling when I think of her, that one front tooth crookedly overlapping the other just a little. What am I to read from her visit to the schoolhouse this afternoon, a Saturday?

It would be easier if I had never met her. But I have met her, and now she is all I can think of. I do not know quite how she feels, but I know that above all else Iris must be seen for who she is. Not for who people want her to be or expect her to be, but simply as Iris.

She has crept beneath my skin and informs my movements. As I chew slowly, without pleasure, I think of old Father Dutton, the single moral compass I have had in my life. What would he say to these thoughts that knock up against one another in my head? He would, of course, say it was wrong to desire the wife of another man. Yet he also thought with his heart as well as his head and he was wise enough that he would have been able to read the truth: that Iris is an unhappy woman.

I push my plate of food aside and stare up at the star-streaked sky, listening to the rustles, hisses and squeaks of the creatures of the night. It is impossible to enjoy this food or to concentrate on anything else. *Do not go*, my head tells me. *Do not go.*

CHAPTER TWENTY-SIX

IRIS LAWRENCE

When the chill of the evening becomes too great (the temperature of the Nairobi nights never fails to take me by surprise, so sharply in contrast is it to the day), I take the kerosene lamp and visit the lavatory. I cannot help but smile whenever I go to the long-drop, thinking how horrified Mother would be to see this, a makeshift hut, not even attached to the house, of wood and corrugated iron, housing a crudely constructed lavatory poised above an eight-foot pit.

I am accustomed to it now, but I cannot deny that in those early days of being here, if I needed to go in the middle of the night, I felt far more comfortable holding it than risking going outside in the dark. But now? Of course I still check for snakes – I would be unwise not to – and I still listen out for those unfamiliar rustles from the nearby bushes. But I am not afraid. Rather like Alice in her wonderland, the longer I am here in this strange place built upon dusty plains and papyrus swamps, the less hostile it all feels.

I walk back into the bungalow, lock the door, ensuring the rifle sits behind it in its customary place, and stretch luxuriously, wondering what to do with the rest of my evening. It is not late and I am not tired. All the cooking is normally done in the outside kitchen, but there is a small stove in here for boiling water, so I begin to make tea.

I set a cup on the side, then stop. I can hear a soft, rustling noise coming from outside, quite unlike the murmurs of the night creatures I am accustomed to. Is someone outside? Surely not, it is too late. I must be imagining it. I frown and take my cup of fresh tea over to the table. But there it is again and this time, a voice.

'Mrs Lawrence,' I think it says. It sounds like Kamau, gentle and low. I hurry to the door and make out his features on the other side of the screen, accentuated by the dull glow of the hurricane lamp that hangs above the door.

'Kamau!' I whisper sharply, fumbling with the padlocked door and pulling it open. 'Is there something the matter?'

He walks through the door, his tall frame stooping slightly to enter the bungalow, taking his hat off as he does so.

'What are you…? Are you…?' Truly, I do not know what to say. I close the door behind him and look at him expectantly. But he simply looks at me and smiles.

'I am sorry,' he says gently. 'I hope I have not disturbed you.'

'Disturbed me?' I say, unable to keep the nervousness from my voice. My heart is thundering and I am excited and scared and confused. 'Not at all. As you can see…' I trail off and desperately gesture around the room, 'I am quite alone this evening.'

'Yes,' he replies before we lapse into an awkward silence.

'How are—' we both begin at the same time, then both break off. The paraffin lamp is flickering, changing the colour of Kamau's skin from slate to copper to ebony within a single second. The varying shades of brown, just as I said to him earlier as we walked back from the schoolhouse.

'How are you?' he repeats first.

I bite at my bottom lip and take a deep breath. 'I am happy to see you.'

'You are?' Relief paints his features and his shoulders relax a fraction.

'Of course,' I say quietly. 'I am always glad to see you. Well, you and the children and…' I flail around for words and, finding none, fall silent.

Kamau takes a small step towards me and the reality of this situation, his nearness, causes me to move backwards. 'I have just made some tea,' I say hurriedly, as though it is the most normal thing in the world to be receiving visitors at – I glance at the clock hanging on the wall – nine fifteen in the evening.

'Tea? Yes, why not? You and our mutual friend Fazal certainly drink a great deal of this.'

'But of course,' I reply. 'I am English and he is Indian and surely we are the two greatest tea-drinking nations in the world. Though his tea, naturally, is rather different and though I had not tasted it before coming here, I am wondering if it is not superior to our own. All those spices and subtle flavours and—' I stop. Take a deep breath. 'Kamau, how did you know…'

'Yes?'

'How did you know that Mr Lawrence would not be here this evening?' I swallow hard, stunned that these words have left my mouth.

'I knew because… well.' He walks over to the table, pulls a chair out and sits down before looking up and smiling. 'I knew because I saw Fazal earlier and he mentioned your husband was away, hunting.'

'I see.' I walk to the stove. The water in the pot is still warm enough and, hoping that Kamau is unable to see the tremor in my hands, I place some more peppermint in the crested silver teapot and pour the water over the top of it.

I stand there for some time, not knowing what to think. 'Mrs Lawrence,' he says softly. I do not want to be Mrs Lawrence to him. I turn my head back over my shoulder.

'Please. Please call me Iris.'

I will myself to not tremble and then bring the silver teapot to the table, pour tea into a tin cup, place it in front of him and then draw my own chair up so that we sit opposite one another. I drink. He drinks. A distant animal howls beneath the nearly full moon and I am acutely aware of his presence near me. I feel that somehow I am connected to every part of him and aware of every movement along the surface of his skin.

'Iris,' he says eventually, breaking out into a smile.

'Yes?'

Still smiling widely, he clasps his hands round the tin cup. 'You were very brave this morning.'

'Brave?'

'Yes. Eating those termites. I never imagined you would actually do it. The boys weren't expecting it either.'

I feel my cheeks flushing and I look down at the table and smile before I too cannot help myself and begin to laugh.

'I know. I am not sure what I was thinking. But I never managed to eat one. Slippery little thing.'

He chuckles at the memory and takes another sip of his tea. 'This is good. What is it?'

'Peppermint. I grew it myself. But it is not as good as Mr Ahmed's.'

'*Just* as good as Mr Ahmed's.'

'Kamau,' I say, so suddenly and loudly that I even take myself by surprise.

'Yes?'

'Kamau. Why have you come here?'

I wait for him to answer and the entire time he does not take his eyes from my face. I do not need him to answer this question, but I feel I must ask anyway. I need to hear it from him.

'Can I ask you something in return?'

I nod.

'Why did you come to the schoolhouse this morning?'

My breath catches. Of course, my being near the schoolhouse is no stranger than him turning up here this evening. We are both acutely aware of this, but how to put it into words?

'I was not at the schoolhouse.'

'Near enough.'

'Yes…' I pause. 'Near enough.' My fingers instinctively reach out to drum on the tabletop. 'I – I suppose I wanted to see you.'

I am not looking at him but I know that his eyes are upon me.

'Yes,' he says. 'So you also have the answer to your question.'

I cannot bring myself to look up at him; to read what I know rests in his eyes. I know what exists between the two of us because I can feel it, deep in the pit of my stomach, and it would serve no purpose to deny it. *Iris*, I say to myself, *all you must do is ask him to leave. Ask him to go and he will. He respects you, he will leave without a fuss.* And as I continue to drum my fingers on the tabletop, I form these words in my head but they do not come out of my mouth, as though my thoughts and my physical body are not connected at all, not unlike the walk I took this morning.

Kamau reaches a hand out and places it over mine to steady the drumming of my fingers. The sudden physical contact takes me by surprise and I take a sharp intake of breath.

CHAPTER TWENTY-SEVEN

BENEDICT KAMAU

We sit in quiet stillness as I feel her fingers, beating like the wings of sunbirds against the table, calming and settling beneath mine. She does not have to say a word; I know she is agonising over whether or not to remove it. And now? Now what happens? Of this, I am unsure. But her face, before so solemn, breaks slowly into a smile.

Slowly, I lift my hand away, but rather than stretching it back to my side of the table, I draw it up alongside hers and lay it against her warm cheek, my fingers intertwined with hers. Her skin feels exactly as I imagine it would: smooth as the river's surface on a windless day. I look into Iris's eyes.

I take her hand away from my cheek and turn it over slowly in both of mine, carefully, inspecting it as a precious item. Against my own hands, hers looks whiter than ever. It is the white of the moon and of the snow that Ngai spills from the sky onto Kirinyaga's peaks. And then I bring her fingers to my lips and close my eyes. I am not sure if I have ever been as happy as I feel at this moment and I want to reach deep within me and store this moment in my memory for evermore: the softness of her fingertips, the gentle grace of her pale hand.

CHAPTER TWENTY-EIGHT

IRIS LAWRENCE

Kamau opens his eyes and moves my fingers along the length of his soft mouth, his lips. I place our interlaced hands back on the table, looking from Kamau's face to our fingers, and there is something so strange but so comforting about seeing them intertwined with mine. He looks at me searchingly.

'What is it?' I ask quietly.

'Iris,' he breathes. 'Iris.'

'Shall I make some more tea?' I ask, slowly pulling my hand from beneath his. I am struck by the sudden absence of his touch.

'I have barely started my first cup yet.' He laughs softly and stands up, pushing back his chair and walking round the table so that he is standing a handspan away from me.

'Iris.' He says my name again. I like the way he says my name. I am turned away from him, staring unblinkingly over the tabletop. But I slowly turn my head and look up.

He places a hand out to me and for a moment I just sit there and stare at it as though it is a foreign object. I sense that he is about to let it drop. But I cannot let it and I stir, steadily placing my hand in his. Gently, he pulls me up.

And now we stand opposite one another. He is about half a head taller than me. He still has one of my hands in his and now he takes the other. I am trembling slightly and he squeezes both my hands.

'Are you alright?' he asks.

'No. I mean—' I break off and frown. 'What I mean is, not that I am unhappy you are here. Quite the contrary.' I shake my head, causing the light from the hurricane lamp to flicker. 'I am scared of my feelings for you.'

'Why?'

'You know why, Kamau. I am married. I am scared, and confused. Like Alice in Wonderland.'

He smiles. 'Who is Alice in Wonderland?'

'She is the heroine of a book I have loved for a very long time.'

'I would like very much to see that book.'

'Shall I go and get it?' I ask.

He squeezes my hands. 'Yes. But not now.'

My smile fades and I turn my face towards him. Very slowly, he moves closer and brings his lips to mine.

How to explain how it feels? How the weight of the air around us changes, becoming lighter? All I know is it is the first time I have truly been kissed. I think of the picture of the sunbird that Kamau drew and I imagine it taking flight from the page, being steeped in colour and life and flying away.

My hands raise of their own volition and they feel the warm ring of his neck above his shirt collar and below the graze of black hair. His mouth is soft and tastes of peppermint tea and, suddenly, he pulls away and stares at me, eyes wide, lips broadening into a smile.

He has a small scar on one side of his nose, a line of skin a fraction lighter. He has a habit of flaring his nostrils slightly. He has high, defined cheekbones that, even when he is looking down, lift his entire face. He is extremely handsome.

'Iris,' he murmurs again.

I push gently past him, turn and hold my hand up to him. I am walking on water, gliding upon the swell of waves. There is no urgency to our movements, only a sense of knowing, of belief, of inevitability.

In the bedroom, the mosquito net is doubled up with stretched colobus monkey skins to protect against the cold of Nairobi's nights, hanging down from the roof all around the narrow wooden bed. I walk around the bed, pushing the net upwards on all sides, a task made more difficult and cumbersome by those skins. But once I have achieved it, I turn back to him. He is standing beside the window, the curtains mostly drawn and the pale, silver moonlight filtering through the space and catching the gleaming sheen of his ebony skin.

I return to his side and move close to him so that we stand a breath apart. He reaches for both my hands again and they feel warm and safe inside his.

'What is that bird?' I whisper.

'Which one?'

'That. That sound. Listen.'

We both fall silent as we take in the depth of silence in the bedroom and then the small sounds, cries and echoes that begin to transcend the quiet stillness. We hear a shrill calling sound that rises and falls and I pull gently at his hands. 'That one,' I breathe.

'A nightjar.'

'What does it look like?'

'It's small. Smaller than you would imagine with that call, with a tiny little bill and large, spreading wings.'

'So nothing like the sunbird.' I edge a little closer to him.

'No,' he breathes. 'Nothing like the sunbird.' He brings his lips closer to mine until I can feel his warm, sweet breath feathering out across my cheeks. His eyes narrow as the deep blackness of them is lost. Then I place my hands against his smooth cheeks and bring my lips to his. The kiss we share is wondrous: rays of sunlight and streaks of moonlight against the steady symphony of nightjars. I never want this to end. I think that I should like to be locked in this embrace with Kamau for hours, days.

His hands move down my face and rest lightly on my shoulders before continuing, down my arms until they sit cradling my waist. I feel the unmistakable stirrings of desire from somewhere deep within me and I press my mouth deeper on to Kamau's. His tongue, caressing mine, is soft and immeasurably gentle and I almost cannot feel my feet, my legs, my arms. My entire body feels numb.

CHAPTER TWENTY-NINE

BENEDICT KAMAU

It is her hair that I long to touch now. For I have never touched the hair of a white person and I have little idea how it will feel. Will it be coarse like the *m'tama* we use to make flour with or fluid as the linen sheets the *mundu mweru* sleep under?

It is parted at the centre and hangs down in two curves over her forehead in such a way that they look like wings. First I let both hands run over these wings and, somehow, it seems so appropriate, for my first impression is that they feel like nothing more or less than water. She is smiling at me as I do this, with a lovely combination of shyness and curiosity, her beautiful jacaranda eyes resting on me, containing, I am quite certain, trust.

I move both my hands and run them through the dark hair at the top of her head that ripples and yields to my touch, just as I imagined. As my hands move across the waves, hard little ridges reveal themselves. Pins. At least, I think that is what they are. I move my fingers in to manipulate them and tug at them, though several are stuck in hard. She doesn't reach up to help me and I am glad of this.

We are not far from the bedside table and I place each pin carefully on top of it. Fourteen... fifteen... sixteen... Her hair now lies in disarray, one side up and the other side down; she looks muddled and beautiful. Now, with one final tug, the last pin is out and the rest of Iris's hair tumbles down, far longer and thicker than I could ever have imagined.

I simply stare at the dark waves in wonder and disbelief and then gather up one handful that hangs loose over one of her shoulders and, with the other hand, run my fingers through it. Water. Flowing water. And then, for I cannot help myself, I raise the handful and lower my head and take a deep breath.

I close my eyes. And there it is, the unmistakable smell of the red dust and warm earth of my land that I have been born into, cried into, grown on, danced on and walked upon. I had imagined a smell of English soap or those strange slabs of bread and butter her people eat but no, she smells of my land. She is of my land.

I look upwards and my mouth is the width of a whistling thorn from hers. I do not want to think what I am doing, to dwell too closely on the implications of this.

She is, I think, the most beautiful being I have ever seen. Her hair falls through my fingers like sand and her lips are curved into a smile. I think that I have never seen her looking so happy or so radiant and feel a deep well of gratitude and joy that I may be a part of the cause of this. Abruptly, she pulls away from me and unbuttons her blouse, pulling it over her head and dropping it so that it lies on the floor like a gleaming white puddle in the moonlight. Then, with unsteady fingers, she unties the clasp that keeps her skirt up and this, too, drops and lies in a heap before she pushes it away with her foot.

I have never seen this thing before that binds and ensnares a woman and is tied up at the back. 'What is this?' I ask.

'A corset,' she murmurs.

'It is for what purpose?'

'I suppose to make our waists look thinner than they truly are.'

I cannot help but laugh. 'Your waist is thin enough. You do not need this.'

'I know,' she replies. 'But this is what I must endure for the sake of fashion and convention.'

'Even here in Africa?' I continue. 'You are not walking down the streets of England now. Nobody would know if you were wearing one or not.'

'My husband,' she says, her voice catching on the word, 'my husband would know.' I sense she does not want to say his name, but now that he has been mentioned, I cannot help but notice the sudden heaviness that falls upon her shoulders and her face compacting and clouding. I do not wish to dwell on Mr Lawrence either. I run one finger down the length of her cheek. She sighs again and looks directly at me; she is unsmiling but her eyes are shining and she brings her mouth close to my ear and whispers, 'Help me untie my corset.'

She turns round and pulls her long hair that falls like a rope down her back over one shoulder and I tug at the strings round her slender back with my trembling fingers so that this strange and unnatural thing she is forced to wear loosens. Once I can do no more she turns back to me, places her arms above her head and smiles at me, willing me with her deep blue eyes to take it off. So I do, lifting it above her head, and now, without this strange, restrictive device, Iris looks entirely different, freer. Yet there remains beneath her corset a thin cotton garment that hugs her breasts.

'And this?' I whisper as I place my hands on her waist. 'What is this called?'

'A chemise,' she whispers back. Once more, she lifts her arms above her head and I pull her garment over them, as soft as camphor leaves, and leave it on the steadily mounting pile of clothes on the floor. She is now naked from the waist up. She has small, firm breasts and her skin is as white and untainted as the linen sheets that lie upon her bed. I sink my head between her breasts and draw my hands up on either side so that they rest lightly on her skin. I don't want to hurt her. I want to do nothing that would hurt this woman in any way. I want only to cherish her in the way I know she deserves to be cherished but has not been, I sense, for much of her life.

Reluctantly, I pull my head back and look at her closely. 'You,' I say slowly, 'are beautiful.' She says nothing for several moments, only continues to stare at me intently, the faintest hint of a smile on her lips.

'And you,' she murmurs, 'are also.'

CHAPTER THIRTY

IRIS LAWRENCE

For he is. And as he begins to remove his own clothes, it takes my breath away to see his body. Items fall away one by one – his long-sleeved shirt, his trousers – and then he pulls off the vest that clings to his chest like a second skin. He wears nothing beneath his trousers. And whilst I have, of course, seen both African men and women almost naked, as is often their custom, it is entirely different to be standing before a man who has unclothed himself only for me. A man with smooth skin the colour of the sharp and flat notes on the pianoforte at The Old Vicarage; a man with full lips I should like to linger on with mine pressed against his; a man with a gentle dip embedded in each cheek that only show when his mouth curves into a smile; a man with a gift for capturing and recording the birds of Africa on paper; a man who, at this moment, belongs to me and me only.

Kamau hooks one firm arm under my waist and another around the higher part of my back and lifts me onto the bed, as though I am light as a bird. We kiss again, more deeply this time, almost as though we wish to feel the very essence of one another that we have so yearned for in the past weeks, wanting to draw out one another's very life force so that we may claim a portion of it and hide it in a secret chamber of our own being.

I am lying back on the bed, my hair splayed out against the pillow, now wearing only my undergarments. Slowly and with infinite tenderness, Kamau unties the bow round my waist and I arch my back up to allow him to slip the undergarments seamlessly down. I lift myself up on my elbows, look at him long and hard and, as I move closer to him, he presses his lips softly to my neck, to my ear, to my mouth.

I have never known before what it is to feel pleasure of this kind; for a body to fit to mine; for warm, supple skin to respond to my touch or my own skin to ripple and sigh when he touches me. Nor have I ever seen anything to quite equal the beauty of his strong, confident body, two shades lighter than the night sky. In Kamau's arms, I feel instantly safe, needed, cherished, and that serves only to make me kiss him more deeply and to reach for those secret parts of his body to make them come alive.

Even if I feel shocked at my own behaviour at first, it does not and cannot last as my own desire for this man overwhelms me. Sitting with my legs wrapped round his waist, I ease myself down on to him and Kamau moans softly, pulling my body in closer and placing his lips against my breasts.

'Iris,' he murmurs. 'Iris, Iris.'

I smile to hear him say my name so, with such tenderness, and I tighten my legs round his waist as we rock back and forth, something building inside me. It is a feeling so foreign that I do not know what to do with it, but it is stronger than me and I can do nothing except let it carry me. I hear breathing, loud and laboured, which I come to recognise as my own mingled with Kamau's, and as the feeling of intensity grows, so too do the sounds that escape my mouth.

With a sudden, sharp sensation, I experience release as he grips me firmly to him, his lips at my neck and my hands clasping his back. My eyes are clenched tightly shut but in this new moment of quiet, I slowly open them and see my hands gripping his dark back, slick with sweat. After some time of sitting like that, still, marvelling at one another's presence, I draw back and look into his eyes. I can just see my outline and the glow from the hurricane lamp mirrored in their black intensity and he moves his mouth onto mine, kissing me with a new tenderness.

CHAPTER THIRTY-ONE

BENEDICT KAMAU

This woman with skin the colour of a Nairobi dawn, she is a marvel: from the grace of her hands to the turned-earth shade of her hair to her ability to let go, she is a marvel. I think I shall never tire of feeling her lips part against mine, as though she has been waiting to be opened like this to the world. When I slowly, reluctantly ease out of her, we lie beside one another on the bed, listening to the distant cry of hyenas. I lightly move my fingertips up and down her arm as she nestles in beside me, her long hair tumbling onto my stomach. The night has grown cold and I pull the sheet over both of us.

My heart might burst with longing for Iris if I leave her now, not knowing when I might see her again, but it is only a matter of time before I must do so. Her breath grows heavier and I look down to see her face, but beneath her dark lashes she is still awake. I wonder what she is thinking.

'Iris,' I whisper. She tilts her beautiful face sleepily up towards me and smiles. 'Iris, I must go.'

Her arm, flung across my chest, tightens a fraction. 'Don't go,' she replies, not taking her eyes from mine for a moment. 'Don't.'

And so I do not. We remain in silence for some time, our arms and legs entwined. I have no right to be here and with each minute that passes I feel the knowledge of that weighing on me. Yet, at the same time, I feel as though I don't want to leave Iris's side ever again. What has been building between us, this feels sacred and right, almost as though I have been searching for her all my life.

'Kamau,' she says in a soft murmur. 'Who do you live with?'

I sweep my fingers through her silken hair. 'Nobody. I live alone, in my *thingira*.' I smile to myself, a sad, ironic smile. For only I know how far I have turned from my traditions and that my home no longer, in the Kikuyu sense, constitutes a true *thingira*.

She inclines her head towards me. 'What does that mean?'

'*Thingira*? It means bachelor hut.'

She nods and sighs gently, a sigh of relief, I'm sure. For she wasn't to know that I am unmarried, though the fact that she is would not have made matters any less complicated.

'And your family?' she asks. 'Tell me about them.'

I take some strands of her hair and wind them round my finger. 'I don't have any family left,' I say. I thought I had managed to keep my voice even while saying the words, but the way Iris squeezes me tighter makes me realise that still, after all these years, I am unable to keep the emotion hidden when I think of them.

'You don't have to talk about it if you'd rather not,' she whispers, and I instinctively bend down and kiss her smooth forehead.

'I do want to talk about them.' And it is strange, for I really do. For the first time in I do not know how many years, I want to bring the spirits of my dead family alive again.

'I was the youngest of five,' I tell her, 'the *kehinganda*. This is the last child, the one who closes the womb and is nurtured by everyone in my family: my three elder brothers and one elder sister, both my parents and also all my grandparents. I was happy. I was given a small garden to tend and I grew maize, sweet potato, a few stalks of sugarcane. Life was simple and I knew no different. My mother made pottery and also baskets, with great skill, from the strings of small shrubs called *mogio*. I would help her to chew the bark to make it softer before laying it outside our hut in the sun to dry and then when this was done my mother would wind the strings together to form a ball, ready to start making the basket. When she was trading at the market, she could get a lot in return for those baskets because they were so finely crafted.'

I pause and blink as I see the ghost of my mother walk across my mind, her unlined skin and the colourful beads encircling her wrists, neck and strung through her long earlobes, her wide, open smile that I always felt was mine and mine only.

'My father. *Baba*. He was skilled in playing the *motoriro*. This was a flute crafted out of bark and was only played at leisure time. Although he spent most of his time rearing our wealth of sheep and goats and tending to the ancestral land, the memories that stay with me most are those of when he was playing his *motoriro*. I remember him so well, standing

on a high platform beside one of our fields. He had his cata-
pult slung over one wrist to scare away the birds when they
tried to come and eat the millet. But during the periods of
quiet, he would stand up there and play. It was the most
beautiful sound I have ever heard.'

I fall silent again. The truth is, I knew my father little.
He had four wives, my mother being the second, and a great
many children. I respected him, but the feelings I had for
him never came close to the bond I shared with my mother.
I sigh. Which parts of this story to share with Iris? Which to
keep to myself? I look down at her arm, pale as moonlight,
encircling my waist, marvelling once more that she should
want me to stay with her. Emboldened by this knowledge,
I take a deep breath.

'There was a man, long ago, a great man in Kikuyuland
by the name of Mogo Wa Kebiro, who practised medicine
and his task was to foretell important events that were to
come. Well, the story goes that one morning, he woke up
not being able to speak and he was also covered in inex-
plicable bruises and trembling uncontrollably. The wives
of the great medicine man were so beside themselves with
worry that they immediately summoned the elders and offered a sacrifice to Ngai.'

'Who is Ngai?' asks Iris. Why it should be a surprise that
she has never heard the name Ngai being spoken, I do not
know. And yet, in a small, strange way, it pains me.

'Ngai.' I exhale. 'He is the divine being and creator of
the Kikuyu tribe. He resides in Mount Kirinyaga. After a
thenge, a male goat, was sacrificed and Mogo was seated on

the animal's raw skin, a senior elder took the blood of the goat and mixed it with a little oil before placing it on the great medicine man's head. All the while the elders recited ritual songs and it wasn't long before Mogo found his voice again. He told them that whilst he slept the night before, Ngai had revealed the future to him.'

Iris pushes herself up and turns to me, her eyes gleaming. 'Is this a true story?'

I laugh lightly. 'As I said, it's how the story goes.'

'Carry on,' she says, her face enraptured. I breathe it in, this beautiful face, her lips parted slightly and her dark hair spilling over one breast, leaving the other bare. 'What did Ngai reveal?'

'Well…' I pause. In no way do I want Iris to read any culpability from this story. I reach out and run a finger down her cheek. 'The medicine man dreamt that a strange race of people would arrive in Kikuyuland, with clothes like the wings of butterflies and skin the colour of *kiengara*, a light-coloured frog.'

'Us,' she breathes, her eyes wide.

CHAPTER THIRTY-TWO

IRIS LAWRENCE

He nods. I love watching him talk: the slight flare of his nostrils, his full lips curving and dark eyes flashing with intelligence and intensity. Glancing down and seeing our legs wrapped up in one another's, I think of the skin of a zebra and smile.

Kamau takes a deep breath and continues. 'The old medicine man Mogo's prediction continued that not only would they wear peculiar clothes and have strange-coloured skin, but they would bring with them magical sticks emitting streams of fire that can injure others far more severely than the poisoned arrows we were accustomed to. Following this, a long iron snake would appear, bellowing smoke and fire and cutting through the heart of our land. And then…'

Kamau pauses and turns his head slightly away from me and I know that this is the part of his narrative that is not easy for him to share with me. It is peculiar to be sitting here and listening to this because whilst he is not referring to me personally, it is the story of my people in these lands. And the more he talks, the more I am filled with a sense of

foreboding for what is to come and how my people have
wronged his.

'And then,' Kamau says after some time, 'Mogo predicted that the Kikuyu would suffer a great famine and a disease
called *ndigana*. It would kill all the cattle and the crops and
this time of hunger would signal that greater numbers of
the frog-coloured people were almost here.'

He falls silent again as he turns his proud face back, entwines
his fingers with mine and brings my hand up to his mouth.

'Was it this famine – did your family…?' I cannot finish
my question, but I see in his eyes that this is how Kamau's
family perished. 'How old were you?'

'I was eight,' he replies. 'The *kehinganda*, remember, the
last child of my mother who closed the womb and, in many
ways, the most cherished. First there was a terrible drought,
the worst in living memory even of my *guuka* and *coco*, my
grandparents. Next the crops failed, even my small garden
that I had loved and cherished and worked on with my
moro, the digging stick *Baba* made me, it all withered up
and died. Of the little food that there was, most of it kept
coming to me. I tried to protest, I tried to share it equally
round all my family but I was hungry, so hungry. I…' He
breaks off and sighs and I squeeze his hands tightly.

'It's not your fault they died, Kamau,' I say quietly.

'I know.' He smiles weakly and chews on the inside of
his mouth for a moment. 'But sometimes that is not easy
to believe.'

I run my hand up and down his arm, long and smooth
and strong. I sense that he wants to talk about this more,

that this is a great burden he has carried with him for many years. And I am right, for he presently continues, almost as though he has started this story and now he must finish it and tell me everything; all of it.

'Nobody survived in my immediate family except me. They all died, every last one of them. My grandparents, my parents, my brothers and sisters... Wanjiku, she was my favourite, the next child up from me. She was just one year older and we would do everything together. She had a doll with hair made from *mogio*, the same shrub used to weave baskets, and she would carry it around all the time and make clothes for it from goatskins and beds from river clay. Wanjiku...' He pauses. 'You know, this is the first time I have talked about all of this.'

I open my eyes wide with surprise. 'The first time ever?'

He nods.

'But what about the man, the priest who cared for you all those years?'

'Ah.' He nods again and smiles sadly. 'You see, when Father Dutton came across this scene of devastation, all these dead and dying people – for I was, I suppose, dying myself – and he took me back to his mission, first of all I did not speak a word of English, only Kikuyu. And by the time I was sufficient enough in English, I did not really want to talk about it. And then I learnt how to read and write, taking the white man's power that I had always feared. And I was given the white man's clothes. And by the time Father Dutton died, I was different. I was no longer the Kikuyu boy I had once been.'

I look at his face, so transformed with pain and a wrenching guilt that I draw him into my arms. Feeling him pressed up against me like that, I hope that I am able to offer him a little solace and, in return, his nearness and warmth comforts me, for the emotion I feel at what this man has endured in his life overwhelms me.

'Mogo's predictions were right,' I whisper into his neck.

'Yes,' Kamau replies. 'But, he tells the people not to fight against these *orori*, the strangers who come, but that they must be treated with courtesy. So my people, who were generous in spirit, fed these wandering white spirits, whom they believed to be lonely, offering them temporary occupation on their land. But it wasn't long before the Kikuyu realised they had been tricked and that the frog-coloured people would not return the land.'

Kamau pauses, draws back from me slightly and looks at me. How can I possibly understand what he has been through? What his entire people have endured? He strokes a finger down my arm and says, 'You do not have skin the colour of a frog. It is not a flattering description.'

I laugh softly, possibly in relief. 'What colour *is* my skin?'

'Your skin,' he responds as he continues to run a finger gently up and down my arm, 'is the colour of the moonlight. See…' He reaches back and pulls the curtain open a fraction and the light of the near-full moon falls down upon us, a pool of pale light resting upon Kamau's shoulders and my arms. 'The colour,' he repeats, tracing the light on my arm with his fingertips, 'of moonlight.'

I look down at it, marvelling at the contrasting shades of our skin. I wish for a moment that Kamau did not have to leave; that Mr Lawrence might never come back and he could stay in this corrugated-iron-roofed bungalow with me and how happy we might be.

'What happened to everybody else in your family?' I ask. 'Your half-brothers and sisters, I mean, and the other wives of your father?'

Kamau shakes his head. 'I don't know. For a long time whilst I was at the mission, I wanted to go back and look for them, for anybody who had been a part of my old life. But with each year that passed, this desire grew less and less. But I saw some of them, that day…'

'That day?'

'Yes. I won't ever forget it. You see, there is a belief amongst the Kikuyu that illness and disease is brought about by evil spirits, carried from one homestead to another by the wind. But you don't have to passively accept what the spirits bring and if you choose to fight them, you should do so in the evening, around the time when the moon rises. After so many people in my community died, the elders believed we were fighting the very worst kind of spirits.'

'Do you believe that?'

He smiles again, his eyes smouldering and still sad. 'I'm not sure I know what I believe any more, Iris.' He entwines his fingers with mine. 'But all our people, not long after my family died, we came out to fight the evil spirits. I don't know if this is what my people still do, but the war horns were sounded and people took up their sticks and clubs and ran from their huts, beating the sticks together and shouting as loudly as they could to scare the spirits. I remember beating the bushes on either side of me as I moved towards the river and that I was crying uncontrollably, so much that I could barely see the path before me. I wanted to kill these evil spirits that had killed my family more than I'd wanted anything in my life. At the river, we had to shout as loudly as our voices would permit once again and amidst the war horns and the beating of the sticks, all the weapons and clubs were hurled with great force into the river whilst we cried that we had defeated the evil spirits and all the sickness held in them. We then beat the dust from our feet and our clothes to remove the remaining vestiges of spirits and return to our homesteads. The custom dictated that we must not look back when we returned, not for an instant.'

'Why?'

'So that we could turn our backs on the evil spirits and cast them entirely from our minds once this ritual was over. But I did, you see. I did look back, because I was still crying as though I might never stop, my heart breaking over and over again, and I felt that as well as leaving the evil spirits to perish in the river, I was also abandoning my family. And when I looked back, I saw a few of the other children of my father and I could not understand why they were alive but my own family were not.'

He falls suddenly silent and I can see that recounting this painful period of his life has cost him dearly. He leans back on the pillow, one arm resting above his head, and closes his eyes briefly. I watch him, the shadows of the evil spirits moving behind his closed lids, until he opens his raven eyes again and smiles sadly at me. 'And now,' he says, 'I think we have talked enough about my family. Tell me about yours.'

And so, as the moonlight fades and begins to mingle with the approaching dawn, I talk. I talk as though my words have no beginning and no end and I realise how important this has been for me, for *both* of us, to share our disappointments, our injuries, our joys wrapped up in our families and how they have embraced us and wounded us.

By the time I have finished talking, dawn has broken. We lie entwined on the sheets. My head is on his chest and he strokes my hair, the contrast of our skin starker than ever.

'Iris,' Kamau says softly, tilting my chin up so that I am looking into his eyes. 'When will your husband be back?'

The mention of my husband causes a physical pain to clutch at my chest. 'Not until this evening.'

'Are you sure?'

'Yes,' I nod. 'I am sure.'

'I think…' he says slowly, '…that I must go soon. Before there are too many people about.'

I nod again. 'Will you take this book with you?' I reach beneath the mosquito net and pick up *Alice's Adventures in Wonderland*. 'If you read this book,' I say, 'you will understand who I was as a child.'

'I would like to understand every part of you.'

'You already do,' I reply, and I feel surprise and recognition even as I utter the words.

We stare at one another for a long time, not smiling, just a deep understanding passing between us. I reach out and touch his face with my fingertips and he moves slowly towards me and kisses me deeply.

We make love again, in the breaking dawn as the sound of the whistling thorns carries across the plains. And this time, it is not the lovemaking of two people unsure of one another, but something so profound that I cry out from the depth of my being, winding myself around him and never wanting to let him go. When it is finished, he draws my face away and tenderly kisses both of my closed eyelids.

'Sunbird,' I whisper in the silver light of dawn. 'You are my sunbird.'

❧ ❧ ❧

Mr Lawrence comes home triumphantly that Sunday evening, tired, filthy and ravenously hungry. When he appears I am sitting out on the verandah, a blanket covering my knees. His face, even beneath his hat, is sunburnt. He looks pleased to see me; no doubt he thinks I am waiting for him. I look up at him as he approaches; the shock of his presence after what has passed between Kamau and myself delivers a physical pain to my chest. And then I notice it: the slash across one cheek, a smouldering raw pink wound.

He must notice the direction of my gaze, for he touches his fingertips to his right cheek and an oblique, ghoulish smile twists onto his face.

Instinctively, my fingertips reach up and graze my own cheek. 'What…'

'It is nothing,' he replies, still smiling. 'Or rather, these are the claw marks of a lion.'

'A lion,' I repeat numbly. 'You mean…' My voice trails off at the same time as I notice his entire stature widening and lengthening in pride.

'Yes,' he replies, a tremor in his voice. 'I killed a lion. *What*,' he adds, 'do you think of that, my dear?'

I continue to stare at him. I feel only disgust. I purse my lips, look down to my lap and reply quietly, 'Well done.'

'Well done,' he echoes and sniggers. I do not want to look up at him, for I know I have irritated him. He wanted a great welcome-home ceremony, the return of the sensational, triumphant hunter. But he knows I am not the one to give him this. His precious Nora no doubt would have given him a different welcome.

He takes a step closer to me. I smell whisky on him, but something else besides. It is desire, perhaps the triumph of the kill, exuding potently from his pores. For the first time, I feel truly afraid of him and I cannot bear to meet his eye. Before I know it, he has taken two further strides towards me. He pulls me up from the chair as the blanket spills across the wooden floor and kisses me hard on the mouth. My lips remain closed, a hard, unyielding line, and I can taste the fury on his mouth.

'Dammit, Iris,' he cries, pulling away. 'What is it?'

Tears sting at my eyes and I gasp for breath, shaking my head over and over again. 'It is nothing,' I plead. 'I am just tired. Please—'

'*You*,' he hisses in a low, sinister voice, 'are my wife and you will not dictate my passions.' A sob escapes from me and I clamp my hand over my mouth, but he yanks it down, pulling me roughly into the house.

I do not know what kind of evil, transformative experience he underwent during his hunting expedition, but a new power-lust has sprung up in him and the pain I experience is unbearable. I sob as he plunges himself deeper and deeper inside me, and then from every angle, but the louder I cry, the more he seems to be enjoying himself. But then I just become numb to it. It appears to matter not whether I am alive nor dead beneath him and so I close my eyes tightly, grasp the sides of the bed and think of Kamau's smile.

❧ ❧ ❧

I have thought of nothing but Kamau since he left; the earthy scent and smoothness of his skin and the low, sanguine voice with which he related his story to me and told me I was beautiful. I long more than anything to find a way to see him again – just to be near him would be enough. But I hear nothing from him over the following week. I know that he must be feeling as afraid as I am, the knowledge that the risk we took to be together as weighty as gravity. I am certain we are both now turning over the very same question, this question with no beginning or end or answer: What now?

Ten days pass and I know I must see him again before something in me bursts. I wait for Mr Lawrence to leave, almost willing him through the door. I loathe the very sight of him more than ever, from the tip of his black-hair-sprouting toes all the way up to his glassy monocle and fair, thinning hair.

When he has left and I let Muthoni into the house, I tell her that I am going for a walk and she smiles at me in that new way of hers. I pause, frowning. She has been behaving a little strangely for a while, ever since that Sunday morning when she turned up unexpectedly to check on me and I felt sick with relief that Kamau had left before she arrived. But this consolation is marred by my having to ask myself whether she may have seen him leaving the bungalow, not to mention my fear of pregnancy. Even if Muthoni *did* see him leave, this is not something we should ever be able to talk about. As I think of her recent loaded smiles, I cannot help but wonder.

'Muthoni.'

'Yes, Memsaab?'

'Do you – did you…' I hesitate.

'Yes?' She is standing very close to me and I can almost sense her holding her breath.

I sigh and shake my head. 'Nothing. Nothing, Muthoni. I will be back soon.'

She nods and smiles at me and I feel her eyes on my back as I walk away from the bungalow. She does not even need to say anything; it is there, unspoken, written into the expressions upon her face and the new, strangely familiar way she leans towards me to hear me speak. But I know she would never say anything; her smiles express complicity and nothing else. I trust Muthoni – she is my friend.

And Kamau? How I have yearned for him the past ten days. I know that I shall be interrupting his teaching but I can wait for him when it is the children's break time. When I approach the schoolhouse, I clear a space beneath an acacia tree and sit and wait for the children to tumble outside, but before much time has passed, I realise that there is no sound coming from inside. Slowly, I approach the long, low building and peer through a window. Sure enough, there is not a single person in there, although it is a Thursday and it seems strange they should not be there.

I walk beyond the schoolhouse, following the Nairobi River, the exact same path I took not long ago when I had watched the termite mounds being built. And in a clearing, not far from there, I see Kamau and his entire class of students, all crouching on the ground, lost in excited concentration on something he is showing them. I stand back slightly so that I may watch unobserved. Kamau is speaking in rapid Kikuyu, pointing and jabbing at something in the circle before them, the children craning their necks forwards to see and squealing. At one point, after one child says something to him, Kamau throws back his head and laughs with wild abandon. Watching the sincerity and openness of this simple gesture, I feel my heart contract. To watch him fills me with joy and pain in equal measure.

After some time, Kamau stands and stretches his hands high above his head, arching his back. He says something to the children and they too stand up and I know they will be passing me soon. So I choose this moment to step out from under the shade of the tree. He sees me immediately, several moments before any of the children do, and he stares at me intently. I catch my breath as I take in his features and I wonder if it was wrong of me to come here, if I should have waited for him to come to me when he was ready. But before I can dwell upon that any longer, his face transforms and he smiles at me in the same way that he laughed just moments before, unrestrainedly and joyously, and I smile back in pure relief and happiness.

We walk back to the schoolhouse together, the children fighting over who is to take my hand, only one or two still scared of me in the way they were the first time I met them all. I am so overcome with happiness at seeing him that I find myself lost for words. How I wish that all these pupils could momentarily vanish so that I might pull him into my arms. But for now, at least, I must content myself with his nearness and listen to his deep, melodic voice as he speaks to the children in Kikuyu whilst they swing on my arms.

When we reach the schoolhouse, I say that I do not wish to disturb him and that I will take my leave. He takes a hurried step towards me.

'You are not disturbing us. Don't go.'

He stands about a metre from me, but it is the longest metre I have ever known. Hearing him say those words, *Don't go*, I am taken back to the night we spent together and how I said those exact same words to him. How clear it is that we long for one another's company, for more precious time with each other.

And so I do not leave. I sit on a bench at the back of the classroom, wedged between two giggling boys, and watch him continue with the nature lesson as he draws the birds and the insects they discovered and the children copy these onto their slates. All the while, I can feel his eyes upon me and it feels like an eternity before he is able to release the children for their break and they pour through the open door like a swarm of bees. He walks to the back of the classroom and sits beside me.

'I have missed you,' he tells me as he gently takes one of my hands. Hearing him say those words, a wave of relief rushes through me.

I smile and nod slowly, not taking my eyes from him. 'And I have missed you.'

'I have been thinking about you, wanting to see you again. I…' He pauses, his eyes scanning my face. 'Thank you for coming.'

Suddenly we see two small heads peering in through the open door and Kamau drops my hand as though it were a hot coal as he shoos them away. He turns back to me apologetically but does not take my hand again. 'This,' he says in a quiet voice, 'is agony. You being so close but not being able to kiss you.'

I pause. 'When can I see you again?'

He doesn't say anything for a few moments, planting his palms on his thighs, and then he looks at me and raises an eyebrow. 'When is your husband going away again?'

I shake my head. 'I only wish I knew.' We remain silent for some time, the enormity of the difficulty of our predicament weighing heavily upon us. 'But…'

'Yes?' he asks, his eyes brightening with hope.

'But, I could come to you.'

'How? I mean, when would you be able to?'

'After you finish school, before my husband returns home. Perhaps…' I trail off. I am shocked to hear myself uttering these words but there is no use pretending I feel otherwise. I do desperately want to see him again, to feel his lips and smooth skin against mine, to watch the contours of his mouth whilst he speaks and relive that sensation of knowing, for the first time in my life, that I am being listened to.

He smiles at me and studies my face. 'We will find a way, Iris.'

He is right, the very nearness of him is tortuous. He suddenly stands. Glancing back briefly towards the entrance, empty of small faces, I stand too and he steers me into the corner where there is a small door leading to a storeroom. Inside, it is hot and pitch black, but I feel his lips on my throat and his hands in my hair. I twine my hands round his neck and blindly seek out his mouth, searching deep to the root of him as I kiss him. I never want it to end but know it must and, as I eventually pull away with great reluctance, he removes one of his hands from my waist, feels for my shoulder in the dark and then moves the hand down so that his palm lies over my heart.

'Iris,' he whispers.

CHAPTER THIRTY-THREE

BENEDICT KAMAU

Iris teaches again that morning and this time it lasts for longer, for neither she nor the children wish it to end. I stand at the back of the classroom, leaning against the wall and watching her. I think I could watch her for ever. She is intent on her task of teaching the names of insects and creatures in English, the pupils captivated. It would appear that each and every person in this room is transfixed by her.

As Iris teaches the word for sunbird, she turns her dark blue gaze towards me. Our eyes lock before she pulls herself back to the children. I wait for her eyes to be directed at me again as though I exist only for such stolen, secret moments and nothing else. What I would give to expand this school with her, build another room and teach the local children from across Nairobi how to read and write and do arithmetic. And speak English. Perhaps above all, speak English. We could construct a small building as a library and fill it from floor to ceiling with books. The only library I have ever seen was Father Dutton's modest one, yet to me, a boy from a tiny village in Kikuyuland, it was the greatest wonder I had ever known.

There is so much, I see, that Iris hungers for. She hungers for learning, for wisdom, for debate, for books. I can understand it. Never will I forget the first time that Father Dutton placed a book in my hands. It was *Treasure Island*. It took me a long time to read, but I barely lifted my head during all those long days as I lost myself in the adventures of Jim Hawkins and Long John Silver and Captain Smollett. How I envied Jim Hawkins; how I *wanted* to be him. How I *was* so often him, in mind, body and soul. And so I understand this connection Iris holds with Alice from her Wonderland book. Before I turned the pages of a book for myself, I never imagined the power it could hold over a person: to transform, to transport. But now I know. Now I understand.

CHAPTER THIRTY-FOUR

IRIS LAWRENCE

I go again to the schoolhouse, and again. For despite having told one another that we can find a way to be alone, Kamau and I are finding it quite impossible. During the day he teaches and at night I cannot leave the bungalow. I long with all my heart and soul for Mr Lawrence to go hunting again and even find myself forcing interest in his revolting mounted trophies so that it might encourage him away for an entire night or more. But my attempts are in vain, for Mr Lawrence is distracted with problems at work: locust swarms erasing settler coffee plantations and potato crops succumbing to beetle-triggered blight. Damn those locusts and *damn* those beetles.

Thus, I must content myself with the nearness of Kamau on those days I go to the schoolhouse to teach, when, save a few chaste kisses in the storeroom, we scarcely touch one another. He does not mind at what time of day I turn up or for how long I stay and I care less and less who may see me walking along the swampy, papyrus-strewn banks of the Nairobi River beneath my parasol. Muthoni, though we have not discussed it of course, knows where I am going. Of this, I have no doubt.

I never think of Mr Lawrence whilst I am there; I think only of the warm, dark eyes upon me and they remain with me long after I have left the schoolhouse, guiding me home in the dying light of the afternoon and keeping me company through the night. But making my way back home along the winding river late one afternoon, I feel physically peculiar. I tell myself it is the relentless heat and nothing more and drink plenty of water from my flask as I walk. But as I reach the bungalow, I am far more out of breath than usual. I grasp the wooden pillar, feeling faint. And then, with my free hand, I clutch at my stomach and bend over, retching.

Muthoni hurries from round the back of the bungalow, her charcoal eyes wide with concern. 'Memsaab!' she cries. And I heave and choke and it spills out across the wooden verandah as though there is no end whilst Muthoni grasps my arm and rubs my back and murmurs soft, soothing sounds in Kikuyu.

No, I think. *It must not be. It cannot be.*

CHAPTER THIRTY-FIVE

FAZAL AHMED

I step out of my workshop and look up at the sky, a thick band of unbroken blue and blinding sunlight. Only a few clouds are needed to give me hope, but there is nothing at all. The long rains have failed again. Whilst I am a tailor, not a farmer, and thus do not rely on the rains for my livelihood, I have lived on this land for long enough to know that the heartbeat and mechanics of Nairobi and everything beyond rely on the arrival or failure of the long and short rains.

As for me, it is a mere irritation because it is so very hot inside this workshop, so tightly hemmed in by the surrounding buildings. My neighbour on one side is a young Punjabi shoemaker and the other is a cantankerous Gujarati selling fabrics, whom I have as little to do with as possible. I stare up at the sky, willing it to cloud over, and wonder, as I have done so many times, what I am doing here. The railway is built, the cost and overspending measured and, like so many of my fellow countrymen, I am free to leave whenever I choose. There is nothing and no one that ties me to this bleak, impersonal town in the middle of East Africa. And yet somehow there *does* exist a tie, of my own making. Perhaps it is pride that I am not yet making the tidy profit I hoped I would be by now. Or that, my wife aside – whom I may in any case bring here whenever I choose – there is nothing truly for me back in my homeland?

As I stand on the doorstep, staring upwards and turning all these things over in my mind, I see a thin funnel of red dust spiralling against the blue sky. Looking down, I see a slight figure making its way along Bazaar Street, head down, the dust churning up in the figure's wake. It is not until several moments later that I realise it is Mrs Lawrence. It has been some time since I have seen her and her appearance is a pleasant distraction from the heat.

'Mrs Lawrence,' I say as she reaches me, holding my hand out to greet her, 'it is a great pleasure to see you.'

She looks up at me and I see that beneath the wide brim of her hat her eyes are red, the normal light in them gone. 'Mrs Lawrence,' I say, 'are you quite well?'

And then, to my great surprise, she begins to cry.

CHAPTER THIRTY-SIX

IRIS LAWRENCE

I am not entirely sure what I am doing here. But Mr Ahmed, though I do not know him well, is someone I count as a friend, a person I can trust. Of that, I am quite sure. But why am I not at the schoolhouse this morning, telling the first person I should tell? Because I cannot, not just yet.

I am handed a cup of Mr Ahmed's delicious chai, of which there seems to be an endless supply, and he pulls half-made garments from a chair and sits me by the open door where there is the very faintest of breezes. To Mr Ahmed's credit, he does not ask me what is wrong but silently hands me a handkerchief and allows me to keep crying until I am quite finished. Once I feel calmer, I sit staring down at the handkerchief on my lap, twisting it around my white knuckles. I take a deep sigh and look up into his concerned face.

'Mr Ahmed,' I say, 'I am not quite sure what I ought to do.'

He waits, his kind face inquisitive.

'If there is anything I can help you with, Mrs Lawrence, you know I shall do everything I am able.'

'You are so very kind.' A sob escapes and I press one hand to my mouth. 'It is not that simple though, I fear. You see, I am pregnant, Mr Ahmed.'

He is silent and I listen to the second hand's interminable journey around the wall-hanging clock and I wish he would say something, *anything*. Of course, there is no way he could know the manner in which my relationship with Kamau has developed and he must, surely, be assuming that the child is my husband's. I know I shall have to tell him the truth, to unburden myself; that, after all, is why I am here. But as the tears continue to spill from my eyes and, with trembling hands, I place the cup and saucer on the table and wrap my arms around myself, I know I cannot talk just yet.

Mr Ahmed sits in his chair opposite me. He is leaning forward a fraction, one elbow upon his knee and a fist propping up his chin. His eyes, the colour of caramel, are so kind and so concerned and I know that I can trust him, but I am terribly afraid now of what he might think of me. How might I explain the feelings I have for Kamau, his friend?

'Mrs Lawrence,' he says slowly as I wipe my eyes with the edge of his handkerchief. 'Your husband is not the father of this child, am I correct?'

I stop dabbing at my eyes, stunned. 'You knew…'

'Knew what?' he asks, smiling weakly.

'You knew that something had happened between myself and…' I trail off and the name hangs in the air between us.

'No,' he says gently. 'But I do now.'

My eyes flicker from Mr Ahmed to the open door, where a shadow suddenly plunges the pool of sunlight on the doorstep into darkness. We both notice it and he murmurs, 'A cloud…' Then he looks back at me, frowning slightly and shaking his head.

'I know what you must think of me.'

'How can you know what I am thinking, Mrs Lawrence?'

'Well,' I say, and I know there is a hint of a challenge in my voice, 'what *are* you thinking, Mr Ahmed?'

'I am thinking,' he replies slowly, 'that yours is a very difficult situation indeed. But it will not help to despair. You must remain strong, Mrs Lawrence.'

'But if,' I say in a whisper, 'if when the baby arrives and it is black, what will happen?'

'But there is every chance that it *is* your husband's, is there not?'

'I think not.' I feel one large tear steal down my cheek. 'You see, his first wife never conceived. And the timing would also indicate that there is every chance it is not.'

Mr Ahmed sighs and rubs his thumb and forefinger around the handle of his teacup. When he speaks again he does not look at me.

'When did you know for certain?'

'A fortnight ago.'

'And you have considered, I suppose… not continuing with the pregnancy?'

His eyes look up to meet mine for a moment before falling again.

'Yes,' I whisper. 'But I do not know those kind of people.'

'There are witch doctors, Mrs Lawrence, amongst the Kikuyu and the Maasai. If you like, I could make enquiries.'

'Witch doctors. I – I do not know if I could go through with something like that.'

He sighs, places his cup and saucer on the table and leans back. 'You must at least consider it, Mrs Lawrence.'

I nod and blink back the tears.

'But you have a long time still until the child is born. You must try not to worry too much for it *might*, my dear,' he leans forwards and grasps my forearm lightly, 'be fine.'

'I do not see how it can be,' I murmur, 'but it is the only vestige of hope I have now.'

'Drink.' He motions to the untouched teacup on the table. 'Drink some chai. It will help refresh you, it's so confoundedly hot.'

I obediently pick it up and take a few sips, wondering how I am to spend the next several months, how I am to endure them with this uncertainty, this fear that my child will have the same colour skin as my husband.

'I am sorry I came to tell you this, Mr Ahmed,' I say quietly, 'but you see, I do not have many friends here.'

'Mrs Lawrence,' he says firmly. 'You must not apologise for that. I am glad you felt you could confide in me. But...' he pauses, presses his finger to a fallen granule of sugar on the table, 'does Kamau know?'

Hearing him say his name like that, so openly, takes me by surprise for some reason and I look at him for a moment, startled, and shake my head.

'And your husband?'

'I think he might have noticed something, and he is waiting for me to tell him. I ought really to go to the doctor, to have it confirmed.'

'Yes,' Mr Ahmed agrees, 'you ought. But in the meantime, Mrs Lawrence, I am here. I am always here. You know how to find me and if you should need me for anything, just come.'

I look into his eyes as they stare unflinchingly at the face of an adulteress and I smile at him gratefully. 'Thank you,' I whisper.

❧ ❧ ❧

'Iris, is there something you would like to tell me?'

Mr Lawrence and I are walking back from church, my arm linked compulsorily through his. A small pied wagtail hops ahead of us on the path and I fix my eyes on it. This moment, of course, was always going to come when I would need to speak the necessary words. But now that it has arrived I am dreading saying them more than I ever imagined possible. I glance briefly towards him and see that his eyes are firmly fixed on my stomach. I take a deep breath and keep my eyes firmly on the rocky path that leads away from the church.

'Yes…' I hesitate. 'I think you already know. I wanted to tell you. I – I was waiting for the right time.'

And then he does something that takes me utterly by surprise. He stops in his tracks, grasps my other arm in an uncharacteristically gentle manner and turns me so that I am facing him. 'Iris,' he says. 'It is wonderful, truly marvel-

lous. I cannot tell you how happy it makes me. I know—'
He breaks off, clears his throat, 'I know that things have not
always been easy between us. I know there have been times
that I have not perhaps been as attentive to you as I ought.
You see, Nora was never blessed with a child. And all I have
ever really wanted was that. I believe this can be a fresh
start for us, my dear, do you not?' He is looking at me with
his pale blue, watery eyes and for a single, foolish moment
I want to tell him the truth. I want to say, *Do you not see?
Have you not noticed? I can never love you for I love another.
You are not the father of this child.*

'Iris?' Concern is etched across his thin, weathered face.
'Are you quite well, my dear? Is there anything I can do for
you?'

'I am merely tired, that is all.'

'Of course you are. You must rest. I shall look after you
from now.'

Firmly, he turns me back so that we continue to walk
along the path and his grip on my arm feels like the clamp
of an iron handcuff, my sentence. As we walk on slowly, I
wonder to myself, *Is this your way of apologising, for trying
to make up for the neglect, the rage and the pain you have
inflicted upon me?* And as the tears silently stream down my
face, I think, *It is too late for this. It is far, far too late.*

The following day, Mr Lawrence comes home straight
after work rather than going to the club. I want to be on my
own more than ever, to think through what I shall do. But
the situation remains the same the next day, and the next.
Mr Lawrence even takes me in his arms, draws me close

and then places a hand on my stomach. 'Iris.' He smiles at me, his pale eyes squinting into slits on his ravaged face. His proximity, this repellent tenderness makes me recoil. I clamp a hand over my mouth, run through the back door as it bangs angrily behind me and I heave out my insides beside the spot where he hacks up his animals.

And then, to my horror, Mr Lawrence decides to work from home.

'It is a quiet period at work, my dear. My employer is a fair man, and he has permitted me to work from the bungalow. Is that not wonderful, Iris? I can take proper care of you now.'

I stare at him, mouth agape, trying to speak. I take a deep breath. 'No – I mean, really, it is not necessary. I am fine, and Muthoni is here. I don't want to inconvenience—'

'Inconvenience me! How can that possibly be the case when you are to give birth to my first child? The first, I hope—' he breaks off, radiating pride and happiness, 'of many.'

Mr Lawrence, I wish you to go, to leave me be during the day so that Kamau can come here or I can go to him. I need to tell him. I must tell him.

Yet no matter how much I will it, this does not come to pass. We leave the house each day to 'take the air', as Mr Lawrence calls it, so that I may remain healthy for the sake of my child. But that aside, I am kept virtual prisoner. At least during these walks he does not insist upon conversation and so I am able to consider my impossible predicament. Yet no matter which way I look at it, I cannot find a solution.

During one such walk, we go to the Stanley Hotel to take tea. Mr Lawrence nods and waves over my head at people he knows whilst I stare resolutely at my slice of Victoria sponge cake and ponder how on earth I can get word to Kamau, forming a plan in my head that I shall take the train to Mombasa. Kamau will come a day after me in order not to arouse suspicion. Yet how can this work when the European community here is so small? Mr Lawrence greets his umpteenth acquaintance in the hotel. The stationmaster himself is a personal friend of Mr Lawrence's and it is quite impossible that I would be able to board the train unnoticed.

All Mr Lawrence talks of now is the arrival of the child – 'the child', for it is impossible for me to think of it as 'our' child. That and the upcoming Race Week. Mr Lawrence fills me in on the minutiae of this week with a gleam in his eye; the races aside, there will be parties, plays, polo, cricket and tennis and even rooster fighting, of all things, near the railway yards.

I feel nothing but impending dread. I do not wish to go to a thing. It's hardly Ascot; the racetrack is really just a patch of bare ground near the railway station. Besides, it is too hot and the churning sickness I feel is relentless. All I wish to do is see Kamau, to unburden myself to him – yet how am I to visit him when Mr Lawrence will not leave my side, either enthusing about the child or waxing lyrical about the joys of Race Week?

Tradition has it that everyone rides to the racetrack in one way or another. Before we reach to the bazaar, Mr Lawrence and I witness on Government Road a strange sight:

several Europeans seated in wooden, hand-pulled rickshaws whilst natives drag them over the potholed street in what appears to be a race. Two or three of the ruddy-faced Europeans are leaning far out of the rickshaws and shouting at the poor men to, 'Go Faster! Go Faster!'

Mr Lawrence hoots with laughter, clapping his hands together and calling out 'Come on! Put some welly into it!'

I stand, wincing, at the roadside as the dust churns up from the turning wheels and I close my eyes as I feel it settling over me. When I open my eyes again, I see that Mr Lawrence is staring at me in concern. 'Iris, is there something the matter?'

'You keep *asking* me that,' I snap, 'but the simple fact is that I am pregnant, and quite often I do not feel at all well.'

He is taken aback by the directness of my words and frowns, opening his mouth to reply. But he must think better of it; he closes it again, instead taking a handkerchief from his pocket and wiping his brow.

'Of course, my dear. I cannot imagine how it must be, particularly in this heat.'

I grimace. The thoughtful Mr Lawrence is just as abhorrent to me as the caustic, cruel version. Nothing he can say to me now can possibly endear me to him in any way. In fact, this new solicitude only serves to pit me against him even further.

'You know, in your condition, it might make sense to attend only the *evening* events of Race Week, such as the banquets and private dance parties and amateur theatricals. They are bound to entertain a young woman of your age and you will not be affected by this terrible daytime heat.'

What is wrong with this man? What on earth makes him think I should like to *dance*, now of all times? The headache I woke up with this morning is worsening and my nerves are fraying. I feel sick, hot and I slept terribly the previous night, dreaming of my child being born with skin the colour of night. Perhaps, I thought upon waking, I can tell Mr Lawrence that somebody broke in that night he was away hunting and forced himself upon me. Would he have any compassion in such a situation? Allow me to keep my child?

I do not respond to his last comment and we continue to walk along Government Road as I think about the answer to the question I asked myself that morning. No, if I had been raped, Mr Lawrence would never allow me to keep the child under our roof. But what would he do with it? What action would he *physically* take? This, I do not know and the uncertainty of it terrifies me.

We reach the point where we are to take our various means of transport: Scotch carts, rickshaws, two-wheeled bullock-drawn tongas, ponies, donkeys and even camels. Mr Lawrence and I board our Scotch cart and take off in a flurry of scorched dust. I look around me. The KAR officers and government officials carry ceremonial swords and wear plumed helmets, the medals on their jackets glinting in the sunlight. Even the settlers seem to have scrubbed up for the occasion; they wear Norfolk jackets and wing collars, frayed as they are. And of course the obligatory regimental or school ties, though on the whole they are rather stained. Yet I fail to be moved by any of this pageantry, and only wish to lie down.

'Heavens,' comments Mr Lawrence. 'Even the Asians appear to have washed for the occasion.' I turn my eyes bleakly towards him. 'That revolting odour of sweat does not emanate from them as strongly as usual,' he continues. I should like to push him out of the cart but instead I take a deep breath and slide my hands beneath me as I turn away from him. The Asian women are dressed in saris of many gay colours and the men wear high-collared, white linen chogas and turbans.

It is not long before I spot Mr Ahmed and I feel a little cheered by this. I am even more surprised when I notice that not only are Asians permitted into the event, but even Africans. During all the months I have been here, this is the first occasion on which it appears that the different races are permitted to freely intermingle. The Africans are carrying shields and spears, their ankles, wrists and ears adorned with heavy ornaments and their bodies wrapped in red and green blankets. I find myself scanning the crowd for Kamau, though I know this is not the kind of event he would ever come to.

Arriving at the track, Mr Lawrence helps me down from the carriage and I stare at the racehorses lined up nearby, a motley, unhealthy-looking selection, though Mr Lawrence is muttering something about the Somali and Abyssinian breeds being marvellous for endurance.

'Are you feeling quite well, Iris?' Mr Lawrence asks.

'Hot,' I snap. 'I am terribly hot.'

He grasps my elbow decisively and leads me towards the shaded grandstand that has been set up, with wooden chairs neatly lined up on different levels. 'Sit here,' he tells me, steering me towards the front. 'You will have a good view of the races from here. I will fetch you some water.'

He vanishes somewhere and I sink into a hard chair and press my forehead into my fingertips.

CHAPTER THIRTY-SEVEN

BENEDICT KAMAU

The heat today is unbearable. This is the latest I have ever known the rains to come. I feel like a fraud, dressed in traditional Kikuyu garb of tanned leather and adorned with cowry shells and glass beads, brass wire wrapped round my elbows and ankles. I have even daubed my hair and body with red ochre that is mixed from the castor-oil plant with a little animal fat to retain the colour. I wear a headdress of ostrich feathers and carry a broad, painted cowhide shield as well as a long spear with an iron blade. To be here amongst these Europeans, I must play my role and dress as a native, *not* as one of them. Besides, there is one reason alone that I am here.

But so great are the crowds that it is not until after an hour or so that I see her. She is sitting beneath the shade of the grandstand, her hands clasped round a tumbler of water, staring ahead at the races. Though, from where I am standing, she in fact appears to be staring right through them. Mr Lawrence perches beside her, drinking what looks like whisky. It is the first time I have seen him properly and the difference in age strikes me first; he could quite easily be her father. Despite not being able to see his face very well beneath his sun helmet, I can see that it is thin and pinched, reddening from the heat and no doubt the alcohol as well.

'Is he what you were expecting?' I hear a voice behind me and turn to see Fazal.

'My friend,' I say, shaking his hand. 'How good to see you.'

He returns the compliment, and then asks, 'Well?'

'To whom do you refer?'

He smiles, a little strangely I think, and nods in the direction of Iris and her husband.

'Oh. I don't know.'

I would love to take Fazal into my confidence but cannot. I run a handkerchief over my brow and stare up in to the arc of blue, now lined with a thin band of cloud. And it is then that I hear the commotion and the frantic shouting. For quite out of nowhere, it seems, an enormous rhinoceros has ambled up, half-heartedly charging a racehorse.

'Does anybody have a gun?' I hear somebody shout. 'Who has a damned gun?'

And then, simultaneously, I feel the first drop on my bare foot. I look up to see that the sky has clouded over and it has begun to rain, lightly at first, but rapidly building in intensity so that it transforms, within seconds, into a downpour.

Mr Lawrence is looking from the rhinoceros to the sky and then, suddenly, he jumps over the barrier and is gone. He helps to bring the table laden with tea and cakes in from the rain and then turns his attention to the rhinoceros, which stares myopically about, as though it has made a terrible mistake and wishes to leave again.

This is my chance. My only chance. I do not think twice about it; no, not even with Fazal standing beside me. Without uttering a word to him, I run through the rain towards the enclosure. I do not know how much time I have, but I know it is not long, for those who were around Iris will no doubt return soon to shelter inside. And then I am before the face of this beautiful woman who has haunted my dreams and waking hours ever since I met her.

'Kamau!' she cries, before clamping a hand self-consciously over her mouth.

It is all I can do not to grasp her and pull her to me.

'You look so – different!'

'Yes,' I agree, glancing down at my Kikuyu garb. 'You look beautiful,' I say quietly. And suddenly, without warning, her lovely eyes fill with tears and I see that she is grasping the barrier with such force that her arms are shaking.

'Iris, what is it? What is wrong?'

She does not speak for several moments. Her chest heaves up and down with the effort of trying not to cry.

'Kamau,' she whispers eventually, 'I am pregnant.'

I feel sure I must have misheard her and lean a little closer. 'Tell me again, Iris.'

'I am pregnant, Kamau. I am having a baby.'

I feel drops of rain trickle down my neck and behind my ears and I shiver. 'Is it – is it…?' I falter.

Iris pauses. 'Yes,' she says and the tears finally work their way free and her whole body is racked with sobs. 'I'm sure it is.'

The following morning, I arrive early at the schoolhouse. I try to make notes for the teaching day ahead of me but I keep stopping, drumming my fingertips in a frenzied rhythm on the tabletop. My mind is constantly drawn to wondering what might happen should Iris give birth to my child. The very thought of it grips me with a fear so profound that my breath escapes from me in ragged, painful gasps. What would happen to me? What would happen to *her*? To the child? I can bear it no longer. I stride outside and bang a notice into the door informing my students that I am ill and there will be no school today.

Then I walk towards the bungalow, remaining at some distance. I stand behind a craggy acacia tree, beneath the sky that hangs overhead like a great, grey dischcloth, and I watch and wait. Mr Lawrence is sitting on the verandah smoking his pipe with the *East African Standard* spread out before him, peering at it through his strange, glassy eye. Iris is nowhere to be seen; she is most probably inside the house. But then she comes out and sits beside him. From what I can see from this distance, she is engaged in needlework, but she frequently breaks off from it. Even from here, I sense her unhappiness: the dark circles beneath her eyes and the physical distance between her and her husband. They do not converse once while I stand there and watch and I feel a dull ache from deep inside me; it is *my* place to be beside her, physically and emotionally, and not Mr Lawrence's. I know this, and she knows this, yet in the eyes of society it could not be further from what we are able to achieve.

Mr Lawrence does not leave and I am forced to return home. But I keep going, every morning before school, in the hope that I might find Iris alone, even for a short while. It takes more than a fortnight but eventually I watch as Mr Lawrence strides from the bungalow. I know I have not a moment to waste.

Hurrying to the bungalow, I rap on the door and Muthoni opens it, pausing for a moment as she eyes me fearfully. 'I need to see Iris,' I tell her in Kikuyu, 'Mrs Lawrence. Is she here?'

Muthoni does not move. She just glances behind her and then turns her face back to me.

'*Daakuhoya*,' I say. 'This is very, very important.'

I hear Iris's voice, from behind Muthoni. 'Kamau!' She hurries to the door and draws it fully open. 'Her stomach presses against her pale blue, cotton dress. She is pale and her eyes have lost their dancing light. I cannot bear it. She turns to Muthoni, places a hand on her forearm and nods at her. Muthoni musters a half-smile and then slips away.

'You cannot be here, Kamau,' she says, her beautiful, wounded eyes staring out at me. 'Mr Lawrence will be back soon.'

'How soon? Where has he gone?'

'To the Somali butcher's. He is buying beef for Muthoni to cook tonight. Iron…' she trails off, 'for the baby.'

'Iris. I need you to come with me. Muthoni can tell Mr Lawrence you have gone for a walk.'

'To where?' she whispers.

'I know of a woman, a *nyitwo ni ugo*. She practises traditional medicine. She is a prophetess and healer amongst the Kikuyu. She might be able to help us.'

'Help us?' Her eyes widen. 'You mean—'

'Simply to talk to her. To think about our options.'

She is shaking her head vehemently. '*No*, Kamau. No, no, no. I cannot. I cannot do that to our child.'

I grasp both her hands. 'I loathe the idea every bit as much as you. But we must consider it. We must—'

'No!' She continues to shake her head and I take a sharp intake of breath.

'Please, my dearest. Just tell me you will think about it. Consider it.'

As she continues to shake her head, I squeeze her hands and, eventually, as the tears fall on the collar of her blouse, her shaking motion turns into nodding.

What is it I am trying to achieve? Do I truly believe she might go through with it? I do not know. All I know is that the fear of losing her is greater than anything else, almost punching the breath from me.

We make our way down the hill, I several metres ahead of her so as not to attract attention. We walk down to the end of Victoria Street, past dusty Indian *dukas* and then out along the dust-churned plains without saying a word to one another.

I cast a look about us. There is nobody here in this bleak, rain-soaked landscape and, knowing it is finally safe to do so, I approach her.

'No decisions need be made right now,' I say, taking her hands in mine. 'You do understand that, don't you?' She looks down.

'Yes, I understand.' Her eyes flicker back to mine and she tries hard to smile, nodding a few times. Her head is a flower swaying on a stalk.

We continue to walk in silence, the sun trying to break through gaps in the clouds.

'We are nearly there,' I tell her. 'Just another few minutes.'

The medicine woman, Wairimu, is digging sweet potatoes. She bends double, then comes upright, trims the leaves and throws them to her goats, who are walking around the outside of her hut. We stand at a distance, unobserved, for some time. I feel Iris's fingers wind their way around mine, her touch cool.

'How old is she?' she murmurs.

'One hundred and sixty harvests, or thereabouts.'

'I don't understand.'

'That is the traditional Kikuyu way of saying around eighty years old. The Kikuyu measure age through the number of harvests they have lived through.'

She nods and looks back at Wairimu busy at work, copper bracelets jangling on her wrists and her earlobes stretched down with the weight of heavy, looped and beaded rings. Beside her hut sits a large iron *sufaria*, containing what smells like millet stew bubbling away. I feel suddenly hungry; I have barely eaten anything all day.

'Ready?' I ask.

Iris doesn't look at me, but together we walk towards the old medicine woman, our fingers still threaded into one another's, and suddenly Wairimu stops her task and turns her old, proud face towards us.

'Who are you? And who is this?' she asks, her voice sounding like a door creaking open.

I feel Iris shift uneasily beside me. Wairimu speaks not a word of English and I must translate. Of course Iris must have seen many Kikuyu women walking through the main thoroughfares of Nairobi before and obviously she knows Muthoni, but she has certainly never been so close to a medicine woman.

Wairimu is dressed in the soft hides of a goat and her head is smoothly shaved and adorned with a few simple beaded bands, a sharp contrast to the network of lines that runs across every part of her face. Her wrists and ankles are encircled with brass wire and, on both arms and legs, her skin has been coloured a deep red, ochre mixed with animal fat. She gestures for us to follow her into the shade of her simple hut, its roof made of *mabati*, and as we move inside, I am stung by the knowledge that had I retained the Kikuyu way of life, I would be living in a bachelor's *thingira* not so very different from this.

We sit on a mat on the floor and now, away from all prying eyes, Iris feels comfortable enough to freely lean in to me, her body close to mine. Wairimu stands before us, her face framed by the tanned leather garments, gourds, leather pouches and belts studded with cowry shells that are hung up on the wall of the hut.

'Speak, boy!' she says with sudden force and Iris flinches.

I clear my throat. 'Wairimu, mother. I am Kamau and this is Iris. A small being grows inside this woman and we have come to ask your advice.'

She looks at me intently. 'You have had sexual intercourse with the *mundu mweru*.'

I try to return her gaze but I feel like a child again beneath her scrutiny.

'What is she saying?' Iris whispers, but before I have a chance to reply, the old healer continues.

'The ancestral spirits are displeased with you.'

I feel anger well up inside me. I have not come here to be judged. We have come for assistance, pure and simple. I am about to say as much but Wairimu speaks again.

'You have attracted misfortune to yourself and this woman. But it is good that you have come.'

Iris nudges me again and I turn to her. Her face is pale and her lower lip trembling and I wonder again if I have done the right thing by bringing her here. I translate softly for her as she grasps my arm tightly.

'You said that this woman – you said she might be able to help?'

'It's possible.' I squeeze Iris's hand and she looks, all of a sudden, impossibly young and vulnerable. She clings to my arm.

'Give the girl some of this. She is scared,' Wairimu says, stretching a leathery hand clasping a gourd out towards us.

'What is it?' I ask.

'Sugarcane beer. It will help calm her.'

I somehow doubt that, but I take the murky-looking liquid and translate for Iris. And then, to my great surprise, she takes the gourd from my hand and tips it down her throat in one gulp, grimacing as she finishes but looking, somehow, stronger.

The old healer nods, pleased, and then says 'Now. Tell me what it is you have come here for.'

Now that I have to say the words to the old woman, fear coils itself around my heart and I cannot reply to her. I turn to Iris. 'I would like… to talk about this a little more. Before we make a decision, I mean.'

She shakes her head. 'Kamau. Just tell me what she can do for us. *Please.*'

'But we need to have *all* our options in place and then we can… decide.'

'But we have no options! Tell me, what are they?' Her voice steadily increases in volume and in the dim light her face looks bloodless and waxen. I feel my heart rate quickening.

I remove her grip from my forearm and take both of her hands in mine, squeezing them firmly. 'We do, Iris. We need to think about this carefully. Perhaps…' I glance at Wairimu, who stares at us, her head held high, 'perhaps this is not the place to discuss this. But we must try to stay calm and think of all the possible courses of action. We could try to leave Nairobi, to get to Mombasa—'

'Mr Lawrence *knows* everybody here. It could never work.' She squeezes her fingers into her temples.

'We don't need to go by train. There are other ways we could reach Mombasa. Or go somewhere else? To Tanganyika, or north even. And then—' Iris opens her mouth to speak. I know her words come from a place of desperation, but I fear that she is now so beside herself with worry that it is difficult for her to think clearly. 'Iris, dearest, *listen*. Or you could give birth to the child and somehow get it to me and tell your husband it perished.'

'Or I just do not have it.'

'Yes,' I say quietly. 'There is that option as well. Which is why we are here.' I glance at Wairimu again. She has moved away from us and is making porridge over the hearth. 'To discuss this possibility with Wairimu.'

'If…' she says slowly, staring at me, wide-eyed, but in such a way that she seems not to see me at all, 'we ask Wairimu to help us, then we could have a chance to be together. To just be more careful next time…'

'We have a chance to be together otherwise, to leave Nairobi. We could *do* it—'

'Kamau. Please, we need to be realistic. The two of us, together – we would be like outlaws. This is not Europe, where we could vanish into a crowd. We would be sleeping in the bush, always moving on. *So* conspicuous: a black man with a white woman and a baby—' she breaks off, 'of indeterminate colour. What kind of a life would that be for a child? What would we *eat*? Even if we made it to Abssynia or to British Somaliland, he would track us down. I *know* he would. He simply has too many contacts and he would stop at nothing. And then, if he found us, what would happen to us? To me? To *you*? To our child? The risks are too great, you must see that.' She falls silent and then, in a small voice, 'I want Wairimu to do this, Kamau. To take this child from me.' Her body is rigid and her eyes focus upon mine as she speaks with a steely determination. '*Say* it, Kamau. Translate that for her.'

'But Iris.' Loose strands of dark hair have fallen over her eyes and I brush them away. 'We have not talked about this properly. Today is simply to talk to Wairimu, to discuss what she may or may not be able to—'

'Kamau,' she cuts in, her eyes flashing with such conviction that they unnerve me. 'Do you not see? That it is the only real way forward for us. I *want* this child. But can you not see that it can never, ever be? Not here, not in this world.'

'It might belong to Mr Lawrence,' I say, hopelessly.

Now it is her turn to take my hand and squeeze it tightly between both of hers. 'Yes. It is possible. But it is so, so unlikely. I know you understand that.'

I feel suddenly scared, more scared than I ever have been. For I underestimated the strength and decisiveness of this woman I love. I recognise the glint of determination in Iris's eyes. I realise two things simultaneously: that though Iris cannot communicate directly with the old medicine woman, she does not need to. And that Wairimu understands exactly what it is that Iris wants.

CHAPTER THIRTY-EIGHT

IRIS LAWRENCE

I have no idea what it was that the old woman gave me to drink but I am feeling a little better than when we first arrived here; less scared. Everything, I feel now, will work itself out. Between this old healer with medicine and witchcraft in her fingers and Kamau and myself, it will be alright.

The old woman creaks to her feet, a jangle of beads and shells and wire, and turns her back to us as she walks to the wall of the hut where many objects are hanging. I watch as she extracts from a pouch what looks like the horn of a cow and several strings of herbs and roots. She drops them into a pot bubbling on stones at the back of the hut that I had not previously noticed, and, with a long stick, stirs them round and round, a curious, pungent scent pervading the air.

I turn my head to look at Kamau. He is motionless, his eyes fixed upon Wairimu. Beads of sweat have broken out on his forehead.

'Kamau,' I whisper. 'What is it?'

For a few moments, he does not reply, almost as though he has not heard me. But then he turns and looks at me, the whites of his eyes flickering yellow in the pale light. 'I don't know,' he whispers back, 'I am not sure if we should—'

'Kamau,' I say, with surprising conviction, 'It will be fine.'

His forehead creases slightly and he gives a small nod before grasping my hand and turning back to the old lady. As she continues to stir, she looks towards me and says something.

'She wants you to go to her,' Kamau whispers.

I stand up but am restrained by Kamau's hand, firmly closed round mine. I turn and search his eyes, trying to smile at him with a confidence I do not feel, before pulling my hand away. Wairimu is pointing down at a bed of banana leaves upon the earth floor and, haltingly, I lower myself down on to them. I look up at her, waiting for further instruction, but she is calling something to Kamau in Kikuyu and a heated debate ensues. For the first time, I feel grateful that I am unable to understand this language, for I know it should only serve to make me feel even more uncomfortable.

Kamau is suddenly beside me, kneeling down and gently telling me that she wants me to open up the back of my dress.

'The *back*?' I ask.

He nods. I am not sure if it is the poor light in the hut, but it looks as though a few tears have travelled the length of his cheek. I fumble around at the back of my neck to unclasp the dress and pull it down over my shoulders.

'Good,' Kamau says, holding both my hands as he moves to the front of me. 'She will make a small cut in your back—'

'But I do not understand why anything is happening on my back, Kamau, surely—'

'I don't understand either, Iris. I know nothing of the ways of a Kikuyu medicine woman. But either we go through with this or we do not.'

'Yes,' I say quietly. 'Yes.'

I feel the old woman's presence behind me as she leans in to my back and pokes at a point between my vertebrae with one long, leathery finger. And then, before I know what is happening, Kamau has grasped my head between his hands and I feel the most terrible pain, a sharp suction whirling and craning its way upwards and outwards as the sharpness spirals through my entire body. I open my mouth to scream, but nothing comes and I find myself staring into Kamau's depthless eyes, and seeing only terror reflected back at me.

Wairimu begins to chant in a low voice, strong and clear and persistent, as the pulling sensation in my back lessens. I crane my head backwards out of Kamau's grasp to see that the medicine woman is clutching the cowhorn in her bony fingers, which is what she must have used on my back. Her eyes are closed and she is rocking gently from side to side. I turn back to face Kamau, who almost looks as though he is holding his breath. 'What was she doing to me?'

'She was sucking something out through a cut in your back with the cowhorn,' he whispers.

'What do you mean, *something*?'

'You need to stay still, Iris. She is going to bathe the wound now with the fluid from a sisal plant.'

I frown. 'And then? Then what will she do?' My words escape my lips raggedly and my breathing is uneven. I suddenly feel light-headed and desperately in need of water. 'Will it be over then?'

Kamau places one warm hand against my cheek. 'No. These are just the preparations. Iris, it will be over soon, I promise you.'

I feel a stinging sensation from the same point on my back. The old healer continues to chant and then I see her face close to mine and I turn and stare at her, unable to drag my eyes away. Her skin is smooth and deeply lined at the same time and I am struck with a sudden urge to raise a finger and run it along the deep groove that travels from her eye down to the corner of her mouth. She takes me by the shoulders and motions for me to turn over and lie on my back. I lower myself down uncomfortably onto the bed of banana leaves, the cut in my back still smarting. The woman begins to speak again and Kamau translates for me. She wishes me to remove my undergarments.

The small hut is stifling and with all my will, for I am trembling like an autumn leaf on a windy day, I push myself up and remove everything from beneath my dress, casting them to one side of the banana leaves. I lie back and close my eyes and the unbidden image of my mother comes to my mind, along with the horror I know she would feel could she see me here now. This thought causes me a great deal of agitation and I push it roughly from my mind, turning my head to the side and trying to slow down my rapid breathing. And Mr Lawrence... he will have returned from the Somali butcher's. Will he now be out looking for me?

And that is when I feel it. It begins slowly, lightly, a gentle rippling sensation from deep within me that builds strength until it is unmistakable. My eyes flicker open and I look at Kamau beside me and grasp his hand.

'Kamau,' I say, 'I can feel it!'

'What can you feel, Iris?'

'The baby. I can feel it moving.'

He squints his eyes at me and with his free hand strokes my arm gently. 'Are you sure, my love?'

Hearing him talk to me in that way, his voice so full of warm tenderness, is more than I am able to bear. He has never called me that before and I realise at that very moment that I cannot do it. I cannot allow this child who is part of the man I love to be killed. I push my dress back down over my legs, sit upright and feel the tears spilling down my cheeks as Kamau's arms weave their way round me and hold me tightly. Beneath his embrace, I clutch at my stomach and feel the flutter of a growing life inside me subsiding as suddenly as it arrived.

$$\text{❧ ❧ ❧}$$

In the days that follow, I take to my bed, watching as the rain spatters against the glass of the bedroom window and the mosquitoes come out in thick droves to hiss against the loosely draped net, baying for blood. Through my window, I watch as a kite rends the bleached sky, black against waterlogged grey. For the first three days, Mr Lawrence barely leaves my side. I turn my head to the wall and pretend to sleep, so at the least I am spared the sound of his voice. I think about the date that draws ever nearer; we have exhausted every possibility.

Save one: Muthoni. Somehow, surely, she could help us. Help me deliver the baby without the doctor being here and then get it to Kamau. Yet how can I make this desire understood when we can barely communicate?

On the fourth day of my self-imposed confinement, Mr Lawrence tells me he has to go to the office. This is my chance to go to Kamau, to share my idea with him. I dress and am in the doorway, about to leave, when Muthoni grasps my arm and points to the table. She has made me a poached egg. I smile at her in gratitude, tears stinging my eyes.

Muthoni, how I wish I could talk to you.

But before I even have a chance to sit down at the table, there is a knock at the door and we both jump. I look up – it is Kamau. He must have been watching from a distance, waiting for Mr Lawrence to leave. Muthoni greets him in Kikuyu and then tactfully walks outside to sweep the verandah.

Glancing around him, he produces a piece of paper from his pocket and stares at it before handing it over to me. 'This is for you.'

'What is it?' I ask quietly.

I stand up, take the paper from his outstretched hand and look down. There is his drawing of the sunbird, pulled from his notebook, delicate strokes rendering each line real and perfect. I pass a hand gently over it, as if by doing so it may come alive and fly off the page. Then I turn it over and read the words:

For my dearest Iris, your sunbird for evermore, Kamau.

My eyes fill with tears and I look back at him as he grasps both my hands within his.

'We have to think of a new plan, my love. Time is running out.'

'Yes,' I whisper.

'I was thinking – Muthoni.' He glances out to the verandah, from where we can hear the gentle swish of her broom. 'Do you trust her?'

I nod. 'We need to ask her to help us. I was thinking the same.'

'This is our perfect opportunity. Right now. We bring her in here, explain the situation and ask—'

'…that she help deliver the baby—'

'…and then bring it to you—'

'…and we say it has died in childbirth. Yes.'

Our words trip urgently over one another's and I know this is it, our final hope. We look at one another long and hard and then Kamau silently moves outside and asks Muthoni to come in.

She lays her broom to one side and nods. Why do I feel that she already has an idea of what is about to be asked of her? All three of us stand as I listen to Kamau's low, lyrical Kikuyu words wash over me. I stare at him as he talks, watching his mouth move, beads of perspiration breaking out on his forehead.

Then I look at Muthoni. Her head is slightly on one side. She is listening intently and she scarcely blinks. When Kamau has finished talking, there is a silence so deep and so profound that I fear it may swallow me. What if she refuses? Her eyes dart nervously towards the door and I see at this moment that her fear of my husband runs deeper than I had quite credited. She says something softly and Kamau gasps, nodding his head.

'What?' I whisper. I feel light-headed, the shades of the morning seeming to bleed into one another.

Kamau looks at me and grasps my hand tightly. 'She will do it, Iris. Muthoni will help us.'

I close my eyes as my world spins on its axis. We have a chance. We can have this baby and make this work. I know what Muthoni is risking for us. When I open my eyes again, Muthoni is looking at me. The corners of her mouth raise upwards, but her eyes are pained. She already *knew* this child belonged to Kamau, I am certain of it. She takes a step towards me, places a hand on my stomach and begins to talk in Kikuyu.

'What is she saying?' I ask Kamau.

'She is saying that we are her friends, that she will help us and that everything will work out somehow.'

'Have you explained to her where you live?' I whisper.

He nods. 'Yes, I have.'

I feel choked with deep gratitude.

'*Nĩ ngatho*,' I say. '*Nĩ ngatho*, Muthoni.'

She drops her hand, moving away from us. I take a deep breath and look back at Kamau.

'I must go. Muthoni is right though, everything *will* work out, Iris. We must stay positive. Oh,' he exclaims, 'I almost forgot.' Kamau opens up his jacket and extracts *Alice's Adventures in Wonderland* from a wide pocket before handing it to me.

'What did you think of it?' I ask quietly.

'It was the strangest but most wonderful book I have ever known.' He smiles. 'I have read it three times. There were all kinds of things I had never heard of before or didn't understand.'

'Such as?'

'Such as murdering the time or shutting up like a telescope. But there are parts that I sat and laughed at: playing croquet with flamingos, characters exchanging seats at a tea party and a talking caterpillar smoking a pipe. And now,' he tucks a loose strand of hair behind my ear, 'I can imagine you as a young girl playing croquet on the lawn and pretending your mallet is a flamingo; imagining yourself growing and shrinking after drinking potions and eating cakes. I loved it, Iris.'

'I am glad.'

'Oh, what is a dodo?'

I manage to smile, but it is strained. 'It's an extinct bird. Rather large.'

He raises an eyebrow and nods his head. 'And a porpoise?'

'A porpoise? It's an ocean creature. Not unlike a dolphin.'

He falls silent. He takes the book from my hands, places it on the table and winds his fingers round mine once more whilst he gazes intently at me. 'I have never been to the ocean before.'

I gaze back at him, his beautiful, dark eyes fringed with black lashes. 'One day, Kamau,' I reply quietly, 'I should like to go to the ocean with you. One day we shall go together.'

At this, he smiles and squeezes my hands, but his smile is full of a pain that I almost cannot bear to look at. I want to take his pain away and there are three words, three truthful words – the greatest truth I have ever known – that could help him. 'Kamau,' I whisper. He rests his head gently on one side and gazes at me. I remove one hand from between both of his and cradle it behind his neck, that comforting place of warmth and strength. 'I love you.'

And just like that, the pain in his eyes recedes. He momentarily closes them, and when they open once more, I read in them so many things: I read acknowledgment, I read joy and, above all else, I read the truth of his own love for me reflected back.

CHAPTER THIRTY-NINE

BENEDICT KAMAU

I love her. I think I have loved her from the first moment she appeared at the schoolhouse with Fazal, her face radiant and bright. There are so many things that I love about her: her compassion and intelligence, the dark sheen of her hair and the crookedness of her smile, her ability to stand before a classroom of children and captivate each and every one of them, her easy grace and determined gait. And those dark blue eyes that shine with warmth and wisdom and that smile at me, even when her face remains serious. But never, ever could I have imagined what would grow between us. Yet I can still hope, for Muthoni has agreed to help us. All can still be well. Iris will remain in my life and I in hers and time for us shall continue to stretch as long as the endless plains of East Africa.

CHAPTER FORTY

IRIS LAWRENCE

He insists on staying and working at home more and more. It is driving me to distraction. He tells me he is concerned for my health, and the health of our son, and that I ought not be alone for long stretches. *No!* I wish to scream at him. *Leave me!* He says he should like to call the child Edward, after his father, and all I can do is stare at him, stare *through* him. This child could be a girl. This child will have skin the colour of night.

I long to see Kamau but Mr Lawrence is never out of the house for long enough. Days roll into one another – weeks – and I must endure listening to my husband telling me of his work, the trials of the settlers and the backwardness of the Africans the colonial government are attempting to civilise. How I despise each and every word he utters. How I wish he would stop talking; how I wish to turn away from him and place my hands firmly over my ears. But I do nothing of the sort. I sit beside him and let his words drift past me like leaves floating downstream and I think of Kamau, nothing but Kamau.

There have been times at night, the moonlight slanting through the open windows on the other side of the mosquito net, when I have sat up in bed and watched Mr Lawrence as he sleeps. Without his monocle, he looks more vulnerable, his mouth cast open and his forehead smoother than normal, that perpetual frown diminished. I wonder about a way in which he could die, quietly, whilst he sleeps. If I placed a pillow over his face, might I have the strength to keep it pressed down for long enough? Or if I returned to the old medicine woman, might she provide me with poisonous herbal ingredients to drop in to his open mouth?

These are the thoughts that occupy me each and every night and when I do eventually sleep, I dream that Kamau's strong body is above me, his soft mouth covering mine and his long, graceful fingers in my hair. Upon waking, I almost choke with disappointment and fear, salty, bitter tears staining my pillow. The child I will give birth to, this child conceived in love, will not have skin the same colour as my husband's. My baby will be black, a child of Africa. And all the while, I am reminded of its presence inside me; I feel its growth and movement, its gentle, fluttering pirouettes.

I find myself praying to God for the first time in years as I clutch the St Christopher pendant Papa gave me – to the God of my father, who is good and just – thinking that perhaps, just perhaps, if he hears Papa's prayers, he might also hear mine. *Let everything be well*, I ask again and again until it becomes a single whir of noise like the wheel of a carriage turning on an endless journey.

Let everything be well, please *Father.* And as I continue to pray this, I realise that the word 'Father' becomes increasingly blurred until I am unsure if my words are directed towards the heavenly God or are screamed as an agonising plea to my own papa.

❧ ❧ ❧

I go into labour in the morning, not long after Mr Lawrence has left for work. At first I simply lie in bed, feeling a bland pain deep inside me that is not unlike the sensation of my monthly bleeding. Yet it builds quickly in intensity and I know this must be it. I climb out of bed slowly and as I do so a great howl escapes my lips as a sharp spasm sears through me. I wrap my arms round my stomach and Muthoni rushes through to the bedroom, her eyes wide with concern.

'The baby,' I choke. 'It is coming.'

She beings to murmur, rubbing my back. 'Yes, Memsaab. Is coming. Wait.'

She vanishes and I grope my way out of bed, clutching at the bedpost. How does one have a child? I know nothing, nothing at all. Mr Lawrence has told me that if I go into labour, Muthoni is to fetch Dr Ford. He is a small, disagreeable man with a wiry frame and sunken eyes covered by rounded spectacles. I have had two appointments with him and at least I can feel relief that he will not be the one to deliver my child. The story Muthoni and I are to give to Mr Lawrence is that my labour was so rapid it gave us no time to fetch Dr Ford. Yet as the acute pain bears down I realise that, encapsulated in our lie, is the truth: that we have no time, that this baby is coming – very, very quickly.

Muthoni hurries back in to the bedroom with a sheet, which she spreads out over the floor. At the very same minute, a great torrent of water empties itself from my body onto the sheet and I look down in horror. What is this and where is the baby? But Muthoni is beside me, rubbing my back some more before she disappears again, reappearing moments later with a towel over one shoulder and a bowl of warm water.

The straining – the overpowering discomfort that racks through me – it is too much to bear and I grasp the bedposts, bending over double. I feel an overpowering urge to push and hear screaming, dimly registering the sound as my own as I bear down. But it will not come, it will not come and I feel Muthoni crouching on the floor by my ankles and parting my nightdress; her hand groping around inside me and stopping upon something. 'Yes, Memsaab. Baby, baby.'

But I feel as though I might die with this pain – is this my punishment being meted out to me?

I have a mere two seconds' respite before another sickening contraction floods through me and I wish Kamau were here, to tell me that I will not die. I imagined that labour would take hours, days even, but this has been no more than half an hour and I feel sure something must be wrong. But I have no time to dwell on it further, for with one final tearing, rasping shaft of agony, I push with all my might and I feel my child slide from me, into the waiting arms of Muthoni. I hear myself sobbing in great waves of relief and the high, mewling cries of my child.

I let go of the bedpost and slide to the floor. Muthoni is wielding a knife and I cannot look. Has she seen this happen before, I wonder? How does she know what to do? Then I see her cut the cord with one sharp cut and place it aside. Now she is wrapping the baby in the white towel and my arms, of their own volition, reach out to it. I need see nothing else save the face, for I already know I have a boy. A son. Kamau's son.

I do not know for how long I sit there staring at him, this extension of mine and Kamau's love for one another in human form, but I am unaware of time. I am unaware of where I am, of *who* I am. I am only aware of this tiny, exquisite creature, opening his perfect bow lips into a perfect yawn.

And then, he makes a noise. Not a cry, exactly but a soft, mewling need. Instinctively, I bring him up to my breast that burns and throbs. He feeds hungrily, my son, taking in as much of his mother's milk as he can to sustain him in the days to come. These days that are as unknown as the murky swamp of the Nairobi River during the rains.

I have my hand over my son's head, stroking the softness of his dusting of black hair.

'Memsaab,' says Muthoni. I look up into her eyes, soft with kindness, and she holds her arms out for the baby. I nod, taking one last look back down, drawing my child up and closing my eyes as I breathe in his sweet, milky scent. 'See you soon, my darling,' I whisper. 'See you very, very soon.'

Muthoni smiles at me and carefully takes my swaddled baby, wrapping him more tightly as she turns to leave. At that very moment, we hear the bang of the front door and steps striding across the wooden floorboards. Fear clouds Muthoni's face and I gasp.

'I have decided to work at home today, Iris!' It is Mr Lawrence, in the front room.

'One minute!' I cry. 'I am dressing. I will be out in one moment!'

I gesture desperately to Muthoni and then towards the window, ignoring the pain that screams through my body as I heave myself up and run to unclasp the latch.

'Iris!'

He is outside.

'Wait!' I cry. 'Just—'

But he does not wait. He opens the bedroom door and he walks in, flushed beneath his helmet. He looks at me. Then he looks towards the window, where Muthoni stands with her back to him, holding onto my child for dear life.

'What…' He takes off his hat, runs his fingers through his hair and frowns with incomprehension. 'What is going on here?' His eyes take in the sheet on the floor, the blood, the bowl of water. And then he breaks into a smile that reaches from one side of his face to the other, the widest smile I have ever seen from him. 'You – I – I am a father?' he stutters.

With the window now wide open, I can hear the sounds of the Nairobi plains filtering through: the clink of hammers; the murmurs of the breeze; the sounds of the African birds, large and small, that I have come to love. And then above it all, drowning out all of these sounds that I should like to stay with for evermore, comes the voice of my husband, strident and acerbic.

'Muthoni! Bring me my son.' There is pride in his voice.

Muthoni does not turn round. I look at her and see from her shoulders that she is crying, heaving, silent tears that fall on to my child.

'Muthoni!' This time, sharpness.

Still she will not look at him and I limp towards her, prise her arms away from beneath my baby and hold him tightly to me.

And then I turn, a turn that takes a thousand years. I think of Alice descending into her rabbit hole and I wish that the ground had the ability to swallow us and take us to another world. A world in which we might be safe.

Mr Lawrence rushes forwards, opens his mouth to say something and then stops. His forehead creasing. His eyes narrowing. His jaw dropping open. He walks from one side of me to the other, all the while not taking his eyes from the child that now roots around hungrily again for my breast.

And then, without warning, he cries out and staggers backwards, his breathing laboured as he crashes into the bed. Now, only now, will he look at me. Tears are stealing silently down my cheeks as I continue to stroke my baby's head, soft and smooth as velvet.

'Were you raped, Iris?' he asks me quietly, and I simply stare at him. I cannot bring myself to answer him.

He bangs his fist hard against the bedpost, causing the baby to cry. 'Were you raped, dammit? Answer me!'

He is shaking with rage, a purple vein pulsating in his forehead, and if I have felt scared of Mr Lawrence before, it is nothing in comparison to the sensation I feel now. I look down and guide my son's mouth back to my breast and he stops crying. My tears spill onto the nape of his perfect neck. I brush them away with my fingertips and then look up, straight into the watery blue eyes of my husband.

'No,' I whisper.

For a moment, he stands motionless. Then he picks up the chair from beside the dressing table and hurls it down hard on to the floor so that it smashes. Splintered shards of wood fly. Then he takes two decisive steps towards me and pulls the baby from my breast with such force that the agony of it makes me cry out. He strides to Muthoni, who stands rooted to the spot, terror in her face, and thrusts my son into her arms.

'Get this fucking nigger child out of here!' he roars. And I am crying, wailing, staggering and reaching out for my child. But Mr Lawrence is pushing Muthoni roughly through the door. 'Out!' he is roaring. 'Out! And you!' He turns back to me and jabs a long finger at me. 'You will return to England immediately. Do you hear me?'

'With my baby!' I hear a thin wail escape from my lips and I move towards the door, but Mr Lawrence blocks it and sneers at me, showing his teeth stained with tobacco. 'No. Without the nigger child. You fucking *whore*.'

And then he is gone, slamming the door behind him as I hear the Muthoni's sobs, intermingled with the cries of my baby, receding into the distance.

PART TWO

CHAPTER FORTY-ONE

IRIS LAWRENCE

1922

20 Hawthorne Terrace
Durham
28th June 1922

Dearest Papa,

I cannot tell you how much your visit meant to me. I know it cannot have been at all easy to have kept this secret from Mother, but please try not to feel guilty. You did not lie to her, you just did not tell her.

Sheena & Leonard have not stopped talking about you since you came. They have been asking when you will come again, particularly Leonard, who wants to show you his new train set. Do you think you might be able, at some stage?

Jonathan, also, was delighted to finally meet you and spend some time with you. I know that the two of you would be firm friends, were circumstances different. I was so pleased to hear that you remain lively and challenged through your work, but far less happy about your hacking cough. I know you said that it was not bothering you dreadfully but even so, dear Papa, I think it is well worth a visit to Dr Warren, simply to put your mind at rest, not to mention my mind.

And yes, I miss you dreadfully too, Papa. Still, after all these years – and that feeling of deprivation that we have not been able to have our walks and our conversations persists. I still have the St Christopher pendant you gave me when I left for East Africa, the patron saint of travellers. I keep it in a small silver box on my dressing table and often take it out and run my finger over its fine grooves. It is something I shall always treasure.

I send you all my love, Papa. The garden at The Old Vicarage must be looking beautiful now. As you saw, we only have a very small back garden but, nonetheless, Jonathan is rather green-fingered and Sheena seems to be also and they planted tomatoes, sweet peas and some flowering field pansy in pots last week and it all looks very pretty.

Yours affectionately,

Iris

I place my pen down and glance at the clock above the mantelpiece. If I hurry I will catch the afternoon post and be back in time for the children to return from school. But then I see through the morning-room window the rain streaming down and think better of it. I can post the letter tomorrow.

I stand and stretch and move through to the kitchen, where I place the kettle on the stove and light it. Then I reach up to the shelf and bring down several tins. I open each one carefully, breathing in the aromas of cardamom pods, cloves, black pepper and cinnamon. One by one, I remove a few of each from the tins and drop them into a pan, adding a liberal amount of milk and sugar.

Sugar with tea is vulgar, Iris. Will that voice ever leave me alone?

I stand at the stove for fifteen minutes, letting the chai simmer. It is patient work, making it taste just right. But it is worth it, for each and every sip.

When it is ready, I pour it into a teapot, place a cosy over it and tread carefully back to the morning room. I sit down at the desk, rain spattering against the windows, and look at my looped handwriting on the front of the envelope addressed to Papa. I run a finger over the dried black ink. 'The Old Vicarage, Bourn, Cambridgeshire.' A house that watched me grow for the first eighteen years of my life. And now, I realise with a sudden jolt, I have lived for the same amount of time here in Durham.

I pour a cup of the chai into the teacup and take a sip. As the first sip does every single time, it causes me to close my eyes for a moment. To lose myself in memories.

❧ ❧ ❧

After Mr Lawrence pushed Muthoni out, my son in her arms, I staggered to the door, numb with pain. But he had locked it behind him. I pounded against it, screaming of my need for my child, my grief. I moved round to the back door. This was unlocked and I flung it wide open. I wore no shoes, no petticoat, no underwear. But none of this occurred to me as I staggered round the house, up the hill, past my croquet pitch, with its bent hoops and discarded mallet. But I could not see them. How could they have moved so quickly?

Sobbing so fiercely that the path blurred before me, I could feel the pain of sharp stones tearing at the soles of my feet but I continued, screaming Muthoni's name, again and again. But nothing. Nothing. They were gone. I fell to my knees, my hair covering my face and my body shaking uncontrollably as I stared up at the grey blanket of sky, wringing my hands as I pleaded for mercy.

He returned about an hour later. He would not look at me. He poured whisky after whisky and pounded up and down the wooden floorboards of the bungalow. When I tried to talk, to ask him what he had done with my child, he stared at me, a drunken snarl in his eyes. 'Please,' I whispered, 'please, just tell me. I—' But I could say no more, for he struck me across my face with his full force so that I spun round, falling hard on my back. I lay there, staring up at the whirring ceiling fan, and I wondered to myself: *Is this it? Does my life end here?*

That night, I slept outside on the verandah on a thin rug, if it can be called sleep, considering the nightmares that assaulted me each time I drifted off. I wanted to go to Kamau, but I did not know where he lived. I could have tried the schoolhouse, but the physical pain that tore through me each time I tried to take a step was overwhelming. *Without the nigger child. You fucking whore. You fucking whore. You fucking whore...*

In the morning, I heard the door bang and opened my eyes to see Mr Lawrence standing over me. His eyes were red and bloodshot and his voice was thick with whisky and bitterness.

'You will take the train to Mombasa this evening,' he said, so quietly I could scarcely hear him. 'From there, you will travel back to England. I will cover your fare home, but after that, you are alone.'

I heaved myself upwards. 'No.' I shook my head. 'No. Please. Tell me where my baby is. *Please.* I will do anything, anything at all—'

'It's rather too late for that, is it not?' He emitted a sharp, bitter laugh. 'There is no debate. No discussion. You will begin your journey to England this evening. *Without* the nigger child. I will put you on the train myself, do you hear me?'

I stood up so that I was opposite him. 'No.' I kept shaking my head, repeating that same word, over and over again. 'Where is Muthoni? Let me talk to her, *please—*'

'For Christ's sake, Iris!' he shouted, in such sharp contrast to his previous quietly spoken words that I staggered backwards, banging against the posts of the verandah wall. 'Have I not made myself clear?'

I stood there, my head hanging and the tears working their way free as I sobbed as though I could never stop. He walked slowly towards me so that only a breath separated us.

'Though perhaps we can make a compromise.' His voice was quiet again, terrifyingly so. 'You tell me who the father of the nigger is and I let you see Muthoni.'

I choked on my sobs, lifting my head and staring at him imploringly. 'What will you do to him?'

He walked round so that he was standing beside me. He brought his mouth close to my ear so that I could feel his hot breath on my skin. 'It is not so much what *I* would do to him, but more what the *law* would.'

I was trembling uncontrollably. Despite the warmth of the morning, I felt colder than I ever had in my life. Nor could I breathe properly; my breath was tearing through my lungs. Everything ached – between my legs, my face, my lungs, my heart. I squeezed my eyes tightly shut. 'I cannot tell you.'

He took a step back. 'So be it. I will find out anyway, after you have gone. You have made your choice, Iris.'

Those words, again, just like my mother's.

I remember screaming, turning to Mr Lawrence and pummelling my fists against his chest. And then, once again, his fist against the same smarting wound on my cheek from the day before. Falling, falling. And darkness.

❧ ❧ ❧

Sheena is the first to appear, kicking her shoes off in that untidy way of hers and slinging her damp satchel down in the corner so that it opens and pencils spill out.

'Hello Mother.' She walks to me and places an absent peck on my cheek before turning away towards the grate. 'It's so cold! May I light a fire?'

'A fire, in June? I think not.'

'*Please*, I'm frozen. Look how wet I got walking home.'

She pulls the red ribbon from her hair and holds up a wet clump of her thick, strawberry-blond hair in front of me.

'Oh dear.' I soften. 'Well, perhaps we can then, just this once. Where's Leonard?'

'I'm here, Mummy!' he calls from the kitchen. 'Just warming in front of the Aga.'

'Mummy says we can light a fire!' Sheena shouts back at him, falling to her knees in front of the grate and starting to arrange pieces of kindling.

'Why don't I make you something to warm you up?'

'Can we have crumpets and toast them?'

'I don't think we have any—'

'We do! I saw some yesterday in the larder. Len!' Sheena shouts again, 'do we have crumpets? Check, would you?'

'Right-o,' Leonard calls back. I sigh and stand up, moving through to the kitchen. Sometimes I think this household would function perfectly well without me.

'Hello, darling,' I say, ruffling my son's dark hair. He ducks away from me. 'Oh, *please* don't do that, Mummy. You know how I hate it.' But he is grinning at me crookedly. He has the exact same teeth as I.

'So, *do* we, Len?' we both hear Sheena shouting.

'Do we what?'

'Have any crumpets?'

Leonard takes his dripping shoes off, leaves them beneath the Aga and pads in his grey socks towards the larder. 'Just looking!'

🕊 🕊 🕊

I hardly recall being taken to the train station, I was so racked with pain and anger and bitterness. I do remember trying to kick out against Mr Lawrence as he heaved me into the railway carriage, screaming at him to 'Stop! Stop!', trying to climb down from the compartment, but Mr Lawrence fetched two men to hold the door closed until the train pulled out of Nairobi station, thick smoke billowing as I choked and heaved and wailed.

On the lengthy sea crossing back to England, I was violently sick with rage and raw grief. I heaved bile overboard, my blouse dampening against the hot, wet tightness of my breasts that would never again be nursed by my son and the sea spray that covered me.

Once I arrived in England, numb with shock and fatigue and the biting cold, I stood at Tilbury Docks with my cases and blinked uncomprehendingly into the angry wind. With the icy, salt-laden air whipping around me, I threw open my cases and sorted through them, placing only a few items in one and abandoning all the rest. And then I walked, weak with hunger and thirst, stopping to sleep beneath viaducts and scavenging discarded food when I could find it.

I knew it would be quite impossible to get all the way to Bourn; I had neither the means to get there nor the strength. And so I walked instead to Mayfair, past the dock labourers, the road sweepers and the flower sellers, who took one look at me and decided not to implore me to buy their posies of violets and primroses. Walking through the hard-

edged, impoverished areas of London and along the stinking, open sewer of the Thames, I passed broken windows
and open doors with ill-clad women standing in them. Poverty stretched on for what felt like miles on end, but at least
in those areas people did not stare at me. For as the dank
streets finally gave way to the more genteel neighbourhoods
of hanging birdcages, lace curtains and scrubbed doorsteps,
people stopped and stared in undisguised, open-mouthed
horror. I had not seen my reflection in many days, but I did
not need to. The state I was in was only too apparent.

It took me some time to find my aunt and uncle's house.
I stood before it, with its immaculate plants in hanging baskets, and rested my head against the door for several minutes
before I could bring myself to knock. The butler answered
and he would, at first, not permit me entrance. But then
Aunt Josephine appeared behind him, peering at me myopically before gasping, a thin hand clutched to her mouth,
as she realised who I was. She took me into the drawing
room and I was given tea. I would not talk. I could not talk.
I was unable to stop shaking. My parents were summoned
without delay and I was taken to a bedroom to sleep, the
very same bedroom I had slept in after the debutante ball.

My mother and father arrived that same evening, without
my brother or sister, and when I heard their voices downstairs
– or rather the voice of my mother, verging on shrill hysteria
– I squeezed my eyes tightly shut. What could I say to them?
Which elements of my story could I possibly leave out?

I needn't have worried about any of that, for Mother of
course steered the entire conversation, if it could be called

a conversation. Clearly during her journey to London she had settled upon the questions that would be asked of me, the minimum information required to carry out what she had, I knew, already decided. In many ways, I was grateful that she was not interested in the particulars of my tale. She wanted to know, first and foremost, if Mr Lawrence had sent me home. I looked her directly in the eye, Papa standing some distance behind her, his face contorted in pain, and I nodded.

'Will he have you back?' Mother asked, her chest heaving up and down as she took uneven, ragged breaths. I shook my head.

'For heaven's sake, Iris, what did you *do*?' she cried. 'In fact –' she placed a hand up in front of her – 'no, I am not sure I wish to know. The fact that you are here, and not there, tells me quite enough. You are not fit to be in our family. You do not belong. You do not belong anywhere. You have shamed me and you have shamed the good name of our family. You will not return with us, Iris, do you hear me? Not today, and not at any point in the future. You are—' she choked on her words, '…you are no longer my daughter. That is all I have to say on the matter.' And with that, she rushed out, a flurry of taffeta and silk and heaving sobs.

Her words did not touch me at all, for it was impossible to be wounded to any greater extent than I already had been. I only felt a deep, heavy numbness. Papa was clearly struggling to form the right words. For some time, he was silent, standing by the window as I lay on the bed and gazed helplessly at him. But then I rose unsteadily and walked towards him. He seemed not to hear me, to be lost in his own thoughts, and I reached a hand out and touched his shoulder.

He started, turning to face me, his eyes that were my eyes taking me in solemnly. 'Will you tell me?' he said quietly.

I breathed in sharply and dropped my hand to my side. 'I—' I broke off and made every effort to stand up straight, to push my shoulders back. 'Not yet. I cannot.'

'Iris,' he said. 'Did you hear what your mother said? She will not take you back. She—' He broke off, and I was horrified to see that tears were rolling down his cheeks. I had never seen my father cry before.

'Dear Papa,' I said. 'I am sorry for not being the daughter that you and Mother wanted. I only—'

'Don't say that, Iris, *please*. I do not know what has happened, what you have done. Or what he has done, or not done. But what I do know is that it is quite impossible now. Your mother…'

I shook my head. 'You do not need to explain. I know. I understand.'

He stared at me, deep grooves lining his forehead. 'What will you do?'

'I will go to Miss Logan.'

'Miss Logan, the chaperone?'

I nodded. Curious, as I had not thought of it until that very moment, but now this sudden decision felt like the most natural and normal thing in the world.

'Where does she live?'

'Durham.'

'Durham...' Papa cast his eyes down.

We were silent for a few moments, the weight of our situation bearing down upon our shoulders. I studied my father's face: he had aged considerably and now had lines in places where there had been none before and more grey hair around the ears and temple. Eventually, he looked back up at me.

'Arthur's terribly upset. He wanted to come and see you, but your mother forbade it. Iris...' He shook his head. 'I don't have much money, as you know. But I never want you to be in a situation where you cannot make ends meet. First of all, though, have you enough money to reach Durham?'

I shook my head. Papa looked furtively around and, ascertaining that the door to the bedroom was closed, pulled his leather wallet from his pocket and emptied a number of florins, half-crowns and shillings into my hand.

'That is too much, Papa.'

'No. I want you to have it. It will make me feel less... less dreadful if you do.'

I suddenly remembered something and walked to my packing case beside my bed, rooting around in it until I found what I was looking for.

'Let me copy this down, then you can have this paper,' I told him. 'It is Miss Logan's address in Durham. So you can write to me.'

Papa nodded sombrely.

'Charles!' We both heard Mother's shrill voice from downstairs.

I bit my bottom lip, fighting back tears, and set about copying down the address. 'I do love you terribly, you know,' I whispered. 'And I am sorry I have made you suffer.'

He shook his head and looked at me hard and I wondered when the next time would be that I would look into those navy blue eyes.

❧ ❧ ❧

'How was school today?' I ask Sheena and Leonard as they toast their crumpets. Leonard is sitting cross-legged on the grey, tassled rug and Sheena is sprawled out on her stomach, swaying her legs in the air.

'Mmm,' Leonard mumbles, his mouth full of crumpet and damson jam.

'Don't speak with your mouth full, Leonard,' I chide.

'Well, don't ask questions when we're eating then, Mother!' Sheena fixes me with a steely look. When did my twelve-year-old daughter become so imperious?

Leonard makes a great show of finishing off his mouthful, chomping and swallowing noisily. 'What time's Daddy back?'

I glance at the clock over the fireplace. 'In an hour or so, I should think.'

'What are we having for supper?'

'Fish pie.'

'Oh, not *again*,' groans Sheena.

'I *like* fish pie,' Leonard says and gives me a small smile. I smile back and look away. I find my daughter's quibbling about what I cook tiresome, particularly as not very long

ago, when the war was still on, we were not eating anything vaguely resembling fish pie. But Sheena can be very
quarrelsome, and I have no wish to argue with her. Besides,
cooking is not my strong point and everybody in my family
knows it. To say that I grew up being cooked for would, I
know, sound terribly spoiled. But the truth is, I have never
quite warmed to the fine art of cooking.

I feel like saying to my daughter, *You cook, then*. But I do,
of course, nothing of the sort.

The fire crackles in the hearth as the rain continues to
teem down outside.

$$\text{\textbf{\textit{y y y}}}$$

Penelope Logan, unlike my aunt in Mayfair, recognised
me immediately. It mattered not that my skin hung loosely
from my body, that my hair had lost its sheen or that dark
shadows were etched beneath my eyes. Thankfully there was
a map of the city at Durham railway station and I found my
way to Miss Logan's Victorian terraced house beneath the
viaduct without difficulty. She stared at me long and hard,
betraying nothing in her expression. Then she folded me
into her arms, right there upon her doorstep.

For some days we did not talk about what had happened
to me. She fed me with nourishing soups and broths, provided me with an abundance of the reading material I had
been so starved of and we wrapped up against the wind and
took brisk walks over the old stone bridges of Durham, along
the Old Bailey and the River Wear. The first time I saw the
great cathedral from Framwellgate Bridge, I stopped walking

and stood and simply stared. It took my breath away, with its ancient spires and intricate arcades, and I breathed in its majestic profundity, wondering about the hands of faith that had crafted this structure from nothing.

After several days, I began to talk of my own volition. We were sitting on a wooden bench by the river, watching the university crews row past.

'I fell in love.' I did not look at Penelope, but kept my eyes fixed upon the blades as they sliced into the cold water. I waited for her to say something, but when she did not, I continued. 'I fell in love with someone I should not have done.'

My gloved hands were clasped in my lap and I could feel Penelope's eyes on me. After some time, she said, 'We do not choose with whom we fall in love, my dear.'

'Don't we?' I turned to face her. There was no judgement in her eyes, of course, only gladness that I was finally confiding in her. 'I could have been stronger. I could have avoided his company. My feelings were clear, and I suspected how he felt also. He... I loved him, Penelope. I *love* him. And I do not think I shall ever see him again.' I turned back to face the river and felt my chest heaving with pain. She took my hands in hers and squeezed them gently. We sat quietly for some time, the silence punctuated by the gentle swish of blades and the breeze carrying birdsong.

'And what else?' she asked me quietly. 'Do you think you are ready to tell me?'

I stifled a sob. 'I had his child. Mr Lawrence took my baby from me.' It was too much to be recalling that episode; it cut through my memory like a knife wound. I released my hands from Penelope's, dropped my head into my hands and relived that moment, that terrible moment when my baby was pulled from my arms and an iron fist clamped around my heart.

The tears spilled out, endlessly, a raging river bursting its banks, a grief with no beginning and no end. Penelope rubbed a hand over my cloaked back in firm, rhythmic motions. 'Cry, child, cry,' she said.

Ten minutes, maybe more, I remained like that, my thin body hunched over my legs as I felt again that pain of separation as keenly as though somebody had removed my own heart, my lungs. For I could not feel freely; I could not breathe freely. My emotions were frozen, encased in ice.

Bent over double on the hard, wooden bench, I turned my head to the side and looked at my friend, this woman who was more of a mother to me than my own, this woman who had saved me.

'Thank you,' I whispered as I looked into her small, shrewd eyes, which glinted in the pale sunlight.

'For what?'

'For this. For everything. For helping me believe I could come to you.'

'Iris. You have nothing to thank me for. Nothing at all.' She continued to rub my back and her steady hand felt comforting, necessary. 'The truth is, it was clear to me from the very beginning that things could not go well for you and Mr Lawrence.'

I nodded and forced a small, tight smile. 'Yes. I should have stayed in England and married Lord Sidcup. But then...'

'Then?'

'Then,' I took a deep breath and closed my eyes, 'then I never would have met Kamau. He loved me. I loved him. I shall never know that again.'

'Iris,' Penelope said firmly as she gently grasped one arm and drew upright, 'I do not know the pain you are going through. But you cannot know now what life will bring you. You must grieve both of them and then you must continue with your life. You are young. You have so much to offer the world. You are *strong*.'

A small, bitter laugh escaped my lips. 'It's strange; people often say those words to me. You yourself have said this to me before. Yet never have I felt less strong in my life. So powerless.'

She shook her head and pulled me into her so that my head rested upon her shoulder. The long, wooden boats cut through the water before us and I wished my life were as quiet, as uncomplicated and full of hope as those students'. Black-necked grebes swam to safety at the side of the river, heads bobbing. 'One day,' I said, 'I shall go back and find him. Both of them.'

She squeezed my shoulder. 'Yes. You must.'

Ya Ya Ya

As the children finish off their tea and crumpets and spread their homework out over the floor in front of the fire, I look at the framed monochrome of Penelope Logan on my desk. It is the only picture I have of her. She is dressed in the Victorian clothes of her day, a dark bonnet framing her small face, yet her humour and wisdom shine through the picture. I still miss her, each and every day. If I had had a different kind of chaperone, a less learned or sensitive woman, I do not like to think what might have become of me.

We all hear the key turn in the lock at the same time. Leonard's eyes look up from his books, gleaming. 'Daddy!' But it is Sheena who jumps up, hurtling round to the front door and, by the sound of her father's reaction, hurling herself upon him with wild abandon.

Jonathan staggers through to the parlour, Sheena attached to him for dear life.

'Sheena,' I say, 'let your poor father take his coat off, at least. Hello, Jonathan.'

He makes his way laboriously over to me, bends down with Sheena between us and kisses me on the cheek.

'Hello, love. Hello Leonard. Doing your homework, are we?'

'Yes. Geometry.' Leonard pulls a face.

'There's still tea in the pot,' I tell him.

'I'll get some for you,' Sheena says, finally disentangling herself and skipping off to the kitchen.

'Are we having chai special today or just normal tea?'

I smile at him. 'I finished the last of the cardamom pods earlier, I'm afraid. So it's just old Earl Grey today.'

'Well,' he grins, 'as you know, I'm partial to the Earl too.'

Jonathan. My Jonathan. Is he possibly the most good-natured man in the world? Just occasionally, I imagine what he and Kamau would have made of one another, had they met. But I am unable to follow these thoughts through as the truth is I have no idea how they would have got along. Two men from such different worlds, quite impossible to place together. But I sometimes think I must *learn* to imagine them together, for the idea of returning to Africa never leaves me. The war is over and I have enough money. But then I look at this man who loves me, whom I care for deeply. And I look at my children and I think, *How? How can it ever work? Have I left it too late?*

✷ ✷ ✷

All I could think about in those first months in Durham was how I could return to Africa. I knew how much my passage to Mombasa had cost and though I did not have that kind of money, I discussed at length with Penelope the kind of jobs I could take on around Durham to earn enough. I was prepared to do anything at all: be a charwoman, work in a factory or as a chambermaid. I went to interviews and factory owners and housekeepers looked at my unchapped hands and neat nails and asked if I had ever done a hard day's work in my life.

'I can work, I promise you,' I implored them.

'Oh, la-di-da, you can now, can you?' they scoffed.

Nobody would give me a chance, not with my polished voice and smooth hands. So I had to try something completely different. I went to the university and asked for a job there.

'Can you cook?'

'No.'

'Can you clean?'

'Yes.' How difficult could it be? And I was given, to my great delight, a job in the student library on Palace Green. I worked at night, cleaning the lavatories, the book-lined walls and the silent, wooden carrels that smelt of old paper and oak tables. Although it didn't make me happy – nothing could make me happy in those days – my job served to numb my grief a fraction. For when I was dusting tomes by Chaucer and Ovid and walking down whispery aisles surrounded by so much wisdom, I could remove the pain of my heartbreak for whole moments at a time, whereas at home my child and Kamau were all I could think of.

I worked from six each evening, when the library closed, until ten. After a few months, I started coming earlier, at five o'clock. I would spend that hour sitting in a corner carrel reading. Nobody questioned what I was doing, so I kept coming, earlier and earlier. To begin with, I wasn't sure how I wanted to focus my reading, but it wasn't long before I naturally gravitated towards women's suffrage, as this was what Penelope was so heavily involved in. I believed in it all, yet it was impossible to commit myself to such a worthwhile cause wholeheartedly. For I could bind myself to nobody and to nothing – all I could focus on was getting back to Africa.

Even so, I enjoyed the reading. My carrel had a tiny window beside it and I liked to break away from my books on occasion and watch the throng of students gathering outside, chattering gaily, the sleek covering of snow in the winter months and the dappled sunlight on the green in the summer.

And then the day arrived. I had earned enough. It was almost seven months since I had returned to England. I sat on my bed at the top of the long, narrow house, looking out to the tiny garden and towering hawthorn tree, and I counted it all out three or four times. All I had to do was book my passage. But at breakfast the following morning, when I shared my news with Penelope, she did not react in the way I expected.

'Iris, my dear.' She wiped a spot of marmalade from the corner of her mouth and placed her napkin on the table. 'Are you certain that you have thought this through? That this is wise?'

'Thought this through?' I placed my teacup back in its saucer with a clatter and stared at her, wide-eyed.

'Yes. What I mean is this: I understand your motivation, of course, for wanting to go back. And I quite agree, it is important that you *do* return, to locate Kamau and your child. But is it the right time now?'

'I don't understand what you mean.'

Penelope sighed. 'Mr Lawrence… I am certain he will still be terribly angry. Is it wise to embroil yourself in all of that once again?'

I frowned. 'But he will *always* be angry. He will *always* hate me. And the more time I spend away from my child…' my voice catches, 'the more he will not know me. It eats me up, this knowledge. Every single day.'

Penelope placed a hand over mine. 'But perhaps his anger will abate, over time. Imagine it, Iris. Try to imagine it on a practical level. You arrive back in Nairobi, everybody will recognise you, from the stationmaster to the shop owners, and most probably know what has taken place. I can guarantee that it wouldn't take long for word to reach Mr Lawrence. And then what? He will find you, Iris. And what will he do to you?' The upper half of her body is convulsed with a small shudder. 'He is a violent man. I understand your motives, my dear girl. Truly I do. But I fear for your safety back there.'

I stare down at my half-eaten bowl of porridge and watch as a single teardrop splashes into it. 'It is a risk I must take. I have no other choice.'

'You do, Iris. You can wait.'

'Until when?' I look up into the small, kind blue eyes of my friend. 'Until my child has another mother? Until Kamau's schoolhouse is closed down and he is ostracised from the entire community? Until I have forgotten how to feel anything, anything at all?'

Penelope scrapes her chair across the wooden floor, moving it closer to mine. She encircles my shoulders with her arm and pulls me gently into her.

'Did you not have a friend there? The tailor, what was his name?'

'Mr Ahmed.'

'That's it. Mr Ahmed. My dear, why not write to him? To ask him for news?'

I paused and thought about her words. 'I could, I suppose. I do not know his address but I could…'

'Guess it. Yes, you could. There cannot be so very many Mr Ahmeds who are tailors in Nairobi. And you knew the street he worked on?'

I nodded my head against her chest. 'Mr Lawrence knew the postmaster,' I said. 'As *well* as the stationmaster and countless more,' I added bitterly.

'But it is worth a try, is it not? Write to him, with your address. See if he responds.' We are both silent for a few moments. 'Iris,' Penelope says very softly. 'This is an abominable truth, but one you must face. Several months have passed already, have they not? Your child will be somewhere, *with* somebody. You must hope and pray that he is being cared for well. As for Kamau, from what you have told me, Mr Lawrence will have wheedled the truth out of your housegirl, do you not think?'

I shake my head. 'She would never tell him.'

Penelope sighed and placed her chin on the top of my head as I nestled against her warmth. She was silent for a few moments. 'You once told me that he hit you, twice, towards the end. And that he was violent throughout in one way or another. I am sure she was wonderful, this girl of yours, but that does not mean she would not tell him the truth. And whatever is going to happen to Kamau – prison or whatever it is – most probably has already happened.'

'But I can visit him there,' I whisper.

'You have voiced it yourself, how small the European community of Nairobi is. Would you be permitted to visit him, really?'

The tears begin to flow freely. For she is right. She kisses the top of my head and smooths back my hair. '*Wait*, Iris,' she says gently. 'Wait a few years, three years or so perhaps, until people are talking about something else and not expecting you.'

'But all this money I have saved,' I sob. 'What was it all for?'

She squeezes my shoulders. 'It was to start living again. It was to feel a part of this world again.'

❧ ❧ ❧

As I serve out the fish pie to my family, Sheena begins to grumble again.

'Sheena!' Jonathan reprimands, 'none of that, thank you very much. Your mother's fish pie is delicious.'

'Yes, but we had it last—'

'Enough!' Jonathan fixes her with a glare and she frowns, falling silent and staring irritably at her plate. 'A strange thing happened to me today at work,' he continues, changing the subject.

'What?' Leonard asks.

'Well. I was asked if I would like to head up the department. Edmunds, it turns out, is leaving at the end of the year.'

Three pairs of eyes turn to him. 'Oh, but that's *marvellous*, Jonathan!' I grasp his hand on the table.

His eyes shine. 'Yes, it is rather marvellous. Pay rise and everything coming up. More work, though, but...' He shrugs, 'I'm sure it will be worth it.'

'Well done, Daddy!' Sheena enthuses as she stands up and throws her arms round him, planting a kiss on his cheek.

'Yes, well *done*, Daddy!' says Leonard. 'Does it mean we can go somewhere different on holiday this year other than Northumberland?'

'Well...' He hesitates, glancing at me, 'I won't *have* the pay rise until towards the end of this year. But...' his face softens and he beams. 'As a treat, or a celebration, perhaps we can. Where would you like to go?'

'Blackpool!' screeches Sheena. 'Wales!' cries Leonard.

Africa, I think. *I would like to go to Africa.*

۶ ۶ ۶

I took Penelope's advice. But every morning as the daylight filtered in through the gap in my curtains I asked myself if I was making a terrible mistake. *Today you will be nine months old,* I said to myself. *Today you will be one year. Do you know it is your birthday?* I drew sketches of him, the newborn baby I never had a chance to know. I sketched Kamau: his full lips, his almond-shaped eyes, his prominent collarbone. A sunbird hovering in mid-air behind him. But each time, I tore the paper up before I finished, angered just as much by my lack of drawing skill as by the fading contours of his face.

I started taking an interest in the birds of the hills around Durham and along the vast stretches of white-beached Northumberland coast. Penelope bought me a book of British birdlife and I studied it tirelessly, searching within its pages for anything resembling a sunbird. I did not find anything close, but I did see swallows and house martins, ospreys and white wagtails, and I recorded each and every bird sighting in my book in neat, black ink beside its picture.

And I continued to work and read at the library and take a mild interest in women's suffrage. I so wanted to feel more about it and I knew that in another life, in another set of circumstances, I would have been the one marching with banners on the streets, demanding equal rights for women. As Penelope talked about her involvement, her eyes glittered with feverish optimism. I envied her optimism. I longed to capture it for myself. But I repeated that 'three years' that Penelope had suggested like a mantra, counting down the days on a calendar.

'Now you will be one and a half. And now you will be celebrating your second birthday. But who will know it is your birthday?'

Two years after arriving in Durham, I agreed to go to a meeting with Penelope. She had been asking me to accompany her for a long time and I had never yet found it within myself to say yes. We walked together one light, summer evening to Durham Town Hall and as I walked into the old stone building, nothing could have prepared me for the number of women amassed there; a teeming pulse of vibrant femininity and potent dynamism. Everybody seemed to know Penelope and greeted her enthusiastically, as well as me. 'Ah, you are Penelope's lodger! We have heard so much about you!' I glanced at Penelope in discomfort, but knew in an instant that she had revealed none of my past to these women.

We sat at the back of the hall listening to speeches by working-class women, by educated women, by ladies from the northeast and others still who were visiting the region. As I sat there on my hard, unyielding seat, the sinking

summer sun casting fractured light on to the faces of these
women with a cause – who *believed* in something – I noticed something curious: I felt the unfamiliar fluttering of
excitement, as small as an apple pip but unmistakably growing, taking root and craning for the light, rubbing against
the cold, dark edges of my grief.

Of my own accord, I very slowly started to attend more
talks and meetings. Not once did I consider militant suffrage action, like so many of the women, nor hunger strikes.
I admired them, but there was no part of me that wished
to find myself in prison, for my soul already resided there.
Instead, I joined the Durham WSPU and embroidered the
occasional banner. My head was in it, but my heart had
yet to be captured. Could it *ever* be captured by something
other than Kamau and my child?

In 1907, the National Union of Women's Suffrage Societ-
ies arranged a huge march and demonstration to the Houses
of Parliament in London. Penelope urged me to go, but I
was unsure; London was not a place that held happy memories for me. Yet eventually I relented and a large group of us
travelled down by motorbus. At one point, we passed not far
from my aunt and uncle's house in Mayfair. I broke off from
the mass of women and stood to one side beneath the frozen, driving rain, staring in the direction of their house and
remembering my desperate walk there from Tilbury Docks.

We walked, on and on, thousands of us there for a unified
cause: the grave injustice of our sex not being represented in
parliament. I thought of Penelope, who owned her house in
Durham, who paid her taxes, but for what? Her needs and

her views were neither enquired after nor represented and she, like women up and down the country, were unable to vote on matters that affected them each day of their lives. Of *our* lives. Marching there on that day, I felt it again, that small stirring of excitement. It was shrouded in guilt, for how could I feel joy when my child in Africa needed me? But it was there nonetheless and I could not deny it. When we had been walking in the driving rain for hours, the hem of my skirt and my boots muddied, the mounted police began to ride amongst us, jostling us aggressively and tearing banners from hands, waving their truncheons. I felt anger build up inside me, an unspoken resolve hardening. For too long, women had endured being second-rate citizens, being subjugated and spoken down to and sidelined, having marriages brokered as though we were chattels. And a well burst inside me and I began shouting, *screaming*, my banner held high as the wind and rain carried my voice: 'Votes for Women! Votes for Women!'

There were times when I thought I might actually hate men. But then I remembered the gentle tickle of my father's moustache as I sat upon his knee as a child, him reading me poetry and stories, his navy-blue eyes gleaming in the candlelight. I thought of my brother Arthur, his kind smile, straw-blond hair and infectious chuckle. I thought of Kamau, his strong, dark arms and tenderness and his love for me. And I thought of my son, that dusting of tight, black curls crowning his head, his ten perfect fingers and toes, his curved, Cupid's-bow lips and his tiny, mewling cries and I thought my heart might break all over again.

My father was as good as his word. He continued to see that I was provided for, without Mother knowing, of course. I was dead to her – but the truth was I had never been truly alive in Mother's eyes anyway. He wrote when he was able, sporadically, as did Arthur. Violet, I was told, had married and moved to Nottinghamshire. She busied herself, as Arthur once wryly wrote, with receiving guests in her morning room and redecorating it with burgundy trim, the colour that was all the rage amongst respectable ladies the length and breadth of the country. And Mother, with no children in the house, held more and more At Homes. Strangely, I thought of her more than I ever had in Africa, sitting in the parlour with her rose-patterned tea set and small, fancy cakes. I wondered what she said when people asked after me. Presumably my aunt and uncle were sworn to secrecy and, as far as anyone knew, I was still abroad, married and settled and producing children for my husband. Did my mother concoct an elaborate fantasy world for me during those At Homes? Or did she simply change the subject each time my name was mentioned? Of that, I would never know.

❧ ❧ ❧

By the time we finish dinner, the rain is teeming down outside stronger than ever and I am afraid Hawthorne Terrace might flood. The drainage isn't terribly good in our street. I make the children some cocoa and, after placing some more logs on the fire, they return to their homework whilst Jonathan and I sit on the sofa.

'Would you like that, Iris?' he asks, taking my hand, 'to go somewhere different on holiday this summer?'

I pause. 'Well, yes. But you said it yourself. This pay rise won't come in for a little while still. It is wonderful news though, Jonathan. You deserve it, you have worked so hard.'

His warm hazel eyes glow in the light of the fire. 'You deserve it too, Iris. You have worked tirelessly at the library, especially with all these outreach projects.'

I smile and stare into the flickering embers. I am never quite sure how I earned the attention of this man; his unconditional love.

'Come. You deserve a break. When was the last time you left this county?'

I ponder his question a little. Truly, I don't know the answer to this. It has been many, many months. And yet, staying in Durham holds a great advantage for me and this is something that none of my family could ever guess: it allows me to hold at bay tender, painful memories of another time, another place.

I shrug. 'That is not important, Jonathan. If we *do* go somewhere else, though, perhaps we could go north? To Scotland? To Edinburgh and Inverness and some of the islands? I should like to show the children where Penelope was from.'

Jonathan squeezes my hand. 'Good idea,' he says. 'Very good idea indeed.'

❧ ❧ ❧

Over three years passed. I had more than enough money saved from my work and I began to make enquiries about

my passage to Mombasa. What I had always hoped most
fervently was that Muthoni had never revealed Kamau's
identity to Mr Lawrence. She could easily have said that
she did not know who the baby's father was and he would
have had to believe her. This was the only way I could bear
to imagine it; not, as Penelope intuited, that Muthoni had
given Mr Lawrence his name, with the consequences that
would have unleashed, but that Kamau was still working as
a teacher, that he was unharmed and unhindered and that
he had found our child and was caring for him. Three times
I had written to Mr Ahmed… but nothing came back. Not
a word. I could only assume he was not receiving my letters,
for I was certain he would have replied otherwise.

But then something happened. It started one morning
when I came down for breakfast and Penelope was not yet
up. This was curious in itself. Penelope was an early riser
and all the time I had been living with her, she was without
fail up and about before me. I thought little of it, however,
but when she did eventually come downstairs, she looked
pale, her eyes not shining as brightly as normal.

'Are you well, Penelope?'

'Yes, yes.' She waved a hand through the air. 'I slept badly last night, that is all. I was terribly hot, were you not?'

I shook my head. It had, in fact, been a very cold night,
during which I had had to fetch another blanket from the
cupboard.

The following week, I noticed that Penelope was looking
thinner than usual. She had always been small and wiry,
but now her skirt was loose round her waist and her cheek-

bones more defined. She did not like it when I enquired after her health or fussed. She simply kept going about her usual business: to her WSPU meetings and talks; I accompanied her more than I had previously, just to keep an eye on her. Nobody else noticed a thing. But I noticed. I knew Penelope so well and her tiredness, the way she kept coughing and the thin sheen of perspiration that often covered her forehead were all clear signs to me that something was not right.

It came as no surprise that Penelope bore her illness stoically. But it reached a point at which she could keep the truth from me no longer when she began to cough up blood.

'I may still be fine, you know,' Penelope said as she lay in bed late one morning after another bad night. 'Tuberculosis does not always mean the end.'

I gazed, stricken, at her beautiful, wise face, framed with tight grey curls.

'Iris, you must not worry about me. You need to go back now, to Nairobi. I know you have been waiting for this.'

'Oh no.' I shake my head. 'I cannot. Not while you are like this.'

'Iris,' she sighed and then began to cough furiously again. I hurriedly brought a handkerchief to her mouth and watched in horror as she choked out a thick clot of blood. When it was over, I gave her a glass of water, which she drank in one gulp before laying her head back on the pillow. 'This illness… it is contagious.'

'I don't care about that,' I cried. 'I will look after you, help you to get better.'

'You should care. You *must* care, Iris. You have so much of your life yet to live. And you need to go back, just as you said you would, to look for Kamau and your child. There are sanatoriums for people with TB. I am going to make enquiries.'

I paused. 'Are you more likely to make a full recovery if you go into a sanatorium?'

Penelope was quiet for a few moments, closing her eyes. I saw tiny blue veins threaded across her eyelids. 'Probably not.'

'Then you will not go anywhere. You will stay here, and I shall nurse you.'

She opened her eyes and turned her head to me. 'I will not allow it, Iris,' she said in a soft voice. 'I do not want you to get ill. You must return to Africa. *Please.*'

Despite the pain my words brought me, I knew I could act in no other way. 'I'm afraid,' I replied, 'you do not have a choice.'

Caring for Penelope in her illness was tortuous; watching the health of this mountain of a woman deteriorating, little by little. Not once did she complain, not once did she lament that she was unlikely to reach her next birthday, her sixtieth. Yet I never allowed myself to believe that could be the case. No, she would survive. How could a woman with her strength of spirit possibly not? The doctor visited her at home every few days and said that she was doing very well, but outside her room, he looked at me grimly and said I must do everything I could to help keep her comfortable.

'But she will get better, won't she?' I pleaded with him as we both heard her hacking cough from inside the bedroom. He blinked several times in reply and was gone.

I continued with my job at the Palace Green library and on rare occasions, upon Penelope's insistence, went in an hour or so early to read. I noticed that there were often a number of women amongst the crowd on the green or bent over the oak desks. They seemed to emit a scent of wisdom and learning and contentment and I wondered why, now that I could finally study, I chose not to. There was not a single practical thing in the world stopping me, unlike when I was eighteen years of age and surrounded by insurmountable obstacles. I had the time, the support, the freedom, the intellect… yet I could not bring myself to apply. The reason, of course, was because I could not do anything properly until I had returned to Africa. Yes, my life was on hold.

But whilst I continued working in the library and caring for the woman I loved with all my heart, watching her fade away from me, my life took another unexpected turn. Jonathan Kingsley was a postgraduate student at Durham, studying ancient history. I am not sure when I first noticed him; I think it is fair to say that he was the one to notice, and then approach, me.

One late afternoon as I was arriving for work, a silver dusting of frost covering the green in the chill of a Durham December afternoon, I was standing just inside the entrance of the library pulling off my gloves when I heard a cough coming from in front of me.

I looked up and saw a man standing before me, presumably about to leave. He was huddled within a thick winter coat, a lopsided smile upon his face and kind, chestnut eyes peering at me through spectacles. He cleared his throat.

'Good afternoon,' he said. His voice was deep, shot through with the rich accent of the northeast that I could scarcely understand when I first arrived in Durham. He held his hand out to me and, hesitantly, I took it. I was eager to start my cleaning and unsure why this gentleman was talking to me.

'Jonathan Kingsley,' he said

'Hello. Iris La— Johnson,' I corrected myself quickly.

'I have seen you working here…' He hesitated, shifting a little on his feet, 'but also studying. Are you a student at St Mary's?'

'No.' I unwound the woollen scarf from round my neck.

'Oh, it's just that you always look so studious that I thought you must be.'

I raised an eyebrow. 'Can one not be studious without being a student?'

He blushed, a deep crimson creeping up his cheeks, all the way to the roots of his hair. 'Ah, no. I apologise, that is not what I meant—'

'Don't worry,' I replied, smiling at him. 'I don't mean to be rude, but I need to be getting on with my work.'

'Yes,' he agreed. 'Quite. But…' Mr Kingsley took a step towards me. 'There is a teahouse not far from here, just round the corner on the Old Bailey. Perhaps you might permit me to accompany you there one day after… after we have both finished studying?'

I was taken completely by surprise; frankly it was the last thing I had expected him to say. I stared at him rather blankly, wondering how I could politely decline his offer. And yet… it was only a cup of tea.

My hands flew up to my velvet hat, fiddling nervously with the edge of the silk fibre braid before pulling it off my head.

'Very well, Mr Kingsley,' I surprised myself by saying. 'No doubt we shall meet again here soon.' Before giving him the opportunity to firmly secure a day, I nodded my head at him and bade him farewell, for I did not wish to commit myself quite to that extent yet. He smiled warmly and I walked past him into the library.

It was a few weeks before I saw Jonathan Kingsley again. During that time, Penelope seemed stronger and I spent as much time with her as I could, reading to her, taking short walks with her and even accompanying her to a WSUP meeting. When I did spy him heading towards me, my first reaction was irritation. For I did not wish to be pursued, and I had all but forgotten about our previous conversation. We talked briefly, then I mumbled an excuse about being late and left him. The disappointment written across his face was palpable, yet I refused to be affected by it. I had never promised him anything.

Over the following weeks, as winter thawed into spring and Penelope's health did not improve – and yet, miraculously, did not deteriorate – I often saw Mr Kingsley in the front hall of the library. We would converse for a few minutes about nothing of any consequence before I took my leave. He asked me for tea a few more times, but I always managed to steer the conversation onto another track. Yet eventually the question presented itself so directly that I could think of no way around it.

I shrugged and replied in the affirmative for the following Saturday and he beamed at me, his goodwill and sincerity washing over me in waves. As we sat in the teahouse, we sipped at a steaming blend of Lady Grey and shared a plate of fruitcake, which felt strangely intimate. I did not want to talk about myself, but it was clear he was curious about me. I responded to his questions in fits and starts, fragments of information making their way over the fruitcake to him, whilst trying my very best to keep turning the conversation back to him.

I wondered how old he was. It was difficult to tell, for he had smooth skin and clear hazel eyes but his fair hair, I saw, was thinning at the temples and delicate crow's feet webbed outwards from the corners of both eyes.

'What are you studying, Mr Kingsley?'

His eyes gleamed with enthusiasm. 'Ancient history. I am specialising in classical antiquity. I have spent considerable time conducting research in the regions of the old Etruscan kingdoms of northern Italy.' Ah, that possibly accounted for his slightly olive complexion.

'And you, Miss Johnson. Do you think you would like to earn a degree one day?'

'Oh.' I lifted the lid of the teapot and peered down into it. 'I don't know. I should think not.'

'I am sure that you would be more than capable. And now that so many more women are earning degrees—'

'That may be so. I shall just have to see.' I smiled tight-ly at him and poured him more tea. That tense moment aside though, I must confess I enjoyed passing that hour with Mr Kingsley over tea, more than I thought I might. Returning home to Hawthorne Terrace, I commented to Penelope, in as offhand a manner as I could muster, 'I think there is a gentleman I met at the library who wishes to court me.'

Penelope, with her customary tact, scarcely raised an eyebrow. After a length of time, she turned her pale, wise face towards me and asked 'How do you feel about that?'

How *did* I feel about it? How did I feel knowing that in all probability Mr Kingsley would invite me out for tea again, or a walk, or something similar? He was not Lord Sidcup, nor Mr Lawrence, that much was for certain. And yet… nor was he Kamau, the man I still loved, the man whom I imagined was waiting for me in Nairobi with our son.

And yet, did I *really* believe that or was it just a gentle story I had to tell myself to keep the pain at bay? As time went on, I continued to meet with Mr Kingsley, to take walks over the cobbled streets and alongside the river and sip hot drinks at various teahouses across the city. I felt *something* for him, but I was entirely unclear about what form this 'something' took. He often walked me home and on one occasion I invited him in to drink chai with Penelope and myself in the morning room.

'This is astonishingly good,' Mr Kingsley remarked as he sipped at it. 'Where did you learn to make this?'

'Oh,' I said breezily, 'a friend once made it and I asked for the recipe.'

He nodded, satisfied, and Penelope smiled at me.

'I like him,' she told me later. 'He is a good, kind man.'

'I know he is,' I replied, 'but... oh *please* do not look at me like that. You know that I cannot have feelings for him in that way.'

'Cannot or will not? No – let me speak, Iris. There is no crime in a friendship growing between you and another man. Or something more, even. You are betraying nobody, my dear.'

I cleared my throat and felt the hot pinprick of tears stinging the corners of my eyes. 'You really believe that?'

'I *know* that.'

'I admire Mr Kingsley a great deal, but I can never love him.'

'It is impossible to surmise that now. You have a long life ahead of you.'

I frowned and stared out of the window. Hawthorn blossom covered the tree, pale petals floating to the ground.

I didn't know what I believed any more.

❧ ❧ ❧

Finally, it has stopped raining, but Sheena and Leonard's bedroom has a chill to it and I light a small fire to remove the dampness. Sheena doesn't like to be read to any more but Leonard does. Jonathan and I are taking it in turns to read to him from *Robinson Crusoe*.

'Do you think, Mummy,' Leonard asks as I tuck him up in bed after I have finished reading to him, 'that if we go up to some of those little islands around Scotland, they will be like where Robinson Crusoe was shipwrecked?'

'I imagine so,' I tell him, sitting on the side of his bed, 'but a good deal colder.'

'I wonder what it's like to live in a very hot place,' he says, scrunching his eyes up.

'Horrid,' interjects Sheena from the other side of the bedroom. 'You'd be sweaty, all the time.'

'Have you ever been to a very hot place, Mummy?' Leonard asks me, ignoring her.

I smooth back his dark fringe and trace my fingers over the paintbrush flick of freckles over the bridge of his nose. 'No,' I say. How does this lie slip out so effortlessly? 'Though London can be horribly hot, especially in the summer months. You have to go and cool down in the bathing ponds in Hampstead.'

'Have you been there?' Leonard asks.

'No,' I admit. 'I have only heard of them.'

'Why don't we ever go to London, Mummy?'

'Because it's a very, very long way,' says Sheena, ever practical.

'That's right,' I say. 'But don't worry, Leonard. You're only eight. You have your entire lifetime to go to London.'

'I want to go everywhere, Mummy.'

I smile at him. 'You will.' I bend down and kiss his soft cheek. 'But, you know, you might just go everywhere and then realise that Durham, truly, is the best place in the world.'

'It is,' says Sheena.

'There,' I say. 'Now, time for some sleep.'

꙳ ꙳ ꙳

Mr Kingsley's proposal came six months later. Yet it arrived earlier than I had expected and it took me by surprise. We were standing in the centre of Palace Green, flanked by the castle, the library and the looming spires and arches of the cathedral, about to bid one another farewell for the afternoon. But suddenly he caught the crook of my arm and whispered, 'Wait.' And then, with fingers that trembled ever so slightly, like the wings of a dragonfly, he reached into the pocket of his overcoat and drew out a small box. Of course from this point on I could be under no illusion as to what was happening.

But the question remained: would Mr Kingsley still wish to marry me, knowing the truth? I could not decide how much to tell him or at what stage. The fact remained that I did not wish to talk about any of it, but to keep him entirely in the dark about my past would be deceitful. Thus I chose the coward's exit. I put my hand out, lightly placing it over his.

'Mr Kingsley…' I said quietly. 'There is something – a very painful CHAPTER of my life I have told you nothing about.'

He paused, looked at me intently and replied, 'I know.'

'You know?' A flock of geese flew directly overhead and I looked up, shielding my eyes with one hand as I stared into the whiteness of the sky.

'What I mean to say,' he continued, 'is that I don't know what it is. But I know you have suffered.'

He uttered these words with such direct simplicity that they stunned me. I had never considered how apparent it might appear to others that something was amiss in my life. Perhaps my pride was wounded; it was not that I ever minded how others viewed me. More to the point, I had always

believed that I had successfully kept my pain to myself –
yes, I may have come across as quiet, or aloof even, disinter-
ested, but was my suffering that clear to those around me?

As though reading my thoughts, Mr Kingsley peered at
me in concern with his gentle, hazel eyes.

'Please do not misinterpret my words, Miss Johnson.
I find you... remarkable, tenacious.' His neck reddened
slightly. 'I do not believe for a moment that others would
have noticed this, for you carry yourself admirably. It is only
that – that *I* have noticed.'

I smiled at him gratefully and realised two things simultaneously: firstly, that this Mr Kingsley would take care of
me and, secondly, that he would demand nothing of me. I
did not love him. But I respected him. As I scanned his kind
face, I knew I felt safe with him.

'I'm afraid,' I said hesitantly, 'that it may be some time
before I feel able to... to share with you what happened to
me. I need you to know, Mr Kingsley, that you might think
differently of me if you knew.'

He straightened up and pushed back his shoulders,
grasping his hands solemnly behind his back. 'I do not believe this could be the case, Miss Johnson. After all, we all
harbour skeletons in our closets. Besides, I am not easily
shocked.'

Looking at him with his tall, stiffened collar and four-in-
hand necktie, he seemed to me so terribly English. It was
difficult to think of him not being just a little shocked by
the fact that I had given birth out of wedlock and that the
father of my child was an African. But perhaps I underes-

timated him; I considered his words, wondering what his own skeletons might be. More pressing was the issue that I was still legally married and did not know what to do about it. I had no desire to renew contact with Mr Lawrence to initiate divorce proceedings, but what else could I do? It was then that a thought occured to me.

'The ring,' I said cautiously, 'the ring that is in this box. I should like you to put it on my finger. I should like to be your wife.' It was curious to hear myself say those words and Kamau's dark eyes flashed through my mind as I said them. I winced, willing myself to stay focused upon Mr Kingsely. 'But…'

'Yes?' he pressed gently.

'But must we get married? In the official sense, I mean. I realise this is not at all conventional. But could we not simply live as man and wife? I should try my utmost to be a good wife to you.'

It was Mr Kingsley's turn to be distracted by a bird; a starling, to be precise, that landed on the grass beside us and puffed up its delicate plumage, pecking at the ground with its yellow beak. I wondered to myself if Mr Kingsley cared at all for birds. He stared at it, deep in concentration.

Eventually, he tore his eyes away from the starling, looked up at me and smiled. I tried to trace any rancour in his smile and yet, to my relief, found only warmth.

'If that is what you wish, Miss Johnson, I must respect that. For I know you must have your reasons.' He grasped my hand, the one not holding the box. 'You need never tell me, you know, if it is that difficult for you. That, I shall leave entirely up to you.'

'I *shall* tell you.' I nodded effusively. 'Only not yet.'

He smiled softly, his whole face lifting and brightening, and at that very moment I thought that yes, I might love him just a little.

➤ ➤ ➤

A thin band of pale light is still present, even at ten o'clock, when Jonathan and I have finished washing up and go to bed. Our room is at the very top of the house, with a view of the tip of Durham Cathedral spire. Perhaps Sheena is right. Perhaps Durham *is* the best place in the world. It is where Penelope chose to make her home, it is where Jonathan comes from and it is where my children feel a deep sense of belonging, despite Leonard's dreams of Robinson Crusoe-style adventures. And me? This city, with its narrow cobbled streets, gentle, winding rivers and warm, unpretentious people, has been kind to me. It has kept my secrets safe within its stone walls and whilst I feel gratitude for this, it also stings me. For I have never told Jonathan what happened to me. I have always meant to and on a number of occasions I have come very close. But I am so terrified of hurting him and of this comfortable, safe world we have created crumbling down around us were I to tell the truth.

I feel it most in the darkness of the night when, on occasion, I still cry. It happens tonight, I think because I told an outright lie to Leonard. When the light finally fades from the midsummer sky and we are plunged into comforting blackness, Jonathan reaches out to me and traces my tears beneath my eyes. He is still waiting for me to tell him something I know I never can. I have left it too long now. And he accepts me; he loves me, despite that. *If you knew, Jonathan,* I think, *would you love me as much?* Strangely, even knowing that the answer would be a resolute yes, I still cannot tell him. I do not understand what is wrong with me, when I have every opportunity to release my burden.

You will be eighteen years old now, my son. What are you doing with your life?

'I love you, Iris,' Jonathan whispers in the darkness.

'I love you, too,' I say. And I mean it.

※ ※ ※

My sister Violet visited me just once, towards the end of the war. Naturally I was not expecting her; besides which, I had thought so little of her over the years that her presence in the front room of the house I shared with Jonathan came as a great shock. She told me that Father had given her my address and that she was sorry she had never written to me but Mother had forbidden any contact. I blinked into the harsh sunlight and invited her in.

'Why are you here, Violet?' I asked abruptly. She looked hurt and pouted in that manner that used to irritate me so.

'I wish I didn't have to tell you this.' She cast her eyes down. 'But I do, I'm afraid. There is no getting around it.'

'Just tell me, Violet. Tell me quickly.'

'It is Arthur. He has been killed.' She lowered herself into a chair whilst I gripped at the sideboard I was standing beside to steady myself.

'Where?'

'In France. The Battle of the Somme.'

I could not look at her. Did she know that I had received a letter from him just three months previously? A letter from France in which he cheerfully told me he should be home soon? That throughout all of this we had remained in contact? My brother never acquiesced to our mother's demand that there be no contact with me. He was not a coward; he went against Mother's wishes. Not like Violet.

Arthur. My dear brother. I blinked back the tears and rose to make tea. How many more? How many more would be lost to that senseless violence before we could once again live in peace?

Violet was still beautiful in her own vain, steely way. She told me about her husband and two children. Although I had two small children of my own upstairs in the nursery, I found I did not want to introduce them to her. For I did not want them to ask questions about their aunt. So I said nothing about Leonard and Sheena, only briefly mentioning my husband. Nor did I ask her whether she had married an earl or a lord or someone of the landed gentry, as Mother would have desired – she was dressed so stylishly I could only imagine that she had. She looked deeply uncomfortable perched on the edge of my front room armchair, without a maid pouring the tea. The room looked too small and too shabby for her.

'Will you stay the night, Violet? You have come a long way,' I said, with little conviction.

She shook her head and told me she was booked into a small hotel close to the railway station.

'Why did Papa not come and tell me?' I asked.

She hesitated, sipping her tea daintily. 'He was going to, but I offered. I wanted to see you.'

'You did?' I was surprised.

'Well, yes,' she said simply. 'It has been such a terribly long time.' She turned her face away from me and spoke towards the window. 'Iris, what happened to you in East Africa? Nobody will tell me.'

'That's because nobody knows, Violet,' I replied quietly.

'Not even Papa?'

'Not even Papa.'

She turned her translucent blue eyes back to me, so like Mother's that I felt a sudden jolt.

'Won't you…' she faltered, 'won't you tell me?'

'Why do you want to know? To help me, or to assuage your curiosity?' As soon as the words were out, I regretted them. The old unkindness towards my sister had returned so effortlessly, yet I was angry with her, angry that she had never tried to make contact before and angry that she had brought such dreadful news with her. 'I am sorry,' I said irritably. 'That was unfair. But the truth is Violet, there is no part of me that wishes to talk about it.'

She looked crestfallen in that exact same way she always did when we were younger and I would not take her into my confidence. When she left, I stood for some time with my back against the front door, my eyes tightly shut as I recalled that cheerful, straw-haired boy whom I had played hide-and-seek with in the secret corners of The Old Vicarage garden.

The curtain finally closed on the vile war, after it had cut through the heart of communities and swallowed thousands upon thousands of our country's men, my brother amongst them. Yet one beacon of hope shone through the grief that wrapped around us like a heavy mantle: women householders over the age of thirty finally received the vote. It was not all that we had wished for, but it was a start. It was a very necessary start.

Penelope clung tenaciously to life for far longer than any doctor imagined possible. She never went to a sanatorium, she never infected me or anybody else with her illness and she was lucid until the very end. And, not long before she died, she was able for the first time in her life to vote. I walked with her very slowly to the town hall and after she had cast her ballot, she turned to me and smiled proudly, her entire face coming alive and looking very much like that same Miss Logan who had escorted me to Africa all those years ago. Her fever was constant by then and I could see what a physical effort it was for her to have walked there. But the joyful brightness of her eyes spoke volumes. *We have done it. We have* done *it.*

Jonathan and I have lived as man and wife for fourteen years now. As my life with him and our children grows, entrenching its roots more deeply into the ancient soil of this cathedral city, the impossible question that I once breathed to myself countless times a day releases its steely grip on my heart and floats along the winding River Wear and over the stone bridges of Durham, the trace of a whisper in its wake. *When will I see Kamau and my son again?*

PART THREE

CHAPTER FORTY-TWO

IRIS KINGSLEY

MAY 1952

I grip the wooden handrail of the *Dunnottar Castle* and turn my face into the wind, the calm ocean glittering palely beneath me as the ship muscles the waves aside. This is the furthest I have travelled in forty-eight years. Five years ago, when Jonathan was still alive and before he became too ill, we went on a motoring trip. We drove through Paris and then all the way down to Provence and through the Pyrenees. We had not intended to go any further than that, but we had nothing to get back for and we were so enjoying ourselves that we spontaneously booked a ferry crossing to the north of Spain. From there we continued, spending our nights in small hotels that ranged from luxurious to dingy and eating *paella* and *boquerones*, tiny, tasty little fried fish. It was a terribly long journey, but since we were in Spain, I wanted to visit the Alhambra in Granada. Jonathan, ever-obliging, acquiesced and several days later we found ourselves in this enchanting palace, perched on a hilltop, being shown round by a charming English guide with fair hair and eyes that were lost in creases when he smiled. He told us he had married a Spaniard and now lived in Granada with his family. It was strange, but I knew from his eyes that there was another story there; one that, of course, I would never know.

And now, here I am, taking the same route I did all those years ago, feeling sick with anticipation. I have no idea how I shall find Nairobi and even less of a plan for once I arrive. It is now a capital city, a great metropolis, and motorcars have no doubt replaced the oxen, horses and donkeys that once trudged its thoroughfares.

Leonard and Sheena think that I have quite lost my mind. I had not been looking forward to telling them, for their reaction was all too easy to predict.

'You're doing *what?*' Leonard had said, looking at me with an expression of unashamed horror upon his face, quite at odds with his ever-immaculate appearance of two-piece tweed suit and winklepicker shoes. I had invited him and Sheena round for tea and it was only when we were all eating our second piece of cake that I found the courage to tell them.

'Yes, Leonard. I am going to Kenya.'

'But why, Mother?'

Sheena. Dark blue eyes, the same shade as mine. Her father's pointed nose and high forehead. I placed both my hands on the kitchen table to stop them from trembling, which I could only hope neither of them had noticed.

'Why?' I said and rooted my slippered feet into the ground. 'Why? It's not an easy question to answer.'

Leonard and Sheena continued to stare at me and their scrutiny made me uneasy. We were all silent for several moments as I heard the second hand of the grandfather clock tick interminably from one second to the next.

Leonard put his finger in his mouth to wet it and then dabbed at the leftover crumbs on his plate. He always did love cake, even as a boy. I remembered the times I had found him in the larder, hiding behind the door, telltale traces of strawberry jam around his mouth from my Victoria sponges. He leaned forwards and placed one hand lightly over mine. 'Try, Mother. *Try.*'

I sighed and looked at my son's hand. I longed to tell my children, to take them into my confidence. Since their father had died, this urge to share my past with them had strengthened, and yet...

'I've always wanted to visit Kenya,' I told them and tried to smile brightly at them. 'More tea, either of you? I can put the kettle on again.'

Sheena and Leonard looked at me blankly. 'Have you, Mother?' Sheena asked. 'I've never heard you talk about that.'

'Really?' I said lightly and stood up, walking over the tiled kitchen floor to the kettle. I shakily refilled it and placed it on the stove.

'Have *you*, Leonard?' I could hear Sheena asking behind my back. 'Have you heard Mother talk about wanting to visit Kenya?'

I didn't hear him reply and I imagined them making faces at each other, grimaces of surprise and horror, just as they always used to when they were young. There was an invisible line that connected my children and whilst I always felt gratified that they had a close relationship, at that moment I felt more distant from them than ever before; on the periphery of their wordless closeness.

I turned away from the kettle as it boiled and faced them, my back against the kitchen countertop. My feet were hurting. They were often hurting these days.

'Why didn't you go when Daddy was still alive?' Sheena asked. 'Go together?'

I gave a small smile and shook my head. 'Jonathan, in Kenya? I don't think it would have been quite his thing, do you?'

'True,' Leonard said, leaning back on his chair. 'Dad hated the heat.'

But it's not always hot in Nairobi, I thought to myself as the kettle whistled behind me. It can be cold, surprisingly cold.

'But what is it you want to see there exactly, Mother?' Sheena asked. She was looking at me intently, suspiciously. I knew I had to tread carefully with both of my children, but particularly Sheena.

I had, thankfully, anticipated this question and prepared an answer. 'Birds,' I said stoutly. 'I've heard the birdlife there is quite sensational.'

'Go to Berney Marshes in Norfolk, Mother. It's far closer,' Leonard said with a smirk on his face and I should have liked to clip him round the ear, the way his father, playfully, used to. But I did not. I turned back to the kettle and refilled the pot, adding more tea leaves.

'I suspect she was thinking of a more *exotic* variety, Len,' Sheena chided.

I returned to the kitchen table with the teapot and drew my chair out. 'That's right,' I said quietly.

There was a pause whilst I looked from my daughter's face back to my son's. There was another thing, I was aware, that might happen at any moment and just as though Sheena was reading my mind, she said brightly, 'Well, I could come with you, Mother. I'm sure David wouldn't mind looking after the children for a week or so. If it really means that much to you.'

I wanted to keep the desperation out of my voice but I couldn't have Sheena coming with me. I didn't want either of them to come with me.

'I don't think so,' I said softly, after a while.

'Why not?'

I cradled my hands round the warm teacup, 'I... I think this is just what I need. Some time away, on my own, doing things at my own pace.'

Leonard now looked outwardly concerned. He poured more tea for us all, barely taking his eyes from me. 'Mother, you're seventy-two. Do you really think this is the right time for you to be going to a country like Kenya on your own? France, I could understand. Italy. Switzerland. But Kenya?' He was shaking his head emphatically. 'Besides,' he added, scrunching his nose up as though trying to remember something, 'isn't it rather unstable out there at the moment?'

'Unstable?'

'Yes. I read something in the paper. Mau Mau, a group stirring up trouble, trying to reclaim land back from settlers.'

'That doesn't sound good, Mother.' Sheena frowned.

'No,' agreed Leonard. 'I think I'd worry about you too much being out there alone.'

'Oh, but I shan't be alone.'

Both their eyes widened. 'You shan't?' Sheena asked.

'No, of course not. I was thinking of having a proper tour booked through the travel agents. Itinerary, hotels, guides, all that sort of thing. So really, I shall be well looked after. And I don't think Kenya's quite as backward as you think it to be.'

'Nobody's saying it's *backward*, Mother, just that it might be a challenge for you to be alone there. But if you have it all organised…' His voice trailed off as he glanced over at his sister, who continued to look unconvinced. 'At least you will be in good company.' I raised an eyebrow at him. I had no idea to whom he was referring. 'Princess Elizabeth.' Leonard smiled. 'She's going on a royal visit to Kenya soon.'

'She is?'

The smile crept into his eyes. My Leonard. Always the royalist. As a child he would cut crowns out of cardboard boxes and pretend to be King George and his eyes would go all moony whenever Princess Margaret was mentioned. 'Yes, it's her and Prince Philip's first time there.' I digested this information. It was hardly going to make much difference to my trip. But for Leonard's sake, I gave him a bright smile. Little did either of us know when we had that conversation that King George VI would die soon and Elizabeth would no longer be a princess, but a queen.

'So,' I said, trying my best to sound cheerful. 'If it's safe enough for Princess Elizabeth, it's safe enough for me.'

Leonard looked convinced by this argument, Sheena, who was still scrutinising me, less so.

'I knew you would be supportive. Anyway, it's a while away still. I shan't travel until the end of May,' I added. Before either of them had a chance to respond to this, I asked them how the children were, a sure way to change the conversation as there was never a shortage of things to talk about on this topic. I have four grandchildren, two of them Leonard's and two Sheena's. Four little girls; on my good days I find their tears and demands endearing and, on my bad, tiresome. I half listened as Sheena and Leonard chattered away but the truth was, all I could think was, *Africa, Africa, I am going to Africa, after forty-seven years.*

Fazal Ahmed once told me that he would never leave Nairobi, that East Africa had become his home and that he would raise children and grandchildren to thrive and be successful there. Knowing his character, as I once had, I do not doubt he could achieve this. But whether he has stayed in Nairobi all these years… and even if he has, how difficult will it be to find him?

I feel it more likely that Mr Ahmed will still be in Nairobi than Kamau. I would love to try to find Muthoni but I have only a single name for her. I would not know where to begin. As for Mr Lawrence, occasionally over the years my thoughts have reluctantly turned to him. I wonder if he stayed on in Nairobi – if he is still there. Fear pricks at me and I hope that the city has grown enough that there is no chance I will bump into him. Though, of course, even if I walked past him in the street, after all these years, would we know one another?

I shake my head and pull my attention back to Leonard and Sheena. The tour I told them I had arranged has no truth to it. The single thing I have booked is a hotel for a week following my arrival. There is only one hotel I remember from my time there, the Stanley, though there was one other place that opened just before I left, but I cannot remember the name of it. And so, just one week ago, I went to the travel agents and asked them to telephone Nairobi and book me a room at the Stanley. The young man behind the counter was clearly unaccustomed to such requests and his dark-fringed eyes widened with something between surprise and respect. After some investigations, he discovered that its name had changed to the New Stanley and duly booked me a room.

As the ship pulls out of Tilbury Docks, I stand on deck watching as England, with her patchwork of pastures and farmland, skirted by neat little villages, slowly recedes into the distance as I move further south to a land that continues to visit me in both my dreams and nightmares. Kenya. Though, of course, it was not called that when I was there; it was simply the East Africa Protectorate. It was not until many years after I left, in 1920, that this land was renamed after Mount Kirinyaga, the region's highest mountain, a name meaning 'mountain of whiteness'. But my people could not say Kirinyaga, so to placate our soft tongues it was changed to Kenya. It still sounds strange to me. The name lacks the melody that Kirinyaga possesses, but I shouldn't think they would change it back on my account.

I remain detached from the sea voyage, as I do the journey by train from Mombasa to Nairobi, which, if my memory serves me correctly, has changed little in fifty years. More settlements perhaps, more children running alongside the train, churning up dust with their bare feet. The whirring clack and the smell of the steam that blurs the glass of the window stirs a long-forgotten memory in me: that voyage all those years ago. It does not feel like it was me at all, but something I watched at the picture house: a girl leaning far out of the window and breathing in the shimmering African dawn. That withering look from Mr Lawrence as he surveyed my face covered in soot and red earth. When I think of him, I cannot remember what he looks like, only a few disparate features that hover in mid-air, but do not come together: his monocle; the fair, receding hair; the groomed moustache hanging above thin, pinched lips.

When I awake from an uncomfortable, almost sleepless night, I pull my sleeve up over my fingers and rub a circle on the glass before pressing my nose and forehead against it and peering outside. Birds flash past the carriage. Trees everywhere. I do not remember the names of these trees, nor the particular type of antelope that darts gracefully through the long, yellow grass.

We pass tiny villages and shops made from sheets of corrugated iron, painted bright crimsons and blues. Clumps
of bananas hang up outside them and women run towards
the train holding out bags of sugarcane, calling up at this
hulking iron beast that pulls us through their land. But all
I can think of, all I can focus on, is my son. I wonder if he
lives in this village, or that village, if he has inherited his
father's love of nature, and birds in particular, and whether
he looks more like Kamau or myself. I can feel my mouth
set in a hard, determined line, my jaw scarcely relaxing for
the entire journey, which passes in a tangle of salt-whipped
wind, strengthening sun and arid plains.

And then, Nairobi. By the time I arrive, I am so exhausted by lack of sleep and the tension that has been building in
my body that, standing at the train station, I am flung into
confusion. For though a great many years have passed since
I was last here, I still remember the day I arrived, clutching
Pearl Rivers and *Alice's Adventures in Wonderland* and a hope
for a better life than the one Lord Sidcup could offer me.
And yet, standing here amongst the clamour and noise and
motors and concrete, nothing looks familiar. Nothing at all.
Where are the shacks that line the street up from the railway
station, the rickshaws pulling people towards Government
Hill, the bullocks and donkeys that throng the potholed
thoroughfare?

As I stand outside the station, I feel my stomach heaving, a sensation I can only identify as nerves. Yet at least, I
think to myself, I am feeling *something*. All too often I have
become inured to feeling nothing at all, a cavernous void

where happiness or fear or sorrow ought to sit. Men surround me, dozens of them, in trousers and buttoned shirts;
this too, is new, for the last time I was here the vast majority
of Africans one saw wore traditional dress.

'Taxi, Mama!'

'This way, Madam!'

'Your bags are where?'

'You want to go where?'

The faceless voices come at me from all sides, a cacophony
of tones and timbres, and I force myself to take a deep breath
and swing towards the man standing closest to my luggage.
I nod at him and mutely follow as he swats his competitors
out of the way. Battered old lorries, donkey-carts, gleaming
new motorcars fight for right of way as we plough through
the chaos. Nairobi. Is this *really*, can this truly be Nairobi?

The New Stanley Hotel is, indeed, new. Rebuilt, I am
told, after a fire back in 1905 destroyed the original premises
and, indeed, much of Victoria Street. When I tell the young
African man behind the desk that I was last here in 1904,
well before he would even have been born, he looks at me
in bewilderment and murmurs something about Nairobi
being a very different place now. Different indeed. For after
resting in my hotel room for a while, I take a short walk. I
see the names Victoria Street and Government Road, which
I remember. Yet nothing, *nothing* is familiar. Of course I
expected the small township to have expanded, but nothing
prepared me for this.

I stand on the roadside, blinking into the sunlight as
motorcars and motorbuses roar down the gum-tree-lined

avenues, past offices and shops, department stores and public buildings and suddenly I feel terribly old. The size of this city, I feel with a sinking heart, is unnerving. How am I to find anybody within this maze of streets? I take a deep breath and keep walking, keep placing one foot in front of the other, and eventually I find myself outside a film hall. I look up and see the name of a film I have not heard of, but impulsively I enter anyway and buy a ticket. Everything inside is comfortingly familiar, no different at all from the picture house in Durham. There are not many people in the audience, but it is clear that we are exclusively white. Though the boy who sold me the ticket was not and that is something, I suppose. When the heavy, red curtains swing open, the film does not start. Rather, upon the grainy screen, Queen Elizabeth appears, smiling broadly, astride her horse outside Buckingham Palace. Behind her, a Union Jack flutters in the breeze and I am taken by surprise when the small audience jumps as one to their feet, placing their hands on their hearts.

I am in no mood for this and frown, staring ahead of me. But it is not long before I hear somebody coughing behind me. I turn to look and see that an elderly gentleman is motioning for me to stand. He is dressed in what looks like military uniform and wears, of all things, a monocle in one eye. A shudder passes through me involuntarily as I stare at him. But no – it is not him.

Reluctantly, I get to my feet and stare ahead of me, waiting for this show of patriotism in this British colony to be over before sinking back into my seat again in relief. Once the film is over, a nondescript sentimental romance, I decide to return to the hotel for a cup of tea. It is not terribly hot outside, cooler in fact than England at this time of year, yet I feel as though all the moisture has been sucked from me.

Before I go to the restaurant area, I decide to ask the young fellow at the desk about whatever form of Yellow Pages they have here. He eyes me curiously, that same look of bafflement he gave me earlier, as though surveying a relic.

'Yes, Madam,' he tells me, 'we have Yellow Pages,' and he produces a thick, bound copy from behind the desk. 'Name?' he asks. I am so surprised that the Yellow Pages even exists here that I am unable to answer for a short while. He raises an eyebrow at me.

'Kamau,' I breathe. 'Benedict Kamau.'

The young man licks the tip of one finger and flicks through the phone book until he reaches K. He turns it round so that it faces me and runs his finger down through the Kamaus, of which there are a great many. But no Benedict. I bite my bottom lip. I know I am being watched, intently, and I wish that I could be alone to do this, to take this hefty book up to the quiet privacy of my room.

'May I... May I borrow this book for a short while?'

'Does Madam wish to make telephone calls?'

'Yes,' I nod. 'May I do this from my room?'

He smiles indulgently. 'Yes, Madam. But you will be charged on your final bill for these calls. It is cheaper if I make them for you from here.' His accent is impossibly polished and clipped, his black buttons gleaming upon his smart blue jacket. Pleased as I am to see an African engaged in work of this sort, it is impossible to match this image with that of the Africans in Nairobi when I was last here. For it was a European town then, Africans only working as labourers or farmhands. Or teachers— A memory of Kamau rises, unbidden, his dark, warm hands over mine, and it takes my breath away. I gasp. The young man eyes me, both eyebrows rising, and I frown, shake my head. I have not got off to a good start with him, with – I eye his name badge – Edward.

I reach out for the book. 'I shall bring it back once I am finished. May I have a pot of tea sent up to the room, please?'

He hands me over my key. 'Dial 2 from your telephone Madam and this will reach room service. You can order it that way.'

I nod, clasping the book to my chest and hurrying off beneath his gaze.

There are also a number of Fazals in the phone book. Thirteen, to be precise, I count as I run my finger down the list. Yet close to the bottom I see it: 'Fazal & Sons, Tailors, Tentmakers, Upholsterers'. My breath catches and my hands feel clammy. Fazal & Sons. Could this possibly be him? Could it possibly be so easy? There is a phone number but I do not ring it. I drink my cup of tea and pour myself another. It has been almost half a century since I have drunk this peculiar, milky Kenyan tea.

And then I stare at the telephone, blink several times, lift the receiver – and immediately replace it. I find I cannot call the number. Tomorrow, I think, after I am better rested, I shall walk to the address given in the book, to see if it is really him. But before I do that, I will visit the police station and see if they can help me with Kamau.

I do not even eat dinner that evening, I am so tired. And I forget to return the Yellow Pages to Edward, remembering only in the middle of the night. Throwing the sheets off me, I place the heavy book by the door so that I do not forget to take it downstairs in the morning, and climb back into bed. But then, as though my legs are separate from my brain, I find myself rising once more and turning on the dim bedside lamp. Crouching down by the door in my nightgown, I turn to the letter L in the book. I run my finger down the page several times but it is not there. I cannot find the name Lawrence. I close the book with a heavy thud and stumble back to bed, sleeping deeper and sounder that night than I have done in many months.

Edward directs me to the police station. It is not far and we worked out on a map together at reception the direction to Biashara Street afterwards. I can see he is itching with curiosity as to why I should want to go to a police station, but I just raise an eyebrow at him and walk outside into the clamour of this city from which I've been so long estranged.

Women are carrying babies, tied tightly to their backs with colourful strips of material and sometimes covered in blankets, their tiny heads capped by knitted hats bobbing as they stare around them, blinking. Hawkers sell roasted maize, battered books, newspapers, paper cones of peanuts.

Everywhere there is noise, so much noise, and the number of motorcars careering down the street is astonishing – far more, even, than in Durham.

The police station is a dark, squat building with grand lettering painted over the entrance. A man in a uniform and cap sits behind an iron grille picking at his teeth and poring over a huge book containing spidery black handwriting. I think that he cannot have seen me as he does not look up, but after several minutes of clearing my throat, I realise he is simply ignoring me.

'Excuse me,' I say to him. Lazily, he draws his eyes up and stares at me. He inclines his head slightly. 'You are fine?'

Is this a greeting? 'Oh. Well. I am fine, thank you. And you?'

The man grunts, his eyes falling back down to the interminable lists he appears so engaged in.

'I wonder if you can help me. You see, I am looking for somebody.'

'You are looking for somebody?' he echoes.

'Yes. That's right. If a person is missing, I imagined this is something you can help with.'

The man sighs, stands up and rifles through a cupboard behind him until he finds a piece of paper and pencil.

'Name?' His eyelids droop disinterestedly.

'Kamau. Benedict Kamau.'

'Relationship?'

'I beg your pardon?'

'Relationship.' He sighs again. 'How do you know this Benedict Kamau?' I pause, biting my bottom lip. 'Friend,' I eventually reply.

He frowns and squints at me, then shakes his head and continues.

'Last place seen? Date?'

Heavens, how can I answer such a question? 'Well, it is not quite that simple, I'm afraid.'

He places his pencil down on the table and leans back in his chair, surveying me.

'The trouble is, I have not seen him for some time.'

'How do you know he is missing, then?'

How, indeed?

I run my fingers through my hair. It is hot and airless inside here and clumps of my fringe are starting to stick to the sides of my face. There is nothing about this man that I feel comfortable with, but I am left with no other option.

'Can I be frank with you?'

He stares at me, bewildered, as though I am quite mad, or stupid. Or both.

'The truth is, I have not seen Mr Kamau for a very long time indeed. Years, in fact.'

'But you are wishing to file a missing person's report?'

'Yes, you see—'

'You are a time-waster, Madam.'

'No, I—'

'*Yes*. You must waste no more of my time. I am a busy man.' He reaches for the piece of paper, screws it up and throws it towards a waste-paper basket, missing.

I refuse to be fobbed off so easily. 'Could you please just look for me, in your files? To see if you have any information on a man of that name.'

He shakes his head resolutely. 'I cannot do that.'

'Why ever not?'

'*Because,* Madam, it is not my job to do that. It is the job of my superior. And I tell you right now, he dislikes time-wasters even more than me.'

I want to snatch his cap off and hurl it across the room in frustration. But I see that I shall get nowhere with him.

'You have been most unhelpful,' I tell him and turn on my heel, walking back outside into the dazzling light and clamour of Nairobi.

Now what? What other avenues are there for me to locate Kamau? Perhaps I could go to Nairobi's central prison to ask about archives. But should archives for former prisoners even exist, what are the chances of my being able to access them? First, I will try Ahmed Fazal, and *then* I will go to the prison.

❧ ❧ ❧

A small bell rings overhead as I enter the shop on Bi-ashara Street. Shelves of neatly piled cloths and fabrics line one entire side, reaching all the way to the ceiling, and framed verses of Arabic calligraphy dot the walls. A young Asian man and woman stand behind the counter and I stand, numbly, in the doorway, simply staring at them until the young lady smiles at me warmly. 'Can I help you, Madam?'

'Yes.' I clear my throat, take a few steps away from the door. 'I am looking for a Mr Ahmed Fazal. Have I come to the right place?'

Now it is the young man's turn to speak, leaning eagerly over the counter. Can I be imagining it, or do I see Mr Ahmed in him?

'That is my grandfather. He rarely comes into the store these days. But he will be in this afternoon to speak to one of our customers. I can call him, if you wish, Madam. Ask him to come in earlier?'

'Oh no,' I say hurriedly, 'I can wait. Really.'

The two of them glance at one another. 'Are you sure?' He continues. 'Perhaps Madam would care to sit in the back room, where you might be more comfortable?'

That flawless English, so polite that one wouldn't even hear it back home, save for in the smartest of establishments.

'I don't wish to be any trouble...'

'No trouble, Madam,' the young woman says. She has a sleek, black plait hanging over one shoulder and as I follow behind her, she leaves a faint trace of jasmine.

And so I sit and I wait. I hear customers come and go and the kind young woman, who tells me her name is Hasina, brings me cups of tea. But it is not like the tea I have been drinking at the hotel; it is stronger, spicier. Like the tea that Mr Ahmed used to make me and that I have tried to emulate all these years. I must have been waiting for a few hours by the time I hear the bell and the young man, the grandson, comes to tell me that Mr Ahmed has arrived. My nerves flip and the soggy bacon and eggs that I ate that morning sit uncomfortably in my stomach. Moments later, the bell rings again and from where I am seated in the back room I hear a loud, gruff voice, unmistakably British.

'*Thaatha*,' I hear the young man saying, 'there is a lady waiting for you in the back room. She has been here some time.'

'Who is it?'

'I don't know.'

'I'll need the back room to talk to Mr Madingley. I'm afraid I'll have to deal with her afterwards.'

He enters the room, followed by a portly Englishman, who nods brusquely at me. I cannot meet his eye. I can only stare at Mr Ahmed. It is, unmistakably, him. He looks back at me, smiles warmly, yet without a glimmer of recognition in his eyes. He apologises for keeping me waiting for so long, but he will have to keep me a little longer if I would not mind waiting in the shop for him. I stand, barely able to take my eyes from his face as I nod and walk outside.

I listen as Mr Ahmed is talked down to like a schoolboy, the British man picking fault with the suit he is having tailored for him. Mr Ahmed replies in gentle, appeasing tones, telling him he has every confidence in his grandson's abilities but as he is a valued customer, they can together consider a small discount. The stout man is rude, derisive. Clearly he has no respect for Mr Ahmed or his grandson and I do not wish to listen to the way he is addressing them, but it is impossible not to hear him, his voice raised.

Eventually, the meeting draws to a close and the man blusters out, his nose and ears pink. I heard the discount offered and I only hope that Mr Ahmed has not lost too much money in the transaction. He soon walks out of the back room, shaking his head, and then, stopping in his tracks, he remembers my presence.

'Good afternoon, Madam,' he says. 'It is a great pleasure. I am terribly sorry to keep you waiting for so long. Now,' he goes on, his face lit up into a sincere smile, 'how can I be of assistance to you?'

I blink at him, taking in the kind face that has aged so much over the nearly fifty years that have passed and yet, somehow, not altered at all. I part my lips to speak but, as I stand there, I find I cannot.

'Madam.' He raises an eyebrow. 'Are you quite well?'

He looks at Hasina and his grandson but they do not say a word, both as bewildered as Mr Ahmed looks.

I clear my throat and breathe again. Strength, Iris. Have strength. 'Mr Ahmed,' I say eventually in a voice scarcely louder than a whisper. 'Can it really be you?'

He puckers his brow. I can see him thinking, *Who is this person?* I take a step towards him and then another. My eyes flicker over his face and I watch as he stares back at me as though trying to read me, before he takes a sharp intake of breath.

He looks as though he is not breathing and I hold a hand up, reaching towards his arm. 'Mr Ahmed…' I say. 'Do you know me?'

'I…' He falters. 'Are you…'

I nod and take another step towards him until I am standing close enough to grasp both his hands lightly in mine. 'Yes. It is me. Iris.'

'Mrs Lawrence,' he whispers.

'Iris,' I repeat firmly and his eyes, one shade darker than the setting sun, cloud over. I feel a tear escaping lightly down one cheek, but I am smiling. I am happy, so happy. 'I found you. I never imagined – never believed I could find you so quickly.'

'But Mrs – *Iris* – how long have you been in Kenya? Where are you staying? What are you—' He stops abruptly, squeezes my hands between his. 'This is absurd, talking like this, asking such important questions beside my shop counter.' He shakes his head. 'You have already met my grandson, Tajim? His wife, Hasina?' Both of them are staring at us, baffled. Mr Ahmed does not even wait for a reply. 'Please. You must come home with me. Have something to eat. Meet Maliha.'

'Maliha,' I breathe and I find myself smiling broadly.

'Yes.' He smiles back. 'Maliha.'

Without waiting another moment, he fetches his over-coat from a peg, holds the door open for me, and together we walk out on to the street into the misty May Nairobi morning.

🕊 🕊 🕊

The truth is I have never imagined what Maliha might be like. But now that I meet her, here at their home in Park-lands, I find she is exactly as she should be; the only kind of open-hearted woman that Mr Ahmed could have married. She has aged beautifully, her hair still dark and oiled, with only a few streaks of silver threading their way through her long plait. Her face is round and dimpled and full of mirth and the gentle folds of her stomach are concealed beneath her simple but elegant sari. Her liquid eyes are dark and laughing and I trust her instinctively, just as I always trusted Mr Ahmed.

She bustles through from the kitchen, putting dishes I have never seen before down in front of me. She calls them dal gosht and dahi bhallay. All this, though she knows nothing about me or even who I am. And then there is tea, so scaldingly hot that it almost takes the roof of my mouth off, but so wonderfully fragrant and delicious,

He keeps looking at me, shaking his head and rubbing a hand over his eyes as though I might vanish. Then he opens and closes his mouth as he watches me eat, before frowning and shaking his head again. Astonishing, how a man can look the same after half a century. For his skin remains smooth and taut across his cheekbones and his light brown eyes still gleam with humour and kindness. Only the salt-and-pepper greyness of his hair belies his real age. As for myself, I am under no illusion that when Mr Ahmed looks at me he does not see before him that same girl from those years gone by. When I look in the mirror, what do I see? I see regret, pain and loss woven into each white hair, each line that traverses my face, each blotch and blemish. The years have done nothing to alleviate this loss, only to entrench it deeper.

And yet now, by some miracle, a man sits opposite me at a table who may provide hope and answers for me; a man who was my first friend in Nairobi, whom I entrusted the making of my clothes to, but, more significantly, the weight of a heavy secret.

Maliha's food is delicious, but I find I have little appetite. She hovers in the doorway, her dark, laughing eyes glinting at me, and I look up and smile at her. How much, I wonder, does she know of me? We have barely spoken, Mr Ahmed and I, and yet I know that the unspoken question upon my lips hangs between us, as weighty as water. Yet I cannot ask it, not yet. For in these moments of not knowing, hope may still be present, the wings of sunbirds hovering in mid-air as they use their long, curved beaks to extract nectar. Eventually, I break the silence.

'You look so well, Mr Ahmed.'

He chuckles, self-consciously removes his spectacles from his nose and blows on them, hot round moons. 'If I am to call you Iris, I think it is a fair exchange that you call me Fazal, hmm?'

I smile and agree.

'You also look well.'

'No.' I laugh. 'You are kind. But we both know I have not aged as gracefully as you.'

The smile fades from his face and he sighs deeply. 'What you must have suffered. When you left here.'

I feel sharp tears stinging at the corners of my eyes. *Do not cry. Do* not. *You have just arrived here.* 'Yes,' I agree.

'And…' He pauses, 'I have no doubt it did not end there. That the suffering continued. Or continues, I should say.'

He says it so simply and yet, as always, in his words lie deep acknowledgment and understanding. To think that all these years have passed without me benefiting from the integrity and warmth of his friendship. But I take a deep breath and think, *I am here now. I always said I would return one day, and here I am.*

'Iris,' he says, replacing his spectacles, looking directly at me. 'Why have you come here? Why now?'

At that moment, Maliha appears by my side, laying a creamy-looking delicacy down on the table. It looks like a dessert of some sort and I am embarrassed, for I have scarcely touched the rest of her delicious food.

'Gulab jamun,' she announces.

'Gulab jamun?'

'You have to try Maliha's gulab, Iris,' Fazal enthuses, his eyes crinkling. 'It is marvellous. If you do not eat anything else, you must try this.'

My stomach protests, but I do not wish to disappoint and so remove a corner of the round ball with the teaspoon. It is, indeed, delicious. Delicate and intensely sweet, yet somehow not sickeningly so, infused with subtle flavours. I find myself going back for more.

'Wonderful,' I say. 'What are the ingredients?'

'Milk, flour, syrup, cardamom, rose water and saffron,' Maliha says.

'Gracious.' Once I have started, I cannot stop and this appears to please my hosts inordinately. It feels curious, having two people intently watching me eat but I try not to pay too much attention to this, instead casting my eyes about the room, adorned with tasteful floral-patterned rugs, framed photographs and verses from the Quran.

'More?' Fazal asks.

'Oh no.' I laugh, drawing my eyes back to him. 'No. Thank you. But you were right, it is marvellous. Thank you, Maliha.'

She beams at me and I feel certain that, had I stayed in Nairobi, Maliha and I would have been friends. She takes my plate away and I shift in the wooden chair.

'Fazal,' I say, 'that question you just asked me, about why I am here… do you mind terribly if we do not talk about that just yet; if I can ask you some questions first? You see, this isn't terribly easy for me and…'

'Of course,' he says. 'Forgive me. I cannot imagine the courage it has taken you to make this journey.' He pauses and smiles reflectively. 'Though, saying that, you always were a courageous soul.'

I smile back at him gratefully and close my eyes. Was I? I cannot remember the last time I felt truly courageous. Even making this journey now does not feel like an act of courage, for I have concealed the true reason for it from the two people closest to me in the world, my children. Just as I have concealed so much of my past from them.

'Iris, may I get you some more tea, my dear?'

My eyes flicker open. 'I am alright, Fazal. Will you tell me about your family? Fill me in on your life from the moment I left up until now?'

He smiles and nods his head slowly.

And so, though I am a ghost from his past, he tells me. He begins with Maliha arriving in Nairobi a mere six months after I left; his first son was born nine months later, another following four years on. And then a girl, a little girl who looked just like him and is now forty-eight years of age. Around the same time as the birth of his daughter, he finally had sufficient funds in the bank to extend the workshop, to turn it into something he could be proud of.

Fazal's children did well at the Asian school, all three of them, his eldest son excelling so much at mathematics that Fazal questioned on more than one occasion the wisdom of drawing him into his business rather than allowing him to follow his own path. His soul-searching, however, was unnecessary as both the boys, when they were old enough, came of their own free will. They needed no cajoling from their father. They worked hard, the three of them, their client base and reputation expanding. All the while, Maliha and their daughter sold Indian sweets from the house, this side business taking on a life and income of its own.

He tells me that here he is, many years later, with his eldest's younger son and his wife now running Fazal & Sons. They have been happy for many years in this comfortable house on Limuru Road in Parklands, not far from City Park, so there is plenty of greenery around. He is proud of himself, he tells me, of what he has achieved.

'You knew me when I was just starting out as a young tailor. I never imagined in my wildest dreams that all this would come to pass. And all the while,' he says, 'Nairobi has continued to grow. I am sure you barely recognise it, am I right?'

I have not taken my eyes from my friend all the time that he has been speaking. I laugh a little, the flow of Fazal's monologue broken. 'To tell you the truth, I have been a little scared, walking around Nairobi. Nothing looks familiar at all.'

'Scared?' He chuckles. 'That I find hard to believe. You were always so fearless. I remember when you walked down to Bazaar Street to see the dresses I had made you. Walking to Bazaar Street! I tell you, in all the time I worked there, until the shop was renovated, not one single European lady came to my workshop. Not a single one, apart from you!'

I smile wryly, dabbing my finger in the remaining crumbs of gulab jamun and placing it in my mouth. Then I stand and walk over to the window, staring out at Fazal's small garden and the bright oleander bush. Finally, I turn, my arms crossed protectively, and I feel a shadow pass over my face.

'What happened to Mr Lawrence?'

Fazal looks shocked by my question, though I am not sure why. Perhaps this is a past that he also does not wish to revisit.

'Mr Lawrence,' he repeats slowly. Maliha has come into the dining area with more tea, quietly sitting at one end of the table as she pours it into the ornamented silver goblets. 'I am sure this will come as a great relief to you, Iris, but there is no chance that you will come across him whilst you are here in Nairobi.'

I expel a large breath of air. 'He left.'

'Yes,' he replies quietly.

'When? When did he leave?'

'Oh. A long time ago now. He stayed after – after what happened. I didn't see too much of him; he threw himself into his work and hunting, as far as I could gather. But then he went back to England, several years after you left.'

'Do you know why?' I ask hesitantly. Do I want to know? Do I care? I know I do not, but my curiosity overtakes me.

'It is not a pretty story, Iris.'

'I see.' I look down. 'Perhaps you can tell me another time.'

He nods. 'I heard nothing of him after his departure,' he continues slowly, 'so I cannot tell you if he still lives. I take it you heard nothing of him back in England?'

I shake my head, sunlight slanting through the open window and falling upon my hands so they gleam white.

'You never divorced?'

I turn my face away to look out of the window and then shake my head again, blinking several times. I wait, whilst Fazal stares at me with a look of such deep empathy written across his face that it makes me want to weep. It is clear he knows the question that must come, eventually. Yet of course he cannot, and am sure he does not wish to, pre-empt it.

'Did you find happiness again, Iris?' Fazal asks gently.

I look him directly in the eye, walk back to the table and sit down. 'I lived with a man for many years. Jonathan. He died a little over a year ago. He was a good man. He was kind to me. I have a son and a daughter, and grandchildren.'

The relief that is written upon his face is palpable. In turn, I feel my muscles loosen. I wonder about the extent to which Fazal has thought of me over the years. He was a friend to me and as well as grieving the loss of Kamau and my child, I also grieved for him for some time. Did he grieve for me? I find myself relieved that Maliha came so soon after I left and wonder if my sudden banishment played any role in this.

'Fazal.' I smile sadly. My voice, even to me, sounds soft and distant, as though I am hearing myself speak through a long, hollow tube. 'You must tell me now. You must tell me what happened to Kamau and my son.'

He stares at me, wide-eyed, unblinking, and I feel guilt stab at me that I have entered his life again so suddenly like this. Fazal swallows hard and asks Maliha to fetch a jug of water.

'Fazal.' I say softly, 'Please, just tell me. *Please.*'

He taps his fingers on the tabletop as he turns his head and looks the window. After some time, he looks back at me, eyes narrowed.

'Iris,' he says. Maliha brings the water and three tumblers and I drink thirstily. 'I wish there was another way to say this. I wish I could tell you anything… anything else at all besides what happened. But –' he sighs deeply – 'I cannot.'

I nod, urging him with my eyes to continue. I am almost holding my breath.

'After you left, Mr Lawrence was in a blind rage. Everybody knew about it. Everybody was talking about it. He vowed to find the father of your child and he involved the police, who questioned everybody you had come into contact with since your arrival. Me included.'

I widen my eyes.

'No,' he says quickly. 'I did not say a thing. I told them about making clothes for you, but that I knew nothing more.' He pauses and digs a thumb deeply into his temple, massaging it. 'Somebody though,' he says quietly, 'somebody revealed Kamau's identity.'

My head hangs and I place both my palms flat on the tabletop and press them down. I am silent for a few moments as I stare at my hands as though willing them to steady me and then I look back up at Fazal, my eyes boring into his.

'Muthoni,' I whisper. I look away towards the open window, where a pied wagtail has alighted on the sill.

From the corner of my eye, I see Fazal exchange a look with Maliha. No doubt she knows this story.

'We cannot lay blame on Muthoni, though,' he says. 'I do not need to tell you about your past husband's temper or his tactics of… coercion. Muthoni was fond of you, that much was clear. She would not have revealed anything lightly.'

I nod tightly. 'I know. I do not like to think how he extracted that information from her.' I stand up again and walk to the window, placing a single palm against the glass. 'And then?' I ask with my back to him. 'And then what happened?'

'And then…' he continues slowly, 'whether it was Muthoni, or somebody else, we shall never know for sure. But Kamau was identified as the father.' I hear Fazal's words catching, a single sob bursting from his mouth. 'And then… and then he was hanged.'

And then he was hanged.

I rest my forehead lightly against the pane and close my eyes. I think of his neck, of the smooth skin and the graceful curve over the Adam's apple.

'I'm so very sorry,' Fazal says eventually. 'He was a good man.'

'Yes,' I force myself to say, my voice distant and hollow. 'He was.' I pause. 'And my son?' I ask. 'What happened to my son?'

It is only at this point that fear grips me, winding me of all my breath. I take my palm and forehead away from the glass and stagger back slightly, breathless and aching. Within seconds I find Fazal and Maliha at either side of me, murmuring small, unintelligible, soothing words as they draw me back into the chair.

'If my son is also dead,' I gasp, 'just tell me quickly. *Please.*'

The kindness and sympathy in Maliha's eyes is unbearable and I find I cannot look at her.

'Iris,' Fazal says quickly, placing a hand over mine, 'I do not think he is dead. At least, I don't know.'

'You do not know?' I look up at him – hope, that terrible, necessary thing, welling in my soul. 'But what happened to him? Do you know anything? Anything at all?'

'I made some enquiries,' Fazal says, 'around the same time as Kamau…' His voice trails off. 'I wanted to find him, to somehow get word to you. But he just… vanished.'

'Vanished?' I look at him desperately.

'I wanted to try to speak to Muthoni, to see if she knew of his whereabouts—'

'Muthoni was the one to leave the house with him. She was carrying him, when Mr Lawrence pushed her out.'

'I see,' Fazal says, his face solemn. 'Well, I thought she would be the best person to speak to. But…'

'But?'

'But I also could not find her, and nobody could give me information about where she might be. Mr Lawrence employed a new maid and I once tried to talk to her. But she knew nothing of Muthoni. Of course, there was also the issue that had I even obtained information, I had no means of contacting you. There was no forwarding address for you. Iris…' He pauses, runs a hand over his face, 'I truly believed I would never see you again.'

'You never received my letters?'

'Letters? No! Nothing. I would have responded immediately if I had. I cannot believe it. Why—'

'Mr Lawrence,' I say quietly. 'He knew the postmaster. He knew the entire European community.'

I fall silent, take a sip of water, look from Fazal to Maliha and back to Fazal again, these good, kind, quiet people.

'Where are you staying, Iris?' Maliha asks me.

'The New Stanley Hotel. The Stanley was the only hotel when I was here before, so it was the only name I could remember when I made the booking.' I laugh mirthlessly.

'You must come and stay here with us,' she replies. 'We have a spare room.'

'Oh no.' I shake my head. 'I do not wish to impose on you. Truly. I cannot.'

'It is no imposition,' Fazal says. 'It would be a great pleasure.'

'Thank you,' I reply quietly. 'But all the same, I think it makes more sense for me to be in the hotel.'

'At least tell us you will think about it. Agreed?'

I pause and try to muster a smile. 'Agreed.'

'And for how long,' Fazal continues, 'do you plan to be in Nairobi?'

'Well,' I reply, 'that all rather depends.'

Fazal and Maliha look at me expectantly and I am aware of the heavy silence and the small, subtle noises filtering through it: the distant horn of a car; sporadic banging, hammer against nail; the whistling of birds.

'On what does it depend?' Fazal asks softly.

I take a deep breath. 'On how long it takes me to find my son.'

Fazal stares at me, a pained expression upon his face. 'I see.'

'Even if he is dead,' I say quickly, 'I need to know, Fazal. I must. It has haunted me all these years, the not knowing.'

'I understand. At least, I cannot fully understand. But I can only imagine how painful this must have been for you all this time.'

I nod briefly. I long to ask him something, but I know it is not fair of me. And yet, he is my friend. He was my friend all those years ago and has, in a way, never stopped being my friend. Besides, I have nowhere else to turn.

'Will you help me find him?'

The words have escaped my lips and they hang there, vast and weighty. It is Maliha who eventually speaks.

'Of course, my dear. Of course we will do everything we can to help you, won't we, Fazal?'

Fazal takes a deep breath and smiles at me, though his eyes are sad. 'Yes, Iris. Of course. It will be a great pleasure to assist you. We cannot promise any miracles. But we can try. We can try. Maliha and I will pray for you. Oh, and Iris – there is one thing that I remember, something that is particularly important now. It could have just been hearsay, but…'

'Tell me, Fazal.'

'Though I never saw him, they say that the child was named Maitho.'

'Who is "they"?' I whisper.

He waves a hand through the air. 'People. Just people. There was talk of little else at the time.'

'I see.' I pause. 'Maitho.'

'Yes. It is a Kikuyu name. It means "eyes".'

Fazal does not need to say as much, but it is clear that he thinks it highly unlikely I will ever find my son. He tells me that several million people reside in this country now, not to mention the numerous shantytowns, home to thousands more, that dot the length and breadth of Nairobi and beyond. Yet I have come all this way. True, I have no idea even where we ought to start. Nairobi is unrecognisable as the small township I once inhabited. Yet start we shall, somehow.

But how much do I know, how much do I really understand of what is happening in this country at present? Fazal tells me that the truth is he feels scared for the first time in the fifty-something years he has lived in Nairobi, scared of how volatile it feels, as though they are sitting on a pile of wood that might burst into flames at any moment.

'Who are these Mau Mau?' I ask quietly, though I am not certain I can listen to the answer. All I can think of now is his neck, Kamau's neck, and my son, out there, somewhere.

Fazal shakes his head. 'Whether they are truly freedom seekers, fighting for land and liberation from the colonial regime, or simply men and women with a proclivity towards violence and blood on their hands, I cannot say, Iris. I really cannot.' He sighs deeply. 'I can't deny that the Africans have been subjugated for too long, made to suffer humiliation and prejudicial treatment at the hands of their colonisers. But how can violence, and particularly violence at this level, ever be the solution? This is not my struggle, yet…' He trails off and runs a hand through his salt-and-pepper hair.

'Yet?'

'Yet, it also is. I belong here. This is my country and has been for many years. And it's not just the whites these people are turning against; it is anyone who is not black. It doesn't matter how long we've been here for. If these bands of marauding thugs can turn so easily on people they have served for years – the parents of the children they helped to raise – how much time will pass before they also turn against the Asian community? For in the eyes of these people, we shall never truly belong on this land either.'

Maliha has left the room and gone into the kitchen. The door is closed and through it I hear an Asian song blaring out on the radio.

'Would you ever go back, Fazal?' I ask quietly.

'Back? Back where? My country is not my country any longer. When I came to Africa, I was from a country called India. Now Karachi is in Pakistan. It is as foreign to me as…' He shakes his head, plants his hands squarely upon his knees. 'No, I cannot go back, Iris. I think… that would be even more painful.'

We are both silent for a few moments, Fazal no doubt lost in his memories of a Karachi he once knew and I trying hard, but failing, not to think of very much.

'I find I am being increasingly wary with whom I talk to, what I say. Maliha says I am being paranoid. But my wife has a good heart and there is no room in that heart for suspicion or prejudice. She believes in each person's inherent goodness. Sometimes I fear for her naivety. "It will blow over, Fazal," she tells me, "all this Mau Mau nonsense. What kind of a name is Mau Mau anyway?" But Maliha does not read the newspapers as I do; she merely skims the front page. No, this will not blow over as quickly as she predicts it will. I pray, every day. But I fear the worst is to come.'

Abruptly, Fazal rises from his chair, walks to the window and flings it open, momentarily relieving the stultifying atmosphere in the room. I rise and walk over to him and we stand there together, our shoulders not quite touching, looking out on to Nairobi's grey mist, joined by a silent grief that is impossible to enunciate. We talk for a little longer before I return to the hotel. Before exhaustion overtakes me.

❧ ❧ ❧

Maitho. Maitho. *Eyes.* It is curious that both my son and I have names connected to vision. I lie on my back on the bed, curtains drawn, the rain hammering against the window, and I try to conjure a vision of these eyes. There must be a reason why he was given this name. Is it possible my son inherited my eyes rather than dark brown or black? Of course it is possible. He is a combination of myself and Kamau, so just as his skin is likely to be different from that of those around him, so are his eyes.

Kamau.

How to grieve for a man I have not seen in over fifty years? A man whom I have scarcely allowed myself to think of all this time, suppressing his face, his memory, his warm touch each time it rose, unbidden, like smoke from a fire. Yet he died because of me.

A physical pain grips my chest and I take a vast breath of air, my eyes squeezing shut. The enormity of this is too great. A public hanging, no doubt the European community flooding out of the club in droves to witness it and chattering gleefully of the excitement and gossip-worthiness of the event. And all the while, the noose tightening round my sunbird's neck. I brush a tear impatiently from my cheek and think of the drawing he gave me.

I still have it. After many years of carrying it in my purse, it had started to look scruffy, so I took it to a special shop where they were able to put it in a plastic casing and there it has remained all these years. And now. Now what? My son *might* be dead. I feel my heart contracting and tightening and conjure the other voice, the voice that tells me, *But he might also be alive.*

Yet how to find him? Where to begin, particularly now that Kikuyu are enlisting in the Mau Mau cause, either of their own volition or under duress? And those who do not submit, those who stay loyal to the Crown, are tracked down by the rebels and brutally murdered. Maitho, if he lives – where does he stand in all this? That morning over my breakfast of fried eggs on a chewy piece of toast and Kenyan tea, I pore over the *East African Standard*, reading of both white settlers and loyalist chiefs butchered in their beds and tightening security measures. I lean back, take a deep breath and close my eyes. Where is my son?

CHAPTER FORTY-THREE

MAITHO

NYERI
JULY 1952

Nyeri showground. Hundreds of people. No, thousands. Men with Kenyatta beards and long hair. Women, their faces shining. Children, babies. Buses decorated with Mau Mau banners and KAU flags. Singing, there is so much singing of Kikuyu songs. And then Kenyatta speaks on stage. Jomo Kenyatta. He has a strong voice, a powerful manner of speaking. 'Land and freedom,' he cries. He calls the British *biltis*, donkeys. He says, 'The tree of freedom has been planted. It is the dry season and the tree must be watered with human blood. Democracy has no colour distinction.'

Everybody around me shouts, 'Yes! Yes! Yes!'

Me? I do not shout. I do not like the feeling here. The tension. Men going through the crowd, wanting more. Wanting anger from people. They say, again and again, 'The day of action has arrived, it has arrived!'

And I wonder: why am I here? Why did I board bus this morning from Nairobi? I have no political feeling, no belief in Mau Mau, in bloodspill. I only want to see. Maybe to understand what my people are doing, what they believe in.

But… the Kikuyu. Are these my people? Sometimes I do not know. My skin, it is almost as black as theirs. But my eyes – dark blue. The colour of sky at dusk. Always, I have been different from others. From mother, father, brothers, sisters, boys at school. They treat me differently. So I feel different. Me, I only want to do my job. Keep quiet. I am a gardener; I have been for more than one year now. I am happy with this. I work alone. No questions. No people staring at my eyes, wondering. I tend garden and work outside all day. I watch birds settle on mgumo tree in garden, on frangipani, on jacaranda. So many colours. Here, I feel free. I feel alive.

My boss, the bwana, his name Tobias Edmunds. Bwana Tobias. He treats me fine, fair. He pays my wage. He lives with sister, Dorothy Edmunds. She is not married, nor he. I do not like Memsaab so much. Her face is like thundery sky. She always looks cross, annoyed. She doesn't like my work so much. Well, I think it is Africans she does not like so much. But he, the bwana, he has no problem with it. I am very, very lucky to get this job. Edmunds, they have farm in Kinangop, cattle farm, then they have house here in Nairobi. Sometimes I think to ask Bwana if I come to Kinangop with him, to a place with less people, more earth, more sky. But for now, I just think of my luck and I continue quietly with work.

There is one time only I ask question of my mother why my eyes are colour of dusk. And she says nothing, only hugs me tight and I smell sweetness of arrowroot on her skin. There is something more, I know. Untold story. But I do not know what and nobody will tell me. At eighteen years I go to the great medicine man, *mondo-mogo*. I bring goat as he asks and we sacrifice it under most holy of mgumo trees. Then I ask him. I say, 'Tell me my secret.'

He looks at me, long and hard. Then he tells, 'You always alone. Always were. Always will be.' I wait. He speaks truth, but I must know *why*. Why I am different. He waves smoke from burning goat carcass over his face, my face. Then he says one day I will know truth, but I must wait more years to find it. I am angry. This *mondo-mogo*, he is very best. But I give up one precious goat, for what? For him to tell me wait, even more time.

Back on the bus to Nairobi. I look outside at green hills, wrapped in cold mists of July. Man next to me, he stares at me. When I look, he whispers, 'You take the oath?'

I shake head.

'You must take the oath,' he hisses. 'For our Kikuyu people. For land and freedom.' I turn back to window. I do not like his voice; sugarcane beer thick on breath. Back in Nairobi, I walk through crowds to home. I sense him, this man, in crowd behind me. Following me. But I look back and all I see are faces, pyramid-piled oranges, women carrying babies, children running.

At home, later, I make millet porridge. Grains swell as water boils, thickening. I have taken only one mouthful when he bursts in, man from bus. I know stinking breath before I see face. He with two others, hair in long dreadlocks, crusted beards, chewing miraa leaf stems to stay alert.

It happens quickly, too quickly. Stinking man knocks the porridge from my hands whilst others twist arms behind back. Bind them. Steaming porridge spills on my arm and burns me. I open mouth to shout. But big, coarse hand clamps on mouth. Cloth tied round eyes so I cannot see.

'Money,' I hear someone hiss.

Footsteps towards me. 'Where is your money? You need to pay your fee to the movement.'

Hand removed from mouth.

'Which movement?'

Of course I know which movement. I feel sharp kick on spine and I fall to floor.

'You know which fucking movement! You tell us where your money is. Then we take you for ceremony.'

Nothing I can do, no way out. I motion with chin to hole in ceiling. Money in box up there. They jump up, empty box – all my wages – and now I am pushed, from house, through alleyways round home. And all I think is, why nobody is helping me? Where are they taking me?

Scarf taken from eyes but hands still tied. I blink, everything dark, blurred. I hear a voice. 'Do not be scared. We are waiting for an important visitor.' Do not be scared? Taken with violence from house in darkness and they tell me to not fear?

Now eyes are used to darkness and I see figures, huddled round room on floor: sitting, crouching, standing. All men like me, some old, some young. But all have fear in eyes, all have hands tied with rope. One or two whisper. Strange, but whispers comfort me more than anything.

I know why I am here. I know why we are all here. Hurricane lamps brought in and now I see better. Look round. Thirty men here, maybe forty. Everyone told to stand and one man kicked hard because sleeping. He moans, staggers to feet. We are pushed towards door in one side of hut. In single file, we walk through and here, we are in bigger room. Like hall, hurricane lamps all around. First we must go through arch, made from banana leaves. On each side of arch there is banana tree on which eye, looks like sheep's eye, impaled on tree by thorn. Three men with long hair, dusty beards stand guard with *simis*, traditional Kikuyu swords.

My legs, trembling like leaves. Why me? I only want quiet life. I only want work, my salary to buy maize and plantain and sweet potato from market. Not trouble, no trouble. I feel anger, at myself only. For going to Nyeri, to meeting. I only wanted to see Jomo Kenyatta, man himself, man everyone is talking about. To have trip away from Nairobi. But see, see now price I pay. All men are in hall now and behind us, I hear door bolting. This is only way out. I look around – there are windows, but all barred. There is no escape.

Stinking-breath man whom I sat beside on the bus, he is now talking loudly. He smokes cigarette, tip glowing. He says we must make line by arch, to remove shoes and coins, watches, other metal objects. On floor, I see calabash, split.

And inside, there is meat, raw meat. I do not want to think about what kind of meat it is.

'We want you men to join us in the struggle, for freedom and the return of our stolen land.'

Man behind me, young man, a brave man (or maybe foolish), he shout, 'I will not take the Mau Mau oath! I will not!'

Stinking Man nods at another and young man is pulled out from behind me, dragged to side of banana arch. Cigarette pressed into his cheek. Young man screams but is still pushed then thrown to ground. Rope around his wrists is cut with *simi* then both arms twisted back, so hard they look like they will break. Young man screaming and screams twist through me like *simi* pushing into my gut. Then he is slammed, hard, against wall. He falls like crumpled paper on ground. He is lying there, unconscious, blood trickling from his cheek and cut on forehead.

'Anyone else here who doesn't want to take the oath?' shouts Stinking Man. 'Well?'

We are all quiet. My legs, they still tremble badly. Two Mau Mau, they come and pull unconscious man from room, trailing blood.

'What will happen to him?' someone asks.

Stinking Man smiles, then laughs through cracked teeth. 'Nothing you need to worry about if you take the oath.'

They will kill him. Of this I am sure.

'Anybody else want to join him?' Stinking Man shouts again. No words. Heavy silence. So we are all brought forward, hands untied. One by one, we walk through banana leaf arch, then again, and again. Seven times in total. Hall, it is too hot. Need water. But there is no water here. We are put in lines. Me, I am in second line. First line, cuts made on arms of men. Then blood mixed with millet and put on their lips before they made to swallow greater amount. I cannot watch more. I close eyes, try big breaths but water, need water. I hear murmurs of oaths, words spoken and repeated. I do not want to listen. But cannot close my ears. 'Brain… bitten… seven times… dead European.' *No, no, no*, I am screaming inside. *Please, no, I cannot listen.* I think of a Kikuyu lullaby Mama sang me when I was little: '*Kanyoni gakwa wihithahithe, Kanyoni gakwa wihithahite, Nawonwo nduri wakwa, Nawonwo nduri wakwa…*'

But now I am pushed forwards. Must open my eyes. I feel sharp pain as blood drawn from my arm with *panga*. Oath given and now I must repeat. I open mouth but nothing comes out. My voice frozen in fear.

'Speak.' His face close to mine, stinking breath like garbage and thick beer.

I want to tell him I cannot. Trying to speak, but I cannot. No words coming.

'Speak!' His voice is like roar of lion, like waterfall I once saw. Words stuck in my throat. Tears are on my cheeks, crying like a small boy. I am scared. Too scared to speak. His face is closer, closer to mine. Black eyes flashing at me. They flash pure evil. He calls something to others, I do not hear what. They come, either side. Strip me of clothes, everything, everything.

I stand naked like day I was born, naked and crying. And Stinking Breath, now he presses *panga* into stomach. I feel sharp pressure and warm trickle of blood. There is metallic smell. Water, I need water.

'You going to take this oath, pretty eyes, you worthless piece of shit?' He is shouting at me, pressing *panga* harder and now I am sobbing louder. Not quiet cries but noisy cries. Heat, pain, thirst, it is all too much. Too much. And then memory, it comes to me quietly. I have not thought of this for so many years. Boy at school, he throws small stone at my head. I turn. He says, 'Who is your mother?'

'You know answer,' I tell him, then keep walking.

'She is not your mother. You do not have her eyes.' I do not look back again. I keep walking, but tears running on my face. But that night, I ask her. I tell Mama what boy says and she only reply, 'Cha! You no mind these silly boys, they know nothing.' But she will not look at my eyes, my blue eyes, when she talks. And for first time, I think this: maybe she lies to me.

I feel warm trickle on stomach. Look down at line of blood from *panga*. I cannot stop crying, crying, tears mean everything blurs. Then next thing I feel is something around neck. First I think he is choking me, his hands there, tight tight. But now I see through blur it is not hands but rope. I cannot breathe, I cannot see, I cannot even cry now. Slowly, slowly, my feet leave ground. Lifted up and rope is tightening. Hands fly to neck to pull rope away. But it is no use, too tight. Choking, I cannot breathe, I am lifted up higher higher. My legs are swinging, kicking. But this only makes rope tighter.

Stinking Man, he is shouting at me. What? I cannot hear. His mouth, nose, eyes, voice, all swimming. I realise now, I will die. One minute more and I will be dead. But to die this way, it cannot be. I must concentrate on what he is telling me or it is certain, I will die.

Focus, focus, focus. Maitho, listen to words, what he is saying.

'You taking oath now, you fucking coward? You taking oath?'

It is simple: if I take oath, I live. If I do not, I die.

'Yes,' I croak. 'Yes.'

And the rope is cut, I fall hard, smash to floor. I fight for breath, panting, gasping. I am kicked hard in the stomach and cry out, twisted moan.

'Good,' says Stinking Breath, 'because we have a job for you.'

CHAPTER FORTY-FOUR

IRIS KINGSLEY

I know that Maitho could be dead. Dead, like Kamau. He could be many miles from Nairobi. He could be swallowed into the belly of a slum, spreading like an inkblot across this city's landscape. But I have waited all these years and I need to be able to tell myself that I tried. I at least *looked* for my son.

Fazal and I have agreed to meet two days hence at the hotel.

'First place,' he says, pointing to the top of a list he has made with his fountain pen, 'is Kibera.'

'Kibera?'

'Yes.'

I inhale deeply.

'Nairobi's largest informal settlement. A kind of native reserve. It was formed around the time you were here, originally allocated this site by the Britishers for Nubian soldiers returning from service with the King's African Rifles. It was designed as temporary accommodation but of course has grown and grown, illegally in the eyes of the colonial administration and they've been trying to demolish it for years, to relocate everyone. But really, where would they all go? Thousands of people live there.'

'Thousands?' I ask, panic gripping me. 'But it will be like searching for a—'

'Needle in a haystack.' He nods. 'Yes.'

'Why Kibera?' I ask. 'Why start there?'

'Well,' he replies, not quite meeting my eye. 'It's where Nairobi's poorest live. And we have to start somewhere.'

I nod, continuing to look at Fazal.

'The other thing, Iris,' he goes on, 'is that I don't think you should come. I think I must go alone.'

I narrow my eyes, shaking my head and frowning deeply. 'That is quite out of the question, Fazal. I have not come all the way to Kenya to let you do my searching for me alone.'

'Iris.' He takes off his spectacles and wipes them with a handkerchief he pulls from his pocket. 'I am not sure if you appreciate what it is like in Kibera. How filthy it is. How... dangerous.'

I tap a single finger on the tabletop. 'You are probably right, Fazal. I don't think I am at all prepared for it. Nairobi is a different place entirely to the one I remember. But that does not mean I should not come. Do you know anybody who lives there?'

'One person. James Ndegu. Incredibly resourceful fellow. He supplies virtually the entire slum with their footwear, along with a Sudanese he works with. I know where he lives but... you do realise I might be able to extract more information from people without you there?'

I look at him mildly. 'Do you really believe that, Fazal?'

'Many locals are distrustful of the *wazungu*. Particularly poor locals. You are a symbol to them of the white colonial government and what they have, or have not done, to help people. There are, of course, no white people living in poverty here. But you need only go to Kibera to witness human depravity.'

I swallow. 'I understand what you are saying, Fazal. But my conscience will not permit me to allow you to do this alone, on my behalf.'

Fazal chuckles and I look at him in surprise. 'Iris,' he says. 'Still as fearless and headstrong as ever.'

I give a tight, rueful smile. 'Or foolish, one might say.'

'No Iris,' he replies firmly. 'You are many things, but you have never been, and never will, be foolish.'

He is right, of course. This is quite unlike anything I have ever experienced. One time, many years ago, I went to the very poorest part of Newcastle. It was through an outreach programme with the library, to take books to the underprivileged of the northeast. I was horrified that, on the doorstep of genteel Durham, people were living like this, in stinking, squalid conditions. It was not difficult to see why books were not a priority in their lives; people needed to survive, first and foremost. But if I was shocked at Newcastle, it was nothing in comparison to Kibera. I step over narrow rivulets of urine and piles of human excrement that scrawny chickens peck at. And the flies! The air is thick with them and they buzz around my face, my throat and my hands, which feel as though they belong to a conductor, beating in frantic time to try to keep them away.

Everywhere I look, there is movement. People are busy, selling *sukuma wiki* and chai from small kiosks, scantily clothed children running out from dwellings made of rusting iron sheets and boards of wood, women stirring large pots in doorways, charcoal glowing beneath them. We are being stared at, unsurprisingly. I cannot quite read the expressions on the faces; they seem neither hostile nor curious. But as we pass, people stop what they are doing, a ripple effect of quiet calm upon the previously noisy clamour of the slum.

How do people live here? I know they probably have no choice, but to live in these conditions… how can the British government say they have successfully colonised this land when thousands live squeezed into these narrow, fetid alleyways? I feel as though I have jumped into a squalid Dickensian world, though somehow far worse, for there seems to be no beginning or end to Kibera. We walk and walk, Fazal occasionally turning round and asking me if I am well. I nod, though I long for water and fresh air, for the air here is thick and oppressive. But he warned me. I have chosen to be here today.

After what feels like an age, Fazal tells me we are entering the Kikuyu district.

'There are separate areas for the different ethnic groups?' I ask in surprise.

'Of course,' he replies.

'And your friend,' I call after him, 'the supplier of shoes. He is Kikuyu?'

'Yes.'

I step over rotten banana skins, and brown paper bags congealed in mud. Smoke curls round the open doors of shacks. How Fazal is able to find his way within this sunless labyrinth is a mystery to me. But eventually, we reach a house at the end of a track of surprising proportions and actually built from brick rather than the customary tin and wood.

'Here,' Fazal says, turning round. 'This is James Ndegu's house.'

I nod my head, relief flooding through me that I need not, for now, walk any further.

Fazal knocks firmly on the door and before long a young, long-limbed woman opens it and looks at us in surprise. Fazal speaks to her in Kikuyu and she responds, a rapid staccato of words spilling from her mouth.

'James is out,' Fazal says as he turns to me. 'This is his daughter but she says we can come in and wait, take some tea.'

I nod gratefully and muster a smile, following Fazal and the girl through the narrow wooden doorway.

When James Ndegu returns he greets Fazal like a long-lost friend, though Fazal told me earlier it had been at least two or three years since they had seen one another. He looks surprised, to say the least, to see me sitting in his house drinking tea, but also delighted. Not many *wazungu* make it out to Kibera, that much is certain. Fazal looks on edge the entire time we are there and, as I have on so many occasions, I feel a flash of guilt for putting him in this situation. It seems that white people are not the only unusual sight around here.

Fazal tells James, as quickly as is polite to do so, the purpose of our visit. He doesn't react, sitting on a wooden stool, stroking his chin.

'His name is Maitho, you say? No idea of other names?'

'No,' I tell him. 'The truth is we do not even know if he kept that name or was given another.'

'Maitho,' he repeats. 'You know what that means in Kikuyu?' He is looking at me as he speaks and I nod my head. 'It's not a common name, you know. Not at all.' He pauses, calls to somebody in the kitchen to bring more tea. 'What year was he born?'

'1904,' I say.

James lets out a long, high whistle and raises his eyebrow. 'So long ago? So that would make him... forty-eight.'

Fazal glances at me. I feel slightly ill, light-headed, my hands clasped tightly in my lap and my mouth set in a fierce line of grim determination.

'Well,' James continues, 'I certainly don't know of anybody of that name in Kibera. It doesn't mean he isn't here.' He motions to a young boy wearing a clean white shirt to pour the tea. 'But you must be prepared for the possibility that he is not.'

'We know,' Fazal says hurriedly. 'You are well connected, James. That is why we have come here first. To see if you can make some enquiries.'

'Of course,' he replies, waving a hand through the air. 'Always happy to help an old friend. Although...' He pauses, eyeing me with curiosity. 'You have told me you are looking for this fellow. But not *why*. I do not mean to pry, but I am interested.'

Fazal is about about to open his mouth to say something, when I beat him to it. 'He is my son.'

James whistles again. 'I see.' He blows on the tea and then sips at it. 'And I'd wager this Maitho has your eyes, Madam?'

'Please. Call me Iris. Whether or not he has my eyes I cannot say. But it is possible, of course.'

James squints and looks at me hard for a long time and I wonder what he is thinking. 'It is a Kikuyu name, so I take it he is Kikuyu?'

I pause. 'His father was, so yes… I suppose so.'

James nods. 'I shall do my best to look for your son. How long will you be here for?'

My shoulders, which had been tensed up around my ears, relax a fraction. 'As long as necessary.'

James nods, satisfied. 'Leave it with me. I can certainly tell you within a day or two whether this Maitho lives in Kibera. And there are contacts I have outside the settlement who can make enquiries.'

'Thank you,' I say, smiling at him. 'This means… a great deal to me.'

James nods solemnly. 'I see that. Now, what do you make of my house, the largest in Kibera?'

🕊 🕊 🕊

Whilst we wait to hear from James, Fazal urges me to relax a little, do some sightseeing perhaps to pass the time or go to the Lyric Hall to take in a comedy or drama whilst he is at the mosque or dropping into his shop. But I am adamant:

I am not here to spend money on tourist attractions. I am here only to find my son.

'And what if you don't find him?' Fazal asks one afternoon as we walk around the Jeevanjee Gardens. He turns a strained face towards me. He looks tired. I know I am not entirely to blame for this; he is growing increasingly fearful of the threat of Mau Mau that is spreading like wildfire. He has told me he would be sticking his head in the sand not to acknowledge that the ire of these people is directed not only towards the whites, but also towards the Asians, the in-between race, neither white nor black but still regarded with suspicion by many.

I stop in front of the statue of Alibhai M. Jeevanjee, the great Asian philanthropist and entrepreneur, and stare at it. 'Yes,' I say. 'If I do not find him? Well, in that case I return to Durham, to my life there, to my children and grandchildren. And at least I can say I have tried.'

He clasps his hands behind his back, nods solemnly. 'Yes. I can understand that.'

We walk silently back towards Parklands, passing on the way men selling newspapers that I throw only a quick glance at. When I first arrived, I immersed myself in the papers each day, but now I have stopped reading them so fully, for they are full of the shadows of the dead: hamstrung cattle, mutilated dogs and innocent people, both Africans and whites, though primarily the former, massacred by the Mau Mau. At darkness, the settlers barricade the windows and doors of their homes and encircle their properties with barbed wire and even electric fences. There is talk of a curfew coming soon to Nairobi; we shall not be allowed outside between six in the evening and six in the morning. What is this country coming to and what, I sometimes find myself wondering, would Kamau have made of all this? For his own people to have turned on themselves and be slaughtering one another as well as the settlers would have been, to him, intolerable. And as I think this, it occurs to me for the first time that this country is at civil war; that the Mau Mau are waging battle both inwards and outwards. I feel a chill run down the length of my spine as I double-bolt the hotel bedroom door and rest my head against the warm wood and think to myself, *Iris, what are you doing here?*

❧ ❧ ❧

Over a week after our visit to Kibera, Fazal calls me at the hotel early one morning. He tells me he has news for me and asks me to join him and Maliha for lunch at their house. I feel like a nervous child as I wash and dress, forcing down breakfast. I make brief telephone calls to both Leonard and Sheena from the lobby, telling them the lie that I am having a wonderful time here, visiting the museums and game parks. The line is dreadful, but over the crackle I detect the concern in particular in Leonard's voice, demanding to know if I am safe.

'Safe?' I echo.

'Yes,' he shouts back down the line. 'The Mau Mau, Mother! That terrorist group. It's not sounding good from this side. Are you keeping safe?'

'Of course,' I reply lightly. 'Such reports are always sensationalised from abroad. When you're actually in the country, you scarcely even know it's going on. Don't forget, Queen Elizabeth was here not so long ago.'

He seems to accept this and, after promising I will call again soon, I place the receiver back down.

The news Fazal has for me is that he heard from James at daybreak that morning. There is nobody with the name of Maitho in the whole of Kibera. I feel my heart plummeting a hundred miles and I look at my feet; my thin, bare ankles and the rivers of varicose veins that cross the skin.

'But…' Fazal says.

'But?' I look up into his caramel eyes.

'But… but he is following another lead. I…' Fazal casts his eyes around the room, settles his gaze upon Maliha before looking back at me. 'I don't want to raise your hopes too much. It's not that I don't believe we have a possibility of finding him, it's just that—'

'Fazal,' I interrupt. 'Don't *worry*.'

He looks anxious.

'Yes,' he continues. 'Well, as I said, he is following another lead. From outside Kibera.'

I wait, but Fazal does not offer up more information than this. 'Do you know what kind of lead?' I ask quietly.

'He didn't go into too many details. Said to sit tight and he'd get back to us as soon as possible, so…' He spreads his hands and shrugs. 'I suppose that's what we must do.'

'Yes,' I reply and I look back down at my feet.

Fazal is not telling me everything; I know him well enough now to be aware of that. But I must trust him. I *do* trust him. He will tell me in his own good time. Which, of course, he does, sharing the news with me that through James Ndegu's large network of contacts he has discovered there may be a Maitho living somewhere in Eastlands, outside the city centre. It may not be the Maitho we are looking for – although the fact that his name is not common plays in our favour, Fazal tells me – and James could tell him nothing more about this person: his age, his ethnicity. But it is something, it is *something*.

Once again, Fazal and I have the same conversation. He does not wish me to accompany him to the 'insalubrious' district of Eastlands, as he calls it. It runs along from the railway station and down Doonholm Road, bisected by steely grey shunting yards and the long worn gleam of railway tracks. Fazal tells me this is a land of sickening poverty; of illegal trading and criminal gangs trading anything they can think of on the black market. But I *must* go. I would prefer to draw Fazal into this as little as possible but, of course, I need him to come with me for I am a fish out of water even in central Nairobi, let alone outside of it.

First, we walk through an area of Asian residences that is ordered and calm, neat little stone houses with wooden verandahs carved in Indian scrollwork. I wonder if Fazal has exaggerated the turbulence of this area; yet minutes later we are plunged into the dense native quarter, seething with humanity and commerce. Fazal reaches into his pocket, pulls out a handkerchief and a small bottle. He unscrews the bottle top and empties a small amount of it onto the cotton before refastening the lid.

'What is that?'

'Cologne.'

'Cologne?' I frown. 'Why?'

'The smell, Iris. I'm afraid the smell here will not be pleasant.' He presses the handkerchief into my hand. 'When it gets too much, just press it to your nose.'

I nod briefly and put it into my skirt pocket. We walk through the muddle of cardboard, sacking, stone and tin, music blaring out of decrepit speakers from the flyblown shopfronts that line the filthy roads and hawkers selling mangoes and sugarcane. Donkey-carts and barrows are being loaded all around us and battered old lorries that have squeezed themselves down the narrow, fetid lanes are having goods taken off them. There are a few larger, public buildings but these are encircled by barbed wire, armed police standing in front of them. I also see a number of armoured cars prowling along the streets, slowing down when they see us.

'I am so glad you are here, Fazal,' I murmur. 'Kibera seems like Mayfair in comparison to this.'

'Mayfair?'

I shake my head. 'Never mind.' I need to focus on where I am going, placing one foot in front of the next while remaining aware of everything around me. Smoke rises and swirls from the small stoves in every slanting interior made of old packing boxes, mud and thatch, lending the area an even more sinister appearance.

Multitudes crowd the dingy lanes, open hostility upon their faces as they stare at us. They are dressed in cloth that hangs from their bodies, blankets, or torn European clothes that have clearly seen many years of being worn. Fazal is jittery. I sense that he wants to find Maitho as much as I; my search has become his search.

Tension has fallen like a black mantle and I realise that neither of us are entirely safe here. For this is the dwelling place, I have no doubt, of a great number of Mau Mau agitators, intent on stirring up discontent. But I am here now. We walk through the district of Bahati, the stench of sewage from the nearby works making me, on occasion, press my handkerchief to my nose.

'Where do we begin?' I ask Fazal.

'I don't know. But we must just start asking. Shopkeepers, hawkers, kiosk owners, men of around Maitho's age, *anyone*.'

'Will anyone speak English?'

Fazal shakes his head. 'Unlikely. Many of these people are uneducated, illiterate – angry.' He sighs deeply and scratches his forehead. 'I am not even comfortable being in Eastlands myself, Iris, let alone bringing you along. It is terribly unsafe, particularly now.

Are you aware that in Nairobi there is one policeman to every one thousand inhabitants? And that in *Eastlands*...' he pauses, 'well, for the entire population of this district, which, believe me, is vast, there is just one African inspector and five constables. That is *it*, Iris.'

'Fazal.' I catch his arm and stare at him. '*Thank you.* Truly. For everything. You have been such a friend to me.'

He looks tired but smiles at me. 'You don't need to thank me, Iris.'

'I do. I am sorry if I have not shown you enough appreciation since I have been here. I know what you are—'

'No, *no*.' He shakes my hand emphatically. 'It is not that, my dear. You certainly have shown your appreciation. And believe me, I want to help you more than anyone. It's just that…' He trails off. I don't say anything, wait for him to continue. 'It's just that I am scared. Not for myself, you understand, but for you. Where this journey will take you and the heartbreak it can bring.'

I am silent for a few moments and then I squeeze his hands. 'I know, Fazal. I know. But it is a risk I must take.'

Moving briskly through the chaos around us, we turn off into a haphazard maze of corrugated iron shacks and narrow streets that the sun never warmed or brightened. I know that everybody is staring at us – at me in particular, an English lady with silver hair tucked up beneath a hat and wearing a calf-length patterned dress, drawn in at the waist.

We enter our first small shop, less dirty-looking than many others, where sweet breads and biscuits are being sold. Fazal takes a deep breath and opens his mouth to ask a question of the old, stooped man selling the goods: '*Wi mwega*, do you know a man called Maitho?'

The answer? No. Then again, and again. 'No, no, no. Never met anyone of that name.'

But then, as we walk further out of Bahati and towards Shauri Moyo, a squalid government housing estate, we find a pineapple seller who does not simply brush us off.

'Maitho…' He squints his eyes and stares into the distance. 'Maitho…'

Then he begins talking, his eyes animated and his hands gesticulating. Of course I understand not a word and yet it is clear this man with his broken teeth and lilting voice knows *something*. My pulse begins to race and I wait impatiently for him to stop talking so Fazal can translate.

After what feels like a lifetime, Fazal looks at me and he says, 'He remembers a Maitho who used to live in Shauri Moyo.'

'Used to?' I cannot keep the tremor from my voice.

'Yes. He doesn't think he's there any more.'

We thank the pineapple seller and hurry on, energised by this information. The estate is grimmer than anything I could possibly have imagined. My son, living here? One windowless cement block follows the next and from within the crowded rooms I can hear the crying of children and crackling of fires. There is not an inch of green or anything vaguely resembling nature anywhere to be seen. We walk past a large, cordoned-off wasteland where charred remains of wooden structures lie in blackened mounds.

'What is this?' I ask.

Fazal runs a hand over his face. 'Must have been Burma Market. I remember reading about it. The police burnt it down the morning after Tom Mbotela's body was discovered. He was a *tai-tai*. Murdered by the Mau Mau in the early days.'

'*Tai-tai?*'

'Kikuyu loyal to the government.' Fazal nods his head grimly and I glance around nervously. It feels like every single pair of dark eyes in the doorways is upon us, upon *me*. There is a tall, thin man standing outside one of the estate blocks, leaning against a door, watching us with curiosity but also with fear in his eyes. I take Fazal's arm and nod in the man's direction and we approach him.

At first, he wants to know if we have come to search the building. Fazal assures him this is not the case. Then, when we ask about Maitho, he asks *why* we are looking for him. He is suspicious and I cannot blame him. Everyone is suspicious, it seems, of everyone. But we must also be careful with our answer and appear impartial to Mau Mau support.

Fazal produces a shilling and places it in the man's palm. His lips curve into a smile and he slips the coin into his torn shirt pocket.

Maitho, yes. A quiet man, unmarried, who kept to himself.

'Anything else?' Fazal asks. The man knows nothing beyond that, but it feels so important, so very significant, and he says he will take us to the building he used to live in; his old neighbours might know.

We step over rubble, a few rats and unidentifiable objects I do not wish to dwell on for too long; the smell says it all. I press the handkerchief to my nose and pick my way gingerly along behind Fazal and the skinny man.

Maitho's old home has a broken stairwell leading up to the fourth floor, where he lived, and only one window, which is smashed. He shared a room with at least ten other men and slept upon a thin, dirty mattress on the floor. I attempt to take in these facts impassively for the pain they bring me. But then I remind myself that every little bit of information we receive brings me one step closer to him.

Only one man who lives in the room knew Maitho – unsurprisingly, people do not stay here for long. Fazal talks and listens until dark shadows force their way beneath his eyes and he is stooping with fatigue. And when he eventually translates, I hang off each and every word.

We discover that Maitho would leave early each morning for central Nairobi, where a bus waited to collect labourers who wanted work that day. He also sold plants that he cultivated himself. But he left over a year ago when he got a new job and nobody knows where he went.

The man Maitho shared a room with beckons us to the floor below to a small room with a stove in the middle where a woman crouches on the floor cooking, four children sitting around her. When the woman looks at me, her eyes are dull and expressionless and I wonder if this is what poverty does to people, sucking the souls from them.

After a brief conversation, the woman stands up, walks out of the room and comes back moments later with an older man. It transpires that he knew my son; not well, it seems, just as nobody knew him well. But he knew him.

'Ask him the man's age,' I say to Fazal.

Yes. The age matches with that of my son and I feel my heart constricting with excitement and hope.

'What does he look like?' I ask, more emboldened every moment with the certainty that this is the Maitho we are seeking.

They speak between themselves and Fazal strains to listen, but the words he turns back to me confirm what I was already starting to believe.

For all of them noticed the single thing that made him stand out from the crowd, that stopped him from being just any quiet, lonesome, strange Kikuyu man: eyes, they said. It was the eyes they remembered. Some described them as strange, others as frightening, or frightened. His eyes were pale, a few said, quite unlike anything they'd seen before on an African. Almost like the eyes of the *mundu mweru*. And with that, I stopped dead in my tracks. *The eyes of the mundu mweru.*

Suddenly, the woman stands up, looks directly at me for the first time and holds a hand up, motioning for me to stay there. She disappears through the doorway and I notice for the first time that she has a fifth child, tied to her back. I stand rooted to the spot and moments later she returns with a large plant, dripping with chilli peppers, between her hands and gives it to me.

Confused, I turn to Fazal. 'Why is she giving me this?'

They have a rapid exchange and Fazal's eyes widen. In them, I read pain and happiness intermingled.

'Maitho grew this,' he says quietly to me. 'He was also a gardener.'

🕊 🕊 🕊

I'm not sure if I have ever been as exhausted as this. I sit in Fazal and Maliha's lounge that afternoon, too tired to even lift the cup of tea to my lips; instead I lay my head back and close my eyes. I do not know how many people we met today. Even though he was quiet and kept himself to himself, in these kinds of tight-knit communities it is impossible, it seems, not to have at least some idea of people's characters and their comings and goings.

My son, it seems, has a feel for the earth, just as his father had a feel for the creatures of the air. From the fragments of information we have gathered together, I have discerned that Maitho grew his own plants from seed. As for the seeds themselves, they were either harvested and dried from previous plants or he would take cuttings from other places, though I have no idea where.

He had found a small patch of space behind the burnt-down market where sunlight filtered through and grew *sukuma wiki*, tomatoes and carrots in kerosene tins and old milk cartons. Everybody thought him a little simple, we were told; because he didn't talk that much, they assumed that he *couldn't*, not that he just didn't want to.

Yet nobody, not a single person, could tell us where he might have gone or anything about his family or where he lived before Eastlands. I felt so close to him, In that fetid place whose dank corridors the sun never warms. And yet, he is still so far from me.

CHAPTER FORTY-FIVE

MAITHO

1952

Police, they come and handcuff me. Metal is too tight round wrists. Behind, Memsaab Edmunds is sobbing, screaming. We pass *askari* on gate and he stares at me like it is first time he has seen me. I look back, Memsaab's face and hair like wild woman. And I look at rose bushes in garden where Bwana still lies, dead. I see only his bare feet, covered in blood. A speckled mousebird lands on feet. It pecks, confused, at his toes. Thinking it is food.

I am put in car by rough hands. And I nearly smile, because I think: this is first time I have ridden in a motorcar. But then I remember situation and cannot smile. Back at police station, I walk down corridor. People stare at me like I am rat or vulture or owl. I am pushed into small room. No windows. White man is there, skin like puffy clouds. He brings face close.

'Why did you kill Tobias Edmunds?'

I have trouble breathing. I am scared, so scared. I cannot talk. Like time I took oath, I cannot find words in my mouth.

'Why did you kill Tobias Edmunds?' He is shouting now, angry, white face turning red. But I think only of bad memory, night when I am almost killed by Stinking Breath. I feel tears again. I cannot cry, I cannot cry. I shake head.

'I no kill Bwana Edmunds.'

Policeman stands. He grabs me by collar, slams me hard against wall. My head throbs.

'You fucking Mau Mau liar,' he shouts. 'You killed him.'

'No. No. No,' I say.

'Well who fucking did, then? Hmm? You're the gardener there, right?'

I do not talk.

'*Right?*' He shoves me hard again, big hand now under my neck.

'*Ndio,*' I whisper.

'Don't speak in Swahili with me, you cunt. Speak English, or there'll be even more trouble. Now, are you or are you not the gardener at Mr and Miss Edmunds' house in Muthaiga?'

'Yes.'

'And were you or were you not the person to find Mr Edmunds dead?'

'Yes.' My eyes are sore, tearing. My neck is sore. It still pains from last time. 'I come for work. I find him in rose bushes.'

'You expect me to believe that?' He speaks in strange, sneering voice. 'You taken the oath? Hmm?'

If I tell him I was given choice of taking the oath or death, I know he won't believe me. I know. So I say nothing.

'You taken the oath, you fucking nigger?' He slams me hard again. My ear catches the wall. I feel blood coming. 'Where's your passbook?'

My passbook. This I must carry at all times. Everybody must carry one. It shows we paying fifty shillings every month, it shows our names, our tribes, our employment. I had to wait hours to get one. So many questions asked, on and on and on. Then board hung round my neck and photo taken, fingers and palms pressed in ink and flattened down. But passbook… it is at home.

I take my mind from body. I am back in garden of Bwana, silent, earth work. How I like it. Firefinches, sparrows, wagtails, sunbirds, all flitting round me. They are my friends. I leave food for them, water. One time sunbird even lands on flower one inch only from my face, sucking nectar from base of blossom. I stay still, still as rock. It feels like blessing, this tiny bird glimmering gold.

For first time in my life, I think I know happiness. Working in Bwana's garden, I think I am luckiest man in Kenya. It is like dream. But now all gone. Everything. Bwana, garden, birds, my life. I am angry with myself. That meeting in Nyeri, why did I go? It was of no interest to me. If I had stayed home that day, would Bwana still be alive? Would I still have my job?

'Well?' White policeman shouts. I see one silver tooth, shining, at back of his mouth. 'You taken it? You taken the oath?'

I close my eyes, tight tight. And nod head. I feel hard, cold fist against cheek. Then I am falling, falling. And there is blackness.

I do not know where I am. But this is bad place, bad place. It is cramped cell, with many other men, black eyes blinking. Nowhere for toilet. We all must go in corner, against wall. Stench fills my nostrils and sticks there, like glue. First night, I lie on cold stone ground and cry. Cry for my dead Bwana, kind man who did not deserve death. And cry for myself, for my life, for my death. For I know this is coming now, no other way for me. But I only wonder, *How? How my life will end?*

They bring me old arrowroot to eat. And water to drink. But water is not fresh and lean over, vomiting. Other men in cell stare at me, *pangas* in eyes. For nobody will clean this up. It will only remain and we must smell it, sleep in it. A few men in here, they have pellagra disease. Not enough vitamins, it affects skin. Lesions all over bodies, too weak. They will die from this. I see they are on journey to death already. And I wonder, *Is this my journey too?* Somehow I think not, for before I suffer this, I will already be dead.

I stare at wall. I speak to nobody. And one time a day I walk around compound. Barbed wire is all round. Beyond it, one acacia tree, long thin spiked branches. One thing of beauty in dark, cold place. I stare and stare and I think about God Ngai resting on Kirinyaga. And I think, *Have I angered you, Ngai? Is it because I have not followed the Kikuyu way that I am being punished?* I only want quiet life to lead. To not disturb people. But now, this is my life. And this will be my death. Before, I always thought each person on earth put here for a reason. This reason must be found. But now? I find no reason for my life. I cannot understand purpose.

Guard comes in. He asks me if I want to write letter. I shake head. 'Parents?'

'*Hapana*.'

'Wife? Brothers? Sisters?'

'*Hapana*.'

He stares, pity in cold eyes. But no contact with parents for many years. Maybe they even dead. It is the same with brothers, sisters. And no wife. I have never loved woman, never have I lain with woman.

Hapana, I do not have letters to write.

One man comes. We fear him more than others. All have nicknames, this one called Blue Knuckle. For when he finishes beating men unconscious, knuckles turn strange blue colour. For Blue Knuckle, beating same as enjoyment. Like for me, digging in soil or sucking sweet juice from sugarcane.

He has blue eyes. Not my blue though. Light, sky of dry season. Skin always red from sun: nose, forehead, arms. He is big man, like he never stops eating. Thick fingers, biggest thumbs I have ever seen. And his voice, this voice it surprises me more than anything. Because he is so big, I think voice will be deep like drum. But no, it comes out as squeaking bird. Every time, it surprises me, for long enough before I forget everything but pain as Blue Knuckle's fist meets my jaw.

Falling, falling, manacles round my legs strain and dig into skin. Then blackness. Nothing.

CHAPTER FORTY-SIX

IRIS KINGSLEY

'Iris,' Fazal say gently. 'You need to tell your children why you are here.'

We are sitting in Jeevanjee Gardens. This has become a ritual, the two of us meeting here. Fazal always brings a Thermos of hot chai with him and we sit on a wooden bench close to the Jeevanjee statue, watching pied wagtails and incongruous, stray chickens pecking about them.

I fold my hands in my lap and stare straight ahead of me, shaking my head. 'I cannot, Fazal. Can you not see this is not the kind of news I can break to them by telephone?'

'But you've been here for over two months now. They must be suspicious, not to mention terribly worried about you. They must know that you are not simply here for a holiday.'

'I have no doubt about that. *But*,' I say firmly, 'I shall tell them when I get home.' I turn to look at Fazal and smile weakly.

'And when will that be?' he asks quietly.

I sigh deeply. 'Fazal. He is alive. We know that, we just do not know where he is. I cannot give up now. I need to keep searching.'

I do have to concede that, after two months of staying at the New Stanley Hotel, I shall shortly be having a cash-flow problem. Fazal has repeatedly insisted that I move into the spare room at his house, yet I feel that I have imposed enough upon his and Maliha's time and kindness. Eventually, however, I relent, and I must confess it comes as something of a relief to not have to return to that anonymous, lonely room in the hotel each day and endure their insipid tea.

I feel we are so close to my son, yet a million miles away. Fazal does not like me to walk around Nairobi too much on my own, particularly now that the situation with the Mau Mau has deteriorated and a curfew is in force. But it is unthinkable that I should stay at the house all day. I require fresh air and exercise; to walk around the Asian playing fields or City Park helps me to think more clearly. The truth is, though, that I cannot do without Fazal. For he knows this city in a way I do not. He speaks Swahili and some Kikuyu and feels the nuances and pulse of this maze of streets in a way that only a person who has been living in a place for many years can.

Maliha open-heartedly accepts my presence in her house. She tells me I am family to them now and I feel tears prick at my eyes that a person can be so kind. 'We will find your son, Iris,' she tells me one day, laying a soft hand on my wrist. 'We will find him.'

I have to find him. But how? The whole city and far beyond have their eyes turned towards the unfolding tensions. The newspapers are full of murder and bloodshed, slaughtered cattle and men who have served settlers faithfully, reared their children, cooked them their meals and tended their gardens, only to cold-bloodedly murder them after taking the Mau Mau oath. I do not like reading of any of this, yet to ignore that it is happening right here in Kenya would be naive. And whilst I do not, of course, condone what is happening, for such abhorrent lengths to be taken, I realise that something important must change in this country, that this discontent has been simmering and building ever since I lived here half a century ago. Just as I fought alongside other women for the right to vote, the Kikuyu are fighting for their land to be returned to them, for equal rights as citizens. And who can blame them? Racism and discrimination is as endemic here as it was all those years ago. I have seen local people having to step off the pavement when a European walks along to give them right of way, removing their hat. I have seen Asian shop owners on Government Road shooing away Africans from outside their premises, simply for lingering too long. I have seen roadblocks halting the stream of traffic into the business district, searching every vehicle; the fear in people's eyes when they see the British army patrols coming in their direction, really no more than schoolboys, savouring the first sweet taste of power in their mouths.

So no, I do not condone the murders and bloodshed, but I feel for the way the natives have been treated for too long. What is far less easy for me to understand is why the Mau Mau are intent on slaughtering their own people: those loyal to the British government, the *tai-tai* who are employed as government clerks, office assistants and cashiers and come into work each day with their polished shoes, fashionable neckties and smart European clothes. They have worked their way up to a respectable middle-class status but are only attacked for it. There are also those innocent women and children, entire villages razed to the ground. It makes me feel sick to the very pit of my stomach and I close the newspaper along with my eyes to try to make the gruesome images disappear.

What this country needs is independence, like India. We no longer inhabit the age of Queen Victoria and British domination of a third of the world and those who believe we can keep living such a life, such a dream of imperialism, are sorely misguided. Ghana, people say, is on the cusp of being granted independence and how I should like to see their brothers on the other side of the continent moving in the same direction. It is not a question of *if* but *when*. The time will come, one day, when the people of this land can once more take control of their own affairs.

❧ ❧ ❧

One week after I have moved into Fazal and Maliha's house, I am sitting at the table eating breakfast with Fazal. Maliha has made a delicious fruit salad of chopped pawpaw, mango and sweet banana. She is in the kitchen, singing in Urdu, and I smile as I listen to her.

The newspapers are spread out before Fazal and I glance at him as he picks up the *East African Standard* and scans the headlines. I concentrate on my breakfast and delicious chai. He knows I do not wish to hear of the daily atrocities in any detail. But after several minutes of peaceful eating, listening to nothing more than the birdsong coming from the oleander bush outside and the distant motorcars, my thoughts are interrupted by violent coughing from Fazal.

Maliha rushes from the kitchen and I look at him in alarm as she thumps him on the back.

'Fazal?'

He will not look at me; for some time he clears his throat, coughs again and looks in every direction except for at me.

'Fazal?' I ask again. 'Are you alright?' And then he does turn his face towards me. But his eyes are full of a pure terror I find it impossible to read, though instinctively my heart starts to thump violently. 'What is it?' I ask quietly.

Fazal finally stops coughing and Maliha peers over his shoulder, staring down at the double page spread of the *East African Standard* before her. And now it is her turn to stare up at me with wounded, haunted eyes.

I place my palms on the tabletop and say in a small, firm voice, 'Please pass me the newspaper.'

There is a photograph of a British settler, the word 'Murdered' in bold print above it. I read under the picture that it is from Muthaiga, a northern Nairobi suburb, but the photograph was taken on his farm in the Kinangop, in front of an enormous sisal plant, broad sunhat partially shading his face and his feet planted firmly on the ground. His hands are on his hips and he is smiling openly into the camera. He looks happy, confident, invincible. There is another photograph, far smaller, on the opposite page that I do not wish to linger on; it is of the same man, presumably, lying face down in a flower patch. I shiver involuntarily. I have never understood why the press are permitted to publish such gruesome photographs. I am still uncertain why Fazal and Maliha have reacted in such a way, though; perhaps they knew the man. Perhaps he was a customer of Fazal's. I look up from the article to ask them as much but they continue to look as though they have seen a ghost.

Fazal shakes his head. 'Look again, Iris,' he whispers.

I frown and cast my eyes back down. The article reads that Tobias Edmunds arrived in Nairobi in 1920 and was joined several years later by his sister. Both unmarried, they had divided their time between their home in Muthaiga and farm in the North Kinangop, where they reared cattle and cultivated sisal. Their Mau Mau gardener has been convicted of his murder, identified by the sister. It goes on to give details of how Mr Edmunds was murdered, which I have no desire whatsoever to read; why anybody should want to know the details of a murder is beyond me.

I am about to turn the page back to see if I have missed something, when I notice, in the bottom right corner of the double spread, a very small photograph. Beneath the picture, I read that it is of the condemned man. I am about to turn enquiringly back to my friends when something makes me look at the photograph more closely, the name beneath it. And that is when it is my turn to choke, my throat constricting.

I finally breathe in painfully and, without speaking, bring the paper closer to me.

'It is – it cannot be…' I whisper.

Fazal comes and stands behind me. 'It is him,' he says gravely. 'Without a doubt. Look at his eyes.'

I peer again at the picture. All the colours and contours around me bleed into one as the world begins to spin.

'The quality is terrible,' Maliha says. 'How can you tell anything?'

'*No*, Maliha,' Fazal urges. 'Look again, look!'

And so all of us look again closely, the paper mere centimetres from us. I feel sick to the core, my entire body shaking. Maliha coaxes Fazal back into a chair and then comes to me and grasps one of my hands. But all I can do is nod my head up and down and look back at my other hand, still clutching the newspaper, at the face of – what is becoming more unmistakable with every passing moment – my son.

The three of us sit round the table in strained silence for what feels like an eternity, as I continue to scrutinise the picture. Eventually, I look up at Fazal and Maliha. 'Yes,' I say in a firm voice that belies my true terror. 'It is him.' I pause and then nod. I rest my fingertips lightly on his photograph. 'But he did not commit this crime.'

I see Fazal frown before glancing uncertainly at Maliha, whose normally composed features also look crumpled.

'Iris,' Fazal says eventually. I can see he is struggling to find the correct words. 'You have suffered more than a human can be expected to, but…' He pauses, wipes his brow with his handkerchief. 'It is impossible to say. The Mau Mau take terrible oaths. Many are forced into committing crimes they have no wish to be a part of. You *know* this. These troubles… they have done dreadful things to people. How can we know what kind of a life Maitho has led? What he has been driven to do?'

'But you said it – you said yourself,' I look at him steadily, 'that the people who knew him where he used to live, they said he was a quiet man. That he kept to himself.'

'What can that possibly say about a person?' he presses.

I shake my head, my mouth setting into a stubborn line. 'He did not do it, Fazal. I tell you, he did not.'

Maliha lays a hand on my wrist. 'How can you know this, Iris?'

'Because he is my son. And the son of Kamau.' I look away and then whisper so quietly that even I can scarcely hear myself, 'the peaceful warrior.'

We are silent, the three of us, for some time. Then, without looking at him, I ask one of the most difficult questions of my life.

'What will happen to him, Fazal?'

He does not reply.

'*Fazal!*' I turn my face to him and see my own fear reflected back at me in his eyes. 'What will happen to him?'

Fazal casts his eyes downwards and massages his temple with the fingers of one hand. 'I know little of the penal system here, Iris. But…'

'Yes?'

'But if he is guilty of this murder, or is *perceived* to be guilty of this murder… I do not like his chances.'

I hear a distant squawking sound from outside the window. I have not thought of the hadada ibis for so long, but the name of this large bird with its iridescent feathers and hawking cry returns to me immediately.

'They will kill him,' I say.

It is a statement, not a question, and Fazal's silence is far louder than any words could be.

🕊 🕊 🕊

This internal war has made monsters of good people, but I cannot and will not believe that Maitho is responsible for the murder of his employer. Fazal has attempted many times to gently suggest to me that it is possible, likely even, that he committed the crime. For the sister of the deceased witnessed the attack from a cupboard she was hiding in and she has identified Maitho as the culprit. But I cannot hear it. I cannot hear these words spoken of my son.

Fazal looks tired and troubled. I know that he wants to protect me, but every single conversation we had that day in Eastlands pointed me towards a truth that I cannot rationalise but only feel deep within me: that this guerilla war has made a scapegoat of many people, Maitho one of them.

'Which jail, Fazal? Which jail will they have taken him to?'

He runs a hand through his hair.

'I don't know,' he says quietly. 'But I imagine it will be the main city prison, Nairobi Jail.'

'I need to go there, to see him.'

'No.' He shakes his head.

'Yes!' I get to my feet.

'Iris. It won't be that simple. You won't be able to get access to him.'

'How do we know if we don't try?' My voice is climbing in pitch and I know I am sounding hysterical.

Fazal puts both his palms up towards me, moving them back and forwards. 'You are right, Iris. We must try.'

❧ ❧ ❧

The man behind the desk is exactly the same kind of person as the one I encountered in the police station on my first morning in Nairobi: officious, obnoxious and entirely unwilling to help.

'*No* visitors.' He knits his eyebrows. 'Did you not hear me the first time? *Nobody.* Not one single person.'

'But why?' I plead.

'He is in solitary confinement. He is a murderer, a dangerous man.'

'He is—' I take a step towards him but Fazal places a restraining hand on my arm and draws me back.

'Can we speak to your superior?' Fazal asks calmly.

He shakes his head at us. 'No point. He will say the same thing as me.'

Fazal lets go of my arm and bangs his fist down hard on the table. Both the man behind the desk and I jump. 'Just let me speak to your superior!'

We are all silent for several moments, shocked by the sudden change in tone and Fazal's outburst. I think Fazal has even shocked himself.

'Well.' He shrugs, beginning to scribble a number on a piece of paper. 'Don't say I didn't warn you.'

As the wan evening sunlight filters through the lounge window, I feel sleep tugging at me and allow myself to drift in and out of this welcome place. I spoke by telephone to the director of the prison when we got back, but he ended up hanging up on me. When I tried to call back, he would not pick up.

'No,' he said in the very same manner as his employee. 'Out of the question. Never been allowed, never *will* be allowed.'

It mattered not what tone I took: wheedling, polite, severe, authoritative – all my pleas fell upon deaf ears.

'Five minutes, that is all I want. Just to see him. Please.'

'It is not possible.'

'Please – I only want—'

And the line went dead.

As I am about to drop off to sleep, suddenly, as though I have been pricked with a needle, I sit bolt upright, letting out a loud gasp. I know what I have to do now; the *only* thing I can do now.

'Iris, we cannot.'

Fazal stares at me with an expression of bewilderment upon his face, as though I have taken leave of my senses.

'Why not?'

'Why not?' He places his hands firmly on his hips and draws close to me. 'I can think of very many reasons why not.'

'Such as?'

'Such as we could be accused of intimidating the prime witness.'

'No, no.' I shake my head and grasp my fingers firmly in my lap. 'You misunderstand. I do not wish to intimidate her, simply to talk to her.'

A small laugh escapes his lips. 'Come, Iris. You know as well as I do how this would be construed. That kind of thing could land us both in jail along with your son.'

I sigh and frown, staring down at my lap. 'She need not know about my relationship with Maitho—'

'But what would you tell her? Why you are there, I mean?'

'I was thinking we could just talk to her and find out if she is absolutely certain that it was Maitho she saw.'

'She has already positively identified him, Iris.'

'Yes, but she is under so much stress right now and she just needs to find somebody, *anybody*, responsible for her brother's murder. I can understand that. My own brother Arthur was murdered. At least, he was killed in the war, as so many others were. But I should give anything to know the whys and wherefores of his death. Just like this Mr Edmunds should not have died, neither should my brother. Do you not see, Fazal, that I could speak to her on a personal level, one woman to another? Besides anything else, it is our last chance.'

A sob catches in my throat and I turn away from him.

'Iris,' he says very quietly, and I turn slowly towards him. 'I cannot come with you. I want to help you, you know I do. But *this*, it is impossible. Nothing can come from it.'

One small tear forms in the corner of my eye and splashes, soundlessly, in slow motion, on the wooden tabletop.

❧ ❧ ❧

A couple of days later, Fazal and I catch the bus to Muthaiga in the late afternoon, the uneven roads bathed in light, shimmering gold and green from an earlier rain shower. I do not remember coming to this leafy, prosperous suburb when I lived here, but in any case, if I did, in those days there would have been far fewer houses and a great deal more forest.

I know the address; it is in the Nairobi Yellow Pages. Winding through the hilly lanes, I think of the bus journeys I have taken back home in and around Durham, also traversing hills. I love fiercely the place I have made my home; yet looking out of the bus window now as we travel, I see again that here there is a different quality of green and that the colours are brighter, the trees taller, the forests more alive and the air sharper, mingled with woodsmoke and tropical flowers. I wonder could I ever live here again? Could I find peace back in this place that has brought me so much pain?

Fazal eventually agreed to escort me to the house, but he does not wish to come in with me. He says that the presence of an Indian will only aggravate Miss Edmunds further, which may or may not be true; but Fazal, I have to assume, knows better than I when it comes to such matters. As we walk towards the house, rising up behind iron gates, I feel nervous. What if I am unable to even pass the *askari*? But more than that, as I stand behind the gate, looking at the garden beyond, I feel closer to my son than I have ever done; he worked here, with his hands in the soil, tending that datura plant, and that clump of green-fronded bamboo, and that flowering bougainvillea.

I stand behind the gate, blinking at the splendour of it all, my heart constricting. And I feel more certain of it than ever before – a person who can care for a garden with such tenderness is not, I am sure, capable of murdering the person whose garden they are nurturing. How can I explain this knowledge, this feeling that comes from somewhere deep within that the son of Kamau is incapable of such an act? I cannot say that the son of Iris Johnson, Iris Lawrence, Iris Kingsley is incapable of it. *That*, I do not know, for I recognise the shape and depth of anger. There were nights, after Mr Lawrence left me sore and weeping in my bed, that I harboured fantasies of killing him and how I might do it. But Kamau's son? No, not Kamau, the gentle warrior. It is not possible.

Two *askaris* approach me at the gate and I feel a surge of panic. Why am I thinking only now of what to say to them? How I am to be granted entrance? They nod, looking mildly surprised that I am on foot and not arriving by motorcar, and I swallow my panic.

'Good afternoon, I am here to see Miss Edmunds.'

'You are a friend of hers?'

I nod, trying to smile brightly at them, and then, just like that, they say, 'Karibu', and begin to unbolt the door. I am so shocked that it could be this simple that I stand rooted to the spot for several moments.

'*Karibu*, Madam,' one of them repeats and I take a deep breath and walk forwards. How is it that I am trusted so immediately? I know, of course, the answer to this – that it is simply the colour of my skin that opens doors for me. This knowledge makes me feel both deeply uncomfortable and relieved at the same time and I edge forwards, clutching my bag as I walk up the gravel drive.

The house is beautiful, with whitewashed walls and a sloping, brown-tiled roof with green climbers creeping up all around it and pots clustered around the front door. To both sides, the garden stretches gently out, sloping into a valley so that the house sits tightly upon a hill. I stand on the front doorstep and am relieved that I am out of sight of the *askaris* as, at this moment, I know I am hesitating, my courage failing me. I think of Fazal waiting for me not far from the gate and wonder if he was right all along – if this is madness, pure and simple. I clasp my hands in front of me and take deep, even breaths, my eyes closed. Then I open them and I knock.

The maid shows me into the house when I tell her I am here to see Miss Edmunds and, once again, I am amazed at the ease with which I am given access to her property. I am shown into a musty drawing room, thick, to my mind, with foreboding from the stuffed animals that line the wall, staring down at us with their glassy eyes.

There are a few photographs in frames sitting on wooden cabinets and I am about to move towards one to take a look when I hear footsteps. The lady who enters the room is not at all what I was expecting. She is slight and small, with a drawn and tired face and a crown of tight grey curls on her head. She frowns at me, realising I am not a visitor she is acquainted with and walks over to me with sharp, precise movements.

Nervously, I hold my hand out to her. 'Iris Kingsley, Miss Edmunds,' I blurt.

'Kingsley…' she murmurs, shaking my hand briskly before pulling it away again. 'Have we met before?'

I shake my head. 'No, we have not. But your late brother was a friend of my late husband. I was in Kenya and I wished to come and give you my condolences. Such a dreadful thing to happen.' I am shocked by how easily this lie slips from my mouth. Her look of suspicion vanishes immediately and she smiles wearily at me.

'I see. Well, it was good of you to come. Mary!' She turns round, calling something to the maid in Swahili; the only word I recognise is 'chai'. 'Won't you sit down?' she says, turning back to me.

I perch on the edge of an ancient, frayed armchair.

'What did you say your husband's name was?' She looks at me with absent, hazel eyes.

'Oh.' I cough. 'I had not yet said, but his name was Jonathan Kingsley.'

'Kingsley, Kingsley…' she murmurs. 'It rings a bell, but no. I cannot recall him.'

'It was a long time ago,' I reply placatingly.

'Where did they know one another?'

I inwardly gulp. Of course there was every chance she would ask this. 'At school,' I reply, hoping that I am on safe ground.

'Heavens! Broadham House, as far back as that.'

I nod, eager to change the subject. 'Your brother's death – of course, it was widely reported back in England. Everybody has been so terribly shocked. These past weeks must have been such a strain for you.'

Miss Edmunds fiddles with a thread unravelling from the upholstery on her armchair and smiles tightly. 'It would be fair to say that. This country… I just do not know what it is coming to. I used to feel so safe here, but…' She frowns, trailing off, and then looks at me curiously. 'What brings you here now, Mrs Kingsley?'

I had hoped to avoid questions of this type, but of course that was unrealistic of me; I know that in order to win some of her trust early in the conversation, I must not appear closed. I take a deep breath and begin to speak, again the lie slipping out with alarming alacrity. 'I came here once as a young woman, to visit a great-uncle who lived in Nairobi. I was terribly taken by the place and always wished to return. So, here I am.'

'I am not sure you have chosen quite the right time to visit, Mrs Kingsley,' she remarks drily.

'You are probably right,' I agree, 'but I did think that if it was safe enough for the Princess Elizabeth to visit not so long ago, or *Queen* Elizabeth I ought to call her now, then it should surely be safe enough for me.' I think, fleetingly, of Leonard. 'Besides, in another year or two my age will be such that I should not feel like making such a journey.'

I shift in my uncomfortable chair, wondering how I can tactfully return to the subject of her brother. At that moment, the maid enters the room with a pot of tea and two chipped cups and I wonder how old everything is in this house. Not that I am priggish about these sorts of things, but some of the items scattered around look as though they might have been here since the previous time I was in Nairobi.

I take a deep breath. 'I read in the press that your gardener is thought to have committed the crime.'

She visibly bristles, staring intently at the maid's hands as she pours the tea. She waits until the maid has left the room before continuing. 'Not *thought*. He *did* murder my brother. I saw him.'

'You saw him,' I say quietly.

'Yes. I was hiding in a cupboard. And I saw Maitho come in and kill Tobias.'

'Maitho,' I whisper.

'Yes.' She shakes her head and I notice her hands are trembling as she lifts the chipped cup to her lips. 'The Mau Mau gardener.'

'Was he with you for long?'

Miss Edmunds places the teacup back down firmly in the saucer. It is clear from her expression that she has no wish to discuss this any further. But I cannot lose her now. She drums her fingers on her lap and chews at her bottom lip. 'Kingsley…' she says. 'I wish I could remember your brother. My memory…' She breaks off and sighs deeply.

I wait a few moments before repeating my question, in as neutral a voice as I can muster.

'Long? No, not all that long. A year. Or a little more.'

'Your garden is beautiful.'

'Well,' she says, clearing her throat. 'Beautiful it may be, but I don't care to spend time in it at present.'

'Did – did you trust him whilst he was working here?'

'Who?' She opens her hazel eyes wide, startled.

'Maitho. The gardener.'

She frowns. 'I didn't have much contact with him, to be honest. The garden was my brother's department. More tea?'

'No, thank you.' I pause. I know that I am edging towards dangerous ground. 'What was he like?'

'My brother? He was… wonderful. I'm sure your husband must have told you that. Firm but fair. Nobody ever had a bad word to say about him. And he certainly didn't deserve this kind of end—' She breaks off, staring down at her hands tightly clasped in her lap, stifling a sob. 'Nobody does.' She looks back up at me, a steely glint in her eyes. 'Apart from the demons who did this to him. They deserve everything that they'll get.'

'Demons?' I ask hurriedly. 'I thought it was just one person – the gardener – you saw?'

'Oh, demon, *demons*,' she replies, waving a hand impatiently in the air and pulling a handkerchief from her pocket to blow her nose, 'what does it matter?'

I place my hands under my legs because I can feel them shaking. Oh, how it matters. Of course when I asked her the question about what 'he' was like, I was referring to Maitho, not her brother. Yet I know I need to be careful if I am to remain in this house talking to her, the only person who can give me the information I need about my son. But how to broach it now that she is becoming emotional? I can see that she still has no wish whatsoever to discuss him. I wait a few moments and then take a deep breath.

'Do you think there could have been others involved?'

'What do you mean?'

'Besides your gardener. You say you were watching it from a cupboard. Could you see other people in your house?'

She looks directly at me, her eyes narrowing slightly. 'I don't know,' she says coldly. 'It is neither here nor there. This information will not bring my brother back.'

I feel myself beginning to panic, my breaths shortening as I return her steady gaze, heavy with scrutiny.

'You seem terribly interested in the gardener, Mrs Kingsley.'

'Do I?' I clear my throat.

'Yes,' Miss Edmunds says evenly. 'You do. Did you know him?'

I frown. 'No, I did not,' I reply, truthfully. 'It's just that…'

'Yes?'

'Just that, I have heard from a number of outside sources what a gentle kind of character he was and I wanted to know whether you are absolutely certain that—'

Miss Edmunds stands up abruptly from her armchair. 'Who are you?'

'I told you, I—'

'What do you want? Why are you here?' Her voice is shrill and panicked and I wonder, desperately, how I can placate her. Yet at the same time, I realise that we have gone beyond a certain point and there can be no return. I have one chance and one chance only.

'Miss Edmunds. I truly do not mean to frighten you. I am exactly who I say I am. I am desperately sorry for your loss, for you to lose a brother in this way. I too lost a brother I cared for deeply. I only wish to ascertain, Miss Edmunds, if you are absolutely certain that it was your gardener you saw break into your house that night.'

'But why?' she cries, her voice climbing even higher and louder. 'Why is this so important?'

'Because,' I try to say calmly, 'a potentially innocent man may die.'

'My brother was murdered!' She shrieks this so loudly that the maid comes hurrying in. Miss Edmunds is now crying openly, clawing at her grey crown of curls. 'I would like you to leave, this instant. Mary! Show the visitor to the door.'

Mary walks towards me to accompany me out. I look at the maid and nod. 'I am coming... but please, Miss Edmunds.' I turn back to her. I am pleading now; I know how my voice sounds, but I am unable to control it any longer. 'Please think about it very, very carefully. Whether it was Maitho you saw that night, or perhaps somebody else. *Please.*'

'Get out!' she sobs, her hand to her mouth. 'Out!'

'Madam,' the maid says firmly and I let myself be led to the door. Once it is closed firmly behind me, I lean back against it and feel myself collapsing into its wooden frame as my own heavy sobs escape. My visit has achieved nothing, *nothing*, but only served to pit Miss Edmunds firmly against me.

CHAPTER FORTY-SEVEN

MAITHO

Never have I had visitor. Not even mother or father. I do not even look up. So when guard shouts my name, first I do not hear him.

'Maitho!' He is shouting again and I look up. 'Out. Now.'

I stand. Dizzy. Cannot open left eye from last night beating. I follow guard down long, dark passage to small room. There are two chairs, man is sitting on one chair, Asian man. The door is closed behind me, locked. I turn but guard has gone, it is only me and this man.

He stands, walks to me. Old. Never have I seen him before. Never have I met Asian man before. He is staring at me, hard.

'Maitho,' he says in voice that sounds like croak of frog. He holds out hand. I do not take it. I do not know what he wants.

'Maitho,' he says again. 'My name is Fazal Ahmed.'

I say nothing, only watch him watching me. But then I think maybe he is lawyer. Maybe he is here to get me out this place. I ask him if this is so. He only shakes head.

'I am not a lawyer. I am a tailor. I *was* a tailor.'

I think, this man is crazy? He wants to make me new clothes in this place? Clothes maybe to die in?

'I want to help you, Maitho. I need you to trust me.'

I stare at him, thick moustache. Light brown eyes. Lighter skin. 'You are who?'

'A friend.'

He says it so simply, it sounds true. This man, Fazal Ahmed, friend. But still, I know nothing.

'Maitho. You are here for murdering your employer. I want to ask you a few very direct questions and I need you to answer them truthfully. Do you understand?'

I stare at him for long time. He is not like guards here. Not like Blue Knuckle. I do not know who he is, but I feel he is different. I nod.

'Have you, under threat or otherwise, taken the Mau Mau oath?'

I think of cigarette burn, of coarse rope against tender skin. I close my one good eye. 'Yes.'

'And did you, under threat or otherwise, murder Tobias Edmunds?'

Eye flicks open. If I tell him, will he believe me?

'No.'

This man, he stares. 'Are you telling me the truth, Maitho?'

'You ask for truth, I give you truth.'

His shoulders, they move down. He sighs deeply. 'Do you know who killed him?'

I shrug. 'Maybe. But no good now.'

'What do you mean?'

'So many people, killing so many others. Nobody mind, nobody care who is victim, who is murderer. I Kikuyu, this all that matter. I Kikuyu. I gardener of Bwana Edmunds, so I murderer, and I murdered for this.'

The Asian man, he frowns like I am not saying right words.

'I want to get you out of here, Maitho.'

I smile at him. Feel sorry for him. 'Why? In two weeks I am dead. I been given my execution date.'

He looks startled, shakes head. 'I cannot tell you why right now. But I will. Miss Edmunds, your employer's sister, said that she saw you kill her brother. Why would she say that?'

Again, I shrug. 'She not see me. She see someone else. Memsaab, she need someone to blame. I, easy person. Kikuyu servants all over, killing their masters and mistresses, small children even. So easy that could be me. But not me.' I shake head. 'Not me. The bwana, he good to me. I like him. They want that I should kill him. I say I do it, but I cannot—'

'Wait, wait.' He is holding hand up. '*Who* wanted you to kill him?'

'Mau Mau General. The only way I let go if I agree to it. But *hapana*, I cannot do it. That night… I only know they looking for me also, after they kill Bwana. But I move house again, I scared they come find me.'

'Who is "they", Maitho?'

I do not answer.

'Maitho,' he repeats. 'Who is "they"?'

'I tell you already. Mau Mau General and his people.'

'Do you know their names? Where to find them?'

I cannot speak. Throat clamped with fear and memory of rope winding round it.

'Maitho,' I hear him saying, again and again. But his voice sounds like it is coming from the end of very long tunnel. From far, far away.

CHAPTER FORTY-EIGHT

IRIS KINGSLEY

As dawn breaks this morning after a long, sleepless night, I feel the heavy mantle of defeat. At midday, I am still in bed. I do not know what to do any more, what course of action I can now take. There is a knock at the door.

'Yes,' I reply.

Fazal walks in. He is dressed smartly in a pressed kurta shalwar suit and is cleanly shaven.

'How are you, Iris?'

I pull myself up slightly. 'Well…' I hesitate, 'I did not know what to get out of bed for this morning.'

Fazal pulls a chair up beside the bed. He looks more lively, better slept. 'Iris, my dear. Please do not be angry with me.'

'How could I ever be angry with you, Fazal?' I brush my hair away from my face, conscious of how unkempt I must look.

'I… you see, I went to the prison this morning. I saw Maitho.'

My hand drops, a leaden weight, and I stare at him, slack-jawed. 'I don't understand… but why did you not take me—'

'Please, Iris. Hear me out.' He shifts an inch closer on the chair and clasps his hands before him. 'I wanted to go back, alone, to see if it would make a difference. I loathe having to say this, but people see the colour of your skin and some are immediately antagonistic. I don't need to tell you that Kenya is no longer a white man's country; the tide is changing. Rapidly.'

'Yes, but—'

'And it *worked*, Iris, it worked. I slept well last night and when I woke up, it occurred to me that it might help if I offered to pay that dreadful man on the desk some *kitu kidogo*.'

'What is that?'

'A bribe. He was probably just waiting for that yesterday; I don't know why I didn't think of it. Anyway, I had to give him a fair amount, but it could have been worse. *Much* worse.'

'And then?' I can hardly breathe. Fazal has seen Maitho. He has met my son.

'Once I had paid the bribe, I was taken to his cell.'

'And…' I say in a muted whisper, 'how is he?'

Fazal pauses and I wish I had not asked that question, for his hesitation crashes down upon me. 'What does he look like?'

Fazal sits stiffly, his hands still clasped.

'He looks like Kamau,' he says softly. 'And he looks like you, also. I have no doubt we have found the person we are looking for. He has your eyes, Iris. Exactly the same shade.'

I try to digest this information, to imagine a forty-eight-year-old man, an older version of Kamau and a younger version of myself, with navy-blue eyes.

'His skin?' I whisper. 'What colour is his skin?'

'He has Kamau's skin. He is dark.'

I nod and rise from the bed, walking towards the window in my nightgown and staring down at a man cycling past on a rickety bicycle, mangoes for sale in a basket at the front.

'Iris,' Fazal says in a firm voice and I turn my head round, looking at him over my shoulder.

'Yes?'

He is silent for a few moments before he speaks again. 'His execution date has been set. For two weeks' time.'

I steady myself against the windowpane, my eyes closing, my forehead resting against the cool glass. I feel a constriction in my throat and windpipe and force a deep inhalation of air into my lungs.

'Maitho did not kill Tobias Edmunds, Iris,' Fazal says.

It is the first time since my reunion with Fazal that I feel angry with him. He does not deserve this, I know; he has been nothing but kind and generous and loyal. But I cannot help it – the surge of irritation combined with the utter terror from the news he has just imparted begins deep in my belly and spews up and out of my mouth like a fire-breathing volcano.

'I knew that, Fazal!' I cry. 'I knew that all along!'

He looks cowed, like a small boy hanging his head in shame, and I regret my outburst immediately. I walk towards him and place a hand on his arm.

'Forgive me, Fazal.'

'No. It is you who must forgive me. You were right – he is Kamau's son, a gentle man. And he is your son, an intelligent man. But…' He hesitates. 'He is also frightened. He would not give me names.'

'Fazal,' I say, my eyes filling with tears. 'What are we going to do?'

CHAPTER FORTY-NINE

MAITHO

It will happen in five days and eight hours.

This man, this man who came last week, he told me, 'I am friend.' I believed him. I wish he would come again. Every day I wait for him. But he is not coming. Strange, I do not know him, who he is. *Why* he is friend. But there is something that connects him to me. To my past, this past of which my questions are not answered.

I keep waiting for this man. If he comes again, I will ask him, 'You know my mother? Real mother? You know my father?'

In five days and eight hours I will die.

CHAPTER FIFTY

IRIS KINGSLEY

If Fazal paid a bribe to get in to see Maitho, this *kitu kido-go*, as he called it, so too can I. The prison is a long, grey squat building and as we drive towards it, it looms ominously in the windscreen of the Chevrolet, the car Fazal has borrowed from his son. But as he climbs out of the seat, I find that I am frozen. I simply cannot move. Fazal moves round to the door and opens it for me, peering in, concern in his hazel eyes.

'Iris.' He stretches his hand out towards me. 'Come.'

I stare straight ahead of me. 'I don't think I can,' I whisper.

'Iris,' he says again, his voice firm. 'Of course you can. We are here now. You have already made the hardest journey.'

I turn and look at Fazal. 'I don't think so. Maitho...' My voice trails off.

Fazal simply nods, holds his hand out again. But something has happened to me. My legs have lost the will to move, my heart is thumping wildly and my head – perhaps through self-protection? – is telling me not to go. A conversation is taking place in my mind, a reel repeated over and over again: *But you are here now. Of course you must see him. But I cannot go; his execution date has been set; to meet him and then to lose him? But you are here now…*

Fazal's hand eventually drops to his side and he peers at me, concern etched into his features. I cannot share with him the rage of emotions that is flooding me, threatening to overwhelm me. I cannot say very much at all. But when I do speak, the steady clarity of my voice takes me by surprise. It is almost as though my head has made the decision before my heart.

'Fazal, I need to go home.'

'I will take you back. We can come tomorrow—'

'No. I mean, *home*. England.'

He blinks. 'But—'

'*Please*, Fazal. This is hard enough. Let us go back to your place now, and I will book my passage for tomorrow.'

He opens his mouth to say something, but then, seeing the determination upon my face, clearly thinks better of it and closes it again. Then he walks round to the driver's seat and climbs into the car, whilst I lean my head back and close my eyes.

'Iris,' he says softly, 'please can we talk about this again when we get back?'

'Yes,' I hear myself say, 'we can talk about it. But I will not change my mind. I *cannot*. I know you are far too polite to tell me that you think I have lost my mind under the pressure of all this. Perhaps you think I am callous—'

'Iris!'

'No, wait. Let me speak. I would not blame you if you thought that. I want, I *need* to meet Maitho more than I have needed anything else in my life. But there must be a level of protection for the two of us; protection for Maitho, who cannot discover the identity of his mother just before all is lost for him, and protection for myself. If I meet my son, and then he is sent to his death, what will that do to me? Where will that leave my relationship with my other two children – my grandchildren? Is it possible that I will be able to find it within myself to continue giving them what they need, loving them even?'

I stop talking, open my eyes and turn my head to face my friend, who sits in the driver's seat, clutching at the wheel as he stares ahead.

'You see, Fazal, how am I to live with myself, how can I continue living with his face haunting my every movement, if I am unable to change the outcome of his fate? For that is the most likely scenario, isn't it?'

Fazal does not say anything.

'*Isn't* it, Fazal?'

He turns his strained eyes towards me. 'I don't know.'

'Yes, you do. And it is. I am under no illusions that as British East Africa has grown and moulded herself into a country named Kenya, she has not done so gracefully. True, this remains a land of staggering beauty. Yet all we need do is turn the coin over to see what makes up the whole of this country and it is every bit as ugly as it is beautiful. It is ugly in deceit, in bribery, in prejudice and racism. It is a country

with blood on its hands and has become this way, through –
I believe – the greed and prejudice of my people, the white
people. The *mundu mweru*, the *wazungu*—'

I break off and stare out of the window at the vast, black
building before me that holds my son, the beautiful child
with the crown of tight, black curls.

'Please, drive Fazal. I need to get away from here. *Please.*'

He pauses for a few more moments, perhaps hoping I
will change my mind. Then he sighs deeply and turns the
key in the ignition and the Chevrolet roars to life.

We move down the winding track, red dust blowing up
all around us. I think, for the first time in many, many years,
of the story Kamau told me on our single fateful night together; the story of the wise Kikuyu chief, who prophesised
the white man coming to their land and changing everything with his ways. But could he ever have prophesised
the terrible bloodshed that would be spawned from those
people; that they could give rise to the Mau Mau, who kill
their own people in droves, burning them alive and slash-
ing *pangas* across children's bodies until their soft figures are
limp, emblazoned with tramlines of blood?

A state of emergency has been declared here. Kenyatta, a
Kikuyu who is believed to be orchestrating the Mau Mau,
though Fazal strongly doubts this to be the case, has been
arrested and interned in some far-flung northern outpost.
Does this mean the violence will cease? Of course it does
not. Fazal said several weeks ago he believed the violence
would only get worse. I was reluctant to believe him; I
wanted not to consider the worst, though it has been so

long since I have truly been an optimist. But he has been proven right, as my wise, wily friend is right about so many things.

You're the bravest person I know, Iris. My brother, Arthur, the beautiful ghost of my youth. I have never forgotten his words; the way they escaped his soft, heart-shaped face so naturally as we stood in the garden of The Old Vicarage what feels like a lifetime ago, swallows swooping over our heads. But he was wrong. I am not brave enough to do this. I cannot meet my son.

I want to take a taxi to the railway station but Fazal insists on driving me in his son's car. Both of them pack the boot with my luggage as Maliha and I say our farewells to one another. I feel heavy-hearted, for it is possible, *probable*, that I will never again meet this gentle spirit.

As Fazal and I drive in silence through the streets of Nairobi, I wonder how I appear to my friend. For my part, I feel entirely broken. As we stop at some traffic lights, a child beggar immediately approaches the car and taps on my window, motioning to his mouth. I turn to look at him and, once the child is satisfied he has my attention, he begins a theatrical dance of hunger. Fazal leans over me slightly and tries to shoo him away.

'Don't worry Fazal,' I say gently, continuing to look at him. I open my bag, but at that moment the lights turn green.

'I need to move, Iris.'

'Wait! Just one moment.' Desperately, I fish around in my bag whilst the boy, fully aware of my every movement, splays both dirty hands against the window and watches me eagerly.

The horns sound behind us and Fazal revs the engine.

'Wait! Please!' I cry as I empty the entire contents of my bag on to my lap. 'My purse – it's not here! Fazal, do you have any money I can—'

'Iris!' he says sharply. 'I need to move on.' And with that, we surge forwards, the boy thrown back from the car. I glance at him in the mirror and he is standing in the middle of the road, staring after us with empty eyes, impervious to the traffic swerving past him.

'I'm sorry, Iris. Where is your purse?'

'I don't know. I don't *know*,' I say again, before bursting into tears, my head hanging. 'I think I left it on the sideboard.'

He pulls up into a side road. 'We shall have to go back and get it.'

'Will I miss my train?'

He glances at my watch. 'Quite probably. But we might just make it if we hurry.'

I knead my palms into my temples where a headache is knocking.

Fazal turns the car swiftly and we begin to drive back towards his home. Thankfully the roads are not particularly busy, but a deep sense of unease makes my head pound. I am gripping the side of my seat as though my life depended on it and I do not know what comes first, the memory of the small, head crowned with tight, black curls as I look down at him suckling at my breast or the smell of him: warm. Sweet. New. Impossibly perfect.

'Fazal!' I cry, making him jump. 'The prison!'

He drives silently for a while. When he does speak, he stutters. 'The – the – prison. What—'

'The prison! The jail that Maitho is in.'

Again, Fazal pulls over to the side of the road. He stops the engine. 'What is it, Iris?'

'I want to go back there.'

'You want to see him?'

I shake my head and sniff and Fazal hands me a hand-kerchief. 'No. I should like *you* to see him again. I shall stay in the car outside.'

'But *why?*' he asks, his forehead creasing into a deep frown. 'What do you want me to say to him?'

'I want you to tell him that you knew his real mother and father. That he was conceived in love and that—' I break off, swallowing down further tears. 'And that I have thought of him every single day of his life.'

Fazal does not move and we sit there on the side of Delamere Avenue, listening to the hum of passing cars.

'Iris,' he says after some time. 'You will miss your train.'

'Yes,' I agree.

Twenty minutes later, we have driven back to Fazal's house to collect my purse, which contains in it enough money for ten bribes over and – I think sadly – to have given that boy on the street dozens of warm meals. But something changed in me the minute I saw that child, his lonely, filthy face pressed up against the window of the car. I found myself beginning to wonder, in those few moments that we stared at one another, what my son would have been like when he was this age. It was difficult to actually know the boy's age, for poverty had blurred the lines of his youth. But sitting there in the car, two lives separated by glass, I was overcome with a new grief that my son's childhood, his teenage years, his adulthood and now his suffering had all been taken away from me. And whilst I could not bear to meet him myself, I needed him to know, I *needed him to know*, that he was loved. How many times had that urchin on the other side of the glass been told he was loved?

And now, here we are, the car pulled up outside the jail once more. 'Iris,' Fazal is saying, an unmistakable tremor in his voice. 'Are you sure that you won't come in?'

I nod my head. 'I am quite sure.'

'But…' He hesitates. 'If he asks about you, which I'm sure he will, I can hardly tell him that you are sitting outside in the car.'

I consider this, turning my purse over and over in my hands, wondering how much money will be considered an appropriate bribe this time.

'Tell him I am in England.'

'You want me to lie to him?'

'Fazal, *please.* Please do not make this harder than it already is.'

'Iris.' He places a hand over mine. 'I just don't want you to regret this decision, some day down the line. You have an opportunity, right now, to meet your son, to tell him these things yourself.'

I turn and stare out of the window at the grey prison towers that rise bleakly into the bleached sky. 'I know. And I *want* to. I cannot tell you how much. But I cannot. Not with things being as they are. Meeting him, knowing what will happen to him in such a short time... I do not know how I could go on living with myself after that.'

He sighs deeply and rubs my hands. 'I do understand, Iris,' he says quietly. 'My only hope is that you will not regret this decision.'

I smile at him weakly. 'Please go now, Fazal. I shall be here.'

I watch as he stiffly climbs out of the car, absently runs a hand over the bonnet before vanishing into the squat grey building, flanked by ominous, looming towers.

CHAPTER FIFTY-ONE

MAITHO

Three days, twelve hours. Not eating now. Want to be weak when I die, then I will not feel it so much.

I think, other day, after Miss Edmunds comes, maybe something will change. Her words maybe mean I can leave this place. I wait and wait, but nothing. Then I am moved to new cell, cell where those waiting execution stay. Smell here is even worse. Less space. But… there is tiny, tiny window, up at top. In my last cell no window. There is dribble of light, coming through. All day, I stare at this, lightening, darkening. Waiting for something, anything.

And then it comes. In the early morning whilst I am still sleeping. I hear it before I see it: small, soft, familiar noises. One eye opens, then other and when I look up, I see small bird in window. Maybe it is lost? Silent as breeze, I stand up. I stretch my hand out towards light, towards this sunbird searching for home, searching for nectar, for plants and trees. And this is my sign, to not fear anything.

So when man comes again, few hours later, I do not feel surprise. This man who tells me last time, 'I am your friend.'

Nobody has ever told me these words before. 'I am your friend.' I have them in my head since that day, turning them round, round. And he comes, of course, after sunbird appears.

We are taken to same dark, empty room as last time. So weak can hardly walk and am half-dragged down passageway.

'Maitho, I have something to tell you,' he says. I see guard who brought me from the cell leaning lazily back against door, but now he gives me curious looks.

'My friend,' I say and cough, rasping cough that comes from chest.

'Yes,' he says. He takes step closer to me. 'I am your friend. I—'

'I have also something to say.'

He blinks in surprise.

'She visit me.'

He leans in close to hear me speak. 'Who? Who visited you?'

'Miss Edmunds,' I breathe. 'Bwana sister.'

He opens eyes wider than I think possible. 'Maitho, what did she say?'

'She say—' I stop talking, my body that must weigh now not much more than small *posho* sack, leaning back against wall. My knees bend beneath me and I slump down.

'This man needs water!' my friend shouting at guard, but guard not moving.

My friend kneels down beside me and pulls handkerchief from pocket, dabbing at my brow and neck. 'Maitho!' he says urgently. 'Please, Maitho! Stay with me.'

Cannot breathe properly but after few moments, open my eyes slowly. 'You my friend,' I croak.

Swallowing hard, he supports back of my neck, angling head so I look straight at him. 'Yes, I am your friend. Maitho, why did Miss Edmunds come and visit you? Please try and talk to me. What did she say to you?'

I look straight at him. 'She say she know I not kill Bwana,' I whisper.

I feel the arms of my friend stiffen. 'She knows you're innocent! She saw someone else do it... We need to get you out of here.'

Still with eyes closed, I murmur, 'She say lady visit her, make her realise she must tell truth.'

'Yes,' he replies quietly.

'This lady...' My eyes open and I stare at man and I do not know why I ask it but question forms in mind and I speak it. 'She my mother?'

For some time, he says nothing, only stares at me with eyes the colour of African soil after rain. 'Yes,' he says, not looking away. 'She is your mother. But... I don't understand. Why are you still in here? We need to get you out.'

Now overcome with tiredness, so intense I feel chin drop heavily on to chest. He has one hand behind my neck; with the other he shakes my shoulder gently. 'Maitho!' he says, again and again.

'She tried.' It is guard speaking from behind my friend. It sounds distant, far away.

'Who tried?' my friend says. 'What do you mean?'

'That woman. That *mzungu* woman who visited him. She tried to get him out of here.'

'So what happened?' he cries.

'What happened is she didn't have enough money. Didn't want to pay, you know.' I look up and half open eyes. I see the guard rubbing thumb and forefinger together.

My friend lays my head gently back against wall and stands up. I hear him shouting. 'If there is nothing else I wish to achieve in my life it is this: I need to get Maitho out of this jail.' I hear something – is it laughter? – from guard. 'I need to save this innocent man from the cruel, unjust fate that awaits him.'

Silence. It is deeper, this silence, than any other I have heard in my life.

'Take me to the director of the prison,' he continues in firm voice.

I see guard smirking, then I look at face of my friend. His face angry and I think for one moment he will hit guard; punch him way I been punched so many times here.

'Why?' guard asks.

'Why?' I shout. 'Because I want to pay him *kitu kidogo*! Come on, man!' he cries, pushing behind his back. '*Twende, twende!*'

And that is it, suddenly alone. I lean my head back and close eyes.

CHAPTER FIFTY-TWO

IRIS KINGSLEY

What is Fazal doing in there? He is taking such a long time. I sit in the passenger seat of the car with my eyes tightly squeezed shut against the glare of the harsh sunlight and my fists opening and closing. Part of me wants to know my son more than anything else in the world, only to see him, to place my palm against his cheek. But there is another part, a stronger part, that recognises that if I do this, the life I shall lead after this will be – what? Agony? Torturous? That I knew him, briefly, made him a part of me, only to know that the same neck I once cradled is snapped beneath the weight of a tightened rope.

But I cannot sit here any longer. Fazal has left the key in the ignition and I pull it out, locking his son's beloved car and walking up and down upon the sun-soaked path that leads to the prison's entrance. I look around me. Could a more desolate spot have been chosen to locate Nairobi's most notorious jail? There is a single, forlorn acacia tree standing close to the main gate. Its branches are stripped bare and it leans away from the prison, as though it wishes, like its inhabitants, to be anywhere but there.

At that moment, I hear raised voices coming from one of the outer rooms. I strain to listen and I could be mistaken, but I am sure one of the voices is Fazal's. I glance back at the guards at the main gate and, surmising that I am just out of their sight, walk hurriedly without glancing back along the shrub that skirts the front of the prison. The voices become louder and I know for certain now that it is Fazal. I stand back from the small window and try to make sense of the words of anger flying like arrows.

They fall silent for some time and I hear items being pushed back and forth across a table. And then, 'But how can you live with your conscience?' Fazal is shouting with rage in a way I have never heard this gentle man speak before. 'How? Knowing you are sending an innocent man to his death?'

My heart constricts.

'You know I don't have that kind of money!' he continues. 'Nobody does! How can you possibly ask such a sum?'

'Everybody in here is innocent. At least, they say they are. I am sorry, my friend. I have stated my terms. It is this or we have no agreement.'

'I am *not* your friend! I am *not*!' Fazal's voice is trembling with fury. 'That man in there, that man you are sending to his death, *he* is my friend. And he is innocent!'

I want to cry out Fazal's name, to alert him to my presence outside the window. Yet somehow I am immobilised. My feet will not move, nor my hands, nor my mouth. I close my eyes and I feel the warm sun beating on my forehead, my shoes planted into the African soil that I have simultaneously loved and loathed. A memory, fleetingly, comes to me, one of so many that I have successfully repressed over the years. It is Kamau. The feel of his hand over mine that night as we sat opposite one another at the table. Nothing in my life until that point had felt so weighty or significant or safe as the feeling of that hand over mine. I had closed my eyes at that moment to experience it more fully and when I opened them, I knew it was the first time in my life I had felt needed.

And now? With the sun beating down upon me and the lonely tree craning away from the horrors inside, the words come to me one by one. Yes. You. Are. Needed. Now... now... now...

'*Maitho!*' His name escapes my mouth in a strangled sob. I hear rapid footsteps. The window is flung wide open as Fazal stands there beside another man, both of their faces betraying their shock.

'Iris!'

'How much money? How much is being asked?' I sob. 'Just tell me. I will get the money, I will get it, no matter how much it is.'

⋙ ⋙ ⋙

Two days remain before Maitho's execution. The director of the prison has asked for a sum of money in exchange for his freedom that will leave me virtually penniless, with no inheritance for my children or my grandchildren.

Fazal sits beside me in his living room, Maliha on my other side, as I pick up the telephone receiver and call first my daughter and then my son. I can feel my friends listening to me intently, almost as much a part of this conversation as I am, whilst I tell my children that *no*, I am not in trouble and *no*, I have not got myself into difficulties with the Mau Mau terrorist group. But yes, I have not been entirely honest with them. In fact, I have not been honest with them at all and I am deeply sorry for that.

'I can't tell you now, Leonard,' I say quietly as I grip the white cord of the receiver in my other hand. 'No… I am truly sorry, but I can't. Please. You need to trust me.'

I twist the cord round and round one finger so tightly Fazal is evidently concerned I may cut off my circulation, for he reaches out and unwinds it, placing my hand back in my lap. I look at him and smile with gratitude. Fazal, the greatest friend I could ever hope for.

'Yes, Leonard, that is exactly what I said,' I murmur into the receiver. 'Yes, all of it. I know, it's a lot of money. Yes, as soon as I get home, I shall explain it to you. Everything.'

After several more minutes, I replace the receiver, exhale deeply and look from Maliha to Fazal. I nod slowly, feeling suddenly more exhausted and older than I ever have done in my life. 'Leonard is going to do it,' I say. I lay my head upon Maliha's shoulder and close my eyes.

CHAPTER FIFTY-THREE

MAITHO

I cannot move. I wonder, *Am I already dead?* I turn neck, head, slowly, slowly and there it is: the small patch of daylight where the sunbird visited me. So no, I cannot be dead. But I wish I were, so I will not have to endure today. This day rope will be tied round neck. Like rope Mama used to weave baskets. Except she not my real mama. My mother is *mzungu*. I have picture of her now – she is there when my eyes close – soft brown hair, smooth skin, pale like reflected moon on river. And eyes my eyes, colour of sky at dusk. Mama, I wish I could have known you.

Guard comes in. But no, cannot move. Too weak. Cannot remember last thing I ate, how many days before. I wanted to die *this* way, by not eating. But have failed. Again, I have failed. Guard puts his hands under arms behind me, pulls me to my feet.

'Maitho, come,' he says. 'Stand up.'

I moan. Legs are like twigs of tree, too thin for support.

'Maitho! Let's go. *Twende!*'

Cannot. He places arms round my waist. Half-drags me through cell door. Faces stare at me through bars as we move down long corridor. Eyes black, not like mine. I am different. Always, always different.

Next thing I know, I am pushed through door. I hear lock behind me. Sunlight, sky, they so bright, too bright, they blind me. I clamp hands over my eyes, bend over. Stay like this for few moments and then, slowly, slowly, pull myself upright. Open my eyes and see three things: I see car. I see acacia tree, branches black and bare against sky. And I see person standing under it.

CHAPTER FIFTY-FOUR

IRIS KINGSLEY

I do not know what I expected. But looking at him now, beneath the painful frailty, beneath the prematurely aged skin and downcast eyes, beneath and beyond it all, there is not the slightest doubt in my mind: this is Kamau's son. This is my son. We stand looking at one another. I take a step out from beneath the shade of the tree into the sunlight that beats ferociously down upon my head. We stand mere metres from one another, but the distance I must cross to reach him is immeasurable. For I am also crossing forty-eight years, winding back the clock to the only time that I held him in my arms.

But I begin to move, slowly, propelled forwards by the invisible threads that have always connected us. By necessity. He is painfully thin. So malnourished and so mistreated that it threatens to break my heart there and then. But no, I must be strong. *You're the strongest person I know, Iris.* Arthur's words come back to me yet again. *Arthur, are you with Kamau? Does all that really exist?*

He is having difficulty breathing, focusing on me even. I reach a hand out, across the space, across forty-eight years, and I touch his arm lightly. This sudden contact appears to revive him a little and he jolts his head back, his eyes opening wide for a moment. And there it is, the recognition as we look at one another.

'Maitho,' I whisper.

Maitho has been released with only the clothes he stands in. He has no other possessions and the shack he once inhabited in Eastlands has been repossessed. None of his belongings remain there. We spend the next few weeks in Parklands, ensconced in Fazal and Maliha's apartment, scarcely even leaving it. I watch him as he sleeps, his painfully frail chest rattling up and down as his hands and legs twitch uncontrollably.

When he is awake, I help him to drink Maliha's chai and her warm, gently spiced food; he only takes the tiniest mouthfuls before pushing it away. He is haunted by the nightmares that flicker across the irises of his eyes; his eyes that are my eyes. I do not ask him any questions. I do not want him to relive his ordeal any more than he has to. And whilst I do not and cannot know how much more time I have allotted to me here on this earth, not a moment passes that I do not feel deeply blessed that I am spending these moments with a son I believed was lost to me for ever. And I believe now, I believe with all my heart, that if it is meant to be, the time for us to talk will also come.

Whilst Maitho lies in bed, slowly regaining his strength, the window flung wide open for the breeze and the birdsong to reach us on the other side of the room, I talk to him, not expecting an answer. Not expecting anything. I tell him about my childhood in Cambridgeshire, about the soft-feathered pigeons and the beautiful garden of The Old Vicarage, about my father and my brother. I tell him about the barren, windswept plains of Nairobi when I came here in 1903, where the Maasai herded their cattle and wild beasts roamed. But most of all, I tell him of his father, of Kamau, the peaceful warrior who was good and kind and noble.

Sometimes he listens with his eyes closed, his greying head resting against the white pillow, and other times he watches me intently with his impossibly blue and beautiful eyes staring out of his dark face, made old before his time. But I know, with all certainty, that the tales I relate of his father give him sustenance, for on more than one occasion I see him smiling to himself when I talk of Kamau.

One afternoon, I tell him, down to the last detail my memory allows me, about his father's schoolhouse, imbued with the love and devotion he afforded his chosen profession. When I finish speaking, Maitho's face cracks into a smile and he whispers something. Yet no matter how many times he repeats what it is he is saying, I still am unable to understand. I call in Fazal and the two of us stand at my son's bedside whilst he says the word again.

'*Ugali*!' Fazal cries triumphantly. 'He is asking for *ugali*!'

I do not even know what this is, but within moments Fazal has left the room and I hear the front door banging and the clatter of his feet outside. He returns with some *ugali* – a Kenyan staple made from maize flour, he explains, which is eaten with stews and beans. Not only has Fazal bought enough *ugali* to last my son several meals, but he has also fetched some packages of other Kenyan foods: *githeri* and *kachambari*, *denge* and *sukuma wiki*. And whilst Maitho is unable to eat large quantities even of these foods, foods he has clearly been craving all this time, the pleasure on his face as he slowly chews is unmistakable.

The very next afternoon, Maitho tells me he would like to go for a short walk. Fazal immediately arranges for his son to bring round the car and Fazal drives us to Jeevanjee Gardens, parking up nearby. I link my arm through Maitho's and as we slowly place one foot in front of the other, a warm sprinkling of rain dusting our faces, we are briefly unaware of Kenya's state of emergency and unaware of the arrests that continue in Nairobi and beyond. Unaware of anything save one another's presence.

We sit on the wooden bench near the Jeevanjee Statue, in the exact same place that Fazal and I have sat on so many occasions, Maitho's thin hand in mine. As I look down at our intertwined fingers, I wonder if I have ever been as happy as I am right at this moment. I'm happier than I was as a girl, stroking the soft down of the pigeons in the woodshed; happier than when living in the deep contentment I felt at being loved and needed by Jonathan; happier even than in my stolen moments with Kamau, for a dark shadow always shrouded our togetherness.

Then, as though in reply to this thought, something hurtles towards Maitho and me through the silver-streaked sky, something that carries on its wings the words, *No, you can be happier still. For here I am.* A bolt of iridescent blue and yellow, that perfectly curved black beak, its soft but urgent call. I know that we both see the little sunbird and that it is significant to us both, for our interlinked fingers simultaneously tighten round each other's. And we continue to watch as the bird gracefully darts from one flower to the next. Our bodies are tensed but at the same time marvellously free as we watch the tiny creature soar away from us into the gently falling dusk.

EPILOGUE

IRIS KINGSLEY

DURHAM
1957

I sit in the front row. I expected to feel nervous, but not like this. I scarcely know where to look as my eyes flit around the hall, which is dappled in the fractured light that streams in through the stained glass windows of the ancient castle. I cannot keep my hands still; they flutter in the unfamiliar blackness of my lap – I never wear black – and my head feels peculiar with the tassled mortar board perching on top of it.

Other names wash over me, names of all the young students who jump lithely to their feet and walk onto the stage, shaking the dean's hand with all the aplomb and energy of youth. After what feels like an eternity, I hear my name being called. I take a deep breath, place a hand down on each side of my chair and rise unsteadily to my feet. More noise, and as I walk up on to the stage, turn and see that the entire hall is clapping and smiling, I realise it is thunderous applause. For a moment, I simply stand and stare, so taken aback am I by the reaction.

Then I am shaking the hand of the dean, his round face beaming at me. I cannot even hear what he is saying. But he hands me my certificate, my degree from the University of Durham, tied up with red ribbon, and I stare at it in my frail, mottled hands and see that they are trembling. I look up into the audience who, like a ripple of waves upon the shore, are rising to their feet, one by one. I see their faces almost immediately: Sheena and Leonard's, clapping and smiling as though their lives depended upon it. And in the middle of them, there he is. Maitho. He is standing completely still, his hands thrust down by his side. But he stares directly at me, his handsome head held high. And he nods slowly at me, his face breaking into a smile.

LETTER FROM REBECCA

Thank you so much for choosing to read *The Girl and the Sunbird*. I do hope that you enjoyed following Iris on her journey through half a century as much as I delighted in writing it. I would love to know what you thought of this story – please do leave a review, even if it is just a few words. It would mean a great deal to me.

You can keep up to date with my writing projects through my blog, via my Facebook page and through my Twitter account.

My third novel is already in the making and I very much look forward to sharing it with you. If you'd like to keep up to date with my latest book news, do sign up here:

www.rebeccastonehill.com/email

With my very best wishes and thanks once again,

Rebecca

P.S. If you enjoyed *The Girl and the Sunbird*, you might like to read my first novel, *The Poet's Wife*, set in Granada during the Spanish Civil War and Franco's dictatorship and told through the eyes of three generations of women from one family.

bexstonehill
RebeccaStonehillBooks
www.rebeccastonehill.com

ACKNOWLEDGEMENTS

I have a number of people I'd like to thank for helping me with *The Girl and the Sunbird*:

Claire Bord and Natalie Butlin for helping me to develop this book and pushing me that extra mile to turn it into what it has become – I definitely could not have created this without your insight and encouragement.

Oliver Rhodes, for believing in me and my writing in the first place – eternal gratitude.

Jacqui Lewis for doing a brilliant job on the copy-editing and Emma Graves for a stunning front cover.

Kim Nash, for her amazing and tireless work behind the Bookouture scenes.

Sue Joiner, for casting her discerning eye over the finished manuscript and her fantastic advice.

Abigail Arunga, for agreeing to let me use her poem at the start of this book.

Bridget Allison, for introducing me to her grandfather and especially to the man himself, Major Paddy Deacon, who has the most astonishing memory imaginable and who told me about his life in Nairobi in the 1950s, as well as sharing many other stories with me. Also to Paddy's great friend Noah Imbogo, for kindly lending me several books which helped in my research.

Chao Maina, her inspiring website *Thee Agora* and her assistance with the railway scene.

Dr Henry M. Chavaka, who allowed me to raid his extensive library at his home in Karen.

Evanson Kiiru from the Nairobi National Archives, who helped me to pull out all sorts of old maps of Nairobi.

The Honorable Tobina Cole for talking to me about her years in Nairobi and showing me her beautiful family albums.

Edward Njenga, the talented sculptor, for showing me his incredible artwork and telling me about life in a detention camp during the Mao Mao Emergency.

Pauline Skaper, Jana Lindahova and Ghulam Samdini for providing me with laptops during my 'crisis' period!

My mother and mother-in-law, the two wonderful Elizabeths, for dropping everything and being there for me when I most needed them.

My children Maya, Lily and Benjamin for having to share me with an entirely different world in my head, particularly during that frantic race to the finish line during their school holidays.

And last, but not least, my husband Andy for being nothing like Jeremy Lawrence and for always being there, especially when the going got tough. As I said in my dedication, *Ya tu sabes…*

Printed in Great Britain
by Amazon

72356301R00285